HAUNTED YOUTH

HAUNTED YOUTH

LARRY MILLER

ARCHWAY
PUBLISHING

Archway Publishing books may be ordered through booksellers or by contacting:

Archway Publishing
1663 Liberty Drive
Bloomington, IN 47403
www.archwaypublishing.com
1 (888) 242-5904

Because of the dynamic nature of the Internet, any web addresses or links contained
in this book may have changed since publication and may no longer be valid. The views
expressed in this work are solely those of the author and do not necessarily reflect the
views of the publisher, and the publisher hereby disclaims any responsibility for them.

Any people depicted in stock imagery provided by Thinkstock are models,
and such images are being used for illustrative purposes only.
Certain stock imagery © Thinkstock.

ISBN: 978-1-4808-3490-3 (sc)
ISBN: 978-1-4808-3491-0 (e)

Library of Congress Control Number: 2016948691

Print information available on the last page.

Archway Publishing rev. date: 09/06/2016

This is the place for any disclaimers to be made. First, this is a work of fiction. Several characters, such as Joe and Mrs. Schweikert and the one called Frankenstein, are fictional. While all the rest of the characters are real, they are only as real as I remember them to be. Some names have been changed.

Obviously the incidents involving the three fictional characters are the result of my imagination. The same can be said of the places involving Mrs. Schweikert and Frankestein. Don't go looking for Mrs. Schweikert's house; it does not exist, although I did use a real part of a real town, a town that I still call home.

Many of the incidents involving my friends are real (e.g. the building of the baseball diamond and the tunnels; attending movies at the Griswold Theater; ice-cream cones from Union Farmers Dairy; nighttime games of kick-the-can; the trip to Briggs Stadium) the bag swings at the Kapankas.

As for my family, I thank them once again for the privilege of involving them in another ambitious scheme of mine: the writing of another novel. It is altogether possible that they may recall events differently than do I. I realize that they have no choice in the matter, so I apologize for any mistakes I may have made. I love them dearly, all of them, friends and family. Without them my life would have been mundane. So, thank you, all of you who find themselves used once again.

PREFACE

THERE ARE VERY few of us who aren't haunted by our youth. We are mystified by the illusion of time, especially that haunting past that at one time seemed so vibrant and real, only to watch it become lost in the passing of years. So much a part of our lives seems to have slipped away, like ghosts that come and go in the darkness of our dreams. We reach for them, hoping, even expecting, to grasp and hold them forever, only to watch them disappear. And when they are gone, we are left wondering how it all happened.

They are the ghosts of aspirations that become merely shadowy memories. But while they remain, ghostly or not, they are still worthy of being held, even if we no longer chase them.

CHAPTER ONE

The Movie of All Movies

I T WAS 1940. And *It* was coming. *It* was the movie *Frankenstein*.

This was the monster of all monsters. He was ugly, horrible, hideous. He walked deliberately, mechanically, slowly dragging his feet across the brick floor of the ancient stone tower. His head was square shaped and enormous, deformed, and plugged with wires of some sort that made him look like a…well, like a monster. His eyes stared straight ahead, as though they took in everything and yet took in nothing. Tall, huge, with a monstrous physique that seemed to bulge in the joints of arms and legs, he was both appalling and magnetic. We would not be able to keep from looking at him.

Frankenstein. Yes, the movie was coming. To our town. To our little part of town.

It was one of those scary movies that all kids want to see. Well, at least all of the boys. I had my doubts about Donna Nelson, or Mary Belle Thompson, or my sister Marilyn wanting to see it. But we boys talked endlessly about it for the two weeks before it was shown.

Mother and, of course, the other mothers in our neighborhood, used the word *horror* when referring to the movie. She-and they-thought that the movie was disgusting and revolting, and she could not conceive of any other mother in Germantown-that was the unofficial name given to our part of Port Huron, Michigan- allowing her children to see it. Of course she and the other mothers had never seen the movie, but they *knew*. Oh, yes, they *knew*. They knew what movies were bad for their precious little ones, and they would go to no ends to make sure that those precious little darlings would not be corrupted.

I don't think it was a conspiracy on their part, about wanting to deny us seeing the movie, although now, after having helped to raise three children of my own, a conspiracy might not have been such a bad idea on their part, after all. When it comes to parents and their children, it is always us against them; one must choose sides.

We finally got our parents to consent for us to see it, although it turned out to be quite a battle. In my own particular case, the battle was drawn up between my twin brother Jerry and me on the one side and our mother on the other side, with my twin brother Jerry and me offering up the usual argument: "The other mothers are going to let their kids go," to which Mother retaliated with the line that so many other mothers before her time had used, and which, I might add, modern mothers are still using: "I don't care what other mothers do. You're not other mothers' kids."

Mother had just come in from the back yard, carrying a wicker basket of clothes, having removed the wash from the clothesline, and there was a bead of sweat on her face. She was a medium built woman, with dark hair, dark eyes, and a temper that was even most of the time but could flare up when she felt affronted. And to be fair to her, we twins were often the cause of most of the flare-ups. And there is no doubt in my mind, and in the mind of everyone else who knew us, especially our neighbors, that I was the usual instigator of the problems that cropped up. It is so difficult to wear one's reputation. It's like a coat that somehow just doesn't fit very well yet seems to look right to others, as ugly as the coat might look.

She made that remark about Jerry and me not being other mothers' kids half in jest, I'm sure, but in looking back at those times, I'm also sure that there were multiple instances when she wished that it could have been true.

Anyway, after moaning and whining all morning long, and probably having committed enough minor infractions of the household to warrant a number of warnings and scoldings, we were finally close to being told to get out of her hair. The battle between kids and their parents is won on the ugly field of perseverance. In other words: wear them out.

"There's nothing to do," I said. Jerry and I were hanging around the kitchen, which was not the usual place for us boys to be on a wonderful late spring Saturday morning. But from a strategic point of view, it was the only place to be if we were to win our battle. We needed to wear Mother down to the point of her having to finally give in. Part of any battle is forcing your opponent, no matter who it is, to finally give in, out of a sense of relief, or frustration, or fatigue, if nothing else.

"I don't care what you do," Mother retorted, "just as long as you get out of my hair." She had both hands on her hips and was glaring at us, as if daring us to aggravate her any further.

"But there's no one to play with," Jerry offered.

"Are you going to sit there and tell me that every single boy in this neighborhood is going to be at that movie today, and that there's no one around for you to play with?" she shot back.

"All of the boys are going to see the movie," I said.

"All of them?" Mother questioned. Her eyes narrowed as she glared at me.

"Everyone is going, Mom," I said.

"Everyone?" she asked sternly, looking me squarely in the eyes, her hands planted even more firmly on her hips, again daring me to challenge her.

"All of our friends are going," Jerry said, in a much quieter and softer tone than I would have used.

"That's a horrible movie," she returned. "A horrible movie," she repeated. "And I am not about to let ten-year old boys see something that might give them nightmares." She was bent over the basket, looking through the clothes.

We had already pleaded with Dad, but he had given us the usual parental response: "You go and ask your mother."

Parents have used that ritual for thousands of years, I suppose, sending their children back and forth from one parent to another. I suppose that's so they can wear you out. But it rarely works, as children-especially boys-usually have more stamina, and thus it's usually the parents who get worn out.

So here we were, anxious to see the *movie of all* movies, the picture that had been touted by the owners of the theater for weeks. There wasn't a boy that I knew who had not stood in front of the glass windows of the marquee of the theater and stared, over and over again, at the advertisement that hailed the movie. After all, this was the one really colossal show! The show of shows! The movie of all time! How could anyone think of missing out on such a stupendous show? That idea was unthinkable to all the kids in the neighborhood. Well, maybe to all the boys.

Most of the conversations of the boys eventually got down to discussing this movie. It seemed as though there was nothing else even closely worthy of our attention. Thus plans were made.

We had even made a critical decision: to get to the theater early enough to occupy the very front row of seats, so that all the really scary parts would be magnified and the terror made even more terrible simply by being so close to the huge screen. Of course, afterwards, when we had left the theater, we expected to be surrounded by all the more timid boys, who would want to know how we had been able to survive being so close to such scenes. We would be heroes, of sorts. At least for a week.

So, here we were, one hour before show time, and horribly scared of something far more dreadful than sitting in the very front row of seats at a horror movie. We just might be denied the chance of seeing the movie. We knew what the results of that parental decision would be. We would be taunted by all of our friends for weeks, ridiculed for having parents over whom we had no control. We would be labeled "sissies," or "momma's boys," or-egads! even worse- "cowards." And at the age of ten, no boy wanted to be called any of those names. There would be no recourse but to take the ridicule, and suffer.

"How can it be a horrible movie?" I asked. "It was written by a woman, Mom. And a woman wouldn't write a movie that is bad for kids."

"Who told you that?" she asked, a glare in her eyes that warned me to not be lying to her.

"Our teacher," I said confidently.

"Miss Sullivan told you that?" she challenged. "Your teacher actually told you that?" But this time the question was spoken with less assurance.

"She said that it was a book by some British writer," Jerry put in. Some Mary something."

"Uh, huh," Mother responded somewhat unbelievingly.

"And she also said that it was a popular book over there," I said, pointing in some meaningless direction that was supposed to point out England, although I'm sure my sense of geography might not have been very accurate. For all I knew, I might have been pointing in the direction of Bolivia, or Alaska.

"And did Miss Sullivan also say that she approved of the movie?" Mother responded, heaving a load of clothes out of the wicker basket from the floor onto the kitchen table in preparation for sorting them.

Dad came in just then from the back stairway. He had been down in the basement fixing something when Jerry and I had approached him earlier. His hands were greasy, and he was wiping them with an old towel.

"Did you give these boys permission to see the movie today?" Mother asked him.

"I told them to ask you," he responded, vigorously rubbing his hands with the towel. Fathers have a wonderful talent for pushing off important decisions onto the mothers.

"They tell me that their teacher told them that the movie was from a book written by a woman. Is that true, Mel?"

My mother's name was Leona Viola. My father's name was Manville Ferdinand. Mother called him Mel. All of Dad's friends and coworkers called him Bing. Often Mother called him Dear when speaking with him, and so when she called him Mel, we knew that she was being very serious. And the reason she asked him about the book was because Dad was an inveterate reader, much more so than was Mom, and consequently she presumed that he would know such things.

"I'm afraid it is, dear," Dad answered, and when he used the endearing term, I knew he did so because he wished to take some of the harshness out of any impending debate.

"The book was written by Mary Shelley, a writer from the nineteenth century," Dad remarked almost casually. "Her husband was a famous poet, maybe the most famous poet of his day, in fact."

"Well, what kind of a woman was she?" Mother demanded. "I mean, what kind of a woman would write such awful stuff? Doctors, and pieces of body parts, and making a human being out of it all. And robbing graves, for heaven's sake!" This last remark was spoken with an obvious sense of exasperation.

"Hilda Schmude told me all about it," Mother went on. "I ran into her the other day. Did you know that that's what that movie is all about?"

"It's not nearly as bad as it sounds," Father answered. He was leaning casually against the kitchen sink, his posture an obvious attempt to make his words sound innocent. "It's about a doctor, actually. Herr Frankenstein was his name. A lot of people think that the creature he built was named Frankenstein, but the name actually was that of the doctor. He was dabbling in a little scientific experiment. I think he was trying to find better ways of helping the body to heal itself."

"Healing a body by stealing bodies from graves?" Mother asked.

"Well, dear, I'm afraid that men of medicine had to rely on that kind of thing, in those days. Unless one belonged to a large university, it was the only way that some doctors could study the human body. And if they hadn't done that, then it's entirely possible that we wouldn't know nearly as much about human anatomy as we do today.

"Besides," Dad continued, "it's just a story."

"And it was written by a woman?" Mother asked. "A woman actually wrote such stuff?"

Mother was standing stiff, her face bent forward as if in disbelief, and there was a flush on her face, which I didn't think was caused by the temperature in the air.

"I understand she was a very loving wife," Dad said, stuffing the towel into his back pocket, and turning to the sink, where he began to clean his hands with Fels Naptha soap. "And I really don't think it is going to do our boys any harm if they see that movie," he said over his shoulder, scrubbing vigorously. "I don't think it's nearly as bad as what Hilda Schmude says about it. Besides, you'll have to admit that Hilda's a little bit of an alarmist."

Dad had not said all this in a belligerent way, but rather in a manner that was meant to deflect undue criticism. Mother's response was predictable.

"Hmff!" she snorted. "Well, if those boys have nightmares, don't come to me about it," she huffed, turning her back on all of us, and picking up the sorted clothes and throwing them back into the basket. I figured that she wanted to take out her anger on someone or something, and better it was the clothes than any of us. And without saying anything else, she left the kitchen, pushing through the swinging door that separated the kitchen from the dining room. She was obviously upset, and everyone knew that at such a time, it was best to leave her to her private musings.

Dad looked over at us and nodded slowly, placing a finger pointed upwards, in front of his mouth, a warning to us to keep our mouths shut and to leave things as they were.

And we were wise enough to heed the warning, and also wise enough to give Mother some room. In other words, to leave her alone.

Boy! Talk about children being weaned from their mothers. Heck, it didn't take mother bears ten years to give freedom to their cubs. We wanted the same kind of freedom that bear cubs enjoyed. And if that included the freedom to see a horror movie, well then....

Jerry and I hurried out of the kitchen and into the hallway, and ran up the stairs to our room, where we had left two nickels on top of the scarred chest of drawers. The two nickels were the result of our having scavenged among the neighborhood for used pop bottles. Our hard work and diligence had paid off, as we had found five of those precious bottles, each worth two cents when taken in to Gillies' Grocery Store, which was situated at the nearby corner of Sixteenth and Minnie streets.

Even though Dad worked at the local Coca-Cola distributor, driving a truck five or six days a week, delivering Coca-Cola to various stores, restaurants, and bars, rarely were there many bottles of coke around. He felt that too much pop was not good for us children. Milk was better for us, albeit a little expensive for our household. Water, we were informed, was wonderful, and we were encouraged to drink a lot of it.

It was 1940, and for most people in our section of town milk *was* expensive. There were several dairies in the greater Port Huron area, most of them delivering milk and cream and butter and eggs from door to door.

The Roth Dairy, one of the principal dairies, was actually owned by people who went to our church. Then, there was Babcock Dairy, which maintained a couple of ice-cream parlors, also. The City Dairy delivered to most of the homes in our neighborhood, and all of us boys knew Fred, the driver, very well. There were times when he allowed one of us boys to assist him in making his deliveries. Fred generously gave a quart of chocolate milk to that day's assistant . Chocolate milk! Most of us boys would have fought for a chance at some chocolate milk.

Anyway, getting back to obtaining the necessary money to pay for the movie, we had to work hard to scavenge the bottles, since we were in competition with all of the other boys in Germantown. Our diligence had paid off, and now we were heading to what we expected to be the greatest thrill of our yet-young lives.

CHAPTER TWO

A Crisis at the Theater

P ORT HURON IS located at the very point where beautiful Lake Huron empties itself into the equally beautiful St. Clair River. Across the river is Sarnia, Ontario, Canada, which makes our city truly a border city.

The town itself is split into two sections by what is called the Black River, although it must be mentioned that there are several Black rivers in Michigan. Our particular river of that name would have been better named if it had been called the Brown River, because that actually was the color of it. And I hate to say what some of the substances were that made it that peculiar color. Let's just say that not all of the private and corporate sewer lines were hooked up to our city's primitive waste disposal system.

Most people in Germantown had very little money to spend on frivolous things like pop; they had a heightened sense of frugality, although some of them managed to buy a few beers now and then. That kind of indulgence was the reason why one local entrepreneur had, years before, opened The German Beer Gardens, a few blocks away. It's still there, although it has gone through several different owners and names, over the course of more than three-fourths of a century.

But there were some neighbors of ours who could afford a few other kinds of luxuries, and we got so that we knew who they were, and we kept our eyes open for the bottles that happened to get *discarded*. Well, maybe *discarded* is not the right word. Bottles of redeemable value lying around were fair game.

Our neighborhood was…well, modest at best. And our house was…well, less than modest. But it was filled with laughter, often of a raucous nature, what with five children gracing the premises. Perhaps *gracing* is not the appropriate word, especially when it came to me and my twin brother Jerry.

Jerry and I were five years younger than our sister Marilyn, and four years older than our sister Sandra, who, in turn, was followed two years later by David. Four of us were born in March, while David almost made it five March-children, being an April child. Our birthdays came within a time span of forty-three days. It figures that Mother and Dad must have had one particular annual time period of marital happiness.

There was joy in the house, as well as a sense of optimism even for those hard times. Much of the same can be said for the entire neighborhood. It was a neighborhood of people who knew each other and who relied on each other and who sympathized and cheered each other, as the occasion demanded.

Anyway, getting back to those good ol' pop bottles. We were able to redeem them at Gillies' store. Good ol' Mrs. Gillies had handed us the two nickels the previous Thursday, when we had turned in the bottles, and she was surprised that we had not immediately spent the ten cents on the penny candy that was prominently displayed in the window of one of her showcases. She knew how much all that candy meant to Jerry and me.

That showcase was not just an ordinary affair. Why, to us boys it was a treasure-showcase of unimaginable magnitude. In that glass-windowed case were Root Beer Barrels, and Milk Duds, and lollipops, and Boston Baked Beans(really candy), and jelly beans which could be purchased by the ounce or pound.

There were paper strips that held dots of candy of various colors, and there were tiny wax bottles that contained sweetened juices, and the inevitable Tootsie Rolls found a place in the showcase. But for me, most importantly there was the famous, luscious, marvelous Holiday all-day sucker called Slo Poke. Although that sucker cost five cents, it lasted longer than did even the slow-chewing Milk Duds, since a careful boy could lick and lick at the sucker, instead of biting or chewing off huge chunks, thus possibly making it last for an entire movie session.

I have to admit, however, that the few times I was audacious enough to spend five cents on that sucker, rarely did I have the patience to approach the sucker in such a slow fashion, which meant that it usually lasted through only the first half of the movie itself. I had such a passion for that sucker that, after working it over for a few seconds with my tongue, I always wound up tearing at it furiously with my teeth, not only losing the chance of letting the taste linger in my mouth, but threatening to ruin all that nature had worked so hard at giving me: strong, white teeth. It's hard to imagine how it was that I got through those pre-teen years with my teeth intact. I'm surprised that I didn't pull some of my front teeth right out of their gums, in my battle to pull the chewy caramel away from its stick. It came away so begrudgingly. But it was so delicious.

That sucker cost me a lot of deep thinking as to the wisdom of paying more than twice as much more for one sucker than I would have paid for so much of the other kinds of candy. And thinking deep thoughts can be difficult for one whose mind was not geared to philosophical ramblings.

Oh, the trauma in making such important decisions.

Of course, there was always the option of buying gum. But buying gum could be a big mistake, if one were going to try to take the gum with him when going to the movie. No gum was allowed! It was the ultimate dictum of the Griswold Street Theater, for there was always the danger of the children chewing their gum until their jaws were tired, or until the flavor had completely disappeared, and everyone knew what happened to the then-used-up, flavorless gum: it would be attached to the under-part of the seats. And the ever-vigilant Mrs. Ort was keen in monitoring every child who entered the theater. Her hand took in the nickels, and her eyes scanned the various faces of the children, looking for possible violations of all sorts.

Of course, over the years there were those who obviously had beaten the inspection. For rare was the seat that did not hold evidence of the worn out jaws.

There was one particular incident that drove home the importance of being careful when trying to outwit Mrs. Ort. That incident involved my good friend Jack. He had decided, one notable Saturday the previous year, to try to get past Mrs. Ort with a wad of gum in his mouth. And a wad it was, since Jack had chosen to shove all five sticks into his mouth at one time. Unfortunately for Jack, Mrs. Ort thought she detected a bulge in Jack's mouth, and demanded that he open his mouth for inspection. And since we lacked laws that prevented unwarranted search and seizure, Jack had no alternative but to stand for inspection.

At that point, standing in line, with a horde of youngsters behind him, Jack probably panicked, for he certainly did not want to display the evidence, since that would have resulted in his being banned from the theater for the day, and without getting back his precious nickel, I might add.

So, what did Jack do? Why, the only thing that he could think of at the moment. He quickly bent his head, and swallowed all that gum, hoping that he wouldn't get caught in the act. Now, to chew five sticks of gum is not such a remarkable thing, but to *swallow* such a prodigious amount of gum took a lot of daring. It also required more throat muscles and a larger aperture than what his nine-year old body could muster.

The result was that the gum got only partly down his throat, causing him to gag. Choking on the wad, he fell to the floor, floundering and flapping around like a fish brought out of water. Instantly Mrs. Ort came to his rescue, she apparently thinking that he was sick, or worse.

Friends of ours later told me that Jack's face was turning a peculiar color: like, blue. It was at this point that Mrs. Ort bent down and tried to find out just what was the matter with Jack, and when she saw the color of his face, she took action.

She immediately bought him to a sitting position, and then she clapped him hard on his back, and instantly, with what sounded like a small-bore gun going off, the wad shot out of Jack's mouth, like some missile shot out of a cannon. A few feet away, the wad struck a hapless girl who happened to be in the wrong place at the wrong time and who was bent over in order to get a good view of all the commotion. It struck her right in the face, and in a matter of two seconds, she realized just exactly what had happened.

To say that she screamed at such a vulgar display of a boy's stupidity is an understatement. Her scream flew back over the heads of all those waiting outside, which caused a great deal of wonder and speculation among them, for it just happened that *The Mummy* was playing that particular Saturday, and many of the kids thought, perhaps, that the monster himself was loose, or that something equally dreadful had occurred.

Of course, her screams became contagious, as many of the other girls-and even a few of the younger boys-added their screams to the furor. It was a matter of panic at the box office, if I can put it that way. It was enough to even make Mr. Ort come out of his cubicle where he ran the projector. That helped to restore some semblance of peace.

Eventually the matter was contained, the furor died down, and everyone was allowed to enter the theater. All, that is, but Jack. He not only lost his nickel, but I understand that part of his lunch had been expelled along with the gum. A quick mop-up of the cement floor of the entrance, by Mr. Ort, was required before the rest of the kids entered. Of course the leftover smell reminded us all of what had taken place; probably it was the smell that one might expect to accompany a horror movie.

Jerry and I were already in the theater when it happened, so everything that I heard about it came from eyewitnesses, as well as by rumors that most likely greatly exaggerated the whole event. And when I tried to question Jack about it later, he asked me to drop the subject. Embarrassment need not be made greater by repetition of the tale.

CHAPTER THREE

Germantown's Environment

B UT, GETTING BACK to the original story...
"Thanks, Mrs. Gillies," I had said at the time that we were
redeeming the empty bottles, "but Jerry and I are going to see the movie
Frankenstein." Everyone knew that the Saturday matinees were five-cents
each, and that they always included a cartoon, a chapter from the currently
running serial, and a feature film.

"Ah, I see," Mrs. Gillies said knowingly. "I'll bet that's a scary movie,"
and there was a bit of humor in her eyes.

"They're even playing it at night," I said, looking hungrily at the rows
of candy in their various boxes, tempted to change my mind from our
intention to see the movie. My whole life has been spent in agonizing over
decisions involving sweets. But that day, the decision to see the movie had
already been made, firmly.

Almost all movies shown on Saturday afternoons were merely for
children. Consequently for a movie to be shown both for the matinee and
at night meant that something special was being shown. And we children
had wondered about that, debating about which parents would dare to
go see such stuff of horror. If any of the parents of our crowd of boys
had expressed the desire to see this movie, they had not let on. I figured
that most of them wouldn't let their children know, for fear of giving the
children ammunition about the movie's merits, or lack of such.

"Well, just maybe I'll see if A.D. wants to see that movie," she said
good naturedly. A.D. was Angus, her husband. I never did know what the

D stood for. He was as grand a person as was Mrs. Gillies, and both of them treated everyone with respect, which made them respected, in return.

It was no wonder that most people in the neighborhood took some of their business to them, even though their store was quite small, especially when compared to the H.A. Smith Grocery Store, which sat just three blocks away, at the southwest corner of Sixteenth and Griswold. In comparison to the Gillies' store, the H.A. Smith Grocery was huge, and its assortment of food was far greater and more diverse than what Mr. and Mrs. Gillies could carry. And, of course, the prices at the Smith Grocery were lower, which was sufficient reason for most families to do the bulk of their shopping there. Yet there was enough business to keep Mr. and Mrs. Gillies going, but barely.

Years later I found out that Mr. and Mrs. Gillies often put people on the books, so to speak, allowing people to get groceries on the promise to pay whenever possible. They were wonderful people. They were kind, and generous, and understanding of the times.

Those were tough times. We had just left the 1930s, and America had just begun to dig its way out of a deep depression, and there were rumbles of impending full scale war in Europe. Some madman by the name of Adolph Hitler was making strong noises in Germany, threatening to undo the tenuous peace that had taken place after what we now refer to as World War I, which strangely, at least to my thinking, was called "The War to End All Wars." Little did, or could, we know at that time that an even more monstrous war was looming on the horizon, and that Germany would be at the very center of it.

Poland had fallen the year before to Adolph's goose-stepping Nazis, in 1939, and the word "Blitzkreig" had become a familiar and ugly part of the world's vocabulary. Czechoslovakia's fall had followed. And by the spring of 1940, those terrible, ugly, murderous Nazis had invaded Denmark and Norway, and had then driven their war machine into Holland and Belgium, and had even penetrated deeply into France.

About the only thing that America had done, in support of its allies, was to allow those hurting nations to buy arms from us, although our official stance was one of neutrality. But everyone just knew that our involvement was only a matter of time. England lay just across the channel from France, and there was no way, at all, that we would stand by and allow our greatest ally from across that vast ocean to be swept up in the Nazi craze. It was becoming a darkened world for many Americans, and especially for the residents of our section of town, since we were all Germans and thus were suspected of being related to the militants back in the *old country.*

But for us innocent boys, war was merely something that the adults talked about, sometimes at the dinner table. Mostly those conversations went right over our heads. We were too young to realize just how terribly imminent it all was. We were still in that blissful stage of youthful innocence. For us, it seemed, life would go on as it always had, full of play and adventure and wonderful surprises. It seems, now, that we must have been already infused with expectations of happiness the moment we were born.

It was a time of life when youth reigned. Parents just did not realize it.

As I said before, we lived in an area known as Germantown. It was called Germantown by both the residents who lived in its environs as well as by the outsiders. Those within spoke the name with what could be called affection; the outsiders often spoke the name with contempt, especially because of that monstrous figure of a Nazi, Hitler.

An Austrian by birth, Hitler had adopted himself into the German nation, having served in the German army during WWI. His Germanic background rubbed its ugly self off on anyone who happened to have been born in Germany or who happened to be born to people of German extraction. Consequently we German-Americans were regarded with a disdain that bordered on hostility. That a small, little-talented painter could get so many people up in arms...well, it was almost unthinkable at the time.

The more that happened over in Europe, the worse became our situation in Germantown, so much so that we often were thought of as being outsiders, as *those foreigners.* That position was tough to understand. We personally felt we were Americans first, Germans second. Even those who only ten or fifteen years earlier had just gotten off the boats filled with immigrants, had been quick to ally themselves with their new country;

and although German was their first language, they tried desperately to learn English so that they would fit in.

It took a lot of work by my cousin Ken Reeves to fill me in with many of the details of my family. He maintains a wonderful web site that I often refer to, and from which I have learned a lot.

According to Ken's research, my father's grandfather, John Miller, had emigrated from Germany to Brooklyn, New York sometime around 1848, at the age of twenty-five. Brooklyn was a rural area in those days, but because many other Germans had settled in parts of the middle section of the country, he decided to move across country to Michigan, settling in what is still called Wales Township. One of his children was my grandfather, Ferdinand, who married Susan Lamb, and they had four children, my father being one of them.

But Susan died young, and after an accepted length of time, Grandpa married a woman by the name of Lillie. She is the only one on my father's side that I knew as Grandma, Grandma Susan having died before Jerry and I were born.

Although most of the German immigrants who moved into the area settled in a neighborhood in the southern half of Port Huron that was called Germantown, Grandpa bought an old house up on Sedgwick Street, in a sparsely settled section of the north side of Port Huron. His father had been a carpenter, and had passed along the trade to his son, my grandfather, Ferdinand, whose first name became my father's middle name.

My grandfather sired nine children by those two wives, five by Grandma Lillie. Time has passed, so that only one of those nine children remain: Aunt Eileen, who is the mother-in-law of my historian-cousin Kenneth. She is a wonder-woman and also a wonderful woman. In her nineties now, one would never know it, as she takes each day as being a blessing from God. She is active in her church, The Salvation Army, and she is as kind hearted as one could ever wish an aunt to be.

Grandpa lived until he was ninety-six, and I hope Aunt Eileen lives twenty years longer than that, and in good health. She deserves it.

I remember Grandpa's old house, with its sprawling garage and shed. I remember the old piano that sat in a corner room off the living room, and how I would bang on it whenever I got the chance. I wanted very much to be able to play like Uncle Bud, who was one of Dad's half-brothers. Oh, Uncle Bud could sure "tickle the ivories," as the saying went.

I also remember the huge cookie jar in the old-fashioned kitchen, and how we were allowed to help ourselves. And her sugar cookies were not the small ones; they were made to satisfy a boy's appetite, although in my case it required two of them.

Grandma was a large woman, typical of many of the German women that I knew. She must not have been a scold, for I cannot recall one time when she complained about my piano-banging, or about our hands in the cookie jar, or about our rambunctiously running through the house in our constant games.

Grandpa Miller, though, was the real reason why I enjoyed our visits to their home. Besides siring nine children, and displaying considerable talent with carpentry tools, he also displayed a wonderful memory, for he never forgot a name. At family reunions, he would recall every name of every grandchild and great-grandchild, and eventually there was a horde of them.

Grandpa was one of the warmest persons, male or female, that I ever knew. It was not surprising to any of us kids in the family that Dad had the same personality: warm and loving. Both of them were just plain fun to be around.

Unfortunately, I guess, my father never did acquire much talent or skills with tools, and after dropping out of school at the end of Eighth Grade, he took on odd jobs, until he was hired as a truck driver for the Gruel and Ott Coca-cola Company. Not only were the Gruels Dad's employers, but they were also members of the church that our family attended: St. John's Evangelical and Reformed Church. Prior to that name it had been called St. John's German Lutheran.

The church was, at first, solely German. The minister was required to speak both German and English, and the early service on Sunday was given in German.

Anyway, the Gruels served the church religiously(excuse the pun) down through the years, two of the men serving as council members, and one very talented Gruel woman serving as the organist. In fact, until very recently, our church organist was another woman in the line, one Marian Gruel Relken, so some things do remain the same.

Fred Gruel, Marian's father, was the son of one of the two owners of the Coca-cola Bottling Company of Port Huron. He often sang solo in church. He had a deep voice that carried up into the cavernous spaces of the building. No microphone was necessary. In fact, the church had no microphone. And he articulated the words very well. Dad not only worked for Fred, but he admired him, both for his character and his voice.

For us boys, Germantown was a wondrous place in which to grow up. We delighted in the total environment: the alleys that ran behind the houses; cinder-covered Sixteenth Street, on which we lived; the tulips and roses and lilacs that grew profusely in many of the yards; the surrounding fields that held large gardens; rhubarb growing wildly along back fences.

But most wondrous to us boys was Pollywog. Every boy should have a Pollywog area in his growing-up environment. Pollywog was a large territory that contained both a creek and a pond(both named after the area), and there were countless willows and maples, and shrubs, and tall grasses in which to hide and play, and a huge oak tree that commanded the attention of everyone who ventured into the area.

My cousins, the Kapankas, who lived two blocks south of us on Sixteenth Street and directly across from the eastern boundary of Pollywog, called the area Indian Woods. I didn't know this until years later, but regardless of what it was called, it was a boy's paradise. But more of this later.

For the moment, the important thing was that Jerry and I were going to be able to see *Frankenstein*. We were filled with excitement, with hopes of being frightened out of our wits, with an anxiety that bordered almost on mania.

CHAPTER FOUR

When Movies Reigned as King

T HE GRISWOLD STREET Theater-we always called it the Guthouse Theater, but don't ask me why, since we inherited the name from those whose lives ran before us-was a small theater, sandwiched between Johnsick's Grocery Store on the east and The Club Bar on the west. For us boys, it was a little piece of heaven, a place where we were able to experience horror, excitement, and humor.

It is difficult to explain how much movies meant to us, not just to us boys, but to most Americans. People across the continent had suffered so much during the Great Depression that they turned to movies for one of the few diversions that they could afford. It was later learned that in the year 1938, more than 65 million Americans went to the movies each week. Considering the explosion of stars and quality movies, it is no wonder that someone later dubbed the 30s as "The Golden Age of Hollywood." And thank heavens for the early films of that era, even though it took about two years, or longer, before the best of those films made their way to our little city.

Port Huron had five theaters in the downtown area, alone, plus one up on Pine Grove Avenue(in the north end section of town), and, of course, our beloved Griswold Street Theater in the south end.

For us boys, there were many wonderful aspects of the experience of going to the movies on Saturday afternoons. Of course the main feature was what drew most of the kids on Saturdays, although the cartoons and serials were welcome diversions for us also.

I don't know if it was the Griswold Street Theater that started me on my love affair with movies, but I grew into what might be called a movie-freak. I even liked watching the screen as the credits for the productions rolled by. It was like living in a different world.

Certain cartoons and serials became favorites. To this day Bugs Bunny remains my champion of all cartoon characters. And The Shadow still reigns as king of the serials.

Not one of us boys wanted to miss out on the current segment of the serial that was playing. It is inconceivable to me nowadays that there might be people out there who do not know what the serial was all about. Yet the truth of it is that, in a sense, there have always been serials, when it comes to movies. How many modern movies have spun off sequel after sequel, simply because we have become hooked to an idea or a particular character? Well, getting a person hooked was what serials were all about.

In our days the serial was a running story that required a person to be there week after week in order to find out just what was happening to the hero, or heroine, as the case may be. Both in film and on radio, the serial was developed way early in the twentieth century. My dad reminded me often about his being "hooked" by The Perils of Pauline, whose portrayal by Pauline White was made even more dramatic by the fact that she performed her own dangerous stunts.

Many of the serials took off because of the popularity of comic books. Dick Tracy, The Green Hornet, Flash Gordon, Mandrake the Magician, and Buck Rogers became greater heroes as a result of the serials that carried on the magic. And sometimes great novels produced characters that took on greater status because of the serials, like Tarzan, and Hawkeye(from *The Last of the Mohicans*).

For most of us boys, The Shadow was largely responsible for luring us, on a regular basis, to our Griswold Street Theater.

Each week The Shadow fought the evil forces of the criminal world. Each episode began with a dark and resonating voice that spoke the immortal words: "Who knows what evil lurks in the hearts of men? The shadow knows." And those words were followed by a haunting laugh that spoke of confidence amidst horror. And each week the Shadow would find himself in the most impossibly dangerous position, one that defied our ability to figure out just how he was going to extricate himself from such an awful plight, leaving us to wonder, each week, if he would indeed escape.

But the following week, we would be filled in with a brief synopsis of what had happened the previous week(for those poor, unfortunate kids who might have missed the previous episode) and then revel in the great skills of our hero when he would escape, once again.

But then he would find himself, once again in a horrible situation. Oh, how could he possibly escape this time? We just knew that he couldn't possibly get away every time! Or could he? We would have plenty of food for discussion during the week, trying to figure out how he might do it. Would he really and truly escape this time? Oh, the wonder of it all!

We were hooked. We felt a necessity to be there Saturday afternoons. Some of the serials would last sixteen week, and pity the lad who missed one of the crucial episodes.

Then, after the serial, came the main feature. Certain of those attracted us more than others. We loved Tarzan, and Charlie Chan, and Laurel and Hardy, and horror movies, and heroic cowboy movies, and more cowboy movies.

Of course there was Roy Rogers, called "The King of the Cowboys," who was one of the original members of a musical group of cowboys called The Sons of the Pioneers. His reign came on the heels of the man known as the Singing Cowboy, Gene Autry. Each had his own famous horse, Trigger and Champ, respectively. I suppose I liked both of them, although most of us boys thought that they spent too much time singing, and not enough time engaged in the battles for justice

Oh, those movies. They allowed people to temporarily forget about dust storms on ravaged farms, and picket lines, and food lines, and the disappearance of Amelia Earhardt, and the kidnapping of the Lindbergh baby, and the tramping of the feet of the Nazis.

They entertained us; and that was enough.

CHAPTER FIVE

The Polk School Gang

JERRY AND I grew up near the corner of Sixteenth and Minnie streets. Griswold Street, on which the theater was located, ran parallel to Minnie, and was three blocks north. Both streets ran from east to west. Our house was almost in the center of Germantown, the territory being an area about ten blocks wide by about eight blocks deep. By that time in our lives, Jerry and I had been allowed to expand our personal wanderings so that the theater had long become part of our adventure land.

Old Mrs. and Mr. Ort owned and ran the theater, and they did not put up with any nonsense. Standing at the door to collect the nickels, Mrs. Ort stood solemnly erect, with fierce eyes that seemed to defy us boys to not even dare to think of misbehaving. Mr. Ort, we knew, ran the camera, and thus was usually in the control room. But we were well aware of a few occasions when he had come down into the theater itself and escorted some mischievous child outside. It was one thing to be frightened and thus to scream, which many of the girls did, as did even a few of the boys, or to laugh loudly, which most of the kids did, but it was quite another thing to poke someone, or to yell at inappropriate times, or to announce beforehand when something frightening was going to happen on the screen. The Orts ruled with a firm hand.

There was a large group of us that afternoon who ran boisterously down the aisle to the seats in the front row. As long as Mr. and Mrs. Ort were busy collecting the nickels and getting the movie ready to run, we were somewhat free to act like the noisy and rambunctious boys everyone knew us to be.

Jerry and I led the way, followed by: Don C.(owner of the best and most recent comic books in Germantown); reliable Jack B; Joseph Patrick Carruthers Kramp(we just called him Joe); John Porter, who often made us laugh at the most ridiculous things; and likable Bob Stoner; and Pete Currie; and the dependable Lester Green.

We called ourselves the Polk School Gang, not because all of us attended that particular school but because its environs were the center of many of our mutual activities.

In truth, Jerry and I shared activities with several different groups of boys during those wonderful years, the activities dependent upon which direction we headed toward for entertainment.

Polk School was located on Eleventh Street. It was named after the country's eleventh president. For a long while I was not able to tell anyone anything of importance about President Polk, and thus he was both an enigma and a source of embarrassment to us. It was much later in life when I discovered that President Polk was pretty much the instigator of America's pursuit of the Territory of Texas and the eventual war that brought much of northern Mexico and also California into the Union. Whether that is something to be proud of, or not, is debatable.

On the one hand, we were pointed to the supposedly God-given doctrine of *manifest destiny*, as though God had given the United States a dogma to pursue our way from one side of the continent to the other, sweeping aside anyone who stood in our way. And the resultant history of the resettlement of various tribes of Indians became a sad and bitter history.

Simply put, we swiped land that did not belong to us. That's stealing. Okay? So the government called it *manifest destiny*, but maybe that's because they didn't have anyone around who could spell *stealing*.

So now, in these golden years that I enjoy, I am torn between two ugly feelings: embarrassment and guilt.

Oh, well, Polk was our school, and we were proud of it, and we were glad to be able to have a gang of boys who shared many things in common, especially our own pursuit, the pursuit of boyish happiness. Whether that pursuit was our own *manifest destiny*, or not, I'll leave to my readers to decide.

Anyway, there we were, that delicious, golden, late spring Saturday afternoon, in a dark theater that was about to be darkened even more. We were all squirming in our seats, smack dab in the middle of the front row, listening to all the comments from those behind us about the foolhardiness we were embarked upon.

"I bet they close their eyes during the scary parts," one unknown observer behind us commented. When a couple of us turned around to confront whoever it was that had said that, there were only averted eyes to be met.

"I wouldn't sit there," another whispered loudly. "My brother sat there when *The Mummy* was playing, and he didn't even want to turn out the lights when we went to bed that night."

"Boy!" came the answer from the darkened depths of the area behind us.

That word said it all. "Boy!" It was an exclamation of wonder and mystery and fear. It signaled that we were about to take part in a grand drama, an awesome event that would forever change our lives.

We were all glorying in the attention that we had drawn, and now and then I would turn around to look at all of the others who were filling in the seats behind us, hoping to be noticed as a peculiarly brave soul. And wouldn't you know it, but there, in the immediate row behind us, who did we see sitting so close to the front? Why, it was Mary Belle Thompson, with two of her girlfriends.

I could not believe it. Girls were sitting precariously close to the screen, immediately behind us. Girls! And for one of them to be my friend, Mary Belle Thompson. Why, she was such a gentle being. And yet there she was, sitting with two other girls, in the second row of the theater while *Frankenstein* was playing. How brazen they were. How nervy. How...what?

And when she smiled so serenely at me, I wanted to choke. Why, Mary Belle had never displayed such temerity before. Nor had the other two. But there they sat, waiting expectantly for the movie to begin, and so close to the screen. Some of the grandeur that I had felt began to leave me.

And then came the notice that the movie was about to begin, for the lights began to dim, slowly but noticeably, and the sounds of squealing and forced laughter and fright filled the very air, when suddenly, yet gradually, the sounds stopped, as though the very stopping had begun at the top and continued on down the theater, until it swept over us forcibly like a wave.

We knew immediately what was going on; Mrs. Ort was making her ritualistic stroll down the right-hand aisle. Although later in life I was to think of her as matronly, stern but fair, at that stage in our young lives we reacted as she wished us to react, with a bit of trembling, albeit mixed with respect. We dared not challenge this lady, for it would not have been the first time that one or two youngsters were ushered out of the theater by her, even without her husband's aid. Those youngsters served as sacrifices on the altar of warning.

When she reached the very front of the theater, only about fifteen feet in front of the stage which housed the screen, and no more than five feet in front of us, she turned, and commanded a look from all of us. There was absolute silence in the theater. There wasn't a giggle, or a sneeze, or a laugh, or whimper, or...Well, suffice it to say that everything was now ready, and after standing there rigidly for a few seconds, with her eyes sweeping across and up and down, she finally gave a little nod of her head to her husband, who was sitting in the control booth in the back, and then she marched resolutely up the aisle, and the Saturday matinee began.

The weekly cartoon was presented on the screen, the first act, so to speak, in the wondrous weekly presentation. And if a Walt Disney cartoon was the feature, everyone showed their delight with low screams of joy, just loud enough to show appreciation but not too loud, lest we get a visit from Mrs. Ort. No one wanted that to happen.

Of course, after the cartoon, we were shown another chapter in the serial that was currently running. Poor soul was the boy who had missed the previous episode, and there must have been quite a few, as we could hear some of the children filling in their ignorant companions as to what had taken place the previous week, although it was done in whispers.

And then it came: the feature we had been waiting weeks for, that horror of horrors: *Frankenstein*.

There were twistings and thrashings in the seats, and a collective gasp from within the whole of the theater, as the movie began. A strange silence crept over us as a hundred pairs of eyes stared ahead at the screen.

On the screen a distinguished looking man in a tuxedo walked out onto a stage and gave us viewers a warning about the movie, inducing in us a feeling of great fright, just in case there had been none before. We watched him intensely, and I stole a look at my companions to see how they were reacting, and I noticed that most of them had their mouths hanging open.

And then the movie began! A Universal Picture. The credits came on the screen, and we learned that James Whale-who the heck was he?-was the director, and that Colin Clive-and who the heck was he?-played the part of Herr Frankenstein, the mad doctor. And wouldn't you know it but that there must be a girl in the picture, one Elizabeth, played by Mae Clarke, someone else we did not recognize. Who the heck were all these actors? How was it that we did not know them?

But, then, we were not really interested in anyone other than the monster, and the credits merely displayed the words: "The Monster," with a question mark after the words. The audience apparently was supposed to guess who played the monster, but that was foolish on the movie maker's part, as every boy in the theater, at least every boy who was interested in horror and terror and fright, knew who played the monster. It was the great Boris Karloff. He of the dark eyes that could penetrate into the very soul of a person, whose menacing walk was meant to scare us into the depths of our seats.

How wonderfully bleak and scary was the opening scene: a dark, bleak graveyard, with a group of men standing around an open pit, and a skeleton hanging from a tree limb, and then the first shovels of dirt thrown down onto a wooden casket, the sound echoing into the far depths of our beings. And there, hiding in the background, waiting for the burial to end, were Herr Frankenstein and his helper who, of course, just had to be a hunchback so that more of a sense of the sinister could be presented.

And when the burial party had finished and gone away, out from their hiding place came Herr Frankenstein and his helper, and they dug up

the coffin and began to drag it away, and then they stopped long enough
to also cut down the body of a hanged man, a criminal obviously. More
bodies for more body parts. Oh, this was getting to be good! What grand
horror this movie was going to bring to us.

And then a cut-excuse me for the technical term, but it gives me a bit
of movie sophistication-to a medical college, where a group of medical
students surrounded an open space in a small amphitheater, where a
professor spoke to his students in humorous tones about the parts of the
body, especially alluding to two particular jars, each containing a human
brain, one jar marked "Normal" and the other jar marked "Criminal." Of
course we all knew just where those brains had come from, having just
witnessed the digging up of the one body and the cutting down of the
other body from the tree branch.

And staring in through one of the upper windows of the medical
building was the hunchback, who had been ordered by Herr Frankenstein
to steal the jar with the "normal" brain.

But of course there had to be a foul-up, which we all expected but
which nevertheless brought grave and frightful, subdued screams from
those who were the more timid. That foul-up occurred when, after the
doctor and students had long departed the scene, the hunchback sneaked
in through the window and dropped down onto the floor, gleefully looking
over the scene with small, evil eyes, and took down from the counter the
jar with the "Normal" brain, only to accidentally drop the jar, where it
broke.

What revulsion and fear swept over his face! He knew he was in for
it. He knew that Herr Frankenstein would be livid with rage and that the
doctor would punish him severely. But with great cunning he took down
the jar with the "Criminal" brain, and crept off with it. He obviously
figured that no one would be the wiser.

Ah, but those of us in the audience knew that awful things would
happen because of that decision. We weren't fooled. Oh, no. Not those of
us who had experienced enough horror movies to know better.

And then the movie cut to the huge, dark castle-like tower in which
Herr Frankenstein carried out his terrible experiments, hoping to build a

human body, using powerful currents of electricity and ultra violet rays. That body was going to be the greatest creation ever wrought by man.

Transformers and generators and electrical wires and glass tubes filled the huge room, causing sparks and man-made lightning bolts to glow and flare and flash through the stifling air. Oh, what wonders! What horrors! What terrors struck our very beings.

And then later, how tremendously dreadful came the scene where the created body first walked onto the screen, methodical but awkward, stiff and menacing. And then the rest of the movie, with the awful killings that were eventually produced, especially that of a small girl who had befriended the monster and whose body was carried, in the arms of her father, into the town for all to see.

And then the powerful ending to the movie, when the monster was consumed in the flames of a huge windmill-like tower, the townspeople all in a rage over the murders.

And we all would probably have accepted it as a first-rate movie, if the producers had not presented a last scene, one in which Herr Frankenstein was seen recovering in the bedroom of his baron-father's estate, not the least concerned that the monster he had built had been responsible for some deaths, and especially the death of such an innocent child, as was that poor little girl. Apparently he was only concerned that his experiment had failed.

We were disappointed. We were left to grapple with so many questions. What had happened to Elizabeth, whom Herr Frankenstein had been about to marry? Why wasn't there justice practiced by locking up the mad doctor for the killings that had happened because of his creation? And, most importantly, why wasn't the movie scarier than it was?

A buzz of voices filled the atmosphere of the theater as the lights came on and all the children filed out. The disappointment that we felt was manifest in the voices of many others.

It was a noisy bunch of kids who ushered out into the sunny sky that Saturday afternoon, many of them declaring their disappointment with the movie. Their remarks were not much different than ours.

"That wasn't scary at all," John said.

"I didn't even see many of the girls screaming," Joe put in.

"How would you know?" Bob teased. "You had your eyes closed most of the time."

"I did not," Joe retorted a little lamely.

Joe took the teasing too seriously, I figured, and when that happened, the guys wouldn't let go of it.

"Yeah," Don kidded, "maybe you're right. You probably were just sleeping." Don looked over at me and winked.

"I liked the part where the monster met the little girl," Lester said, helping to put to rest the kidding so that no one's feelings would be hurt too much. "But I just knew that he was going to kill her," he added. Lester could often be the peacemaker.

"We didn't actually see him kill her," John said.

"I wouldn't want to see that happen, anyway, to actually see it," Jerry said.

"Neither would I," someone else agreed. And there were nods of agreement all around.

"Boris Karloff might be a good actor, but he isn't nearly as scary as Bela Lugosi," I said.

"Or the Wolf Man," Bob put in.

"I think *The Mummy* was the scariest movie I ever saw," Jack said.

"Yeah," Jerry agreed. "I remember when that movie came, we sat in the front row, and then the Mummy came up out of the swamp and he looked so big…"

"He was huge," Pete said, interrupting Jerry. "We were right behind you guys, and you scrunched down in your seats."

"So did you, Pete," Joe said. "I saw you."

"Anyway," Jack put in, trying to restore some peace, "I think Larry's right. Bela Lugosi scared the heck out of me in that one movie, especially when he came out of the coffin, and then when he covered his face with that black cape, and only his eyes showed. And then he turned into a bat. You guys remember."

"Yeahhh," Pete put in, stretching the end of the word out in a dramatic, spooky manner. "I'm Count Dracula," he uttered in a reasonably scary way, "and I'm going to suck out your blood," pulling his arm up and across his face in a manner that resembled Count Dracula with his cape.

And we all laughed, but there was an element of terror in the words, and most of us shuddered a little.

And thus another chapter of my life had passed, with the death of the myth of the terror of *Frankenstein*. Not a truly important chapter, I admit, but all the same...

The first chapter of any importance was the previous year, when my friend Marvin had been killed, when first I was made aware of the tenuous thread that connected me to life.

It was hard for me to understand, at that time in my life, that the chapters would eventually pass me by, and at a much later age I would discover, as so many others before me have discovered, that they seem indeed to fly by.

When I had finished writing about Marvin's death in my first book, I had no idea that I would begin another look at life and what it had to offer.

But here I am. And hopefully there are still many chapters remaining in the saga that makes up one person's experiences.

CHAPTER SIX

A Bag Swing and Warfare

THOSE COUSINS OF ours that I mentioned earlier, the Kapankas, lived in what Jerry and I thought of as the most enviable place in Germantown, directly across the street from Pollywog. Thus they had direct access to a wilderness that was wondrous for boys. It was a mysterious place, where a boy could get lost in what I call "boyhood."

The pond was not a large affair, but large enough to provide opportunities for floating rafts during summer, and a great place for skating in wintertime. It stretched itself westward about a hundred yards, its surface trying vainly to hide the creatures beneath from the prying eyes of all of us boys. Not very successfully, I might add, as most of us boys took home, in old glass jars, enough pollywogs and frogs and snakes to fill a small aquarium. Of course most of the poor creatures died, from either mishandling, or loneliness, or a reluctance to adjust to captivity.

The Kapankas' house was a huge brick affair, of two stories. The house was on a large site, with hardwood trees heavily covering a huge grassy area in back, a shrub-filled area that stretched east for what would have been about three city blocks, had there been a neighborhood east of them by which to measure. It was like a great wilderness, back there. The territory was a wonderful place to engage in warfare, Kapanka style.

South of their house stood two smaller houses, and then some railroad tracks. Taken as a whole, the property was vast, and it offered a wonderful environment for the games that were devised by the boys.

There were four boys in the family: Jack, Don, Bob, and Roy. The first three were older than Jerry and I; Roy was about our age. They had a sister, Betty, who was about the same age as my sister Marilyn, which means that she was about five or six years older than Jerry and I.

All of the Kapanka boys were rough-edged, but great persons. I don't want to imply that they were rough individuals, but that they were hardened by each other in the games that they played. Rough but fair would be the proper assessment.

Since the oldest boy, Jack, the redhead in the family, was an outstanding athlete, it was necessary for the ones that followed to try to keep up in the pursuits that most boys engage in.

After Jack, came Don, who was slender, but hardy, and he gave in to no one in anything.

And then along came Bob, shorter and stockier than either of the first two, but he had a bulldog tenacity that allowed him not only to survive the ruggedness of boyhood in his family and in the neighborhood, but to sometimes dominate it. And while it might not be right to play favorites, I have to admit that Bob was the most popular of the four boys, although all of them were admired.

The last boy, Roy, turned out to be the tallest. He often took it on the chin, both physically and mentally, when taking part in the various rough games that were devised down through the years, but he did all right.

That summer of the Frankenstein movie was the first summer that Jerry and I were initiated in the art of swinging on a bag swing. We had heard much about the swing, but we had not seen it yet.

There was a large, barnlike building in the back yard of the Kapanka property. Formerly it had been used as stables by the previous owner, but it had given way to housing an automobile and sundry articles of tools and equipment that might be used around the house or yard.

Inside one of the rooms of the garage was a long coil of heavy rope, and a cloth bag filled with rags and a little dirt, the dirt having been put in there to give the bag some weight. The whole affair lay there all winter long, waiting to be put into use again, when spring arrived.

Each spring one of the Kapanka boys would climb a huge oak tree that dominated the back yard, carrying with him one end of the rope. He would shinny out on a huge limb that stuck itself out, high off the ground, tie the rope to the middle of the branch, and then shinny down the rope itself to the ground. The other end of the rope was then tied firmly to a loose portion of the bag. Lo and behold, a bag swing. But a bag swing unlike any I was ever to see anyplace else, for the limb of the tree was more than twenty feet high off the ground, and the bag swing itself swung no less than four feet up from the ground, at its lowest point of a swinging action, thus allowing for a long arc when it was set in motion.

The boys had jerry-rigged a wooden tower, of sorts, with wooden rungs for climbing to the top. The tower itself was about ten feet tall. When the swing was ready to be used, a bunch of us boys would climb to the top of the tower, and wait for the supreme moment when each could prove his manhood, or his foolishness.

There was a shorter tower across the yard, and someone on the ground would take the swing and haul it back and away from the tall tower, climb up the short tower, and then let the bag fly, so that someone on the opposite tower could catch the bag, jump on the swing, and try to swing it out as far away from the tower as he could.

Of course, the arc of the swing would take it quite a ways away from the starting point, and the swinger would kick his legs in order to propel the bag as far as he could, resulting in a returning arc back toward the tower from which he had jumped. Oh, it was a wonderful thing to see, the first boy swinging with all of his might so as to make as long an arc as was possible.

Meanwhile, we boys on the taller tower would wait for our turn to jump on. Of course there were arguments about who would be next. And eventually the time would arrive for the next participant, who would try to time his jump just right and then fling himself out into space, grasping for the rope with his hands and for the bag with his legs.

At that point the danger would be increased, for two boys would be riding the swing, both of them trying to find comfortable positions, for each knew that another pass would bring them back to the tower, from where another boy would be waiting for his turn to jump on.

The whole idea was not just to provide an exhilarating ride, but to engage in a contest to see how many boys could ride the swing at the same time, without falling. There were arguments, over the years, as to just how many came to be on the bag at one time, and as to who had been on the swing when a new record had been set. Just about every boy who rode the swing saw himself as one of the record-setting riders. No one wanted to be left out of the record book.

It's amazing how many boys there must have been on the bag during that record-setting ride, what with all the bragging that went on. Or perhaps it is not amazing, considering how vivid were our imaginations and how wonderful our ability to invent heroics.

I vividly recall my first ride. I had been waiting on the tower for some time, hoping for the chance for fame. I am sure that my legs were shaking, not with excitement, but with terror. There were already two boys on the bag, my cousin Bob and another boy, when my turn came. Those two were sitting comfortably, their legs entwined around the bag, their cries of joy sounding ominously to my ears. With each arc, their kicking legs propelled themselves higher at each end of the arc, and I was worried that they would be too high for me to be able to jump aboard.

But here they came again, and everyone behind me on the tower was yelling for me to get ready; they were tired of waiting for a coward, although I suspected that a few of them probably did not relish being in the spot I was in. So I got myself ready, bending in somewhat of a crouch so that I would be able to spring out at the swing.

Jerry was right behind me, at the time, yelling for me to be ready. I didn't need anyone to be yelling in my ears, at that moment, for I was trying hard to gauge both the tempo of the swing and the space that would present itself to me when the bag approached.

And then, there it was, almost within reach; and with fear gripping me, there I went, leaping out into the air and desperately grabbing at the rope with my hands while also trying to find a way to wrap my legs either around the bag itself or around the body of one of the boys already on the swing. Fear held me in its power as my hands held on for dear life and as my legs were wrapping themselves around whatever they could find. I had meant to grab the rope, but missed, and instead I had grabbed at the first thing that was available, which turned out to be the back of Bob's shirt, which made him yell out to me to let go, as it was choking him and it was possible that I just might pull him off the swing.

With desperation, again I reached for the rope, but this time all I could manage to do was to grab Bob's throat, and with a strangling sound, he shook himself vigorously, so that I lost hold and fell to the ground.

As I was plunging toward the ground, all I could about was the great possibility of breaking my neck, or an arm or a leg. Whatever part of the anatomy was vulnerable to breakage, I felt sure that I would suffer some terrible tragedy.

But the ground met me with the distinct sound of an inglorious uumpf, and I crumpled up like a sodden old bag. I lay there for a few seconds while my mind went through the process of taking inventory of the various bones and joints of my frail body. And I noticed that there were a lot of boys hovering over me, all of them seeming to be talking at once.

When I tried to slowly sit up, I found that everything seemed to be in perfectly good working order, so that I was able to stand without the help of anyone else. And there was, it seemed to me, a general kind of relief on the part of the other boys, as well as an expression of admiration, so that I found that I had achieved a little of a hero's status because of the fall. I had failed, yet I had been given acclaim. Go figure!

So! I had made my first jump, as brief as it was, and after tiring of the acclamation shown to me, I hurried back up the tower, and waited patiently for the show to begin again.

There was such joy on top of that tower, that spring day, standing there with the other boys, with anticipation of the shivering sensation of knowing that as we jumped out into space, there would come the thrill of swinging high off the ground, aware of space hurtling by, and gaining the further end of the arc, at which point we would begin the descent and then the following ascent toward the tower, where another boy was waiting for his leap into space; we knew that there would be hands and legs clawing at us in that next boy's furious need to grab on to whatever he could find. And the grabbing was, indeed, furious, for if the boy missed, then he would find himself flailing in the air, grabbing handfuls of nothing but air.

And often, while jumping aboard the swing, the next boy would be grabbing one of our arms, or our waist, or even our neck and head, just as all of us had done. And then it would become a matter of utmost strength to hold on, the air rushing past us as we swung high off the ground.

I found that when I was swinging on the bag, I didn't dare look down, for inattention could cost me my position, and if I lost my place on the swing, you could bet that I would be taking others down with me. The thought of our flailing bodies hurtling toward the ground was enough to make a boy hold on for dear life. And let me tell you, life was very dear to me, so I held on with all of my might.

The swinging was often punctuated by screams and yells of both fear and elation, and there were others who were yelling encouragement to hold on so that a new record could be achieved.

Bob told me, years later, that he could recall as many as five boys on the swing at one time, before at least one of the boys would fall. Five boys aboard at the same time, apparently, was a record. And certainly the thought of setting a new record was always uppermost in our minds, even though our efforts produced numerous falls that were fraught with danger.

Of course the distance to the ground during a fall depended on which point of the arc a boy fell from. The closest to the ground that the swing found itself was still a matter of three or four feet, and at the furthest point of the arc, the distance to the ground might have been as much as ten feet.

The thought of falling was enough to make a boy shudder, and my spine shuddered often through the two or three years that I used the swing. But it was the thrill of the ride that enticed us, as well as the challenge to be part of any record. Records that were set in any of our boyish activities were talked about for years to come, and everyone wanted to be known for having taken part in setting the records.

Dangerous? Sure. But the thrill was too much to resist. As well as the glory. Oh, how we treasured the glory!

Of course I fell, many times, as did Jerry, and Jack, and all of my cousins. Joe never took part in this activity. He had a problem with height.

He also had a problem with the knowledge that each of my cousins had suffered at least one broken arm, through the course of the years. I feel that I was lucky to only have been bruised. The same thing was true of Jerry. How we escaped broken limbs from that dangerous game is beyond me. And, no! I don't believe that Divine Providence saved us. Especially me! For I had no right to expect special dispensation from a God who was judicious, as well as benevolent.

I did suffer a severely broken arm, but that happened the following summer, and it didn't happen because of swinging on the bag swing. Instead, ironically it happened when I turned a somersault while making a flip out of the maple tree that stood in Joe's front yard. Of all the trees that that should happen in, it would have to be Joe's, a tree belonging to the only boy who would not take part in the bag swinging contest. The one boy who was my nemesis throughout those youthful days.

The matter of my broken arm was the result of another attempt at record-setting. A bunch of us boys had, now and then, become engaged in a contest involving Joe's tree. That maple tree had a branch that extended over the sidewalk leading up to Joe's front door. And that particular summer we had invented a Tarzan-type of contest. It involved climbing out over the branch, and then hanging onto the branch with your hands while dropping your legs, thus dangling underneath the branch.

Then you would begin to swing your legs, propelling your legs backward and forward into as wide an arc as possible, and, finally, letting go when you thought you were at the longest and highest point of the swing. The idea was to swing yourself, like a pendulum, as far out as possible, so that you could propel your body out and across the sidewalk, where your landing mark would be duly noted, and argued about, by those waiting down below.

I was overly ambitious that summer day, hoping to gain glory by setting a new record. Of course, looking back, I suppose that I was always unduly overly ambitious those days of my young life. Anyway, there were five or six of us boys on the scene, each of us taking a turn. And when it came time for me to take my turn, I mustered all of my foolish ego, all of my tree-swinging ability, and all of my arrogance, and I launched myself into action with as much enthusiasm as possible. My swinging was vigorous, my athleticism marvelous, and at the height of what I considered to be the ultimate point, I let go, hurling myself across the sidewalk with a great cry: "Look at me, I'm Tarzan."

Woe! At the very moment the last word came out of my mouth, I realized that I was not only hurtling through space, in a path that would take me across the sidewalk, but that I also was inadvertently turning a somersault. That was the last thing I wanted to do.

My first reaction, when I realized just what was happening, was to throw my arms out as a way of preventing myself from falling on my head, which could have resulted in a broken neck. My reaction worked perfectly. I did not fall on my head. I fell on my left arm. But that fall snapped bones in two places, in my arm.

There was pandemonium. Some of the boys screamed. For a moment, I sat on the ground, dumbfounded. My arm was bleeding, and one of the bones had broken its way through the skin and was now staring weirdly up at me. To say that I began to cry out in fear is to downplay it somewhat. I was panic-stricken.

I recall running up to the front door of Joe's house, screaming wildly: "My arm's broken. My arm's broken." And when Joe's mother rushed to the front door and took a look at my arm, her reaction to my plight was predictable.

"Watch out, Larry," she shouted, "you'll get blood all over my living room rug."

While I waited on Joe's front porch, Joe's mother went to make a quick phone call to our home. Mother, of course, did not understand just what had happened, having received only the barest of details from Joe's mother over the phone. And so she had sent my sister Marilyn.

Good ol' Marilyn. If ever a boy needed a sister who was kind and helpful and sympathetic, it should be one like Marilyn.

Marilyn gently cradled my arm in her hands, on our way home, all the while trying to reassure me that everything would be okay, talking to me in a fashion that was meant to comfort me and to divert my attention away from my horribly injured arm.

Poor, dear Marilyn. Often she was like a second mother to us. How she handled that situation is something beyond my understanding. It was hard enough for me to look at my arm, and you can bet that I tried not to. But for Marilyn to make that walk home with me, helping me by cradling my arm with her hands…it must have been a horrible experience.

I don't remember just how I got to the hospital. The events are blurred in my memory bank. The next thing I recall is being on a hospital surgical bed, in an operating room, with a nurse hovering over me and telling me to count backwards as she was in the process of administering chloroform. I remember that the chloroform had a most unpleasant smell, and that it also had remarkably unusual effects, as I found myself spinning around and around in a vast circle, with either the nurse chasing me or me chasing the nurse. The nightmare ended, and eventually I awoke to find myself on a bed in a hospital room. The room was shared by a boy who, I later found out, had been badly burned in a fire at his home.

According to Doc Martin, who handled the case-just in case you are interested in this particular story-it was a horrible break. My arm was, indeed, broken in two places, and what with the severe fracture of my forearm, Dr. Martin was concerned that I would never be able to play baseball again, much less swing in the trees. While I was lying on my hospital bed, after the operation, he came for his post-operation visit, and told me that it was necessary for me to begin using my arm as quickly as possible, else I would become somewhat crippled. His methods were far ahead of his time, as I am told that other doctors would have prescribed complete inactivity.

My mother and father also feared the worst. I know for sure that they worried that I would be greatly limited in my future actions. I fooled them all, except Doc Martin, of course. I was determined to play baseball again, and I recovered quickly and very well, and was in the trees of the neighborhood again, although I kept knowledge of those activities to myself.

I did not dare tell my mother that on my first day home from the hospital, my arm in a cast and a sling, I climbed the apple tree belonging to the Wingardens, a family a mere half-block up on Sixteenth Street. It seems

I spent much of my youth trying to impress my friends by performing foolish acts. Jerry warned me not to try climbing the tree.

The tree was in the back of the Wingardens' property, and might have been visible to my mother, had she taken the time to look, for there was an open line of sight between our front porch and the tree. But I knew that Mother didn't have time to keep watch over five children all of the time, and I suspect that she felt that, for once in my life, I would not do something stupid. Poor Mother!

The tree was an easy climb for a boy with two good arms, but it was somewhat of a challenge for a boy with his left arm in a cast and sling. But I carefully worked myself up into the tree, where I sat in one of the higher branches, taunting Jerry to join me. But Jerry decided not to climb, not because he was afraid, for he climbed as many trees as did I, but I think he did not want to do anything to encourage me in my foolishness, for if he had, then I might have been emboldened to go on to even higher branches, and fallen, which might have proved to be disastrous. And knowing Mother, Jerry would probably have been punished for not telling her about my climbing.

So when he turned and walked away, leaving me up in the tree by myself, I felt foolishly abandoned, and so I climbed back down, since I had no one around to display my foolhardiness to. I craved attention. I longed for glory. I was, to put it bluntly, stupidly foolish at times.

Anyway, that all happened a year later than when this present narration takes place.

One particular day in the summer of 1940, after we had had our fill of the swing, a bunch of us boys began a game of *war*. Usually this game was nothing more than using cap guns, or using make-believe guns(pointing our fingers at our *enemy* and making sounds that were supposed to simulate gun shots, which often produced a great amount of argument over whether a person had been shot, or not), or using handmade rubber band guns, which were accurate for no more than about twenty feet.

But this particular day, we found ourselves in a much more perilous game, for my Kapanka cousins brought out a couple of BB guns, one for each of the two sides. Thus the game brought to it a far more serious dimension: we would have to be very careful in trying to outflank our adversary.

There were rules involved. For instance, anyone using one of the BB guns had to make sure only to aim at a person's buttocks or legs, and only then when from a considerable distance away, thus lessening the possibility of great harm. I didn't relish the idea of being shot any place on my body, even on my buttocks. I never did have much weight, and thus my buttocks were merely an area in which skin was stretched taught over bones and tendons and muscles. A BB struck there was apt to hurt.

There were about ten of us involved in the game that day. My cousin Don was the captain of our team, while his brother Bob was the leader of the opposing team. A coin was tossed, and our side elected to be the ones in hiding, which meant that we would be given about two or three minutes to disperse and find safe hiding places.

The idea of the game was either to *kill* our opponents with our imaginary guns, or to be able to get back to and inside the stables without being *killed* ourselves, for the stables were deemed to be *home, or safe territory.*

When the signal was given for the game to begin, all of us on Don's side took off, running around and behind the stables, where a large field stretched out, with both small and large trees among tall field grasses. As we dispersed, I yelled to Jerry to follow me, for I had an idea that I figured would enable us to get to the stables without being detected. We had to hurry, for supposedly we were only to be given a count of fifty before the chasers came after us. And I doubt there ever was a game when the counting was accurate. It was cheating, but we all expected it. So we all ran as fast as we could, running into the grassland, hoping to find some place to hide in the weeds or among the trees.

About fifty yards south of this wilderness area was Cypress Street, a dirt street that intersected with Sixteenth Street, just across from Pollywog. I figured that if Jerry and I could get to Cypress, we could crawl, unseen, along the bottom of the ditch that ran alongside the road, and then we could cut across Sixteenth Street, into the sedge grasses of Pollywog, and wait in the grasses for a chance to get to the stables from the front of the Kapanka property. The frontal attack would not be expected, I figured.

Everything went well, and we were not seen. At least we thought we weren't seen, for no one raised an outcry. And like seasoned soldiers, we crept our way through the grasses, raising our heads only high enough to survey the surroundings. At times we could hears cries of other members of the teams, but since the sounds seemed to be quite a distance away, we became encouraged enough to spurt across Sixteenth Street and make it to the front of the Kapanka house, where we threw ourselves to the ground, underneath some hedges growing there. We hugged the foundation of the house, crawling slowly to the corner of the house, where we lay silently.

After a minute or two, and not hearing anybody, I peeked around the edge of the house, and all I could see was the limp bag swing, hanging from its high overhead branch. There was no one there, no one that we could see.

I whispered to Jerry to wait a few minutes longer, just to be sure. And I kept peeking, from time to time, making sure that everything was okay. And after about three or four minutes of absolute silence from the back yard, I motioned to Jerry to be ready to run for the stables, which were about fifty feet beyond the bag swing.

He nodded, and we jumped to our feet, running lickety-split, a feeling of triumph filling my soul as we rushed through the back yard.

We were no more than twenty feet from the stables when it happened. A sharp pain on my cheek, just under my left eye. I hadn't heard anything, so I wasn't sure just what it was. It might have been a hornet sting, but it felt harder than that, for it felt as though something had struck me with a hard and sharp force.

And then I realized what had happened. As sure as there were apples in apple trees, I was sure that I had been shot with a BB. And for once in my life, I felt abject fear, for that BB had struck me just beneath my eye, and the idea of nearly having my eye shot out was too much for me to handle.

I felt for the spot where the BB had struck, and my fingers came away with blood on them, and Jerry was screaming, realizing what had happened. When he screamed, I imagined the worst, and thought that perhaps I had lost an eye, indeed. So I began to scream, and to cry, not from pain, but from that horrible fear. It didn't take but a moment before I realized that I was seeing everything okay, but still I cried.

Just then Bob came out of some tall grass that grew along the south part of their property, and he was holding his gun barrel pointed toward the ground, and I could see the worry on his face. Come to think of it, he bore a look of anguish.

Bob hurried to me, yelling over his shoulder for anyone within hearing to come in.

"Are you all right? Are you okay?" Bob asked, rushing up to me, his voice filled with anxiety.

By then, my crying had been reduced to a sniffle, for I did not want anyone to think that I was a crybaby, but I was still fingering the spot where I had been shot.

Meanwhile, those near us had begun yelling out loud, calling for everyone to come in from the game. It was like calling "Timeout" during a football game, except these yells were filled with greater urgency.

Soon, others poured out of the woods, and the whole gang gathered around, everyone talking at once, and everyone taking a look at my face. If I had had a handkerchief, I would have dabbed my wound, but I don't think there was a boy in the neighborhood who carried such a thing.

Bob was saying whatever he could to make me feel better, telling me that my eye was okay, and that the bleeding would stop eventually. He was so solicitous that I began to feel some relief, but then I realized that there was something else that he was worried about, as well as my eye. He was more worried about what his father would say if he were to find out what had happened. For if his father, Hugo, were to learn that Bob had shot a boy in the face, there would be all heck to pay. It was one thing to shoot a boy in the seat of his pants. But his face? Absolutely not!

It was at that point that I was presented with a peace offering. Bob offered to let me shoot his gun five times, at an accepted target, of course, if I agreed not to tell on him. Obviously I would not have told on him, anyway. That was not my way of doing things. It probably wasn't the way of any of the boys. None of us wanted to be known as squealers. Well, that might not have been true about Joe, but the rest of us were sworn to the honor code of keeping really important and personal things to ourselves.

Anyway, there had been nothing malicious in Bob's shooting me. There was nothing malicious about any of the Kapanka boys. They were all great guys. They were fun-loving, generous, and likable. And while it might turn out that the matter would be talked about among the boys themselves, there was no question about the matter remaining quiet, in regards to all of our parents.

Looking back on it all, there might even have been a bit of selfishness on the part of all of us boys. None of us wanted to be shut out of the privilege of swinging on the bag swing, and if Uncle Hugo had found out what had happened, then...

The end of the matter was when I let Jerry take two of my shots, a generous gesture on my part, I believe. Neither one of us had ever shot a BB gun before, so I just felt that I had to share the honor. Of course we shot at stationary targets in the woods, at something that wouldn't shoot back at us, and thus were initiated into just a little bit of what we felt real war must be like. It was an activity that only boys would understand.

And I was always of a mind, from that time forward, especially when I myself became a father of a boy, to just let boys be boys. Although I have to admit that I never saw the BB guns again, while we engaged in "war." And I never allowed my son to have one.

CHAPTER SEVEN

Awakening in Germantown

D AD USED TO tell us that things were "tougher than nails" in the early years of the 1930's. I don't know where he got the phrase, probably from some book that he had read, but if he said it, then it must have been true. He wasn't always blunt about things, but he was honest, both in facts and in his appraisal of things.

When I look back on those times, I think that all I can say about the early two-thirds of the decade was that times were slow. Of course, that appraisal is from a boy who was only ten years old by the time the decade had ended. I do know that there were a lot of people out of work, especially in the East, where the hammering of the loss of profits from Wall Street was greatest. Apparently suicides of businessmen, especially stock brokers, had become so common that comedians made jokes about men waiting in line on the highest ledges of skyscrapers in New York City in order to jump off. At first the jokes were laughed at, but eventually no one saw anything funny in people's lives being horribly wasted.

Throughout that era, there were bread lines, and soup kitchens, and work lines in which men who had formerly been business executives were now reduced to crying out for any job, even menial ones. And eventually America discovered that we had a busy President who was accused of being an autocrat, a tyrant, a dictator, because he passed executive orders that, in reality, bypassed what he regarded as an ineffective Congress.

But later, by 1940, Germantown followed the rest of the country in seeing a little progress in the number of people who became employed.

Especially was this true in industry, which was beginning to capitalize on orders for manufactured goods, which were needed by the European sector, since their war demanded things that only America could manufacture, which America was most willing to do.

Meanwhile, in 1939, in England, their Prime Minister had tried futilely to deny that a war was approaching, but there were some politicians there that worked hard to bring America into the discussions that were taking place. But back home the good ol' boys in the U.S.A. were resisting those overtures, at least for awhile. And in good ol' Germantown, our section of Port Huron, Michigan, the people seemed hardly aware that anything of world importance was taking place. Or maybe they just appeared that way.

For us boys, life went on as usual. We went on blithely as though we had not a care in the world. We had no such worries about the state of the globe. We were happy in our unconcern, delighted when we found old pollywogs or frogs or snakes to keep in glass jars, or movies to critique, or new rafts to build, all truly important adventures that our young minds dreamed up.

In the Sixteenth Street gang, Jerry and I found different boys than those of the Polk School gang. It was with this gang that geography was the determining factor. Our boundaries somewhat overlapped that of the Polk School gang, since the school was only five blocks away, but here the boundaries were more fixed for this particular gang, with a little leeway to allow for some democracy in selecting friends.

Directly across the street from our house were the Nelsons. They had no boys who were strictly close to the age of Jerry and me, but two of them, Chet and Kenny, who were a few years older than Jerry and I, sometimes found themselves engaged in our activities, especially when it came to sports.

Kenny was handsome, and slightly cocky, especially when baseball was involved. He also had been a marble champion of the neighborhood (piggy-in-the-pot style), until I found enough spunk-or foolhardiness to challenge him the year before and won more of his marbles than he ever wanted to admit to having lost.

As I recorded in my earlier book, piggy-in-the-pot was a game that was played by opponents rolling marbles on the ground toward a hole.

The contestants could play for only the single marbles thrown, or they could bet a number of marbles on the throws. I suppose the game may be compared, somewhat, to boccie, except that the winner was the one who was able to throw his marble into the hole. And if a tie occurred, then another attempt was made, until one competitor was defeated.

It is impossible to describe the elation I felt that day when I won a very large pot, not only winning all the marbles that had been bet, but also winning the title of Marble Champion of Germantown. In fact, I remember the anger Kenny showed that fateful day when he lost, for he threw a handful of marbles to the ground in disgust. They were the very marbles that he had bet against me, and while he had lost them fairly, he wasn't going to make it easy for me to collect them, for he threw them so that they scattered all over the ground where the game had taken place. There they lay, so widely scattered that I had to work hard to get them all. But collect them, I did. And I did so without showing my usually, stupidly displayed arrogance, for I did not relish being physically trounced by Kenny.

But looking back on that incident from Kenny's point of view, perhaps his anger had produced one desired effect for him: I had to get down on my hands and knees in order to pick up the marbles. Thus, in a way, I had to bow to him. Consequently my victory was bittersweet, as I did not like bowing to any person. But bow, I did. What's a little humility when it comes to owning precious marbles and victory?

Chet was warmer. as a person, easy to like, and a fair athlete in his own right. In fact, he probably was as genuinely likable a person as any person I ever knew. Everyone liked Chetty, as they called him even into adulthood. It seemed that he always wore a smile. His good nature was genuine, and his sincere kindness was something that he carried over into adulthood. Years later, after he retired from Detroit Edison, a utility company, he put his talents to use with Habitat for Humanity. And I know for a fact that he found it almost impossible to turn down a friend who needed him.

Donny Bailey lived in the back of a house owned by the Warren family, two doors south of our house, and was occasionally involved in our games. Donny was tall for his age, had dark black hair, and was admired by all the girls for his good looks. I always had the feeling that Donna Nelson, sister to Kenny and Chet, had a crush on Donny, and I recall calling out: "Donny and Donna! Donny and Donna" whenever the two of them were in the same area together." He took it all good naturedly. But Donna didn't take too kindly to my teasing, probably because I teased too much. I'm sure it's true that I did too much of most everything that was annoying.

Fred Graham and his older brother Wesley lived five houses south of our house, with their sister Barbara and their parents, but apparently they must have been too old for any of our affairs, as I can't recall their ever taking part in them, not even when we lit up the night air with bonfires in Pollywog in the dead of winter. Maybe they were merely uninterested. And when the war eventually came, as it most surely did, both Fred and Wesley went off to various military camps with many of the other older *boys* in the neighborhood. That contingent included Bud Warner and Chuck Nelson and Clyde Warren. And their parents all hung the famous star-flag in their front windows to indicate the sacrifice that was being made. And we younger boys were immensely proud of all of them. They were good, dutiful German-Americans who were ashamed of all the calamities being caused by the Fascists of our grandparents' homeland. But all that lay in the future, although a very near future. We just did not know that Pearl Harbor was only a little over a year away.

Around the corner, over on Seventeenth Street, lived Albert "Knobby" Pugh. Now there was a guy! Talk about handsome! He was movie-star handsome. He was personable. And he was liked by everyone, young and old, male and female. He was about eight years older than Jerry and I, but he sometimes found himself a part of the street baseball games, where he quite often took up the cause of the underdogs. And I remember him for one especially wonderful deed: helping to clean up Pollywog in late autumn in preparation for ice skating when winter would arrive. Old logs had to be dragged up onto the banks of both the creek and the pond, and the wild grasses that invaded the pond during low water times had to be cut down so that skates did not find stubble-like obstacles. As was true about Chetty, everyone liked Knobby.

I remember one other older boy in the immediate neighborhood who left an impression on me. That was Jim S., from over on Fifteenth Street.

He had a unique ability. He could wiggle his ears. One at a time. Or both at the same time.

It was a wonderfully warm late spring day when I went there, along with a few others of our gang, and watched him do his thing. Oh, it was magical! It was a great performance, one that rivaled the greatest baseball or football skills. He sat before us, waiting for us to give our commandments. "Wiggle your left ear, Jim," one of us would shout, and he would screw up his face in concentration and wiggle that ear, and only that ear.

Whereupon another of the boys would yell out for him to wiggle both ears, and again he would concentrate, until both ears were wiggling in perfect rhythm. Oh, but that was a wonderful skill to have, and all of us spent much time trying to duplicate that skill, but none of us ever could master it. Oh, how life's disappointments could invade our young lives.

While Germantown slowly woke up to the changing times, we boys went happily on our way, content to go on with activities that could only possibly interest young boys.

One Saturday I caught a garter snake out by our back fence. To this day I don't know why it's called a garter snake. I knew, even then, what a garter looked like, although I confess to never having actually seen it worn. I supposed Mother wore one, but I never saw one on her, although I have to admit that I wouldn't have been looking for one, anyway.

The point that I want to make-although I seem to be belaboring the issue-is that there just did not seem to be any connection between women's apparel and snakes. I don't even remember who it was that informed me as to what the snake's name was; probably it was some older boy who felt it necessary to indoctrinate the younger boys into the institute of "Boyhood." That institute is a school of sorts that has been inclusive of most every boy who has ever lived.

So! It was a garter snake. Jerry watched as I held it by its tail, watched it as it coiled its head upwards in an effort to convince me that it was dangerous and thus make me let it go. But I wasn't about to be fooled by this creature. I had already had a lot of experience with garter snakes. I knew that it wasn't poisonous. I knew that its efforts were in vain, that it really had nothing that could really harm me. I had even been informed by old Germans in the neighborhood that they were beneficial creatures to have around, since they loved to eat harmful insects and mice.

When I grabbed the snake just behind his head, with my thumb and two of my fingers, I teased it into sticking its tongue out, which it did, but again it was a futile effort to look dangerous. It was all a bluff on the snake's part to appear menacing. It wasn't fooling me.

"Careful, Larry!" Jerry shouted, backing away a few feet. "It could bite you."

"It's just a garter snake, Jerry," I replied. "It can't hurt you." And I pulled the snake's head close to my face, to prove my manliness, or foolhardiness, or stupidity. Take your choice.

Jerry was not as intrigued with the snake as was I. After the encounter the year before with the rattle snake, which I wrote about in my first book, I held a high regard for reptiles, especially for snakes. I have always felt that they have acquired an undeserved reputation. The mere mention of *snake* brings on, in most people, and especially in girls, a picture of ugliness and sheer terror.

But I looked this creature over carefully, admiring the long stripes of faded yellowish-green and black, and noted the small red spots that also decorated it. It wasn't ugly; it was, to my eyes, remarkably beautiful, and so I stuck it in one of the front pockets of my pants, and went out to the front of our house to see whom I could enchant with it.

In other words, I was looking for some helpless girl to frighten. I knew better than to carry my creature home with me, having had that one unfortunate encounter with Mother because of a garter snake that had gotten loose in our house the previous year. Jerry followed me around to the front of the house, where I began to survey the neighborhood.

Sure enough, there were two girls, Donna Nelson and Rita Upleger, playing in front of the Upleger house, just down a couple of houses and across the street. They had skip ropes, and they were singing and laughing and practicing their skills, enjoying the beauty and innocence of the day.

Donna was beautiful. Every boy in the neighborhood was enraptured with her. She had blonde hair, and pretty eyes. We boys weren't supposed to be interested in girls, at that stage in our lives, but we couldn't help it, when it came to Donna. There were times when we made fools out of ourselves, trying to impress her.

This was one of those times, when I saw an opportunity to let her know how much I really felt about her. I would do some boyish thing, something, I was sure, that would strike her as being daring. Something impulsive, yet awe-inspiring.

I wandered over nonchalantly, as though there wasn't a single thing of importance going on in my life, as though I might possibly be interested in their girlish activity. They both were both jumping and singing, almost in rhythm, but I noticed that Donna kept her eyes on me as I approached. She did not trust me. Most girls in the neighborhood did not trust me, and I guess I couldn't blame them, since I had given them, over the years, a number of reasons to look at me with suspicion.

"What are you doing?" I asked innocently, a foolish question in light of their activity.

Both of them stopped, their eyes focused on mine. I knew that they intuitively looked for trouble.

"What do you think we're doing?" Donna asked in a manner that showed doubt in my intelligence. "We're jumping rope, you idiot."

Idiot? She called me an idiot? Wow! You talk about somebody who was asking for trouble. My ulterior motive was picking up strength.

I felt the snake wiggling in my pocket, but I had a hand over it, to prevent it from popping out.

"Want to see something neat?" I asked.

Again the suspicious look.

"You'd better not pull another of your stupid tricks, Larry," Donna warned, "because if you do, I'll tell on you."

"Yeah?" I replied. "Who are you going to tell?" I asked. "Your mother? Always a crybaby," I added.

"You'd better take that back," Donna retorted. She had her hands on her hips, the rope dangling alongside of her leg, and she was glaring at me.

"Crybaby, crybaby," I said in ridicule.

"You stop calling me that," she ordered.

"You make me."

"Come on, Rita," Donna said then in disgust, and turned her back to me.

"I just want you to meet my new friend," I said, and when they both turned to face me, I pulled the snake out of my pocket and dangled it in front of the girls. Of course it immediately uncoiled itself and wiggled and twisted in my hand. It must have appeared to be menacing, as I moved closer to where the girls stood in fright.

Both of the girls screamed, and loudly. Theirs were louder than the screams that I had ever heard in the theater during scary movie scenes. These were the screams of genuine fright.

Within seconds, doors opened all up and down the street, including ours. Mothers from nearly every home stuck their heads out to see what on earth was going on. And now it was I who was worried. I hadn't considered the idea of attracting so much attention.

The girls had fled, each to her own home, and even Jerry had left, so that I was abandoned there on the sidewalk, with my twisting snake, which I no longer held so confidently.

Donna, I noticed, was conferring with her mother, and shortly after their conference, I noticed Mrs. Nelson heading my way. By now my mother was also heading across the street, and she met Mrs. Nelson about half-way toward where I was standing, and I felt much like an actor who was taking part in a surreal scene. This couldn't possibly be happening! Could it?

After all, it had been such a harmless prank.

"You've got to do something about that boy of yours," Mrs. Nelson said loudly. She was a medium-built woman of fair complexion, but the rage on her face was unmistakable. She was angry! She was frustrated! She was just plain mad!

"I will," Mother answered. "I will," she promised again. And she continued toward me, while Mrs. Nelson turned and went toward her house, her anger practically lifting off her in heated waves.

Of course by this time I had let the snake go free, depositing it into the shrubbery that bordered Mr. Warner's home, where it slithered off in freedom. It didn't want anything more to do with me, either, or with what was about to take place. Maybe it had even been embarrassed to have been briefly associated with me.

By now, I noticed, there were many other people out, some on their porches, some on the sidewalks. There were both children and adults who had been attracted to all the commotion. A lot of conversations were taking place, for everyone wanted to know what had happened. Anything that could bring relief to the routine activities of Germantown was welcome, and so it was that word was being spread up and down the street.

Chet Nelson had been drawn to the front of his house, and he was laughing, although not terribly loudly. I didn't know if he was laughing at me, or at Donna, and he was wise enough to realize that his mother wouldn't know which, either, so his laughing was kept somewhat in check so that he would not suffer for his mother's anger.

"What in heaven's sake is the matter with you, Larry Miller?" my mother practically yelled, " her eyes boring into mine. "Can't I turn my back for one moment, for one day, without you causing me trouble?"

The answer was obvious, both to her and to me. It was a rhetorical question, and I was wise enough, for once, to keep my mouth shut.

"You get on home, right now," she said, grabbing a piece of my ear with her thumb and a finger.

"Yipe!" I shrieked. "You're hurting me."

"You deserve more than just having your ear pulled, young man," she answered, pulling on the handle a little harder. "Just what is it that gets into you, anyway? You know better than that. For the life of me, I don't know what it is that gets into you. You're the most exasperating boy I ever knew or ever heard of." Blah, blah, blah, it went on and on, and all the while I was vividly aware of everyone watching me. I didn't know which was worse, my ear being yanked on, or my ego being deflated. Come to think of it, the latter was far worse. My ear would eventually heal, whereas my ego would suffer forever.

I'm sure that the spectators were getting enjoyment out of the entire affair, for I heard waves of chuckles. It was all a bit of welcome relief to the humdrum lives they led.

By now, Jerry was watching from the safety of our front porch. He wasn't laughing, like so many of the other people were. A few adults had disappeared back into their homes, satisfied, I suppose, that justice was about to be administered, although privately, but obviously pleased to have been able to enjoy a bit of a distraction to the day. The public humiliation was over with, so there was no need for them to stay outside.

Even Joe, who lived almost two blocks away, must have heard about what was happening and had arrived, and I saw him smirk with the knowledge that I was about to get it and get it good. I did not like the fact that so many people relished the idea of my being punished, and I especially hated the idea of Joe enjoying it. He was the one boy whom I could label a dubious friend, and he was smiling at me as I looked back before being hauled into the house. Right away I figured that some day, in the very near future, there would be pay-back time. Joe probably knew that, but the fact that he could enjoy my discomfort must have given him great pleasure, at least for the moment.

By now, Mother was pulling on my arm, thereby giving my ear some relief, and I found myself standing before her in the kitchen, far in the back of the house so that, I imagine, the neighbors would not be privy to what was about to be said or to take place.

She was seated on one of the kitchen chairs, and I had been pulled to a standing position immediately in front of her so that she could stare directly into my eyes while we *talked*.

"Now, young man," she began, "could you please tell me just what could make you do something like what you did?"

"It was only a garter snake, Mom," I protested. "And I only held it up in front of the girls. I didn't throw it at them."

"Only a garter snake?" she said. "Only a garter snake?"

I hated it when she repeated things. It meant something ominous lay in my future.

"Larry, Larry, Larry," she said with something more than mere disappointment in her voice, and shaking her head in obvious frustration. Again the repetition. "What am I going to do with you?"

I had a lot of answers for that question, but I wisely kept them to myself, knowing, first, that they were not what she wanted to hear, and, second, that they would only add oil to the fire that was getting hotter and hotter.

She sat there for a few minutes, shaking her head back and forth, and I knew full well that she was pondering her options. Finally, she said:

"Well, for right now, you go up to your room for the rest of the day. And when your father gets home, I'll let him handle it."

"Go on," she commanded, as I had not moved as quickly as she must have wanted me to. "Get up stairs to your room. And don't let me hear one peep out of you. Do you hear me?"

"Yes, ma'm," I replied as dutifully as I could.

"And when you get up there, you be sure to wash your hands. And wash them good. You hear me?"

"Yes, ma'm," I answered. And I wanted to add that everyone else in the immediate neighborhood must have heard her also.

As I passed through the swinging door into the dining room, I noticed two figures hurrying out the front door.

So! Jerry and my young sister Sandra had been listening in on everything. And while Jerry might, sometimes, have enjoyed a comeuppance to me once in a while, Sandra never would have; that was not in her nature. And I'm equally sure that this particular time, even Jerry was not getting such a kick out of it.

Mother had followed me, and as I walked slowly up the fifteen steps that led to the upper story, I could sense her standing at the bottom of the stairs.

"And don't forget to wash your hands, young man," she said once more. "And wash them good."

She had such a habit of repeating her orders to me.

"Yes ma'm," I said as meekly as I could.

"Going around, handling dirty animals," she muttered just loud enough for me to hear.

It wasn't a dirty animal, I wanted to tell her. In fact, it was probably one of the cleanest animals I could think of.

"And don't go down the hallway and cry to your grandmother, either," Mother yelled up, "or you'll be in even deeper trouble. You hear me?"

Hear her? Hear her? Egads! A person would have had to have been completely deaf not to have heard her. Certainly I heard her, but my answer was unnecessary, of course. And she knew it was unnecessary. So, for one of the few times in my young life, I was wise enough to keep my mouth shut. Oh, I wanted to say something, but as Shakespeare said: "Discretion is the better part of valor."

My grandmother(my mother's mother) lived in her own little apartment in the front section of the second floor. There she had a little kitchen that adjoined a living room, just off a small bedroom of her own.

I have often been told that, for some strange reason that I still cannot fathom, Grandmother liked me especially. Apparently Grandmother felt sorry for me because of all the trouble that I got into and was punished for. She must have had a strange idea of what justice was all about, for I cannot honestly say that I ever received a punishment that I did not deserve. In fact, there should have been more administered, for the times I had not been caught. Yet Grandmother was always sympathetic to my plights.

But I had been given orders. So I trudged wearily up to my room, where I lay down on the bed and commiserated with myself over what I thought were the great injustices of life.

So, there I was. Stuck in my room for what must have seemed like eternity. The blue sky, seen through the window that overlooked our back yard, was remarkably blue, with little wisps of clouds that gave the sky character. The warm spring air gave me little relief; instead it only made my imprisonment more intolerable.

There I lay, on my side of the bed. Jerry's place, of course, was vacant, and that vacancy made me feel lonelier than ever. I had time on my hands. Time to think. Time to ponder life's difficulties.

Time! What an extraordinary thing! Many years later I discovered a most wonderful quote in *Intruder in the Dust*, a novel by the southern writer William Faulkner. Faulkner said that all a person had was: Time.

Boy! Was he ever right! I had time. Time to think about what I had done, which I am sure was what Mother wanted me to do. And I had time to ponder what was going to happen to me, after Father got home.

When it came to intimate events, I used the appellative "Dad." When it came to formal affairs, such as punishment, I thought and used the term "Father." And now I was using time to think of Father coming home, and of what awaited me.

I got up and sat on the side of the bed for a long time, thinking. Then I lay down, but I found myself thinking too much.

Time! Boy! Did it ever pass slowly.

I must have fallen asleep, because the next thing I knew was that Jerry was shaking me by my shoulder.

"Larry, Larry, wake up."

I tried to focus my eyes as well as my mind. Where the heck was I?

Oh, yeah, in my room, waiting for Dad to come home. And for some strange reason, I thought about the snake, how much freedom the snake enjoyed at that moment.

"You're supposed to come down to dinner," Jerry said, and then he left, and I could hear his quick footsteps as he ran down the steps, obviously without a care in the world.

I went into the upstairs bathroom, washed my hands and doused my face with cold water. What I really was doing was stalling. Dad would be at the kitchen table. Everyone would be waiting for me. And I knew that if I didn't get down there in a reasonable matter of time, Dad would be up quickly to get me. I dried my hands and face with a towel, and then slowly trudged downstairs.

I found everyone but Mother sitting around the kitchen table, each one in an established place. Even David, our youngest, who was only two years old, sat quietly in his high chair, as though he knew, even at such an early age, that I was in deep trouble.

I felt as though six pairs of eyes were upon me, but I slowly took my place, next to Jerry, and tried not to look up at anyone.

Dad said grace. Actually what he said was a deep and personal prayer, one that took in people's illnesses and other problems in the neighborhood, as well as a prayer of thanks for the wonderful gifts that we had all received, including the food.

And then Mother placed the main dish on the table, along with the usual loaf of bread.

I couldn't possibly tell you what the food consisted of that evening. My mind was on the punishment that was inexorable. It made me think, humorously for a moment, of the line in the Bible: "And these things shall come to pass." But scripture was of no help. So my humorous thought did not last very long.

After dinner was over, and Jerry and I and Marilyn had taken care of cleaning up the table and *doing the dishes*, I got a look from Dad that told me to go to my room.

"I'll be up shortly," he said.

Time! Oh, the magnitude of it! How slowly it passed as I wound my way back up the stairs. Each of those fifteen steps seemed tortuous. And when I got to my room, I sat down on the bed, and waited for what felt like eternity.

I could hear his steps a few minutes later, quite soft for such an important moment. They were slow and deliberate steps, and each one resonated with foreboding. Then I raised my eyes and watched him come into the room. I just knew that he would have his ever-so-handy razor strap with him.

But he stood there, a short, solid man, with his arms hanging down his sides, and there was no strap.

Our father was a most gentle man, usually. He was well liked by all of his friends, and adored by his family. But he could be firm when he needed to be.

No strap? Was he going to send me for it, as he had done on some other occasions when the trip for the strap would make the punishment even more memorable?

"So," he began, almost softly it seemed, "what was the deal with the snake?" He stood almost casually, it appeared to me.

I looked up at him. He didn't move. But there was something other than a rigidness in his posture. He looked almost relaxed, and his face did not betray a feeling of great anger.

"I'm sorry, Dad," I said. "I didn't mean to hurt them. I just wanted to tease them. It was just a garter snake. It wouldn't have hurt them. I found it in the back yard, and I got this idea, and…" All of this was said in a machine-gun fashion, and if I didn't know better, I could have sworn that there was a slight trace of a smile at the corners of his mouth.

"Snakes!" That was all he said, nodding his head up and down. "Snakes!" he repeated.

I looked up at him, at this man whom I practically worshipped, at this man who held the fate of one small boy in his power. I could see that he was weighing it all, deeply thinking about what he should do.

"Your mother is very upset with you, Larry," he said.

There was nothing I could say that would be meaningful, so I held my tongue.

"And so is Mrs. Nelson," he continued. "I understand that she wants you to stay out of her yard. Completely out. Forever."

All I could do was nod my head, as if in understanding.

"And your mother wants you to be punished. Can you understand that?"

"All I did was show them a garter snake," I offered once more.

"Well," he said, "I'm afraid that most girls don't like snakes. And, besides, I think you knew beforehand that the girls would be scared. Didn't you?" He was looking intently at me, as if defying any effort I might make to defend myself.

I nodded again. Only this time, as I looked at him, the little smile that I thought I had noticed earlier seemed to be spreading.

And then I was surprised, because he began to chuckle.

"I remember doing that to your Aunt Helen," he said.

"You scared Aunt Helen?" I asked incredulously.

Of all of Dad's sisters, I had a special fondness for Aunt Helen, and had spent part of a previous summer at her and Uncle Gordon's house, in Davidson, about sixty miles west of Port Huron. And to think that Dad had once scared her with a snake…well, it boggled my mind.

"I'm afraid so," he answered.

"Did she tell on you?" I asked, hoping for an affirmative answer.

"Oh, yes she did," he replied.

"Did Grandpa punish you?" I asked, hoping that the answer would be "no."

"Well, he told me not to do it again," Dad grinned.

And I grinned back at him.

"But if you ever tell anyone about this," he said, cutting into my thoughts about a possible total reprieve, "I'll not only give you the spanking that your mother wanted you to get, but I'll keep you inside the house for a week."

I could hardly believe my ears. There was to be no severe punishment?

"Am I getting across to you?" he added, with a warning in his eyes that defied any thoughts I might have had for complete exoneration.

"Yes, sir," I said.

"I'll speak to your mother about this, but you and I have an agreement. Do we not?" And his tone was very serious.

"Yes, sir," I said once more, and this time I struggled to keep my grin to myself.

He turned to go, but when he got to the door, he turned around, and said: "Maybe you'd better stay in your room for the rest of the evening. At least I can say I gave you some kind of punishment." And he nodded at me with a wisp of a smile. Then, as if having an afterthought, he said:

"She really was scared? Donna?"

"Yes, sir," I said, and although I tried to say this without showing any pride in what I had done, I could swear that as he turned to go down the stairs a grin had taken complete hold of his face and that he was thoroughly enjoying memories of his own.

"Snakes," I could hear him mutter. "Snakes."

CHAPTER EIGHT

The Day the Police Came

L IFE WAS GETTING better for a lot of people. The sun was a steady companion, beaming its rays down upon a population that was awakening slowly to better economic times. Smiles were slowly replacing the frowns of previous years, and we boys enjoyed increased freedom in our activities; whether the one thing had anything to do with the other is anyone's guess.

Looking back on those times, I have come to the realization that one activity took precedence over everything else, at least for Jerry and me: baseball.

Jerry and I took to the game as readily as fleas to a dog. We would play the game every opportunity we had, with different rules for different places where we played.

At first, probably around the age of five or six, we played one on one, in the back yard, having invented very simple rules. Bases were established by placing what convenient articles we could find in what we established as proper distances from each other, so that a diamond of sorts was set up. Home plate was near the back of the house, with the alley being designated as the line over which automatic home runs were hit.

Whoever was up to bat had three outs, just like in regular games, and he had to hit the ball far enough to prevent the pitcher-fielder from retrieving it and rushing to home plate ahead of the batter.

Any ball hit over the fences of the Deacons to the south or Mrs. Wolfe to the north was cause for an automatic out. And when that happened, we had to go out to the alley and enter the particular yard carefully, so as to avoid damaging the grape vines of Mr. Deacon or the roses and tulips of Mrs. Wolfe. And I had already experienced one bad encounter with Mrs. Wolfe more than a year earlier, which I did not want repeated.

I never really knew Mr. Deacon very well. He was a taciturn man, and rarely ever spoke to any of us kids. Come to think about it, I don't recall him having a real conversation with anyone, child or adult. And whenever Jerry or I had to go into his yard to retrieve our ball, he would look askance at us, as if we were secretly harboring evil intentions. He never said anything to us. Usually he sat on a small bench next to the back door of his house, his eyes following us as we made our way through his vines to find the ball. We were very careful not to disturb the vines.

Mrs. Deacon was a small, quiet person, whom we gradually came to know a little better, especially after Mr. Deacon died. After his death, my parents often called upon Jerry or me to carry out the ashes from her furnace, or to cut her small lawn, or to shovel her sidewalk in winter, for which Mrs. Deacon would reward us with a piece of fruit, and good manners meant that we would thank her profusely. We never expected to receive money from her, for times were rough for everyone in Germantown, especially for widows.

Anyway, Jerry and I also honed our baseball skills by a made-up game in our side(south) yard, that space between our house and the Deacons' house. There was a double roof on that side of our house, one directly over the other, the upper one a few feet short of the lower roof. Jerry and used the same three-out rule for that game, which consisted of one of us throwing an old tennis ball up onto the roof, and the other having to catch it after it had bounced off. If a ball were thrown high enough, it sometimes bounced back so far that a leaping catch often had to be made against the Deacons' house. If the ball hit the Deacons' house, without being caught, it was ruled an automatic home run.

And there was also a way of throwing the ball just high enough on the upper roof so that it became difficult for the fielder to determine if the ball would then bounce off the lower roof, or if it would just barely miss the lower roof and fall towards the ground, in which case the fielder would have to make a diving stab at the ball. If the ball fell safely, then a ground-rule double was ruled. Obviously we became quite naturally proficient at catching hard-to-catch balls.

There was no room for controversy; either a ball was caught, or it wasn't. And Jerry and I could play the game for hours, or until the sound of the bouncing ball became too much for Mother, who would then yell out: "Can't you boys find somewhere else to play? You're driving me crazy."

I can recall many times when, for a variety of reasons, Mother drove us away from the house. And being twins, we had double the opportunity to devise ways of driving her crazy, or for being given our freedom, however you want to put it.

Anyway, as we got older, and got more acquainted with all the other kids in the neighborhood, we took to the street, so to speak. The baseball diamond in our back yard-which by that time had no longer needed articles to designate the bases, since we had worn holes and paths by our constant playing-was replaced by one on the cinder surface of Sixteenth Street, with home place being a manhole cover which was almost directly in front of our house. The other bases were usually old tin cans which we mashed down flat. Since the flattened cans were small in size, there often were disputes about whether a baserunner actually had his foot on the *base.* Arguing was a part of growing up.

The first-base line ran toward the curb of the Deacons' boulevard, and the third-base line ran from the edge of the Warners' yard. We tried to avoid running on the grass of both houses, so as to avoid having trouble with those neighbors.

Old Man Warner-every one of the older men in the neighborhood was referred to with that type of appellation, but not out of disrespect-was very quiet and reserved, so he wasn't viewed as a problem for us. But we did try to avoid hitting his house with the ball.

Out there, in such a narrow street as was Sixteenth Street, we had rules that took into account that there were several houses whose owners did not want to see struck by baseballs. Especially was this true in relation to the windows of these homes. And there were some owners who were very protective of their homes, and who thus voiced their protests about balls that had accidentally been struck their way.

Whenever a boy hit a ball that struck one of the houses, he was automatically ruled "Out," and although we tried diligently to prevent that from happening, there were more and more mistakes as we grew in size. It was just a plain fact that we could hit the ball farther and farther as our size and skill developed. And it also was just plain fact that more houses were hit more often.

One evening, after supper, we had a game going. There were about eight or nine of us playing, including Kenny and Chetty.

That particular evening the police showed up. We did not really know what they had come for. Their light was not flashing, and as we noticed their car approach, we moved over to the sides of the road in anticipation of letting them pass by, expecting to continue our game after they had passed. We were too innocent to anticipate that their arrival had anything to do with us playing ball.

We were used to the occasional police car in the neighborhood, especially since we knew that one of the lieutenants lived no more than six or seven blocks away. The arrival of the car was of no concern to us.

But this time, the car pulled alongside a curb and stopped, and two officers slowly got out of their vehicle. All of us boys merely stood alongside of the street and waited to see why they had come.

They called all of us over to their vehicle, where they were leaning back against the front fender. They appeared casual, their tone almost one of indifference.

"Hi," one of us called out. We liked the police, and had been taught to respect them, to respect their authority. We had always looked upon them somewhat as friends.

"Hello, boys," the older of the two officers replied. He was not very tall, but he was bulky, and although there was a bit of a smile on his face, he looked somewhat serious, as well.

"You boys playing baseball?" he asked, looking at each of us.

Only four or five of us had baseball gloves, as they were in short supply in our neighborhood, so that other than the patched-up ball that Jerry was tossing up and down in his hands, there wasn't a whole lot of evidence as to just what we might have been doing.

"Yes, sir," Kenny replied.

The officer nodded, acknowledging that piece of information. He sat back further against the fender, his jaw twitching a little, as if he were trying to think of what he wanted to say.

"Well, I'm afraid you're going to have to play somewhere else," the officer said. And when we looked surprised, he added: "We've had a few complaints from your neighbors. They're afraid of having their windows broken."

"We haven't broken any windows," I protested, careful to keep the tone of my voice sounding polite.

"That may be true," the officer replied, straightening up a little, "but all the same, you're going to have to find somewhere else to play."

The other officer, a younger and more slender man, continued to lean back against the fender. I thought I could detect a slight smile on his face, although he didn't seem to be paying close attention to all that was going on. He was merely looking off into space.

We boys were looking at each other, trying to reason it all out.

"But there's nowhere else to play," one of the boys said.

"Well, that's not our concern," the older officer answered. "We got a few complaints, and that's just going to have to be what has to be." He was looking much more serious, and he straightened up even more, pulling up on his leather belt, which caused my attention to center on the black holstered gun hanging down his right side.

"Where will we play?" I asked maybe a little too forcefully.

"You'll just have to figure that out for yourselves," he said. "But we don't want you playing baseball in the street anymore. You understand?" he asked, looking at each of us in turn.

There wasn't anything else to say, and after we all looked at each other, slowly they got back into their car, and drove off.

We watched them turn the corner and disappear east on Minnie Street. Then we looked at each other, and turned back to our game.

It must have been fifteen or twenty minutes later when the car returned. This time, a few of the boys disappeared, quickly. Only about four or five of us remained.

Again they pulled their car alongside the curb, and this time they were even slower in getting out, as though it required a lot of effort. And this time there was no smile on the face of the older officer, although I could have sworn that there was a slight grin on the face of the younger one. The older one approached us, while the younger officer again leaned back against the fender.

"I thought I told you boys not to play baseball in the street," he said in a severe tone, pulling himself up straight, his thumbs hitched inside of his belt, so that his whole official self would be more noticeable.

His holstered gun and the heavy nightstick that his right hand fondled made him look more serious.

Not one of us boys said anything. We stood there, cowed, maybe even a little frightened, by the nightstick.

"Now, I'm not going to tell you again, boys. I told you once, and this is the last time. If I have to come once more, you'll take a little ride with us. You understand?" He looked solemn, almost grave.

By now there were a few parents on their porches, watching to see what was happening. I'm sure that all of us kids were aware that our parents would not volunteer to either intercede for us or to interfere with what was going on. The parents were not afraid of the police; they were just plain respectful, and thus would allow the proceedings to go on quite naturally.

I didn't know who might have put in the complaints, although I might have made a couple of good guesses. It might even have been a parent of one of the boys involved. I was sure that it wasn't our mother, since she could watch over us more carefully when we were near the house, whereas when we were not around, it was possible that we were doing things that we ought not to be doing. In fact, it was highly likely.

The older officer stood there a few moments longer, looked down at us with squinty eyes, and then slowly and deliberately turned and nodded his head toward his partner, and the two of them got back into the car.

I could see that they were writing something down on what must have been a sheet of paper, and then they left, although this time the car pulled away more slowly. I knew that they were watching us in their rearview mirror, for this time they headed south on Sixteenth Street, at a snail's pace. We boys looked at each other, then sat down on the front lawn in front of our house, and talked it over.

"Do you think they'll be back?" someone asked.

"If we go back into the street, they will," Chetty replied.

"Boy," Jack put in, "that one cop was sure mean."

"Ah," Chetty answered, "he was just doing his job." And everyone nodded at that remark.

"Someone must have told on us," I said. Of course we kids always had some mistrust about certain of our neighbors. After all, kids have to have someone to mistrust.

"Yeah," Kenny agreed.

"Do you think it was your mother, Kenny?" Joe asked.

"What are you? A wise guy?" Kenny answered quickly, staring so hard at Joe that Joe hung his head. "You looking for trouble?"

Joe shook his head. I could have sworn that his eyes were closed.

No one said anything after that.

We all looked dismal, as though we had lost something precious. And we probably had, at that. The young days of innocence were drawing slowly to a close. I don't think any one of us could have worded it that way, then, or thought it out that way. But it was true.

Kicked off the street! It was like the end of an era. The end of baseball. For Jerry and me, it was like a great tragedy. Baseball was more than just a game to us. It was like life itself, a contest of wills and agility and stamina and ability. We just could not imagine not being able to play baseball.

Disconsolate, each of us drifted off to our separate homes. I was more than downcast. I was devastated. And as night later drew its darkness over the neighborhood, my soul felt as though it had been drawn into a dark pit.

CHAPTER NINE

The Resurrection of Baseball

"WHAT'S GOING ON?" Joe asked.

It was a Monday, the first day of the first week after school had ended for the year, and some of the guys had come over to our house to talk about what we could do with our free time. A bunch of us were sitting on the steps to our front porch.

The days of spring had already pretty much exhausted our attraction to Pollywog, where we watched tadpoles slowly morphing into frogs, and where we had tried vainly to build rafts that would hold us above the stagnant waters.

Jerry and I had talked a lot about what had happened with the police. At first there seemed as though there would be no solution. But then, something popped into my head. And when I first introduced the idea, Jerry thought that I was crazy. But it didn't take long before he saw that the idea wasn't crazy, after all. Some of the other boys had stopped by, as usual. By the time that Joe arrived, we had already told some of the other boys about it.

"We're going to build a baseball diamond," I replied nonchalantly.

"You're going to do what?" Joe practically shouted.

"Build a baseball diamond," I repeated.

Joe probably had been on his way over to our house anyway, since most of our gang's activities usually started in our immediate area. His mother probably wished that Joe could find some other boys to play with, but there were no others; at least there were no other boys who might have come up to Joe's mother's expectations of what an acceptable boy was like.

Whenever someone else had an idea, Joe was the first one to be negative about it, probably because he wasn't the one who thought it up. But he probably would have been against it regardless, since he was the one boy we could count on to not be helpful. Joe was pretty lazy. He rarely had any chores to do around his house. He was spoiled and pampered, and everyone knew it.

"Where you going to build this stupid diamond?" Joe asked. "Out in the street again? So that the cops will come?"

"No," I replied. "Down on Eighteenth Street."

Joe tried to visualize just exactly where I was talking about, and suddenly it came to him.

"Eighteenth Street? Eighteenth Street?" he repeated for emphasis. "That's just a field. It's just a stupid, empty field."

"So?" I queried.

"There's nothing there but a lot of tall grass," he said. "We can't play baseball with grass that tall. I bet it's almost ten feet high. You couldn't even play football in grass like that. You'd get lost in it."

Of course the grass was not that high; at its highest, it usually grew to about three or four feet. But what good is it when trying to make a point, if one can't exaggerate?

"That'd be a lot of fun," Jack put in. "We could really use the hidden ball trick," he joked. At that point I couldn't tell if Jack was for the idea or not, what with his joking.

"We could cut the grass," Jerry said then, in a serious tone. He was trying to drum up support for the idea. The thought of not having a diamond, at all, was unthinkable.

"You're kidding!" Joe said derisively.

"No, we're not," I said. "We can cut the grass, and make a diamond, and maybe even make a dugout."

"Yeah," one of the other boys said enthusiastically, getting carried away by the idea. "We can even give it a name. And it will be ours only. Only our guys will be able to play on it."

"How are you going to cut grass that tall?" Joe challenged. "You can't mow grass that's tall like it is. I'm not going to try pushing a mower through it. That's stupid."

"We'll use some sickles," I replied. "My dad has one, and Kenny and Chet said that they'd help, and they have one too. And Mr. Warner and Mr. Wollen said that we could borrow their sickles."

"My dad has an old scythe," Don put in eagerly. "You can really cut a lot of grass with that. It's got a long handle."

We all watched Joe to see what he would say.

"Anyone who doesn't help doesn't get to use the diamond," I said, and I looked sharply at Joe in order to impress upon him just what that would mean.

"That's right," someone else added.

"You guys really want to cut down a whole field of tall grass?" he said finally, as though the idea was so preposterous that he must have thought that we were only kidding him.

And when no one said anything and he could see that we were serious, he said: "You guys are really going to do it! I can't believe you!" Then when no one replied, he asked: "How much of it are you going to cut down?"

"All the way to Bancroft Street," I replied in as nonchalant a manner as possible.

"A whole block?" he said with skepticism. "You're going to cut a whole block of tall grass?" His eyes seemed as though they were bulging right out of his face.

"Now I know you guys are just kidding. That's a whole block," he repeated. "A whole block!"

"It won't take us very long," I replied. "If everyone helps," I added, once more looking at Joe.

He looked around. There were about five of us there, and I was sure that he was trying to figure how much he would have to work.

"And Kenny and Chet are going to help?" he asked.

"We're going to start tomorrow," I said. "We're getting the sickles today. And, Don, you get the scythe. Then, after breakfast tomorrow, we'll all meet at our house and then head over."

"Okay," Joe said, finally relenting, "but I think you're all nuts."

Tuesday morning couldn't come fast enough for me. Jerry and I had gone down to Eighteenth Street a couple of times later on Monday, so

as to figure out just how much work we would have to do. We knew that
we would have to first cut out the area for what would be the infield, and
then an area for left field, since we could make up rules for a game that
only used half of an outfield. That would save us some work, at first. We
figured that we would tackle the right field portion of the outfield after we
got something of a diamond finished.

Jerry and I bolted down bowls of oatmeal and a couple slices of toast,
and then raced out the back door.

During supper the previous evening, while Jerry and I talked
about the project, we could see a huge smile on Dad's face, and later,
just before Jerry and I went off to bed, Dad told us how he wished he
were young enough and free enough to take part in it all. It was Dad
who had alerted us to the idea, since he knew that the area was vacant
land.

At first Jerry and I thought the idea was crazy. But it didn't take long
for two baseball enthusiasts-baseball nuts, really-to embrace the idea.

And so all that day Monday we spent as much time as we could to
encourage all of our gang that the idea was really worthwhile, and feasible.
Whenever anyone's morale flagged, we reminded them that it would be
worth it, in the end. We had visions of playing both baseball and football
there. Our hearts were elevated

So there we were, five boys in all, armed with our sickles and two
scythes, and even with a machete that Kenny had found and lent to us,
although he, himself, at the last minute, felt that he was too mature
for such boyish ventures. And when Kenny abandoned us, so did his
brother Chetty. I had kind of figured that might happen, since they
were really not a part of our regular gang, being a few years older than
we were.

As we marched west along Minnie Street, we passed Albert Bauman's
gas station, at the corner of Seventeenth. Albert looked up from a car he
was working on.

He wore grease on his face and arms, evidence of his repair work on
people's cars. Everyone liked Albert Bauman. He had a reputation as a
pretty fair mechanic, and he was genial.

"You boys going off to war?" he asked good naturedly. He always was a good person with us boys, letting us use his air pump for our bicycle tires, for example.

"We're going to make us a baseball diamond," I answered.

"I heard about that," he replied. "Down there, on the next block, I hear."

We had stopped, momentarily.

"You going to try to cut down all that tall grass?" he asked.

"Yes, sir," I said.

"Well, good luck," he called, and bent down under the raised hood of the car he was working on, a wrench in his hand.

When we stood at the corner of Eighteenth and Minnie streets and surveyed what looked like a vast wilderness of grass, even I began to wonder about what it was that we were about to undertake. And I had the feeling that everyone was looking at me. I realized that they were waiting to see if I would give up on the great idea.

But after a moment's hesitation, I looked to Jerry, nodded, and moved forward, swinging my sickle in a sweeping motion at the tall grasses in front of me. And I was immediately impressed with how easily the grass fell. The sickle was sharp, and although I had never used one before, I felt encouraged by the ease with which the grass fell. Jerry moved beside and a little behind me, at a respectful distance so that we would not wind up cutting each other up, each of us swinging our sickles, and soon the others joined in.

Don had the scythe, and it was such a long handled affair that it gave him a little trouble, at first, but soon he realized that by shortening up a little on the grip, much like shortening up on the grip of a baseball bat, he was able to cut away fairly long swaths of grass.

Jack used the machete, which Kenny had warned us had been kept very sharp-he said it was sharp enough to cut away facial hairs, but I think he was exaggerating. Regardless, the machete, while not as efficient as a sickle, was still better than nothing. Besides, it made Jack feel a little bit like a warrior.

Even Joe, I noticed, was doing pretty good, for him. I could see that he really didn't have his heart in it, but nevertheless he was cutting away at the grass.

The sun was brilliant that day. There wasn't a cloud to be seen. And summer had a golden glow. And with every blade of grass that fell to our strokes, the glow deepened.

It was surprising that there wasn't a lot of grumbling. And whenever I looked up, everyone was still hard at work, and before very long, I could see that we had leveled an area about the size of what must have been big enough to be an infield, and even a little beyond.

I knew that we needed to cut the grass down even further, but that would have to wait for another day, when we would have to use our lawnmowers. I didn't want to say anything to the others about that part of the job because I figured that they might become discouraged if they stopped to consider just how big the job was going to become.

I was still swinging away with my sickle, when I could see, out of the corner of my eye, four boys approaching. Three of them were about our age, I could see, but one boy seemed to be a little older; at least he was taller, and stockier.

When the rest of our gang noticed the boys, they stopped their work. We moved a little closer together, and warily watched the other boys approach. They were walking slowly, talking with each other, and they seemed to be deferring to one boy in particular, a red headed boy who was walking in the middle of them.

They stopped at the edge of the field, probably no more than twenty feet from us, just beyond what would later be the first-base line. They looked at the fallen grasses, and then at us. The redhead squinted his eyes, as though he was trying to impress upon us the solemnity of the situation. Finally, he said, in a challenging manner: "What do you guys think you're doing?"

There was something menacing in the voice, something menacing about the way the redhead stood.

At first no one responded. We looked at each other, and I noticed that Joe and Don had moved behind me a little. Jerry and Jack had taken places on either side of me. It was at such a time that I wished someone like Kenny or Chetty were there, to bolster our courage. Or to pummel the strange boys mercilessly. I enjoyed the latter thought the most.

But there was no Kenny or Chetty. It was just us.

So! This was going to be showdown time. Two bunches of boys, strangers to each other. Was this a matter of territory? We all stood and stared at each other.

"We're making a baseball diamond," I said, but my throat seemed to tighten up so that the words came out with a little tremor.

"You're making a what?" the redhead said.

I thought it strange that the biggest of the four boys stood almost directly in back of the redhead. He was easily a head taller than all of them, although the redhead was definitely bigger than the other two. I figured right away that the tallest and biggest boy probably didn't really want to see trouble started. I didn't believe it was because he was scared, either. He just looked like the kind of boy who didn't go around looking for trouble. It was something about his demeanor that told me that.

The smallest of the boys was wiry looking, not just thin. The fourth boy was about my size, which was about average for a ten-year old. He kept looking right and left, as though he didn't want to be there.

"A baseball diamond," I said, this time with more boldness in my answer.

"Hear that, you guys?" Redhead asked, turning to look at his buddies. "They think they're going to build a baseball diamond." And there was a distinct note of defiance in his tone.

And it was then that I noticed that there was something wrong with his right hand. The hand was deformed, so that if there were fingers on it, they weren't very obvious. In place of the fingers were tiny stubs. His arm hung down, along his side, and the hand was easily noticeable.

He moved closer to us, two of the others following, but the biggest boy stayed back. They stopped about two or three feet away.

"Who said you could build a baseball diamond here, anyway?" he asked.

I admit that right away I was a little scared of him. In fact, I was probably a lot scared of him. Somewhere along the line I had heard that redheads were fierce fighters. And the fact that here was a redheaded boy with a deformed hand, why, it was entirely possible that he was a natural-born fighter.

I wanted to back away, but I knew that the others were waiting for me to react. Would I defy this boy? Would I turn tail? Would I try to talk my way out of a bad situation? Our boys were all waiting. And although we were closely grouped together, by then, I had the feeling that I was on my own.

One thing was for sure: I did not want to lose face. Of course, there was the alternative of having my face destroyed.

It was as simple as that. I had been in a few minor scuffles already in my short life, and I didn't like the idea of getting beat up. I can't think of anything pleasurable in getting hit in the face. But even more I hated the idea of backing away, and losing face.

"Who said we couldn't?" I retorted. And this time I narrowed my eyes, maybe not in the fierce squint that the redhead had, but still they were narrowed in as defiant manner as I could bring myself to make them.

Bravado didn't come easy for me. I was what one would call a skinny guy, and I was only of medium height. There couldn't have been much to look at that would make another boy cringe in fear, but I tried to concentrate on narrowing my eyes as much as possible, without actually closing them. Of course I was a little worried that the redhead would only be too happy to close them for me.

There was something of a lull then. All of us were sizing each of the members of the other group, and there was a little shuffling of feet, probably from a sense of fear.

"Where're you guys from?" Redhead asked, bringing his shoulders up as high as he could bring them, and moving another step closer. Before I lifted my eyes to his face, I noticed again the end of his right hand, and I could perceive the stubby end as being a club, and wondered if Redhead had ever used it as such.

"Yeah," the smallest of the other boys asked, acting bravely in light of the temerity of Redhead, "where're you guys from?" He had edged to the side of Redhead, and tried to look tough. And maybe he was, although I could see that his shoulder was touching the side of Redhead, as though he was gathering courage from their collective form.

"Where are *you* from?" I asked, throwing the challenge back at them, but being careful to direct my question to the small boy.

The line was being drawn. Territory was territory. And boys, being as territorial as other animals, were willing to defend their turf.

An uneasy silence! If we had had full control of all of our faculties, we might have heard birds chirping, or seen cars passing by on Minnie Street, or smelled the freshly cut grass.

But I don't think any one of us, on either side, was aware of anything else going on in the world. We were in an arena, and the would-be gladiators were caught up in their own thoughts, in the possibility of battles being waged.

"You guys better get out of here," Redhead said, but this time I thought that the voice was not as bold as before. And I also noticed something else: the biggest boy had not moved any closer, and apparently Redhead noticed that also, as he had looked back over his shoulder. Was it possible that Redhead was only as brave as the presence of the biggest boy might make him to feel? I took some courage from that thought.

"Why don't *you guys* get out of here?" I retaliated with as much fierceness as I could muster. "We were here first."

Redhead took a step closer, followed by two of the others, the biggest boy still hanging back.

In what might have been seen as a foolish move, I took a step toward them, hoping that my buddies would move with me and give me moral support. But to tell the truth, I couldn't tell if they had moved up with me, or not. And I really couldn't blame them if they hadn't.

So, Redhead and I stood there for a long moment, no more than a foot apart, glaring at each other, each of us daring the other with our stares, each of us trying to look more fierce than what we felt. Then we inched even closer, so that the distance between us disappeared almost completely.

Redhead and I were so close to each other now that I could hear his breathing. It was loud, a snorting sound. I wasn't even aware if I was breathing at all.

"You guys don't belong here," Redhead said. He was glaring, a message of challenge and defiance.

"Who says?" I returned, and I narrowed my eyes even more, determined to stand my ground. I noticed that my friends were standing off in the background. The distance they stood from me certainly did nothing to boost my courage.

"You see this line?" Redhead asked then. And he used the toe of one of his shoes to draw a line in the ground, between us.

I looked down at the faint impression left by his shoe. And that was another thing: Redhead wore shoes, hard-looking shoes, certainly harder than my bare feet. I suddenly felt even weaker than before, as though his shoes gave Redhead another distinct advantage.

I knew what the line meant. I wasn't ignorant. It was more than a line of challenge. It represented something beyond cowardice or bravery. It was a line of reckless acceptance of war's terms. It was the age-old challenge that had been laid down by countless boys before us. It was boyhood at its most treacherous moment.

"I see it," I answered as forcefully as I could, looking down at the faint line and then back into his eyes. His eyes were green, and they were blinking fiercely. I could almost see malevolence in them.

"Well," he said, "I dare you to step over it." And the look he gave me was so intense that I had to gulp deeply to get air into my lungs,

I tried to look at him as he had looked at me. But I'm afraid that I probably failed. I realized that I was blinking rapidly, and that my breathing had become ragged. My skin was clammy.

This was that supreme moment in a boy's life when he hated himself, for it was that one instance when he either had to own up to a confession of deep fear and the resultant great loss of pride, or he had to consider having his face battered. Either decision was paramount in helping to determine his character. And that decision could haunt him the rest of his life, for the result would either be a battered face...or a battered reputation.

So, summoning up as much courage as I could, I looked down at the line once more, girded up my loins-as the Bible's King David might have put it-and then stepped over the line, inadvertently brushing up against him while doing it.

And it was then that I thought I detected a new look in his eyes, as though he not only was surprised at my action but maybe a little wishful that this whole thing had not started, at all. Could it be possible that he hated the circumstances as much as did I? I took a little more courage from that.

Standing face to face once again, with not enough room for either of us even to wiggle, we looked as defiantly at each other as we could.

The summer day had taken on a harsh atmosphere. Hostility reigned, and two boys stood face to face, ready combatants in the contest of wills.

Then it was that he pushed me. Not a hard push. But still, it was a push.

"Who're you shoving?" I said, and I pushed him, a little.

And suddenly he pushed me harder, and I stumbled back a little, and I could hear a lot of voices, everyone yelling at once. I could distinguish Jerry's voice, and Joe's, until the voices all became part of a general din.

I moved forward, and shoved him as hard as I could, but he hardly flinched. And the next thing I knew, we were wrestling, our arms wrapped around each other, each of us trying to throw the other to the ground.

I could feel the extra weight that he carried, and I feared that he would easily get me down and then sit on me and pound me. But I had one thing going for me: I was quicker than he was, much quicker, and somehow I got my right foot planted behind one of his legs, and I pushed as hard as I could with my whole body. He fell.

Then we were on the ground, with me on top. But that position only lasted for a second or two, and then we were rolling over and over, and the yelling of those around us grew louder and louder, but as yet no real punches had been thrown.

It was then, when I realized that neither one of us had actually struck the other with a fist, that I sensed that Redhead really did not want to fight me any more than I wanted to fight him; and I thought that he had come to the same conclusion, for we both just kind of rolled around and over the ground, being wary of not making things any worse by actually striking the other, until exhaustion set in and we separated, as though by mutual agreement. We both got to our feet, still facing each other, our glares still filled with hostility.

Warily watching each other, we began wiping ourselves off, for the cut grasses had stained our clothes. The yelling of the other boys had died down, and no one uttered anything resembling a threat. And even more of significance was that there no longer existed two lines of boys; rather there was a mingling of bodies, as though two separate bodies no longer existed.

"Where're you guys from?" a voice said. The voice was one that I had not heard before, and it took me a long moment to realize that the one who had asked the question was the big boy who had hung in the background. And I also realized that there was no menace in the voice. It had simply been a question.

"From over on Sixteenth Street," Don said, quick to take advantage of any interruption that might help to prevent even more trouble. For it is well known that as long as opposing forces are talking, there is less chance of fighting.

"Sixteenth Street?" asked the smallest of the other boys, who now seemed relieved that the affair had not turned into a general melee. "We're from over near Nineteenth Street. Over by Oak Street. Well, Charley and I are," he said, pointing to the big boy. "Rich here," he added, nodding toward Redhead, "he's from Eighteenth Street."

"That's not very far from here," Jerry said. "We live just off Minnie."

And it was easy for all of us to see that we were feeling easier about the situation. Why, we were practically neighbors. There were only a few blocks that separated us.

Redhead, I now knew, was looking at his buddies. I turned and looked at mine. The atmosphere had eased considerably. It had become obvious that no one wanted to fight. No one wanted to look timid or sheepish. So, it was with great relief that there appeared to be a peaceful solution.

"Are you guys really going to build a baseball diamond?" Redhead asked then, the former scowl having become a look of wonder. That look was an open invitation to all of us to relax, to accept a chance at peace.

"Yeah," Joe put in, obviously happy that the crisis had passed. "We decided to build one because the cops stopped us from playing ball on the street."

"We!" Jerry said in a tone that let everyone know that Joe had not been any part of the original planning. "You didn't even want to help us, at first, until we told you that you had to work if you wanted to play."

Several of the boys laughed. Even Redhead smiled at that. And the mood became even more relaxed.

"Where'd you get the sickles?" the medium-built boy asked.

"From our neighbors," I said. And it suddenly dawned on me that the other boys were now displaying a sincere interest in what we had been doing.

"You like baseball?" I asked.

"I'd play baseball every day, if I could," Redhead replied.

"So would Larry and I," my brother put in. "Our mother sometimes has to send someone out to bring us home."

There were understanding nods from all around at that remark. We all had been through that kind of behavior with our mothers.

"This boy here," Redhead said, pointing to the biggest boy, "is Charley, and he's the best baseball player that I know."

And suddenly there was a din of noises again, except this was the din of happy voices, of boys all talking at once, of boys talking about baseball and football and favorite players from the Detroit Tigers. And it was then that the big boy moved forward, a genuine smile on his face.

"This here is Charley Miller," Redhead said, introducing the big boy, "and I'm Rich Miller," he added, "but we're not related."

"Wow!" I exclaimed. "Your last name is Miller," I said with surprise. "My name is Miller, too. I mean my last name. I'm Larry," I said by way of introduction, "and this is my twin brother Jerry," pointing to my brother, who had drawn close to me.

"Twins?" Redhead asked. "You're really twins?"

"All of our lives," Jerry put in, and everyone laughed. The tension was lifted.

After that, there were introductions made all around, and the early summer air felt cheerful and warm and welcomed. And there were grins, and laughter, and, handshakes. And birds flitted about, and the sky was full of the sunshine of a summer day.

"Can we help?" the skinny one asked. His name was Carl.

"Sure," Jack said.

"Boy," I said, "with this many guys, we can really make a neat baseball diamond."

And there were smiles all around.

And thus our gang of future baseball stars was enlarged.

The medium sized boy was named Ron. He turned out to be a pretty good baseball player. And Charley? Like Redhead(Rich) had said...well, he really was a great baseball player. He was just plain out and out the best athlete I ever knew personally. Later in life he was made a member of the Michigan High School All-State Baseball Team as well as a member of the All-State Football Team. And after that he went to college went on to coach both sports in a high school near Jackson, Michigan.

And in an ironic twist of fate, not only did Charley become a school teacher, but all of the rest of us Millers in this gang became school teachers: Richard, Jerry, and I. Amazing how life sometimes turns out!

But meanwhile, all of us dug in, and shared our tools, and Rich even went home and brought back another sickle. And I found out something else: having a deformed hand did not prevent Rich from doing whatever he wanted to do, for he turned to the job of cutting the grasses with as much skill as he later displayed toward playing baseball and football, with excellence, and not expecting any special favors because of his hand.

We worked on and on that day, and returned the next day, and the next. And by Thursday we had cut down the tall grasses of the entire ball field, including right field, and had begun the process of mowing the stubble with the push mowers that we brought from our homes.

By late Thursday afternoon, we had finished. We stood there, together, tired, but proud and happy. We had built our diamond.

An official diamond of sorts was made even more official when Mr. Sturmer, who owned a hardware store downtown, and who lived on Minnie Street, overlooking our field, brought over a bag of lime with which to lay out the base paths. And after we had made bases with burlap sacks filled partly with sand, and a home plate out of an old piece of tan carpet, we felt that we had performed a wonderful thing. It would be impossible to explain how ecstatic we boys were when we stood back and surveyed the results of our hard work.

The baseball diamond became a gathering place, a new one for us boys. We were proud of what we had done. And we had the feeling that it belonged to us.

And we played on and on, that day, until the sun began to set on the far horizon, our shadows lengthening across the field. And another day passed us by.

As Jerry and I lay in bed that night, both of us were quiet. Probably Jerry was thinking what I was thinking: Life can't get better than this.

CHAPTER TEN

The Fort

LEAVE IT TO young boys to do stupid things! And I'm not even sure whose idea it was, but we did it.

Eighteenth Street became more than just a baseball diamond. Oh, sure, we improved upon our initial efforts by building a makeshift backstop, as well as a dugout along the third-base line, using some abandoned boards for framing and some *donated* chicken wire for a screen that was more ornamental than useful. I doubt that a baseball hit at the screen would have been deflected all that much, but at least the screen looked good.

From our viewpoint, the dugout looked somewhat professional. From the viewpoint of those who happened to look in on us with curiosity, it probably looked like what it really was: a piece of makeshift.

But Chetty was his usual kindness when he saw it. He stood back a ways, looked the whole thing over, and said, by way of studious commentary: "I don't think the Tigers(Detroit) would care for it, but, you know, it's all right. It really is."

The glow on our faces revealed our appreciation.

Anyway, being the baseball enthusiasts that we were, we played baseball nearly every day, for awhile. Dad even said, one night at the supper table: "I think you boys would live at that diamond, if you had half a chance."

Jerry and I looked at each other, and grinned.

"You're probably getting better and better at the game," he added.

"Not as good as Charley," I said.

"Charley's the best, Dad," Jerry added. "He's so much bigger, and stronger, and he can really run, too."

"As fast as you boys?" he asked. "You two are pretty fast."

"Well, just as fast," I said. "Carl's the fastest. But Charley's not only pretty fast, but he's so much bigger than any of us. And you ought to see him hit the ball. We have to go back almost to the sidewalk along Bancroft Street, to catch most of his balls."

"Yeah," Jerry said. "In fact, we have a rule that if you hit the ball over the sidewalk, it's an automatic home run."

Most of the rest of the family were concentrating on their dinner. They couldn't have been interested at all in our baseball games, although David, at age two at the time, looked up now and then. He probably was dreaming of the time when he would be old enough to participate in our activity.

"How about you boys?" Dad asked, his fork paused half way to his mouth. "Have you hit any over the sidewalk, yet?"

"Almost," Jerry replied. "Almost."

And on we played, nearly every day, for awhile. Sometimes there were more than six or seven of us, but at times there were only four or five. Not every boy had the same enthusiasm for baseball that a few of us had

But before too long, about three weeks into that wonderful baseball season, we were getting base-balled out, so to speak. You know. Just a little bored with the same thing every day. Even Jerry and I were thinking about how we could become involved in something else.

We were sitting around one day, talking, chewing on grass, as boys will do, our minds actively searching for another endeavor, when someone came up with the idea of building a fort, a sort of home away from home. Our Sixteenth Street gang had built a few forts over the years, over at Pollywog. Usually they were of the sticks and branches variety, as it was too long a ways to carry discarded boards and such, although there had been a few times when we had labored with some *borrowed* wood.

"You mean like our dugout?" I asked. The dugout that we had built stood as testimony to our creative talents, even though it had to be propped up from time to time, to keep the thing from falling down. We all looked over at the shambles. I knew that not one of us would be willing to settle for a fort that would be so ugly and flimsy.

And there began a wild discussion of just what the fort should look like. There was a lot of potential building material in Germantown. Most of the families had a carpenter or two, as well as lots of hand tools, and most of the men were constantly working on various projects: chairs, beds, fences, tool sheds, etc. And whenever any boy in the neighborhood had a project of his own going on, it was easy to find the raw materials. Most of the material, like boards, and planks, were usually graciously donated. Other materials just disappeared, somehow.

"Anyone can build a fort with boards," Joe said. "We ought to build something different."

Now, it must be remembered that Joe did not play baseball often. It's not that he didn't have skill at the game; he just didn't care for it that much. He also didn't care for football, either. What he preferred was the tinker toy set he owned, or the chemistry set that he had been given one Christmas.

"Like what?" someone asked.

"Like an underground fort," Joe answered in a somewhat offhand way.

"An underground fort?" I asked?

Sure," Joe said. "No one would be able to see it. And we could keep it secret."

At first, we all looked at each other, as if the idea were preposterous. But slowly the idea began to sound feasible. A place for just us boys, something resembling a secret club.

"How do you build one?" one of the boys asked.

"Simple!" Joe replied. "You just begin digging a hole, with a shovel, I guess, and after you get down a ways, you just keep digging, I guess with your hands, or maybe with garden spades. You know. Build a tunnel. And then you dig out a room, kind of like a cave."

At first everyone thought the idea was crazy, but after the idea had been tossed back and forth, the idea seemed to be pretty simple, and a little awesome.

"Yeah," Rich said with increasing enthusiasm, "we could have more than one tunnel, and a really big room where all the tunnels run off from."

"We could hide things down there," I added.

"And nobody would know about it, because we'd keep it all a secret," someone else put in.

"Yeah," Joe added, "no one would even know it's there. Unless we told them. It'd be real secret."

"Yeah," Jerry said, "and maybe we'd even have a secret club. You know? And anyone who wanted to join would have to know a secret password."

"Yeah," several of the others agreed.

"Yeah," Don said, "and we could have candles in the tunnels."

"And we wouldn't tell our parents," Joe put in.

"That's for sure!" someone said for all of us.

The idea was sounding grander and grander, as the talk continued.

"Where will we build it?" I asked, surveying what most of us now considered to be *our property*.

"How about right over there?" Don said, pointing to an area about twenty feet back from home plate. There was a slight mound, where he was pointing, and in back of it were tall grasses that we had allowed to grow, since they didn't impede our playing baseball and yet gave us privacy.

We all walked over and surveyed the area. I kicked once at the dirt beneath my feet, and noticed that it was fairly soft, and therefore might be easy to dig into. A few others kicked at the dirt, then.

"What'll we dig with?" Jack asked.

We all looked at each other. Finally one of the boys said: "My mother has a small spade she uses in her garden. That's easy to use."

"Yeah," Joe agreed. "We have one, too."

"But don't tell them what we're going to use them for," Jack said. "Otherwise they probably won't let us use them."

"Yeah," Joe replied. "In fact, they probably won't even let us come over here anymore."

"Don't tell them anything," I said. And everyone nodded in agreement.

There was one very important rule that we boys abided by: Never voluntarily give your parents any information about what you were doing. It was their responsibility to deal with their children's antics. It was the responsibility of boys to keep things secret from their parents.

"Let's meet back here in fifteen minutes," Rich said. "And everyone bring something to dig with."

"Let's get them," I said, and we looked at each other, and nodded, and each of us ran off to our homes to get digging tools.

When Jerry and I got home, we first looked down in the basement. Mother must not have heard us come in the back door, or else she would have asked us what we were doing down there. Since Mother had never been one who spent much time working in a garden or with flowers, we were disappointed at not finding what we needed.

"Mrs. Deacon has one," Jerry said.

And we burst up the steps, out the door, and around to the alley, where we went through the wire fence that separated the Deacons' house and the alley.

Mrs. Deacon was sitting on a bench outside her back door, her one spot for soaking up the sun. She was always gracious with us boys. So she lent us the spade she had, without even asking what we were going to use it for. And Jerry and I beat it back to the field, where Rich and Charley and Don had already gathered. Joe and Jack came along shortly afterwards.

And we all stood there, above the slight mound, looking down at the ground.

We looked at each other, wondering how to begin. So, without waiting any longer, I dropped to my knees, and began digging away the dirt, using Mrs. Deacon's garden spade. The dirt gave way easily, and as I got a little deeper, I began pulling it all behind myself. Charley had brought along a regular shovel, which enabled him to dig away large amounts of the dirt. Then the others, surrounding a fairly wide circle, began digging away, and we found ourselves getting deeper and deeper.

Most of the boys dug away with energy, except Joe, which I had expected. Every time I looked up, he was standing nearby, quick to give directions, but with no telltale dirt to show that he was of any help. Of course, he was wearing *better* clothes than most of us, although not much better than what Charley wore. The difference was that Charley was actually helping, whereas Joe…well, he was *supervising*.

Before long we had a sizable hole, about four feet deep and about four feet wide. For the last fifteen minutes or so, we had had to lie on our chests in order to reach down and pull out the dirt. At that point, we realized that we had to begin the actual digging of a tunnel, and that one of us would have to drop down into the hole and dig deeper and on a slant.

"I'll start digging away from the hole, you guys," I said, "but you're all going to have to pull away the dirt. Okay?"

And I dropped down inside the hole, took a spade, looked up once at all of them standing above, and began to dig to one side of the hole and a little deeper. The dirt was fairly soft, and it gave way to my efforts. I would dig my spade into the dirt, then reach out with both of my hands, and pull the dirt under my legs and behind me, where someone else would pull the dirt out of the hole.

The work went well enough, and the deeper and farther away I dug, the more I noticed that I was working in semi-darkness. I looked back occasionally, to see how much I had progressed.

Within about forty minutes, I found myself underneath a ceiling of dirt and actually within a tunnel. Because the tunnel was dug in a twisting manner, when I looked back, I could no longer see any of the other boys, other than the boy who was immediately behind me hauling away the dirt that I had been throwing back.

We yelled back and forth to each other, and like moles we dug away, lengthening the tunnel foot by foot. There were faint exclamations of giddiness from above as I pulled away even more of the dirt and kept getting farther away from the entrance. At that point, the hardest job was waiting for the dirt behind me to be pulled away and out of the hole, so that I could continue my tunneling. The other boys were taking their turns hauling away the dirt, and the tunnel was being lengthened by considerable degrees.

Finally I stopped, not knowing just how far I had dug.

The tunnel was not wide enough to permit me to turn around, so that when I decided that I needed a break, I had to back my way out. When I climbed out, Jack B. asked me how far I thought I had gotten.

"I don't really know," I answered. "Maybe about ten feet, I guess."

"Should we start digging out the room?" Don asked.

"I think so," I answered. "But you know what? I think we could get it done quicker if we started another tunnel and tried to hook it up with the one we're digging. That way, when the tunnels meet, we could haul out the dirt from the room a whole lot faster."

"Yeah," Rich agreed, "and then we'd have another escape tunnel, too." There were nods all around.

So, by consensual agreement, I went back into the original tunnel, followed by Jerry and Jack B., while Rich and Don and Charley began to work on building another tunnel, first marking it out as best as they could above ground with a line, to where they thought it would meet my tunnel.

Joe kept up his job of supervising.

We worked furiously, anxious to complete our goal: an underground fort that would satisfy our eagerness to have a secret place to escape to.

Joe was at his usual best at giving orders, or suggestions. But whenever I came up from below, I still could not see any dirt on either his trousers or his shirt.

My shirt and trousers were filthy, as were everyone else's. As far as shoes went, Jerry and I didn't wear any, since we usually spent most of each summer in our bare feet. I think we had the toughest feet in town. An advantage to that predicament was not having to answer to our parents for abusing our footwear.

Before too long, I was about five feet further along, feeling much like a lonely mole must have felt, and yelling all the while in hopes of hearing the diggers of the other tunnel, when all of a sudden, I stuck my spade ahead of me, and heard a clanking sound, and then I heard a voice cry out: "We did it. We did it." For that clanking sound had been produced by my spade striking the spade of a fellow digger.

Sure enough, after some furious digging away at the wall of the tunnel ahead of me, it gave way, and even in the faint light that was spilling down the two tunnels I could see the face of Rich, dirt all over his features, and he was grinning, and then yelling, and we began to shake hands, and then we began to pull away more and more dirt.

Others took our places, and the dirt almost flew out of the two tunnels, although in reality it all had to be dragged out by hand, and dumped off to the side. Even Joe went down into one of the tunnels, finally, after we had dragged away what must have seemed like mountains of dirt. I found out later that he didn't stay long. The mountains of dirt grew, for we were now in the process of widening the area where the two tunnels had met, making an actual room.

Everyone was excited. We probably were very tired, too, but the joy of making our own secret underground fort was so great that it wasn't until much later that we realized just how tired we all were. All of us except Joe. Throughout life I never knew too many supervisors who got tired.

The work continued, the dirt piled up even higher, outside the fort, and eventually I discovered, the next time that I went down, that we had dug away a room about six feet in diameter and about four feet in height.

I called out to the others, and quickly they all scrambled down, finding spaces around the perimeter of the room. And in the faint light of our little fort, we looked at each other, and smiled, and congratulated each other on what we had accomplished.

"This is great," Don said.

"It sure is," we all agreed.

"Don't anyone tell anyone else about it," I cautioned. "It's got to be a secret."

"They'll know we did it if they see all that dirt up there," Rich said.

"We're going to have to get rid of it," I said.

"How?" Joe asked.

"Well, if we spread it around, maybe over by the base paths, then no one will know that the fort's here," I said. "They'll just think we used some dirt to mark the paths. Most of the lime has gone."

"They'll see the holes," Charley said.

"Yeah," Jerry said, "but not if we cover them up with some boards. Maybe they'll just think that they're just some old boards lying around, and they won't know the difference. Besides," he added, "hardly anyone comes over here anyway."

So we scurried up out of our fort, some of us using one tunnel and others using the second tunnel.

There were some boards left over from when we had built the makeshift dugout, and we dragged them over and placed them over the entrances to the two tunnels, covering them with a little dirt, to make the area look natural. We discovered, then, just how extensive our little network was, for the two entrances were about twenty feet from each other, on opposite sides of where we figured the room was.

Charley was using his shovel to move away the mounds of dirt, and each of us pitched in. An old wide piece of wood served as a kind of scuttle to help us carry away the accumulated dirt. Some of the dirt was carried out onto the baseball diamond itself, and before long we had gotten rid of the evidence that could have betrayed our tunnel entrances.

Just about when we had finished the job, and the area near the fort was fairly level once more, we could hear someone calling.

It was Chetty. He was walking toward us.

"Are we going to tell Chetty what we did?" Don asked.

"We'd better not," I said. "If he were to tell his parents, his parents would tell ours, and then we'd have to get rid of our fort."

We must have looked like a bunch of orphans, what with dirty clothes and all.

"What have you guys been doing?" he asked, as he approached. "Your mothers have been calling for you all afternoon."

"We've been working on the baseball diamond," I said, pointing to the dirt that now blotted out much of the old lime base paths. I worried that he would discover our tunnels.

But he merely looked around, and then said: "Well, your mothers have been calling for you. And your mother wants you to come home right now," he added, looking at Jerry and me. "She asked me to come and get you."

So we split up, and each of us headed home.

When Jerry and I cut up the alley that ran behind our house, we found Mother waiting for us. She was pulling clothes from the clothes line in the back yard.

"Where have you boys been?" she asked, immediately suspicious about our activities. "You look like you've been playing in the dirt."

"We were working on our baseball diamond," Jerry answered. "We made some base paths with dirt."

Although Jerry had given the answer, she looked suspiciously at me. Eventually I was to learn that suspicion is the watchdog for overwrought, conscientious mothers.

"Well, you certainly have been away long enough," she said, obviously miffed with us for being out of her sight for almost the entire day, but probably more upset for not knowing for sure what we had been doing and for not being able to crack our defenses.

"Your father is going to be home any minute now, for supper. So, you two get upstairs and get washed up.

"And take off those dirty clothes down in the basement," she ordered as we were about to enter the back door. "I don't want any dirt tracked up into the house. You hear me?"

"Yes, ma'm," we said.

"And wash those dirty faces and hands real good, not like you usually do," she added just before the door slammed shut on her words.

Using the lone faucet and laundry tub in the basement, Jerry and I washed ourselves better than we usually would have done. We didn't want anyone questioning us about what we had been doing all day long. Dad wouldn't think of grilling us, but Mother was an expert at playing detective. Dad was a believer in the old adage that boys must be boys.

But supper that night held no surprises. Jerry and I usually had great appetites, and that evening we were unusually hungry, since we had not been home for lunch. And so he and I turned our attention to the food, and allowed Mother and Dad to carry the bulk of the conversation.

"What have you boys been doing all day?" Dad asked, during a lull in the conversation.

"Getting themselves as dirty as mud," Mother answered before we could reply.

"You should have seen those boys, when they got home," Mother added. "And I had to ask Chet Nelson to go over to their baseball field, to get them. And when they got home, they looked as though they had buried themselves in sand."

Jerry and I exchanged fleeting glances, afraid to look up at Mother, for fear of giving ourselves away.

"Well," Dad said in a relaxed way, "I guess I probably came home a few times pretty dirty, in my day."

"Well, it's easy for you to say," she snorted. "You're not the one who has to wash their clothes."

"I'm sorry, dear," Dad said in as appeasing way as he could. "You're right. And I'll speak to these boys after dinner."

Even Mother was temporarily appeased by this, as both of them had a rule about supper being an enjoyable time. Neither one of them wanted to bring a little spat to the table.

After supper was over, and Mother left the kitchen, and before we kids took care of our kitchen duties, he took us boys aside and asked us to be a little more careful with our clothes.

And that was the end of that brief encounter with danger that evening. Our adventures with the tunnel went undiscovered, at that point.

After Jerry and Marilyn and I had cleared away the table and washed and wiped the dishes and put them away into the cupboards, Jerry and I ran out to play with the other kids in the neighborhood.

Evening was the most democratic time of the day. The potential activities included hide-and-seek and kick-the-can, and in those games, even the girls were invited, although very few of the girls took part.

It's hard to realize how innocent those early days were in our lives. The only thing that marred or darkened my mood was the memory of Marvin, whose death I told about in my earlier book. And sometimes it was difficult to just push aside my thoughts about him, but I had to if I were to enjoy the innocence of those times.

Next to Jerry, Marvin had been the best friend I had in the world. He had been fun to be with, willing to take up the crazy adventures we dreamed up, and was especially loyal to me.

His tragic death, after he was hit by a car, had stuck me hard. It was the first time that a death had had any deep meaning for me. But for the most part, it is true that life must go on. And so, as time moved on, the accident receded further into the back of my mind. And we, the living, went on with our games and our adventures and our dreams.

CHAPTER ELEVEN

The Band of Baseball Brothers

N O BOY WAS more blessed than were Jerry and I that year, for in July, we got something that practically every boy in the neighborhood, in the whole town, in the whole state, in fact, could only dream about.

Somehow Dad got free passes to a Detroit Tigers game. Certainly we did not have the money to pay for such wonderful things, and I suppose that in some way the free passes were connected with his job with the Coca-Cola Company itself. I'd like to think that it was a reward from the company for outstanding work. Dad was as popular a person as I ever knew, and also a very hard worker, so it would not have surprised me that he would have been rewarded somewhere along the line.

When he told us about the tickets, and how we were to go with him to Detroit, to Briggs Stadium, Jerry and I were flying high. We told everyone about it, with more than a little bragging, hoping, I am sure, to create more than just a twinge of jealousy. Which it most surely did.

To this day, everything about the trip to Detroit seems like a blur. All memories are obscured somewhat by time. Down through the years Jerry and I have talked about that memorable day, but we have found it impossible to form a complete picture. We don't even remember how it was that we got down there, whether Dad drove one of the Coca-Cola trucks, or whatever. For we did not have much of a car at that time. Dad had gotten an old 1931 Ford from my mother's Uncle Fred Harmon, who lived in a home on Gull Lake, a famous lake for fishing over near Battle Creek. Uncle Fred was a very famous fisherman who not only owned records for fishing(bass especially), but he also rented boats and canoes, and was a paid guide for some of the wealthy businessmen in the state. And that car from Uncle Fred, I am sure, would not have been the vehicle which we would have traveled to Detroit, for Jerry and I would surely remember that. Then again, maybe we wouldn't.

Anyway, there we were, standing before the huge, grayish walls of Briggs Stadium(later Tiger Stadium and now, Comerica Park), on a warm summer day, then walking through the turnstiles manned by uniformed ushers, to whom Dad proudly passed his tickets.

I don't know how many boys today can appreciate how awesome this all was to us. Baseball was king. Baseball was the lifeblood of a nation that had gone through, and was still recovering from, a terrible depression. Why, to not embrace baseball was like a cardinal sin.

In those days, Jerry and I could recite the batting averages of all the great hitters in both the American and National leagues. We often hard arguments about who the best players were.

Even though the Tigers were destined to finish in fifth place that year, they were kings, in our eyes. And to think that there we were, in special seats up close to the railing, along the third base line, actually watching the two teams take batting and fielding practice…why, it was unreal.

It was all like some great fantasy. For there, on the field, were the likes of gods. Why, there was Hank Greenburg, arguably the greatest first baseman ever to play the game. And there was Charlie Gehringer, the All-Star second baseman. And Pete Fox. And Rudy York. And alongside the outfielders, were many of the pitchers, shagging fly balls in the vast environs of that magnificent stadium.

Jerry and I consulted our programs, finding the numbers of all those great players, identifying Bobo Newsom, and Tommy Bridges, and Dizzy Trout, and young Hal Newhouser. Why, this was a dream come true.

To this day I don't remember which team the Tigers were playing. For some reason, it seems that I can recall that gentleman of gentlemen, Mr. Connie Mack, manager of the Philadelphia Athletics, out on the field at one point during the game, disputing a call made by an umpire who certainly must not have had as good a view of the disputed play as did Mr.

Mack. Taller than anyone else on the field, slender Mr. Mack always wore a suit, with formal shirt and tie. And he never lost his composure. And if he disputed a call, more likely than not he was right, and often the call would be reversed. And because he was a gentleman, few in the crowd would boo either him or the umpire over the reversal.

I also do not remember who won that game, for there was something that happened before that game that would forever be an indelible part of Jerry's and my past, something that would separate us from the ordinary boys back home.

Before the game started, Jerry and I were standing alongside the railing, marveling at the skills of Pinky Higgins fielding ground balls at third base, calling out his name in appreciation of every ball that he fielded. His movements were so fluid, so smooth. And once or twice he looked over at us, and smiled. And at one point, he even winked at us.

Now, it must be understood that in those long-ago days it was common practice for many of the ball players to interact with the fans before the game. It was not unusual for players to trot over to the seats and chat with appreciative fans, to have their pictures taken with those fans. But Jerry and I were mere boys. We couldn't possibly hope for such as that. It was enough just to be in that ball park, to watch them play a game that was then, and always would remain, America's pastime.

Yet, as some of the players began to move off the field, there came Pinky. I mean, there came the real man, the real ball player, one of our heroes, the deft fielder, the man who even hit an occasional home run(he hit eight of them that year), trotting over toward us. And our eyes must have nearly bugged out of our faces, for he reached out toward Dad, and the two of them shook hands. And they were actually speaking with each other.

"These your boys?" Pinky asked.

"Twins," Dad said proudly.

"Uh-huh," Pinky said, smiling at us. "You boys like baseball?" Pinky asked.

"Yes, sir," we both practically shouted in unison.

"I'll bet you're pretty good at it, too," he said.

Our faces lit up, at that remark.

"We play all the time," Jerry replied.

"I'll bet you do," Pinky said as casually as if we had always been good friends.

"Well," he added, "I'll tell you what. I'll just bet that you'll play even better with this." And he reached out his hand, and in it was a genuine baseball, one that he had just fielded moments before. And he handed it to Jerry.

"Wow!" we both said, our hands caressing the ball, probably hoping not to disturb the fingerprints from Pinky's hand that would have been on the ball.

The moment was so grand that it was like being in some kind of dream. But the moment was about to become even more marvelous, for suddenly we heard another voice.

"Who've you got there, Pinky?"

And there stood one of our all-time favorite players, Barney McCosky. There might have been better outfielders in the American League, but we would have argued strongly about that. He batted over .300, and he moved through the outfield like some graceful gazelle.

"Why, these two boys are ball players, friends of mine," Pinky replied casually. "They're twins. And I just gave them a ball for them to practice with."

Jerry and I were beaming. We couldn't believe it. For here were two of our greatest heroes, two of the men who moved among giants, and they were standing there with us, and talking with us, and talking about us. And what made it all even more wonderful was when Barney reached out and tousled Jerry's and my hair, just as though we had always been buddies of his.

"Well," Barney said, "they just might lose that ball. So I think they'd better have another one," and he handed one over to us.

"Wow!" said it all for us again.

This couldn't be happening, could it? But it was happening. And I recall Dad and Barney and Pinky standing near each other, the railing being the only thing that separated them, and it was as though they had all been long lost friends, so easy the conversation seemed to be.

And if I tell you what took place next, you'll probably think of me as the greatest story-teller who ever lived. But my twin will verify it all, and while I found it very convenient to lie now and then, Jerry was notorious about telling the truth, well, usually, sometimes to my detriment. So you'll have to ask him.

Anyway, coming towards us was a player whom everyone knew simply by looking at him: Birdie Tebbets, the catcher. And his grin was as big as his physique.

"What's going on here?" Birdie asked in such a friendly manner that we immediately took to him.

"Why, we've got a couple of ball players here," Barney answered as casually as one possibly could. "These boys are twins, and they're going to be playing in Tiger Stadium some day. So Pinky and I gave them a couple of baseballs, just in case they don't have the genuine ones back home. We figured that they could use a couple of balls to practice with."

"Is that so?" Birdie said. "Twins, huh?"

"Yes, sir," I said.

"Well, I'll tell you what. I just happen to have a couple more balls for them," and he handed over two more genuine Detroit Tigers baseballs.

Jerry and I must have been mesmerized. We could only stare in wonder. These were the gods of baseball. Oh, sure, there were other great players out there, like a young Joe Dimaggio, who later was to hit safely in fifty-six straight games. And we were aware of the skills of Luke Appling, and the eyes of magnificent Ted Williams, who just might have been the purest hitter in the history of baseball.

And Jerry and I were aware of the prowess of Ernie Lombardi, and Stan Hack(don't throw him a fastball), and colorful Johnny Mize. And both Jerry and I admired a young guy by the name of Bob Feller, who could throw a ball through a closed barn door; we admired him even though our Tigers had to face him, now and then.

But those guys weren't here. They were off somewhere else, wherever the Powers of Baseball had relegated them to play. They were doing wonderful things in places like New York, and Cleveland, and Philadelphia. But here, on this July afternoon, in 1940, were *our* gods of baseball, the Detroit Tigers.

And here were Jerry and I, not only standing alongside of them, but talking with them, rubbing shoulders with them, so to speak. We were being taken into the Band of Baseball Brothers, that band that recognizes the beauty of a ball being run down and caught over the shoulder, or of the sound of "Smack" when a ball was struck by the fat of the bat, and of the "whoof" whenever one of Schoolboy Rowe's sinkers was missed by a hitter.

This was the field of glory, the arena of gladiators, who took as weapons those of cunning and speed and agility, whose nerves could stand up to a fastball thrown over ninety miles per hour, and whose anguish could be felt by forty-thousand screaming fans.

Whatever else happened that afternoon escapes me. I really don't recollect much of what happened on the field, other than Barney McCosky lining a double down the third-base line and sliding safely into second base. And I swear, to this day, that he got up to his feet, and sent a smile our way, although that might only be a figment of an imagination that had already been enlarged by mortals who flirted with the gods.

That was absolutely one of the most glorious afternoons of my life. And when we got home, Jerry and I put the four baseballs in the bottom drawer of our dresser, where they were taken out only occasionally, to be looked at and caressed with our unholy hands. They were never to be used. Or so we originally decided. Sometimes, at night, before we went to bed, Jerry and I would take one of them out and toss it back and forth, there in our bedroom, always careful not to mar the ball.

But the truth must be told. One day, perhaps a month later, when we had worn out the balls that Charley had provided back in June, and had tried and discarded other objects even less round and bearing the signs of multiple mendings, Jerry and I dug out two of the balls, proud to show them to our buddies, proud to let those lesser beings handle them, and ultimately to hit them and field them.

And as time passed, the last two balls were taken from the drawer, and these, too, met the fate of the others, struck by wooden bats, time and time again, until the covers lost their shininess and became unraveled, until the very cores of the balls were taped over and over.

As time passed, the balls were lost, perhaps struck into the ditch that bordered Bancroft Street, perhaps struck by Charley Miller.

But what never passed were the memories: of Briggs Stadium; of an adoring crowd; of three wonderful heroes, Pinky, and Barney, and Birdie; but most of all, of a father who had proudly introduced us to *his friends*. Those memories have never been lost, only fading somewhat into the passage of time itself, but still always there to be pulled out whenever life hangs heavy. They were some of the ghosts that moved through our lives.

CHAPTER TWELVE

A Gang Formed

S OME TIME AFTER we had finished the underground fort, even adding a third tunnel for escape and a fourth tunnel that dead-ended(to confuse any *enemies* that might take it upon themselves to invade it), we gave some finishing touches to the fort. In the walls we dug out small niches, into which we set candles, both in the *great room* as well as in the tunnels. With a supply of matches that we kept inside at many of the candle places, we now had lighted areas. One of the boys had brought a piece of old carpet, which we laid down on the floor of the *great room*, making it all seem so home-like.

At first there was a great novelty about the fort, the feeling of great secrecy in moving in and out of the tunnels, of making sure that the boards that covered the entrances appeared to be merely casually placed.

For the first few days we played very little baseball, so caught up were we with our underground kingdom. Inside the great room, we must have spent many hours just trying to come up with rules and a name for our gang, as well as a password. All kinds of names and words were bandied about, and each one earned positive remarks, as well as criticisms. There was a great deal of arguing, as might be expected.

Finally it was decided, almost by unanimous agreement, that we would call ourselves "The Eighteenth Street Bandits," and the password actually became a motto: "The blood be on your hands." We had no idea what the motto actually meant; it sounded gory, it sounded vengeful, and it sounded fierce. Those were reasons enough.

Of course there was one absolute rule: no one, and I mean <u>no one</u> but ourselves, was to ever know the motto, or the location of the fort. The penalty was banishment forever from our gang. And not one of us would ever want that to happen.

What we never were able to resolve was just what the gang stood for, what its plans were to entail. Were we to go marauding? Terrorizing? Robbing? And, if so, whom or what were we to maraud and terrorize and rob? It was all so sketchy.

But the important thing was that we were a gang. We would always be together. Why, we would be more famous than the Musketeers. We were a band of secret brethren. And to that end, we met secretly, hashing over the plans of the day, which really never amounted to much. But it always seemed as though they might. They just might. Ah, the grandiose dreams of youth.

Meanwhile the world kept revolving. We were not really interested in Europe, even though that seemed to be a constant topic at dinner tables throughout the neighborhood. According to our parents, France had fallen to the horrible Nazis, and some fat Italian by the name of Mussolini had joined his country with the Germans in attacking France, which was Italy's neighbor. So much for neighborliness.

Apparently what bothered Dad the most was the stance taken by one of his heroes, one Charles Lindbergh, the man who had made history by flying solo across the Atlantic back in 1927. Lindbergh was an isolationist, according to Dad, a word that really did not mean much to us boys, but apparently our President did not take kindly to Lindbergh's position. One of Dad's heroes was a fallen hero, in Dad's mind.

But there were good things about the "war over there. " There were events that would capture our admiration for the *good* guys. We learned something about a place called Dunkirk. Dad seemed captivated by the news about the great evacuation that had taken place, and how more than a quarter million soldiers had been saved by "a crazy fleet" of weekend sailors and fishermen and tugboat and ferryboat operators.

"Hitler will live to regret this," Dad pronounced one night. "Hitler made a mistake, and England is going to make him pay."

Thus the war "over there" dragged on, but it was having little impact upon us boys. We were still carefree and innocent.

Mid-summer had turned hot and dry, and Pollywog lost much of its pond and creek. Whoever thought that it would be too hot to play baseball? But the temperature soared into the 90s, and we boys found ourselves taking refuge in our underground fort, where it was much cooler. There, we planned our plundering. And we did, indeed, plunder.

Over on Seventeenth Street lived Leonard Loll, who just happened to be the vendor of potato chips, which he stored in his garage. Ironically the Loll family were members of our church, which should have caused Jerry and me to harbor a little guilt about our plundering. Somehow Jerry and I were able to surmount our guilt; the taste of potato chips can do that to boys.

The two folding doors on the back of Mr. Loll's garage were always closed, of course, but they were never closed real tight. The uneven ground and the years of weather's havoc had caused the doors to be warped, leaving a slight gap that a small boy might venture to squeeze through. And apparently just about every boy in Germantown knew of that gap. Consequently a number of bags of potato chips disappeared over the years.

Once in a while some of those bags found their way into our new fort, although we were never greedy. And we never thought of ourselves as thieves. We were not pilfering. We were a gang. Thus, we were plundering, as any pirate or looter or gang member was expected to do.

Years later I was having a conversation with Carolyn, one of the two Loll daughters. She informed me that her parents were well aware of the missing bags, and that her father had decided that as long as things never got out of hand, and that the loss only amounted to a few bags, from time to time, that he would *look the other way,* so to speak. His refusal to combat thievery was an act of kindness to boys who were usually denied such luxurious foods.

Other than the potato chips, about the only other plunder that made its way into our fort were crab apples from an old tree on a vacant lot on Minnie Street, about a block away; the only problem with the crab apples was that they were late in ripening. We threw more of them away than we ate.

In late summer we enjoyed a delicious watermelon or two from Old Man Thompson's garden from over on Bancroft Street. Those watermelons were wonderful, except for the arguing it produced about whether a watermelon would grow in our stomachs if we swallowed the seeds.

"You guys had better not swallow any of the seeds," Joe said to us one day. "My dad says that if you swallow the seeds, a watermelon will grow inside your stomach." He sat there, smug in his supposedly superior knowledge of almost everything.

"That's stupid," I retorted. "You sure come up with stupid ideas, Joe."

"Okay," Joe replied. "But if you die from some ol' watermelon taking up all the space in your stomach, don't come and tell me about it."

"If I died, then how could I tell you anything, you moron?" I shook my head in disgust. "Boy, you sure are stupid, Joe."

Actually, I recall that I was bothered for some time about that idea, since I had already swallowed a few seeds before the argument had begun. But those fears retreated as a number of days went by without my stomach getting any bigger. Until the fears disappeared completely, I could envision myself looking like a pregnant boy, a horrible picture to hold in one's mind.

The fort turned out to be not much more than a place to hide from the rest of the world, and to pretend. Of course, we never called it pretending; we thought of it as planning, and conniving, and scheming.

Then came the day that the rain poured down from the skies, a thunderous storm that left Port Huron not only soaked in water but practically drowning in it.

At first the bright day of sunshine was darkened by some ugly looking clouds that loomed in the western sky. And when the wind whipped up and began thrashing the trees, all of the mothers came to their front doors and began calling all of their children inside. The sky not only became dark, it turned black. And there was a strange sound to the wind. The wind wasn't whistling; it was more like an ominous howling.

Jerry and I no sooner made it into the house when the rain began to come down furiously. Mother herded all five of us kids into the front room, a place usually denied to us except when the family gathered to listen to the great radio programs. From there we looked out through the large front window, and watched as the rain poured down.

The rain fell in great sheets, striking almost horizontally. It sounded as if someone was pelting the house with a thousand hammers. This was no ordinary summer shower. Mother was strangely silent, and her silence made the whole scene seem even eerier. There we all stood, or sat, watching the rain as it poured, and poured, and poured.

The darkness was just like night. And as the rain continued to pound against the houses and the streets, that very darkness turned strangely dark green. Suddenly Mother yelled.

"Get away from that window." For Jerry and I had been leaning against the sofa that sat before that front window, excitedly talking about the frenzy of the storm.

And just when we turned to look at her, the wind stopped altogether. At least it seemed to have stopped. For there was no whistling. No howling. Just a strange, unfamiliar absence of sound altogether.

"Get away from there," Mother yelled again. And she looked terrified. She was standing with her back up against the farthest wall, and she was staring out over our heads, at the storm that raged outside the window.

Marilyn had taken David up in her arms, and she took Sandra's hand and moved to an easy chair that sat alongside the wall, next to Mother. Mother put one hand down, resting it on Marilyn's shoulder. I couldn't tell if she was trying to reassure Marilyn or herself.

Jerry and I retreated to where they all were, and sat down on the floor. We figured that Mother did not need a disobedient child, at that point.

And then the wind began howling again, a howl that was unlike that of most rain storms. And the dark green of the storm turned to dark gray, even lightening up a bit. And the rain itself seemed to let up, somewhat. It still poured down, but no longer horizontally, no longer in such a vicious fashion. In essence, it became nothing more than a hard summer storm.

Within minutes, Mother seemed to relax. A smile tried to make its way in her face, as she looked down at all of us. And she no longer had that look of fear.

"Can we go out and play?" Jerry asked then.

Mother looked at him, looked outside once more, where daytime had begun to take its rightful place, and nodded. A great sigh escaped from her lips.

When we got outside, we found that the streets were flooded. And just about every boy in the neighborhood had come outside to find some amusing things to do, what with all the water that was in the streets.

Chetty and Kenny had come outside, and Jerry and I met them, and we all began to run along the curb line, swishing our bare feet in the torrent of water that rushed downhill toward Bancroft Street and Pollywog.

We found small branches that had been blown free from the trees, and we stripped them of their leaves, and tore them into smaller pieces, fashioning them into crude boats, and suddenly there were races. We established a point that was mid-block, and using that point as a starting line, we sent those *boats* off along the curbs, in the rush of the water, with all of us boys running alongside, encouraging our private yachts to victory.

But eventually the rain water found its way into the drains and manholes of the sewer system, and we were left to look elsewhere for amusement.

I knew that Pollywog would welcome such a storm. Its water would rise and rise, and overflow the banks of the pond. And the frogs and snakes would be safer and happier.

And then the sky began to lighten even more, and the sun promised to poke its head through the gray haze, and the summer day became less gloomy, and less adventurous. We had learned a valuable lesson: good things don't always last.

Jerry and I wandered over to Eighteenth Street, where we discovered Rich and Charley peering down into one of the tunnels.

Jerry and I quickly scampered down the muddy main tunnel, where we found our little fort's grand room filled with about six inches of water, the piece of carpet ruined. We dragged the carpet out of the tunnel and spread it over the ground. We doubted that it would ever be useable again. The fort was uninhabitable, for awhile anyway. And the baseball diamond was too wet for play. So we all dispersed and headed towards our homes.

Jerry and I sat disconsolately on our front porch. We were out of plans. Bored.

Joe probably was playing with one of his toys. Don probably was reading one of his comic books. Jack could have been practicing at the piano. Chetty and Kenny had disappeared. I didn't know where the rest of the boys were, the ones from our immediate neighborhood.

After we had been sitting and lolling around and doing nothing for a few minutes, Mother came out to see if we were getting into trouble of any kind. Mothers have that intuitive sense that allows them to suspect that things aren't always what they might seem to be. And truth to be known, when twin boys are involved, she had ample reason to be suspicious.

"Where are all your friends?" she asked. She stood at the edge of the porch and looked up into the sky.

"Joe's probably playing with one of his games," Jerry said.

"Well, it's not raining anymore," she said. "So, why are you hanging around here?"

She stood there, her arms across her chest. Jerry and I looked at each other. We both knew that it probably would be a good thing if we went off to play, and left Mother alone. She surely did not want us playing in the house, for we didn't have games like Joe did. Games that we played inside the house often turned into ones of horseplay, occasionally resulting in something getting broken. Consequently those made-up games of rough-and-tumble upset her more than her wondering what we were doing when we off on our own.

"Maybe we'll go over to Joe's house," I said, hoping that Jerry would take a hint, and I jumped down the front steps and started over to Minnie Street. Jerry quickly caught up with me.

"How come we're going to Joe's house?" he asked. "You know his mother won't let us inside."

"We're not," I answered. "It's just that I think we'd better go some place other than around the house."

Of course, Joe's mother wouldn't have wanted us in her house, either. We knew that. Our clothes were usually too ratty and stained for her comfort. And the fact that Jerry and I rarely wore shoes during summer made us seem too much like Huck Finn, in her way of thinking. If she could have had her way, Joe would never have been allowed to play with any of us boys. She was not the most democratic person in the world.

"Want to go to Polk School?" Jerry asked.

"Why not," I replied. "Maybe we'll find something to do there."

Polk's playground included a baseball-kickball diamond, a wooden wall that separated it from the neighbors along Minnie Street and that gave us something to throw marbles against in games of chance, and swings and a teeter-totter.

There was a half-alley off Twelfth Street that ran along the south side of a brown house, leading into the west end of the playground at Polk School. By the time we got there, a number of boys and girls were already there, the younger ones using the swings or the teeter-totter. So it hadn't taken long after the storm for kids to take to the outdoors again.

Jerry and I were pleased to see a bunch of boys playing softball. Fred Kuhr was there. His father owned a drug store on Griswold. John Porter and Les Green and Spurgie Morris and Bob Kushelwere also there, tossing a softball around.

I liked Spurgie, a boy who had experienced a hardship. He had been born with a cleft palate, and had often taken verbal abuse from some of the other kids. It took me a long while in life to realize that children can be very cruel. Compassion, I was to learn, was not necessarily something a person was born with.

Spurgie had gone through a number of operations, and had fallen behind a couple of grades. Thus, when his family moved into Germantown, and he was sent into second grade at Polk, he was already almost ten years old. He was very small, but he was wiry, and a pretty fair athlete, as it turned out.

Spurgie and I had become good friends immediately, from second grade on, as I often took the part of the underdog. On the very first day that Spurgie was introduced to our class, I took issue with one of the bullies in the class, a boy that went by the name of Woodrow.

During recess this bully called Spurgie "hair-lip," and Spurgie had hung his head, humiliated. I called the bully on it, and we found ourselves wrestling on the ground, eventually to be separated by Mrs. Drake, one of the teachers.

Of course we were reprimanded after school, by our principal, Miss Tremayne, the woman we called Old Fussbottom. Just looking at her was enough to inspire great fear, and eventually she was to meet with me several times during the course of my school days at Polk.

But this time it was different, far different than what I had expected, for my punishment turned out to be not nearly as severe as I had expected it to be, merely a couple of raps on my behind with her infamous ruler. Whereas the bully was not only given the same number of raps, but he also had to stay in detention for a half hour, each day, for five days. I kind of surmised that Miss Tremayne found out just what had happened, and had sympathized with me for protecting Spurgie.

Anyway, here they all were, tossing around a softball. The houses behind the wooden fence that bordered left field and left-center field were too close to the diamond for the use of a regular baseball.

"Hey, Larry. Hey, Jerry," John Porter called out. "You're just in time for a game."

Sides were quickly chosen, and I found that one of the boys on the opposite side was Bob K.

Bob K., like Dick Miller, had been born with a similar hand, and thus I had thought it impossible for him to compete with the rest of us, especially in baseball.

Bob lived in the house that stood behind the wooden fence bordering left field. The fact that occasional homeruns struck their house did not bother the family. But the house next to them, in the area of what we would call left-centerfield, was occupied by a childless couple, the Figgs, who had acquired a reputation for detesting kids. And especially did they resent balls that sometimes struck their house. When that happened, it became a race between a fielder hopping over the fence to retrieve the ball and the Figgs. If the fielder was not successful, the ball was lost to us.

I distinctly recall the first inning of that game. My brother had lined a single to left field, which I fielded cleanly, thus preventing him from stretching the hit into a double. So it was that Jerry was waiting on first base when Bob K. came up to bat.

Bob seemed to settle himself into the batter's box with nonchalance, as though he were used to doing just that. He held the bat across the arm that I regarded as helpless, and as Lester, our pitcher, prepared to toss the ball underhand to him, it was immediately obvious to me that Bob intended to swing the bat one-handed. What the heck was going on? I wondered. He really intends to swing the bat like that?

There were no balls and strikes called. A batter simply waited until the pitcher threw him a ball that he liked.

I watched Bob carefully. He held the bat confidently. But he was handicapped, I felt, so there was no way that he could possibly do his team any good.

So I moved in a few steps. This guy couldn't possibly put one over my head, and if he did, it would only be for a few feet, and I knew that I could go back and snag balls as well as anyone.

Bob took a couple of pitches, each time stopping the ball himself and throwing it back to our pitcher.

"Come on," I yelled, "afraid to swing at it?"

He ignored me, and when I yelled even louder, taunting him, he merely turned away for a moment, before settling back into the batter's box. He tapped the plate a couple of times with the bat, his good arm extended, the bat seeming like an extension of his arm.

And then it happened. The pitch was tossed, and Bob's good arm was extended, and there was a blur of a swing, and the next thing I knew the ball was sailing high and deep, and I could tell that it was going to sail over my head.

I quickly turned and headed back, intending to make a spectacular catch of this *lucky* hit. I was running full tilt, keeping my eye on that ball. No way was I going to allow that ball to fall safely! No way was that one-handed boy going to hit one by me!

"Wham!" I felt a tremendous pain, and I fell to the ground, stunned.

It felt as though my whole body was paralyzed. I was so dazed that I struggled to understand where I was and what had happened.

And when I recovered somewhat, I looked up to see what had hit me, and discovered, instead, that I had run into the high, wooden fence that separated the playground from the houses.

And then I realized that there were voices. Someone was yelling something about a home run. And when I came to, I realized what had happened. Bob had hit one over the fence. The ball lay deep inside the Kuschels' side yard.

A home run! A home run!

I couldn't believe it. That guy had hit one over the fence.

I learned very quickly not to ever underestimate Bob K. again. Over the years he hit as many home runs as did any of us. And field? Why, he would snag a ball in his glove, remove his glove in the crook of his *arm* in one easy motion, and then fling the ball anywhere he needed to, and as fast as anyone else could.

He was a ball player! A real ball player! And he was a class guy.

CHAPTER THIRTEEN

Dark Mansions

"WHERE'S JERRY, MOM?" I asked one morning. It was late July, and the sun was shining with beams of possibilities for the day.

"I don't know," she replied. She was cooking oatmeal for Sandra and David. Marilyn, I supposed, was off visiting one of her friends, either Wanda Pipes or Mary Lou Warren.

"But wherever he is, you bring him back home. You two have to get the grass cut before you do anything else. You hear me?"

She wasn't in the best of moods. It was hot. She had a load of clothes sitting in her wicker basket, ready to take down stairs to wash. I knew that doing the wash was not her favorite job. The machine was an old one that broke down regularly, and the clothes, after the washing cycle, had to be put through a hand wringer, an old contraption that took a lot of strength in order to turn the handle. And then the clothes had to be hung outside, on the clothes line; in bad weather, they were hung on lines in the dark basement.

"And I want you to eat something, before you go off looking for your brother. You hear?"

"Yes ma'm," I said, taking a chair at the kitchen table.

She put a bowl of oatmeal in front of me, and a glass of milk. I took the jar of honey from the table and dripped some of it on the oatmeal. We didn't have much actual sugar, so we improvised when it came to sweetening our food.

I began to spoon the oatmeal into my mouth, wanting to get out of there as quickly as possible.

"And stop eating so fast," Mother said over her shoulder. "You act as though someone's about to snatch the food away from you."

How, in heavens name, did she know that I was eating fast? I looked up at Sandra. She smiled understandingly. David was too young to be aware of any possible problems that might crop up between Mother and me.

When I had gulped the last of the oatmeal down, I hurried my dish to the sink, ran out the back door, and began scouring the neighborhood. I don't believe there were more than a dozen days in the first ten years of my life that I would have journeyed out into that vast wilderness of a world without my twin brother. That was one of the great advantages of having a twin; I always had a companion, for good or bad.

But I couldn't find him. I tried Joe's house, and Jack's. And for sure he wouldn't have gone to Polk without me. And a hurried trip to Eighteenth Street was fruitless. It was getting to be a mystery.

As a last resort, I started over toward the area where Charley and Dick lived. I figured that perhaps Jerry had gone to our diamond at Eighteenth Street, looking for a ball game, and then had gone on over to those guys' houses to look for them. At the same time, it just didn't make any sense that Jerry would go off to play baseball without me.

My mind was wandering as I strolled north on Sixteenth Street and then turned west when I got up to Griswold. I had been in this area a few times, but not enough times to really get to know who these *neighbors* were. A few of them looked familiar, those who were sitting on their porches or working around in their yards. I knew some of their names, and being diligent adults and neighbors, they probably knew who I was, since most of the adults watched over each others' children, a kind of collaboration that kept most of us kids on the straight and narrow, at least to some degree. It was hard to get away with much in those days, although I have to admit that I was successful much too often. My reputation was such that the neighbors all kept their eyes on me, whenever I was around.

Anyway, I was walking purposely. Time passed, as did the houses.

Then it was that I came across *the house*. I had passed it by a few times before, without really noticing it. But for some reason that I cannot define, I stopped to really look at it this time. I mean, really look.

Sure, it was a big house, bigger than all of the others that dotted the yards in Germantown. But it was more than just its size that got my attention. It was the curious way it had been built.

It was three stories tall, with each of the upper two stories becoming slightly smaller than the one underneath, so that it resembled a tall, wide ship, like an old steamboat, the pilot house being the upper deck, or story. And that third story was curious looking, with a pinched look about it.

Like a ship at sea, the house had battled the storms of years, and had emerged scathed but still standing, like a valiant warrior ship of old. The clapboard siding was darkened almost to black in places, and here and there were cracks in the boards. Trailing ivy had fought the mildew and had pretty much succeeded in winning the battle; the ivy hung like Spanish moss, sneaking its way into crevices and cracks.

The house was sitting back a ways in the yard, probably about twenty feet or so, and the east, or side, yard was immense. In fact, no one else in all of Germantown-at least as far as I can recall-had as big a yard. It was so huge that it would have been possible to build another house and a half in the yard. And I could also see, through the dense tangles of trees and shrubs, to where a wooden fence ran along what must have been the neighbor's house that bordered the rear yard. And it was obvious that the huge area was no little flower garden and vegetable garden, but a veritable jungle of greenery amid a forest of trees.

One tree stood out, far in the rear yard. It would have given competition to our *sentinel* that stood in Pollywog, so huge was it. It almost overpowered the whole aspect of the place. And it gave off, even in the warm summer air, a shadowy atmosphere. It was almost as if it were a sort of dark guardian of the house, warning outsiders to keep away.

An iron fence surrounded the side and front yards. It was about four feet high, and its iron bars looked formidable, aiding the tree in its protective stance.

In the middle of the front of the property, a walk built of red bricks wound casually from the rear of the yard, through bordering shrubs, until it reached a wide staircase that led up to the front porch. The staircase, also built of red bricks, helped to give the house a forbidding appearance.

I must have been hypnotized by it all, as I failed to notice that a person had appeared from out of the dense foliage.

"What are you looking at, boy?"

The voice was cracked, harsh sounding, and it startled me.

I looked to my left, and there, on the other side of the fence, amidst a bunch of bushes, stood a small, gray haired woman. She wore spectacles, the sort that my grandmother often wore when she did needlework, small ones that seemed to be balanced on the end of her nose.

She wore a long gray dress that was somewhat severe looking. It had a collar that was buttoned at her neck. And she had working gloves on, and was carrying garden shears, almost like they were a weapon.

She must have been kneeling before I got to her place, else I would have noticed her.

Like I said, she was small, not any taller than was I, and I was only an average sized ten-year old boy. She was somewhat slender, but she seemed to have what I would call a firmness about her, like she was a person that few people would dare challenge. My grandmother would have said *feisty* in describing her, as that was a word that she used for old Mrs. Steinmetz, who lived behind us and who had always been regarded as a loner, someone whose independence was clearly visible.

"I asked you, what are you looking at, boy?" Her eyes narrowed, shrewd, but not cold-like, just in control.

"Uh, well, uh…"

"Quit your stammering," she said. "Can't you speak, boy?"

"Uh, yes, ma'm," I answered.

"Well then?"

"Ma'm?"

"What were you looking at?" She had put her free hand on her hip, the other hand still holding the shears.

"Your yard," I replied, not sure if that was what I should have said. It was all that I could think of saying.

She turned around then, as if to survey her property, as if to ascertain just what it might have been that would be of interest to a mere boy. I noticed that her hair was wound closely in a bun, tight to her head, typical German-style.

Then she turned back to face me.

"Don't you have a yard of your own?" she asked. I wasn't sure if she was being sarcastic, or just inquisitive.

"Not like this," I said, pointing to a spot behind her.

At that, again she turned to survey her yard. Then she turned around, and looked me over. For the life of me, I couldn't figure out if she was being critical or just plain curious. Of course there wasn't much of me to look at, but she spent quite a bit of time doing it.

She moved between two bushes that stood in front of her, so that she came close to the fence, so close that she could have touched it. But she stood there, straight, ramrod straight, her posture not so much one of solemnity but rather of dignity, her hands straight down her side, still holding the shears in her right hand.

"Where do you live, son?" And with that being said, I realized that she had dropped the strictly informal "boy" in place of the more intimate "son."

"Down on Sixteenth Street," I replied, pointing in the general direction of my house.

"Sixteenth Street is a long street," she said, expecting me to elaborate. And I noticed that the tone of her voice was no longer quite as sharp.

"We live just off Minnie," I said. And for some reason that I cannot explain, I was beginning to be more comfortable with her. Well, maybe not exactly comfortable, just a little bit easier.

"Big family?" she asked.

"Well," I began, "there's my mother and my father, and I have two brothers and two sisters. My one brother is my twin," I added.

She nodded, obviously digesting it all.

"Two of you," she said then, flatly. "Are you both alike?" The question, I realized, was one of more than just curiosity. If it had been asked by someone who knew me well, then I might have taken it as a question of hope that there could not possibly be two just like me. But she was a stranger, so I felt like I was on safer ground.

"Well, we don't look alike," I replied.

"Hmff. And I'll bet you don't think alike, either. Fraternal, apparently." Her eyes lifted, as if she were querying me in that manner, also.

I didn't know what *fraternal* meant.

"No, ma'm," I answered. "Jerry's not like me, at all. I mean, he's… well, he doesn't get into as much trouble as I do. That's what my mother says, anyway."

And she grinned at that, a full grin, her lips separated.

"Well, at least you're honest about it," she rejoined.

There was a lull, then. I could see that she was thinking something over, giving consideration to something before speaking again. I was trying to find an easy way to leave.

"You have a name?" The abrupt-like tone was back.

"Yes, ma'm. Larry. Larry Miller," I added.

"And your twin's name?"

"Jerry. Jerry Miller," I said, and then I felt stupid for having added our last name, for obviously if my last name was Miller, then so was Jerry's.

She didn't smirk, or laugh at me. She acted as though she had not even noticed my blunder.

"Larry and Jerry," she said, more to herself than to me, obviously mulling it over. "Larry Miller and Jerry Miller," she repeated. "Hmm. Your mother must have had kind of a poetic touch, I gather."

I didn't say anything. And she stood there, deeply in thought, it seemed to me. She no longer was looking at me; instead her eyes were focused on something over my shoulder, or perhaps on nothing physical at all but on something beyond the physical realm.

"I'm sorry, ma'm," I said, interrupting her thinking. I was just about to leave.

"What's to be sorry about?" she asked, and her eyes came back to me, as if by great effort.

"For staring," I replied. "It's just that your place…well, it's…"

"No need to be sorry," she said, interrupting me, and the tone of her voice had changed again. It had become one of almost subtle civility, the words almost soft. Then: "You want to see the yard?" she asked.

I didn't know what to say, or to do.

"I, well, I, uh…"

"And don't stammer," she said, repeating the phrase in the same tone of voice that she had used minutes before. "And quit being timid. Do you want to see my yard, or not?" Her one hand came up once again to rest on her hip.

"Yes, ma'm," I answered, afraid to say anything other than that.

"The gate has a latch on the inside," she said, walking toward it.

I found the latch, lifted it, and the gate swung inward. She waited by the side of the brick walk.

When I walked through the gate, she turned, somewhat abruptly, and began walking up the walk toward the interior of the yard, obviously expecting me to follow. She carried an air of authority about her, as though she was always accustomed to being obeyed.

"And put the latch back in place," she said over her shoulder.

I did, and turned and began to follow her. About twenty feet or so up the walk, there was another brick walk that branched off toward the side yard. There were rhododendrons alongside the house. I recognized them because of some that grew in front of the Wollens' house three houses south of ours. But these were much bigger than those at Wollens'. These were almost wild looking; they stood about five feet tall.

Further on, she stopped in front of some plants that stood about two or three feet in height. There were strange looking flowers on top of the stems, greenish flowers with white around the edges.

"Know what these are, son?" she asked. She shifted the shears to her other hand, fingering the leaves of the plants, actually caressing them.

I shook my head.

"They're called snow-on-the-mountain," she answered. "My husband planted them for me right after we bought this place. They grew in a field near here, and he brought them home and planted them. We had a terrible time getting them to grow. Everyone told him that they wouldn't grow. But they eventually did."

"They're pretty," I acknowledged.

"The neighbors behind me said that they would die."

I looked at the flowers again, not knowing what to say.

"As you can see, they were wrong. But they usually are wrong, when it comes to growing things." She had a stern look when she said this, as though challenging anyone to argue the point.

"Yes, ma'm," was all I offered.

"You know what those are?" she quizzed, stopping and pointing to some plants we had just passed.

I turned back to look.

"Rhododendrons," I replied.

"Hmff," she grunted. "You know something about plants, I guess."

"Your roses are beautiful," I remarked, coming up to bushes that ran along the side and nearly to the back of the house. And, indeed, they were beautiful. There must have been at least ten bushes. Some of the roses were red, others were pink, and some of them were almost purple. They were too overgrown, though. They looked as though they hadn't been pruned in a long time. In my mind, I was comparing them to the well groomed rose bushes that grew in Mrs. Wolfe's yard, the corner house that stood immediately north of our house.

She came up to where I was standing, and stood silently alongside of me, not saying anything. I wondered if I had said something that I shouldn't have said. It would have been very much like me. My mouth had already gotten me into a lot of trouble over the few years of my life.

I looked over at her quickly, but turned back when I noticed that there were tears in her eyes.

"Must be coming down with a cold," she sniffed. "You have to be careful with the thorns," she said, assuming control of her voice, and she reached in among one of the bushes and almost seemed to caress the flowers, like she had done with the other plants.

"My husband planted them for me," she said, her voice cracking a little. "He knew I liked roses."

"Yes m'am," I said.

Then she dropped the shears to the ground, and moved on, toward the very back part of the yard, and I followed, almost dutifully. I didn't feel that I had any other option. I wasn't afraid. I just didn't know how to do anything else.

The whole back yard was indeed huge, like a small wilderness. There were small trees that hugged the perimeter of the yard, away from the massive oak tree that commanded the center of the yard. Underneath the spreading branches of the smaller trees were shrubs of different varieties. Flowers grew in unexpected places, as well. She stood near the edge of where the walk divided off, about in the center of the yard. Near her was a cluster of tall shrubs.

"Know what these are?" she asked, hoping, I was sure, that I didn't know the answer.

I shook my head.

"I didn't think so," she said, a gleam in her eyes probably because she was able to stump me.

"They're viburnums," she said almost proudly. They were almost ten feet tall, and they looked as though it would be impossible to control them. Some of them had clusters of flowers, as well as reddish-colored berries.

"Your husband plant these, too?" I asked, not knowing what else to say.

"He did," she replied in short and succinct words.

"You've got raspberries," I suddenly said, moving over to some low growing bushes further off the walk. It must have sounded like I was surprised, because she didn't reply, but walked over to where I was now kneeling.

"Used to have strawberries, too," she said. But not enough sunshine to keep them all growing. So I had them taken out. Can't eat the raspberries, either," she added. "My doctor says that I'm not supposed to eat anything with small seeds." She stood above me, both hands on her hips, shaking her head back and forth.

"Ah, you get older, and the doctors take away many of your pleasures," she snorted.

"Sit down," she said, pointing to a bench beside the walk. There was another bench across from it, on the other side of the walk, and she sat down on it.

So, I sat. If it had been an order, I hardly recognized it as such. It was more like a gesture of good manners.

"The yard's getting away from me," she offered. "Used to be I could come out here and spend hours working away at everything. But I just don't have the energy any more. And even if I did, I don't think I'd be much inclined to, anyway."

I nodded, I hoped with understanding.

"It's hard to do things all alone."

I nodded once more, and waited for her to go on.

She raised her head then, and looked rather intently at me. She seemed to be studying me, for some reason. Then she shook her head from side to side, as if she were trying to come to grips with something.

"I don't mind the trees so much," she said suddenly. "They're supposed to grow big. It's these shrubs and everything else that are getting to me," she said, looking all around her, at the numerous plants and bushes and flowers and shrubs. "Some of it is supposed to be cut back, now and then."

"Yes, ma'm," I replied, not knowing what else to say. I wasn't sure what she was getting at, or even if she was getting to anything else in particular.

We sat there, in the slanting sunlight that filtered down through the branches of the trees. Birds flitted in and out of the trees, but I hardly noticed them. I was no longer looking over her yard. My mind was on a thousand things, but mainly on how I could figure out a way to escape. Oh, I wasn't frightened of her. I was just being a small boy who had gotten himself trapped and couldn't figure out how to get out of the trap. And I think she realized that, because suddenly she asked: "You do any yard work?"

The question took me by surprise. I began to stammer something.

"Yard work," she said a little gruffly. "Do you do any yard work at home?"

"Jerry and I cut the grass," I replied. "And our grass isn't much, either. We don't have anything else," I added. "We used to have some bushes on one side of our yard, but Mrs. Wolfe had my dad take them out. She lives next door to us. She has rose bushes," I explained.

"Why'd she have him do that?" she demanded.

"She said that we weren't taking good care of them. I guess they were growing into hers."

"I see," she said, absorbing that information. Then, "Are you afraid of work?" The words came abruptly.

"I don't think so," I replied.

She chuckled at that.

"That's an interesting answer. How old are you?"

"Ten."

"Well, at ten, I don't suppose a person is supposed to know if he likes to work, or not."

"We do the dishes each night, my brother and I. And my sister, Marilyn, helps."

"Doing dishes isn't work," she scolded. "It's chores."

I nodded. It seemed to me that I was doing an awful lot of nodding to her comments.

"How would you like a job?" she asked suddenly, turning her eyes squarely on mine.

I didn't reply right away. I was trying to understand what she was asking.

"I need a boy, from time to time," she put in. "Somebody I can count on. Nothing really much. There's a little patch of grass in front of the house, out near the boulevard. That needs cutting about every week or so. And I have a hard time getting up and down a ladder now. Arthritis," she explained. "So, once in a while I need someone to cut away at some of the shrubs, prune them back. Things like that."

I nodded my head, again. I was trying to absorb everything she was saying.

"You interested in the job?" she asked directly.

"Yes, ma'm," I answered firmly, maybe too quickly. I was having trouble grasping all that was going on.

I wasn't sure that I really wanted a job. But the question had come so fast and unexpectedly that I think I said 'Yes' simply as an excuse to eventually get away and think the whole thing over. I figured that I could always escape from any tiresome duties, once I was away from her, in case I decided I didn't really want the job. Besides, the thought of working for an old woman that I had just met…well, I figured that I would probably wind up working for very little pay.

That was just the way it was in those days of the Depression. So many people still out of work. So many men working in distant parts of the country on federal jobs, their families broken up, at least temporarily. I was used to the idea of people working for very little money. So I didn't think there could be much prosperity in working for this old woman.

"I don't tolerate laziness." Her eyes were staring directly into mine.

And again I nodded. Or did I shake my head? I'm not sure. But I do recall that I didn't want to send her the wrong message.

"If you work for me, I expect obedience." Her eyes were still locked directly onto mine.

"Yes, ma'm."

"I pay twenty-five cents an hour."

My eyes must have bulged out of my head.

"That all right with you?" she queried, obviously noticing the look on my face.

"Oh, yes, ma'm," I replied, and the excitement on my face must have showed, because she gave off a faint smile.

Had I heard right? Twenty-five cents an hour? The excitement that I first felt faded somewhat, since what I had heard could not possibly be true. Could it? My hearing must have deceived me, I figured. Why, twenty-five cents could buy more than two quarts of milk or two loaves of bread. And I recalled that Dad had said that one day we might even be able to afford to buy a pork roast, if we could come up with the fourteen cents per pound that it would cost.

"How about this next Saturday?" she asked. "Are you available then?"

"Oh, yes, ma'm," I replied, maybe a little too eagerly.

"And I expect to get twenty-five cents worth of work."

I nodded.

"Nine o'clock," she stated, still looking sharply at me.

"Yes, ma'm."

"And don't be late," she ordered. "I hate people being late." Her eyes narrowed, giving added emphasis to what she said.

"No, ma'm. I mean yes, ma'm. I mean..."

"I know what you mean," she interrupted in a curt manner.

She got up from where she was sitting, and I got up from the bench, following her as she made her way along the walk toward the front of the house. She stopped near a side door of the house, looked at me, and then said: "Nine o'clock."

"Yes'm," I replied.

Then she turned, seemed to think differently about what she was doing, and walked further along the walk and around it to where it went toward the front steps. Following, I quickly walked toward the gate, and when I got to it, I lifted the latch, and then turned around. But she had gone up the steps of the front porch.

I was putting the latch back in place when she was just about to open the front door. She turned back, briefly, and called down: "Nine o'clock. Don't be late," she ordered.

"No, ma'm," I shouted back.

"And be sure to latch that gate," came her call.

"Yes'm," I yelled back, firmly shutting the gate and latching it, taking a last look up at her. But she had disappeared into the house.

And off I ran, back east along Griswold Street, excitement propelling me faster than I had ever run before. Elation was carrying me along, and when I was about to turn onto Sixteenth Street, Mr. Kirby, the owner of the gas station across the street, called out, halting me.

"You running for a touchdown, Larry?"

I came to a stop, my feelings wanting to propel me along. But here was my first chance to share my happiness.

"No, sir," I yelled back. "I just got a job! I just got a job!" And he must have heard the elation in my voice, for I could see him smile and then wave.

And I flew on home. Oh, how I flew.

Chapter Fourteen

A Dream, or a Nightmare?

"Mom! Mom!" I yelled, as I ran up the steps and tore into the house and into the living room.

She came rushing in from the kitchen, flinging open the swinging door that led into the dining room.

"What happened?" she asked, disturbed by the way I had called out to her. "Who's hurt?"

"Nobody's hurt," I said, gasping for air, for I was winded by the long run home.

"For land's sake," she said then, "stop scaring me so. And stop being so rambunctious. You came into the house as though you were hurt, or something. Can't you ever do things in a normal fashion? And what are you using the front door for, anyway?"

"I'm sorry," I apologized. "But I got a job, Mom. I got a job." I was so excited that I wanted to shout out a thousand words.

"You got a job!" she said, as though in disbelief. "What do you mean, you got a job?"

Sandra and Marilyn had come in then. Probably they had been in the back yard and had heard me shouting.

"I'm going to help a lady do her yard work," I explained.

"Let's slow down here," she said. "You sit right there at this table," she added, pointing to the dining room table, and she took a chair on the other side and sat down, herself. I pulled out a chair, but I sat on the edge of it, as I was still so excited about it all.

"Now, let's start at the beginning. And take it slow."

"Yes ma'm," I answered. "I got a job, over at this house on Griswold Street. There's this real neat, old lady, and she wants me to help her keep her yard up. She's got these rose bushes, and some rhododendrons, and some of these bushes she calls viburnas, or something like that."

"Whoa," Mother said, putting up a hand to halt me. "Who is this lady? And how come she asked *you* to work for her? You hardly do any work around this house, for heaven's sake."

"She lives over on Griswold," I said.

"I know. You already told me that. Where on Griswold?" she retorted. "And how was it that you happened to meet her. And what's her name?"

There were too many questions.

"I was over there, looking for Jerry," I replied. "I thought he might have gone over to Charley's house. Or Dick's," I added. "And I was looking into her yard, and there she was. And we started talking, and then we were sitting in her back yard, and she has all these wild plants and trees. And she's got rose bushes, too. And she asked me if I wanted to work for her."

I had rattled on in such an excited fashion that Mother leaned forward in her chair, as if she did not want to miss a single word I had to say. Sandra and Marilyn had moved to one side of the table. Both of them were staring at me, as if I had sprung something incredible on them.

"Well, who is she?" Mother asked. I think she doubted what I was telling her.

"I don't know her name," I said. "But it's a big house," I added. "A really big house. It's on this side of the street, almost down to Nineteenth Street. It's got a huge yard, and she said that she can't do the work like she used to. And she's got all these rose bushes and other bushes. And she asked me if I would like to help her." I was speaking the words so quickly that it must have sounded like I was babbling.

"Is it a big, old, gray house?" Mother asked.

"I guess so," I answered. "I think it's not white. I guess it's gray."

"You mean old Mrs. Schweikert?" she asked incredulously.

"I don't know her name."

"A three-story house?" Mother asked. "With a little dormer on the top floor?"

"If you mean like that thing on Curries' house, I guess so," I answered. The Curries' house had what amounted to what I thought of as a gable, but maybe it was a dormer, or whatever Mother called it.

"That has to be Mrs. Schweikert," she said. "For the land's sake!" she added. And she was shaking her head from side to side, as though she was trying to take this all in.

Then, "How much is she going to pay you?" And there was a suspicious tone in her voice.

"Twenty-five cents an hour," I answered proudly, grinning from ear to ear, I'm sure.

"Twenty-five cents an hour!" she said, this time shaking her head as if she had just heard the most preposterous thing in the world. "Twenty-five cents an hour?" she repeated. "Are you sure? Twenty-five cents an hour? For a boy? She actually said that she's going to pay you, a mere boy, twenty-five cents an hour? Why, there are many grown men who don't make that kind of money." There was great disbelief in her tone.

"There's something wrong here," she said. "Twenty-five cents an hour! You must have not heard her right."

"That's what she told me," I replied.

"Are you sure?" she challenged, for I was one to exaggerate a little. To tell you the truth, I was one to exaggerate a lot. "She's going to pay you twenty-five cents an hour? To work in her yard?"

I nodded. And she shook her head again, as if she couldn't really absorb what I had told her. Marilyn, it was obvious, was having trouble believing it all, too, for her mouth hung open in astonishment.

"I can't believe it," Mother said. "You must have misheard her. You couldn't be making twenty-five cents an hour. Maybe five cents an hour, most likely."

"But that's what she said, Mom. And she said that I can't be lazy, and I have to be on time, and she's really a neat old lady. And she has this big yard. And she wants me to cut the grass, and do some trimming."

I was babbling again. But who could blame me?

"Well," Mother said finally, "we'll have to talk this over with your father, when he gets home."

"I can keep the job, can't I?" I asked, worried that she would shoot down the greatest thing that had ever happened to me.

"We'll see," she answered, and she got up from her chair, still shaking her head, and walked back into the kitchen. But I could hear her mutter, "Twenty-five cents an hour. And for a boy. There's something wrong here." And the swinging door swung shut on her voice.

When she was out of hearing, Marilyn asked: "Are you making up one of your stories?"

"Honest, Marilyn," I answered. "And she really is a neat, old lady."

And Marilyn added to Mother's line, "Twenty-five cents an hour. I can't believe it." And she went into the kitchen, also. Only Sandra was left to stare up at me, and because she was so young, only six years old, probably none of it made any impression on her at all.

That evening, at the supper table in the kitchen, Mother explained to Dad, as best as she could, what had happened to me. I had already shared my story with Jerry, when he had come home. He had been over to Pollywog almost all day, working on a new grass and branch fort, and apparently had expected me to have found him. And because I had gone off in a different direction, I had been offered a job that paid the huge sum of twenty-cents an hour.

Dad had just about finished his dinner, and was sitting back in his chair, sipping at his coffee. This was a ritual with him, his enjoyment of a cup of hot coffee, for when he went off to work every day, he carried a Mason jar filled with coffee that he drank at room temperature. So, a hot cup of coffee was a real luxury, to him.

"So, you've met Mrs. Schweikert," Father began.

"Yes, sir," I replied.

Everyone was watching. This was far different than most conversations that took place at our dinner table. Most of the stuff that we talked about was usually dull, stuff about what was happening with our lives, or about things that had taken place in the neighborhood. It was not often that much happened to be of any great importance.

One day, not long before, for example, the horse-drawn ice wagon had turned over at the corner of Sixteenth and Minnie, spilling all of the blocks of ice onto the street. People had flocked to the scene, where many of the men had helped lift the wagon back onto its wheels, and then helped lift the blocks of ice back onto the wagon. For their help they had received small blocks of ice from the driver, to be used in the ice-boxes that most of us owned; there very few refrigerators in our neighborhood.

So unusual was this incident that the local newspaper, The Times Herald, had run a picture of the accident on the front page the next day. Ah, well, the fortunes of living in a grand metropolis. Such startling news.

But this news, of my getting a job, at ten years of age, for the grand amount of twenty-five cents an hour-well, it was something that was not only newsworthy but was something that bordered on the marvelous. Perhaps even the miraculous. But the use of the word *miraculous* leaves me a trifle concerned, since it would imply that Divine Providence had intervened in my life and had granted me a special dispensation, and those who knew me best, like my family and friends, knew without a doubt that there was no way in God's creation and divine planning that I came even remotely close to deserving of such as the *miraculous*. So we'll leave it at *marvelous*.

"How'd you happen to meet her?" Father asked casually, as though he often had discussions of this sort, then taking a sip of his coffee, and watching me from over the uplifted rim of the cup.

"I went looking for Jerry," I began, looking over at Jerry for support. "I looked everywhere…well, not everywhere, Dad. I didn't think of looking down at Pollywog."

I hesitated. I didn't want this to become a long tale.

"Go on," he said.

"Anyway, I went over towards Charley's house, when I found out there was no one at our baseball diamond, and I was just walking down Griswold, you know, and for some reason I stopped to look at this woman's house…"

"Mrs. Schweikert's," he offered.

"Yes sir. I was just looking at the house. You know how spooky it looks."

"Spooky?" Mother put in.

"Well, that's what it looked like to me," I answered. "I guess I've seen it before, but this time I just stopped to really look at it."

"And you were looking at the house..." Father put in, expecting me to fill in more of the details.

"Yes, sir. I was just standing there. There's an iron fence around the yard, and the house is so big, and there are a lot of trees and plants and stuff. Anyway, I was just looking, like I said, and suddenly I heard a woman talking to me. And that's when I met her."

"Mrs. Schweikert," Father offered.

"Yes, sir," I answered. "I guess it was her. And she asked about me, and who I was, and where I lived, and all about my family, and the next thing, I was in her back yard, and she was showing me all her flowers and trees, and then she asked me if I wanted a job. She said that she couldn't keep up with it all anymore."

He sat back, looking me over, and I was sure he was wondering how it all happened. And to tell the truth, I was beginning to wonder about it all, too. Maybe it *was* too good to be true.

Six faces were on mine; six pairs of eyes. Well, maybe not David's. He was only about two years old, and was too young to be interested in all this. Besides, even if he had been interested, he wouldn't have been able to understand the importance of the conversation.

"Mother tells me you're going to start this Saturday," Father said.

"Yes, sir," I replied.

"Uh, huh." A pause. Then: "Well, I'll tell you what. You go to that house on Saturday, and if she is still going to go through with it, then all well and good. But I expect you home by eleven o'clock. At least no later than twelve. And we'll see how it went."

"That's okay, Dad," I agreed. "The movie starts at 2:00, and maybe I can pay for Jerry's ticket, too." And I looked over at Dad, but he looked a little doubtful about it all.

"That's if you have the money," Father warned. "I have to admit that I'm not sure about all of this. That's a lot of money for a boy your age. In fact, there are grownup men who aren't making that kind of money, and they work for businesses that are…well, let's say, a little more regular."

"Yes, sir. And I know I'll have the money. She's really a neat, old lady."

"Yes, you said that," he answered, obviously mulling it over. "Well, we'll see."

"I can hardly wait," I said.

"There's another thing, young man." This from Mother, and the moment she said it, I knew that something that I would not want to hear was exactly what I was about to hear. That's the way it is with mothers.

"If you do get the money, you're not going to just go out and spend it all, no matter how much it is," she put in.

I have to admit that my mind had run through all kinds of ways to spend exorbitant amounts of money. Besides the theater, there was Union Farmers Dairy, at the corner of Eleventh and Griswold, just a block from the theater; they sold double-dip ice-cream cones for a nickel. Double-dip cones were not a regular part of my dietary pleasures, for a nickel was hard to come by in those days. And I loved chocolate ice-cream. I still do.

Ah, but now! Why, an hour's work could produce huge numbers of ice-cream cones.

But Mother's voice had put a hard stop to all my dreaming.

"You hear me?" she added.

One thing for sure! I never had a hard time hearing her.

"Yes, ma'm," I answered as politely as I could, hoping my change to civil language would help me in the long haul.

"It'd be just like you to want to spend, spend, spend. And I'll not have you doing that."

I can't say that she was glaring at me, but a *glare* is as close as I can get to describing her look.

"Yes, ma'm," I said again, submissively this time.

"If you really do get the job, and if you really do get paid as much as you say, then we'll want you to put some of that money away. You've got a piggy bank upstairs, and I don't remember the last time you put anything in it," she continued.

That was true. Both Jerry and I had piggy banks. They were made of metal, and they were fashioned in the image of the Michigan National Bank building from downtown, and had been given out in hopes of encouraging people to save money. Unfortunately these two particular piggy banks were the possessions of two boys who worked and scrounged just to get the nickels required to see the Saturday matinee. We seldom had extra coins to insert into the slots of the banks. There might have been a sum total of six or seven pennies in either of them, but that would have been about all.

"Yes, ma'm," I said again.

I noticed that Jerry and Sandra and Marilyn were silent during this entire discussion. But I understood why. It really wasn't a discussion. It was a one-sided ruling that invited no debate. And I realized that Jerry and Marilyn-especially these two-were probably feeling some sympathy for me. They were old enough to understand how much twenty-five cents amounted to, and how much it could purchase.

"Your mother's right," Father said. "It wouldn't hurt to put something away for a rainy day."

There was that "rainy-day" axiom. Again! I had heard it enough, even in my short life span. It could make a person wonder if that rainy day was ever going to arrive. Besides, what's wrong about spending money on sunny days?

By the time we had finished cleaning up after supper, and had gone outside to try to find something to do with the other kids in the neighborhood, I instantly knew that my status had changed. There were a lot more kids in the immediate vicinity than there usually were.

This particular evening, there were a lot of kids present. Joe was sitting with Jack on the Nelsons' front porch, with Chetty and Kenny. And Donnie Bailey was approaching from his house a few doors away.

"Hey, Larry," Donnie called.

"Hey, Donnie," I answered. "What's up?"

"Did you really get a job for twenty-five cents an hour?" He was quickening his pace. His voice probably attracted the attention of everyone else in the immediate vicinity.

So that was it! They all knew about it. Word had spread. And suddenly I was the object of everyone's attention and curiosity and wonderment.

"I guess so," I said, trying to sound casual. Mother and Dad had left me wondering whether the job really was going to pan out, so I figured that it would be best if I did not overplay the whole thing. Still, I puffed my chest out a bit, swelling with self-importance.

"Wow!"

"Hey, LayLay," Chetty called out, heading across the street towards me, his brother Kenny trailing along behind with Joe and Jack. My good fortune would have been big news to all the kids in the neighborhood. And to the adults, too.

Chetty and Kenny had called me LayLay and Jerry JayJay for as long as I could remember. He and his brother Kenny were the only ones who called us by those nicknames, and it didn't really bother Jerry or me. In fact, when Chetty called us by those names, it was as though it were with a warm familiarity.

For some reason, it wasn't the same with Kenny. From him it sounded different. It wasn't exactly a put-down, but it lacked the warmth of Chetty's use of the nicknames.

Kenny was a little bit of a wise-guy, although in a likable way. In fact, I kind of thought of him as a hero, of sorts. Kenny and Chetty stopped in front of Jerry and me while we sat on our front porch steps. They were looking at me intensely.

"Are you really going to make twenty-five cents an hour?" Chetty asked in what sounded like amazement. He might have been older and bigger than I, but I felt bigger, now that I was practically *rich*.

Kenny took a place on the top step, just above me. The other boys plopped themselves down on the ground around the steps.

"I'm supposed to," I said somewhat timidly.

"Do you know who she really is?" Kenny asked, a bit of awe in his voice, but a look of questioning in his countenance.

I shook my head.

"She's the meanest lady in Germantown," he pronounced.

Some of the other kids, both boys and girls, had gathered around us. They didn't want to be left out of really important news.

"What do you mean?" I asked, staring wide-eyed at him.

"Sure," Kenny put in, swelling himself up a little bit, as though he owned all the real scoop, "I know Mrs. Schweikert. I know what she's like. She's the meanest woman I ever heard of."

"Well, she wasn't mean to me," I answered, my chest getting smaller, my breathing becoming more labored. I was trying to disassociate Kenny's description of Mrs. Schweikert from the picture I had of her, but I was weakening.

"Sure," Kenny replied, "she'll probably be real nice to you… for awhile. And then the next thing you know, she'll get you inside, and…" he made a cutting motion with his hand, across his throat, accenting the gesture with what could have been understood to be the sound of something being sliced open with a knife.

I cringed a little. Actually I cringed a lot.

By now, there was quite a crowd of kids gathered. And when Kenny made that motion, there were several gasps, especially from the girls.

If one of the younger kids had made that pronouncement, say someone my own age, I might have been inclined to disregard it. But for Kenny or Chetty to say it, the idea must be the straight thing, the real McCoy.

"How do you know that?" I asked, trying to make my challenge bolder than what it came out sounding.

"We went begging at her house last Halloween," Kenny answered, his voice husky and whispery now, giving his words a credence that would have been difficult to ignore. "Chetty and I went. And you know what?"

But no one said anything. Our mouths were open, waiting expectantly for an answer we were sure was to be one of sheer horror. I shook my head.

"She gave out poisonous candy," Kenny said, again in that whispery voice, and nodding his head in an all-knowing fashion, his eyebrows lowered and almost closed.

And again there were gasps. And there were looks of fright, as this information was collected and absorbed. Some of the kids exchanged meaningful glances.

"Did anyone die?" one of the younger kids asked, fear causing his voice to quiver.

Again Kenny narrowed his eyes and lowered his head in a dramatic fashion, and everyone bent toward him, waiting for his answer.

"I threw ours away," he said in a low voice, "into Pollywog Pond." Pause. "And you know what?" And once more he looked around at each of us. And once more we all waited, holding our breaths, and shaking our heads, our bodies tense as we leaned forward, toward this giver of diabolic news.

"I went back the next day, and there were about forty frogs in the water, all lying with their bellies up, and they were all dead." And he straightened up, his head nodding again to reveal himself to us as one who was all-knowing.

"I remember those frogs," Don C. said. "We buried them."

"Those were different frogs, Don," I announced. "The ones we buried were shot with a BB gun. And it was summer. Remember? It wasn't Halloween."

"Yeah, that's right!" my brother agreed.

And we all turned to look at Kenny, wanting more hideous information, more gory details.

"I pulled them up out of the water," Kenny said. "The poison killed them, all right.

"And if I were you," he added, "I'd watch out for anything she gives you to eat. Or drink." And he sat back then, his elbows leaning on the porch floor, and stared down at us, his look traveling slowly from face to face. And when his eyes locked onto mine, I trembled, and I wanted to look away but found myself hypnotized by the narrow slit of his eyes.

And no one doubted what Kenny said. Everyone knew Kenny. They knew he was on top of everything, being as brave and smart as he was. He was a kind of King in our neighborhood. He had a wonderful swagger in his strut, which we boys all admired. And he always kept his head somewhat elevated. Even Chetty, who was a couple of years older than Kenny, appeared to defer to his brother.

After that, some of the kids drifted away, probably to discuss it all. A few looked back at me, as I sat on our porch steps. I knew that they were talking about me. And suddenly I did not feel quite so good about myself, or about my new job and supposed wealth.

Jerry sat beside me, and his silence added to the darkening of the evening. Neither of us said anything. We just sat, and thought.

CHAPTER FIFTEEN

Demon Dreams

NEWS ABOUT MY new job spread. Later in life I was to learn that nothing spreads faster than dreadful or ominous news. It was kind of like chasing an ambulance; no one wanted to look at injured bodies, yet everyone wanted the details. And everyone wanted to be the one to spread the news. So everyone hurried to the accident scene.

The next day, Jerry and I wandered down to Polk School. It was easier to get up a game of softball than it was hardball, since a lot of boys showed up regularly at Polk, whereas the diamond at Eighteenth was only visited by boys who had received personal invitations to play, and going around the neighborhood to collect enough boys to play baseball was time consuming. For some reason that I cannot account for, I can never recall using the phone to contact our friends. Of course, the fact that everyone was on a party-line made the phone system off-limits to children's calls.

Jerry was pretty quiet about my new job, and about the information that Kenny had given us about Mrs. Schweikert. Just thinking about her name caused me to have grave reservations about her. And the more I thought about her, the more I thought about her place. I came to the conclusion that, yes, there was a spookiness about her whole place: the yard, the shrubs and trees, the house. And in my imagination I saw shadows where there probably weren't any.

Jerry and I found several of the regulars at Polk.

Of course they were all interested in what they had heard about me. But when not one of them mentioned anything bad or mysterious about

Mrs. Schweikert, I began to relax somewhat. Apparently her reputation had not spread this far east. Maybe everything Kenny had said was merely made up. Maybe.

We played softball most of that day. And I felt somewhat thankful that my good luck was not brought up.

Later, in the darkness of our room, Jerry and I lay on our bed, each of us caught up in our own thoughts. And I found myself wondering about it all. Reality was mixed with scary wonder. Even an episode of the radio program *Amos 'n' Andy could* not dispel the gloom that I felt. A darkness had invaded my very being. I was pondering just what my life was going to turn out like. I was sure that I wouldn't be able to sleep.

Jerry was quiet. He usually was. That was never my case. I usually spent my pre-sleep time planning the next day's activities. There was always so much to do, so many things that we could do, so many friends to do them with.

But this night I tossed and turned and wrestled with my pillow. I thought for sure that I would awaken Jerry, but I needn't have worried. He wasn't asleep.

"You worried about that lady?" Jerry asked. Apparently he had been lying there awake, thinking, too.

"Yeah," I answered. "You heard what Kenny told us."

"Kenny's always telling us things," Jerry said. "You remember the time that he told us there was a bum who was killing little boys over in Pollywog?"

We only lived about five blocks from the railroad tracks, and we knew the area where the hobos camped.

We had been repeatedly warned by our parents not to go too close to the tracks. Hobos had frequently shown up in our neighborhood, over the years, looking for odd jobs or for handouts, and our parents did not trust them. Occasionally we boys had crept up close to what was called Hobo Jungle, and had spied on these men. We often pretended that we were soldiers who were creeping up on our enemies, and we admired ourselves for the stealth we practiced. We were never discovered.

The Depression had hit America hard, during the 1930s. A lot of men had found themselves out of work, and had turned to riding the rails, free of charge, of course, but uninvited by the railroad lines. Everyone across America knew of the often violent lives led by these men, thus the repeated caution warnings from our parents.

The thought of the supposed killing by a hobo caused my mind to wander, which happened too frequently. And I got to thinking about the trains, and the tracks, and especially about a huge hole several blocks east. That hole was a tunnel that wound under the St. Clair River to Canada, a marvelous piece of commerce that fired most boys' imaginations. It was something that fascinated all of us boys, and many of us wondered what it would be like to be inside that tunnel.

One year, previously, my brother and I had a small paper route, delivering one of the Detroit newspapers two days each week, to people in our immediate area. One of our customers was a man whom I assumed to be a night watchman, whose office was on a hillside near to the tunnel. Jerry and I had split the route in two, and the watchman was on my part of the route.

Often during the two years we had the route, I found that either the man was asleep, or else he was out doing his inspections. My insatiable curiosity about the tunnel eventually concluded in my venturing into the tunnel, on at least three occasions.

The first time I approached the tunnel timidly. In fact, to be honest, I was really scared. I was as much scared at the thought of being caught by the watchman as I was by the thought of being killed by one of the locomotives. Still, my curiosity was so overpowering that I knew I just had to go inside the tunnel, at least once.

Of course I would not want to be inside the tunnel when a train came through. And with that thought in mind, I looked the tunnel over, thoroughly, and I noticed that there was a walkway along one of the sides. Obviously the walkway was intended as an escape for anyone caught inside at the time a train was moving through.

It was a dark and forbidding place, dim in the faint light of lamps that hugged the sides of the tunnel. But I managed, that first time, to venture inside, at least for fifty feet or so. But the thought of a train coming at me was too daunting for me to stay for long. So I hurried out, a lot faster than I had entered.

Scared? You bet. Too scared to go a little further each time? Nah. I was too foolish and reckless for my own good, and thus by the third time that I went into that oval space, I found myself extremely uncomfortable, as I had moved so far inside that I began to imagine the worst of all tragedies: being run over by one of those mammoth engines. Even though there were escape ladders mounted on one side of the tunnel, at various distances from each other, I suffered from the picture that I held in my mind, one that displayed terrible carnage. And when a distant sound that resembled low thunder resounded through that corridor, I beat it out of there, scampering up the steps that lined the hillside.

I waited up on top of the hill, expecting to see an iron giant booming its way out of the tunnel and onto the freight sheds. But nothing happened. No engine came forth, and I stood bewildered, wondering just what it was that I had heard. Whatever it was, I promised myself that I would never enter that tunnel again. It was a promise that I kept. There were times when even I could act wisely.

One of my greatest discoveries in life happened at the railroad crossing on Sixteenth Street. Jerry and I were there one day, at the crossing-we were on our way to the huckleberry patch a block further on-when one of the trains went by. For no particular reason, I stared straight ahead as the train passed us by, and a strange optical allusion occurred. By staring straight ahead at the cars passing, not moving my eyes a bit, instead of seeing the railroad cars pass, I had the allusion that the cars were stationary and that I was moving. It was a most wonderful sensation, a feeling that I was being transported quickly through space. Ah, the memories of youth.

Anyway, regardless of the dangers that supposedly existed in the area of the rail yards, there were many times that some of us boys sneaked onto the track area, out by the depot, where we sometimes *borrowed* the handcar for rides, usually ending the rides when one of the railroad workers discovered us and came running after us. The handcar was a hand-pumped flat car that usually sat on a short section of track parallel to the regular line. It was hard for us boys to man the pumping handles, but with enough boys available we were often successful in making the cars move.

The hobos were another matter. We usually knew when they were there, since we could see or smell the small fires that they lit for their cooking. They didn't look dangerous, but one never knew. Besides, why else would our parents warn us about them?

Of course I never did really believe the story about the killer-hobo. I figured that Kenny had merely been trying to scare us. But I couldn't really be sure, either.

"Yeah, I remember," I answered Jerry. "But maybe he wasn't lying. Maybe it really happened."

"You think so?" he asked, turning over to look at me in the dim light of the bedroom.

"I don't know," I admitted.

There always was the possibility that Kenny was telling the truth. After all, he seemed to have all the facts about a lot of things in life.

That dampened the conversation. I looked out the window, staring at the darkness, trying to pick out pinpoints of stars. There was a dim light from the moon.

"She might even be a nice old lady," Jerry said, finally.

So, he wasn't thinking of the hobos. He had transferred his thinking to that of Mrs. Schweikert. He was worried for me.

"Yeah," I agreed, but there wasn't much confidence in my voice.

The night was going to be a long one.

Saturday morning eventually arrived, and I wasn't sure I was ready for it. I had found sleep difficult the previous two nights, what with wrestling with everything that Kenny had told me. And even the daytime activities had not been enjoyed fully, as I constantly had Mrs. Schweikert on my mind. Just what kind of a woman was she? Where was her husband? Did she have any kids? Where did she get all of her money? How come she called out to me that fateful day and then invited me into her yard? Who took care of her shrubs before I came along?

So many fearful unknowns.

Jerry wasn't in bed. But that was not so unusual, as he often was up before me.

I was slow putting on my pants and shirt. No problem with shoes.

There was the usual clatter in the kitchen. Jerry had already eaten, but he was still sitting at the kitchen table, lingering, waiting for me, I was sure. He and I had always done everything together. And here I was about to embark on a job all alone. If I had been more of a philosopher, I might have considered the idea of *fate*. What was it that awaited me?

I took my time with the bowl of oatmeal that was set before me. Sandra was still at the table, sitting there across from me, and she was trying not to let me know that she was watching me, but I caught brief glimpses whenever I looked up, as she quickly lowered her eyes.

Had she been on the porch a few nights back and heard Kenny describe the possible dread that I might be facing? Was it fear that I noticed in her eyes?

My oatmeal tasted bland, almost terrible. Or was that my imagination also? And would I ever sit around the table and eat breakfast again? Was this all really happening?

"You'd better hurry," Mother said to me, picking up a couple of dishes from the table. "You said that Mrs. Schweikert told you not to be late."

Mother didn't seem to be worried about Mrs. Schweikert. And Dad had not said anything about her. Couldn't I trust my parents to know if I was walking into any danger? Or were they oblivious to what really took place way over there on Griswold, so far away? I mean, they might not even know what took place so far away. Why, it must have been at least eight blocks from our house. What could they possibly know about people who lived at that great distance?

"I don't know if I really want the job," I confessed, my head lowered toward the table.

"What do you mean, you really don't want the job?" Mother exclaimed, her voice loud and filled with astonishment. She turned and stared down at me.

"Well, what if I don't do a good job? What if she doesn't like me? What if…"

"What's got into you, anyway?" she interrupted. "Don't tell me you're afraid of a little work. Because I'm not going to stand for that. You hear me?" And the way that she stood there and stared down at me, with her hands on her hips, caused me to shut up.

"That's all you could talk about the other night. You were so excited that you couldn't talk about anything else. I declare, I can never figure you out, Larry Miller."

I had already learned that when Mother or one of my teachers called me by my entire name, it did not bode well. Those people had a way of making a boy think twice about things.

"Now you get going. And you do a good job. And be polite. And don't forget your manners. And you come right home afterwards."

Jerry was watching all this, but trying hard not to look at me.

Jerry followed me as I went out the back door and headed toward the alley.

"Are you scared?" Jerry asked, a slight tremor in his voice.

"Nah," I answered, but I knew that I didn't sound convincing, that my answer was the typical posture of bravado that I sometimes put on.

"I'll wait for you here," he called. "So that we can go to the movies together."

"Okay," I called back over my shoulder. And I walked away, feeling lonely.

"It's a Johnny Mack Brown movie," he yelled. I think he had meant to offer me that piece of information in hopes of making things sound positive.

I looked back, once, waved, then plodded forlornly up the alley.

It was such a beautiful Saturday morning, and here I was, trudging off to I-didn't-know-what. Why had I even gone up Griswold Street that other day? Why had I even stopped to stare at that house? Why did I always get myself into these ugly situations? Why? Why? Why?

Fate seemed so cruel.

My feet propelled me on, but my mind was reluctantly dragged along. I couldn't even have possibly noticed who all were out and about.

As I approached the house, it looked even darker. And the yard was darker yet, hidden in the shadows of all the trees and shrubs. The

wrought iron fence was even more imposing. The whole place looked…
well, deserted.

Yeah, I thought encouragingly. Maybe something had happened to
the old lady. Maybe she's dead, I thought. Maybe she had to go out of
town. Maybe she…

"Well, I see you're on time."

The voice broke through the morning sunshine, through my gloom.

She had appeared suddenly, rising up from some bushes just on the
other side of the fence. She was wearing the same dress that she had worn
the previous time, except that this time she wore a kind of apron over it,
some kind of work apron, with straps that went over her shoulders. The
apron reminded me of the one worn by the butcher at the H. A. Smith
Grocery Store, except that this one was of tan leather. She was carrying
the same shears that she had carried the first day that I had met her.

"Don't you ever wear shoes?" she asked bluntly, looking down at my
bare feet.

I rarely gave my feet any thought when I was out during summer. I
usually only wore shoes when I went to the theater, or to church, or to one
of the stores when Mother dragged me against my will. Besides, the shoes
I owned had holes in the soles. Jerry and I would put slips of cardboard
inside to keep moisture out during wet weather. And we had learned to
keep our feet planted firmly on the ground, in an effort to hide the holes,
so that we would not be embarrassed by others' remarks.

I didn't say anything. I felt embarrassed, and hung my head.

"Well, let's get started. The gate's unlatched." She turned and walked
back into the forest of her yard, evidently expecting me to follow.

She was waiting for me beneath an overgrowing viburnum.
Considering the shears that she was carrying, I didn't like thinking of
the word butcher, especially after what Kenny had said. And I suddenly
recalled how she had carried those garden shears, almost like they were
a weapon.

"Can you climb?" she asked, pointing to a tall step-ladder that was
standing alongside the brick path.

I nodded.

"What's the matter, boy" she asked. "Can't you speak?"

"Yes'm," I managed to squeak out.

"Well, you take these shears," she said, handing them to me and then retiring to a bench next to the brick pathway. "I want those branches cut short, the ones hanging down over those yews."

She pointed up at the tall plants, my eyes moving along with her pointing fingers.

"You see the ones I'm talking about?"

I nodded.

"And quit your nodding. Use your tongue, boy," she commanded.

"Yes'm," I replied.

I set the shears down, and moved the ladder into position, underneath the branches she had pointed to. She sat there, silent, watching me.

"I'll steady the ladder for you," she said, and she rose and stood by the ladder while I climbed, using one hand to help myself to climb and the other hand to carry the shears.

"These?" I asked, pointing to some drooping branches.

"Those are the ones. We'll get all the ones that are bending down." And she moved back to the bench.

I began to clip away. The shears were sharp, and the branches came away easily. I moved my position from time to time, and neither one of us said anything, and I got used to my work.

I had to come down often to move the ladder. She always retired to the bench after each time that I climbed the ladder, but every time I had to come down, to move to a new area, she was there, alongside the ladder. She seldom commented on my cutting away at the branches, but seemed to be content just sitting there in her garden.

Actually it was quite pleasant up there, among the tall branches. There were the small purple berries that I had noticed the other day, and white flowers that gave off a nice smell, and the air was warm, and I could hear the music of some birds in the nearby trees.

She had me clip all three of the shrubs, and when I came down from the last one, she helped me pick up the branches from where they had fallen on some flowers. She had three or four metal tubs that we put the branches in. I was really surprised at how agile she was, how much energy she showed. I suppose that I was subconsciously comparing her to my grandmother, who never showed any interest in what was going on outdoors. Grandmother spent most of her time in her little apartment in the front portion of the second floor of our house.

And I noticed something else about Mrs. Schweikert. It was very warm, actually a typically hot day for that time of the year. And frequently I had to wipe the sweat from off my face while I was working, yet she was not sweating. Not a bit. And when I thought about that, I was a little perplexed by that fact. I was also a little embarrassed to think of the word *sweat* in relation with her. It just seemed to be too crude a word to use around a lady. Especially this lady.

We finished picking up the branches, filling two of the tubs.

"I have a tree near the back," she said then, turning and leading the way on the brick path toward the very rear of the yard. I dutifully followed, carrying the ladder with me. She stopped near a tall wood fence. It must have been at least eight feet high. We had fences in our neighborhood, but nothing like this one. In fact, there wasn't one in our neighborhood that a boy couldn't just leap over, except, perhaps, that which bordered the Deacons' yard. But this one…, well, it was just plain big.

"That's my neighbor's idea of a fence," she grunted, apparently noticing me sizing up the fence. "I guess he didn't approve of my iron one. He built the wood fence so that he wouldn't have to look at my iron fence." And it was then that I noticed that the iron fence that bordered the front and side of her yard was also carried on around the rear yard, as well, except that here it was dwarfed and almost camouflaged by the wooden fence immediately on the other side of it. I had to admit that the wooden fence looked ugly, in comparison to her iron fence.

"He doesn't like my trees and bushes," she explained.

"Yes, ma'm," I said, trying to sound like I agreed with her, although I didn't really understand the problem.

"He really put up the fence so that he doesn't have to look at my yard."

"Yes'm," I said. "I like your yard," I added, and I meant it.

She looked at me sidewise, not fully. I think she was trying to decide if I had been sincere or was merely trying to make her feel better. Of if I was merely making small talk.

"Anyway," she said, "I want you to be careful with this bush," pointing to a really tall and spreading bush whose branches reached up higher than those of the viburnums.

"Know what it is?" she asked, looking up at the bush.

There were a lot of clusters of berries on it, more than were on the viburnums.

I shook my head. "No, ma'm."

"I didn't think so," she answered. "That's an elderberry bush." She paused to let that sink in.

"My grandmother told me about elderberries, one time," I remarked.

"Not many of them grow around here anymore," she said. "You have to be real careful with this one, when you go up the ladder. I'm going to give you a bucket. I want you to pick off the berries for me, before you trim the branches. And make sure you don't leave any of the berries on my neighbor's side, on those branches hanging over his fence. He doesn't deserve any of them."

I looked at her, waiting for her to explain further. And for the love of me, I couldn't tell why she would want those ugly berries. Or why her neighbor would want them, either.

"He took some off, last year," she huffed. "And I'll be darned if I'll let him get any of them this year. He doesn't like my fence, or my yard, so why should he get to like my berries?"

I moved the ladder underneath the furthest branches, and climbed with a tin bucket that she handed to me. Some of the berries were purple, and some of them were almost black. They pulled easily from off their stems, multiple berries finding their way into the bucket that I balanced on the top step. It wasn't much different than picking huckleberries, something I was experienced at. Except that one did not have to climb a ladder to pick huckleberries.

"Don't squeeze them," she called. "Berries need to be treated with respect."

Yes, ma'm," I answered. "I pick huckleberries. Down at Beard Street," I added, hoping to reassure her that I knew something about picking berries.

"Lots of people do," she answered. "I used to go, myself, but I figure it isn't worth the effort anymore. Too much competition for the few bushes there are."

"Yes ma'm," I agreed, for I could no more think of disagreeing with her than I could with my mother. Well, come to think of it, I guess I did give my mother fits along this line, being the argumentative person that I am, or was, or both.

It took me almost a half hour to get most of the berries picked, and the branches trimmed as she wanted them. The bucket was filled almost half-way by the time that I finished. I handed the bucket down to her, and came down off the ladder.

"Good job," she said, when we both stood under the trimmed tree.

She carried the bucket around to the back door of the house, and I followed dutifully. She set the bucket down, then turned to face me.

"Just one more thing for today," she said. "What do you think we should do about those?"

Where she pointed was a patch of ground with some strange looking plants. They were more than a foot tall, and each of them had three or four stems sticking up.

"Oh, you mean those weeds?" I said, pointing. "You want me to dig them up?" I asked, looking around for a shovel or a spade to dig with.

"For land's sake, boy," she uttered, "why would you want to dig up perfectly good plants?" She looked at me, and I couldn't tell if she was joking or not. So I waited.

"You don't know what those are, do you?"

I had seen some like them, somewhere around my neighborhood, but I figured they were just weeds. I couldn't put a name to them. Weeds are weeds. I supposed that I had pulled a few out of our yard, from time to time, at my mother's request.

I shook my head.

"Those are called plantains," she said. "And they're perfectly good plants for eating. Better than spinach, even, and a whole lot tastier."

"I hate spinach," I said simply and too quickly. Then just as quickly I regretted what I had said. I hadn't wanted to hurt her feelings. "I mean that…" I stopped, afraid of making matters worse than they already were.

"I wouldn't doubt that," she acknowledged. "Most boys do hate spinach. Not many Popeyes around these days," she chuckled.

I smiled. Her chuckling relieved me somewhat.

"Are they really good to eat?" I asked uncertainly.

"Would I lie to you, boy?" She looked directly at me, her hands firmly on her hips.

"No, ma'am," I answered quickly. "I didn't meant to…I mean…"

"You didn't mean to offend me, is what you meant, isn't it?"

"Yes, ma'am. I mean no ma'am," I stammered.

"And quit your stammering," she said bluntly. "You've got to get over that habit of yours. When you want to say something, just say it. You'll find that you'll get your point across a whole lot better." There was a sternness to her eyes, but not so much as to be troubling to me.

"Yes, ma'am."

"And if you're going to work for me, you might as well learn some things. About gardening and whatever."

"Yes, ma'am," I said.

"You'll know some gardening, if you're around me long enough." There was no longer any harshness in her voice, but there was no room for argument with her, either.

"I expect the next time you come across some plants you don't like the looks of, you'll think a little before too quickly calling them weeds."

"Yes, ma'am."

"Like I said, these are plantains. Most people dig them up and throw them away, especially if they're in their lawns. But they are tasty, especially in salads. All the old people know about them. They used to cook the leaves.

"I guess people change. Too much, if you ask me."

I didn't think she expected me to say anything, so I didn't.

"Now, I expect that you've worked a little more than an hour today." She looked up at the sky, as if it was a clock and she was able to tell the time by it. "Does that sound about right to you?"

"Yes, ma'am."

"And I'd appreciate it if you'd stop calling me ma'am all the time. It makes me feel old. You just call me Miss Beatrice."

"Yes, ma'am. I mean, Miss Beatrice."

She reached into a pocket of her apron, pulled out some coins, and counted out three of them into my hand. There were two dimes and a nickel. My eyes probably grew bug-eyed, looking at them.

I was surprised. Shocked, even. Oh, I knew what she had promised, but I hadn't really expected her to go through with the bargain. After all, I was just a mere boy and I knew better than to believe everything that adults told me.

"Do you have time next Saturday?" she asked, holding her head to one side and looking at me, her eyes squinting a little.

"Yes, ma'am. I mean Miss Beatrice," I amended.

"Nine o'clock, then," she said. "And don't be late." And she turned abruptly away from me.

"No, ma'am. I mean, Miss Beatrice." And I watched her small form retreat toward the house.

She had started into the back entrance, but turned and added: "And close the gate tight."

"Yes, ma'am," I said, and I hurried up the path, unlatched the gate and quickly pulled it shut and latched it, and sped toward home. I think I was running fast so that she wouldn't call me back to renegotiate our contract. I held the coins tightly in my closed fist.

CHAPTER SIXTEEN

The Hero

"LET ME LOOK at them again," Jerry said. We were sitting in our room. I took the three coins out of my pocket, and casually dropped them on the blanket as if I had grown accustomed to handling such huge sums of money. He took them up, and looked them over and over.

"Boy," he sighed, "I sure wish I had a job like that. Wow! Twenty-five cents." And he fondled the coins, then carefully put them down again.

"Larry," came the call.

It was Mother. I went to the top of the stairs and looked down. She was ready to yell up again.

"What, Mom?" I asked.

"You put one of those dimes into your bank. You hear me?"

"Yes, ma'am," I answered somewhat sadly, maybe even a little bit angrily.

"You can spend five cents at Gillies' store, but that's all. And you *are* going to pay for your brother's ticket to the show, aren't you?"

It wasn't even really a question. It was more like a demand.

"I was already planning to," I shouted down to her. I felt a little miffed that she should say anything about that. Didn't she give me any credit for doing good things once in a while? Without anyone telling me to?

"And put that dime in that bank right away. You hear me?"

"Yes, ma'am."

"And I mean, right away." She remained standing at the bottom of the stairs, waiting for me to acknowledge her order.

"I will," I said with exasperation.

"And don't get sassy with me, young man."

I went back into my room, took up the demanded dime, looked at it with a bit of disappointment, and dropped it into the slot of the bank. It made a clink at the bottom.

"What time is it?" I asked.

"I think it was about twelve-thirty when I came upstairs. Why?"

"Well, the show starts at two, so we want to have lots of time to pick out the candy."

I could almost see the saliva running across Jerry's gums. Neither one of us had ever had five cents to spend just on candy. Not in our entire lives. Oh, once in a while we had two cents, from a redeemable pop bottle. But five cents? Unimaginable.

We hurried off to Gillies' store. Mrs. Gillies was waiting on one of the neighbor ladies, as we walked in. Jerry and I walked over to the candy display case, and pressed our faces almost to the glass cover. There was so much to look at.

Being such a small store, there was not a lot of merchandise. There were shelves of cereal and canned goods, and a small meat display case. But there was only one part of the store that Jerry and I were interested in: the candy display case.

The customer left, and Mrs. Gillies came and stood on the other side of the case. She was somewhat tall, and slender, and she had a very pleasant face, as though a smile had permanently found a place there.

"How much is that strip, down there near the right hand side?" I asked, pointing with a finger. The strips were dotted with little balls of colored hard candy. The strips were about a foot long. A lot of paper had been used to display small balls of candy, a clever piece of marketing, I realized.

"Those are a penny apiece," Mrs. Gillies replied. She was as patient with children as she was with adults. Maybe more so with children. Her candy case had about ten or twelve kinds of candy, most costing only a penny or two, and she was willing to stand there, on the other side of the case, and wait until we had surveyed all that was there, before making up our minds.

Jerry and I gaped. Five whole cents to spend. It was almost too much for us. How could we possibly choose?

Mrs. Kefgen came in about then. She was a tall, skinny woman. She lived down the street from us. She didn't spend much time outdoors. Her back yard held a few vegetables each summer, mostly tomatoes and beans. The yard was fenced in, beginning part way back on both sides and continuing around the back yard. It might have kept out stray dogs, but we boys could easily have jumped over the fence if we had wanted to, but there was never any reason we wanted to.

Mr. Kefgen was quiet, too. About the only times we boys ever saw him was when he was working in his garden, and even then we could only catch glimpses.

"Good morning, Mrs. Kefgen," Mrs. Gillies said in her usual friendly way.

"Hello, Mrs. Gillies," came the reply. The voice was not a friendly one. Her words were clipped, terse, perhaps even a little abrupt.

"My, isn't this a lovely day?" Mrs. Gillies continued.

"Some think so," came the reply.

I looked up at her, and I swore that she had been looking at me, even when she had been speaking with Mrs. Gillies, but when I looked up at her, she looked away, maybe a little too quickly, at the stocked shelves behind Mrs. Gillies.

"I need some laundry soap," Mrs. Kefgen said. "And maybe just a couple of onions."

I sent my eyes back on their mission inside the candy case. Mrs. Gillies and Mrs. Kefgen talked a little about this and that, nothing of any importance to two small boys.

They went on with their conversation, while Mrs. Kefgen shopped for a few other items. When she finished, she stood before the counter, counting out some coins in payment.

"And how are you boys?" Mrs. Kefgen asked, turning to face us. There was no real friendliness in her tone. It was as if she were merely making talk.

Jerry and I looked up. We were surprised that we had been noticed. Mother had always warned us that when it came to the neighbors, it was better that we went unnoticed, because that would mean that we hadn't done anything wrong.

"We're fine," I said, shifting my attention back to the candy case.

"I hear that you earned yourself twenty-five cents this morning," Mrs. Kefgen said, bringing our attention back to her.

So! Word had passed, as quickly as most other news. I only nodded. I figured that it would be better for me not to comment about the money. In a time when adults were struggling, the subject of money was...well, something left to the adults.

"That's a lot of money for a young boy," she continued, looking at us from under raised eyebrows. I supposed she looked down at us in this manner because she probably felt that small boys did not deserve her full attention.

"Yes'm," I said, feeling a little embarrassed by the attention shown to me by a grownup-neighbor, especially on this particular subject.

"Going to spend it all on candy?" she inquired. And again the words were clipped.

"Just five cents," I answered.

"He's taking me to the movie this afternoon," Jerry offered.

"My, my," Mrs. Kefgen said. "I'm surprised that your mother is letting you spend so much money." She had folded her arms across her chest, and had turned up her face a little more, so that the effect was of someone who would have a difficult time understanding any answer that she might receive.

"I have to save some of it, too," I said. "My mother made me put a dime into my piggy bank."

"Well," Mrs. Kefgen said, sounding a little exasperated, "I should hope so. Twenty-five cents is a little too much for a young boy to spend foolishly. You need to think of the future."

"I think it's okay for a boy to have a little extra now and then," Mrs. Gillies put in, in a friendly manner. "It doesn't happen very often."

It was nice of Mrs. Gillies to defend us.

"I certainly hope not," Mrs. Kefgen fairly huffed. And she picked up her sack of groceries, glanced down once more at me, and went out the door.

"She's had a rough time of it, boys," Mrs. Gillies said, turning her attention back to us. "She really means well."

"Yes, ma'am," Jerry and I both said.

And after choosing four cents worth of candy, and getting a penny change, Jerry and I went off to the movie, feeling a little down about what had happened. I wasn't sure just what had happened, but I felt bad. Adults had often plagued me a little, as if I were never meant to understand them.

We met John Porter, and Joe and Jack and a few others at the show that afternoon. In other words, the usual crew was there. And the movie turned out to be okay. Johnny Mack Brown sure was no John Wayne. And I wished that it would have been a Charlie Chan movie instead; I needed something to laugh at just about then. For some reason, I felt guilty because of what Mrs. Kefgen had said. But for the life of me, I couldn't understand why.

When "The Shadow" appeared, I was able to escape from all of the hullabaloo over my money. I was glad to be able to think about something else, for a change.

After the movie we all poured out of the theater, and I couldn't help but notice that a lot of the boys and girls were looking my way. They were obviously talking about me. I was sure of that.

"How come everyone's looking at me?" I asked.

"You've got to be kidding," John said. "You're the richest boy in Germantown."

"I'm not rich," I replied. "Heck, I don't even have a cent in my pockets. Well, I guess I have one penny left."

"How come you only have a penny?" Jack asked. "You made twenty-five cents, didn't you?"

"Yeah," Jerry said, "but our mother made Larry put ten cents into his piggy bank."

"Boy," John said, "that's rotten."

"I'll bet your mother would do the same thing," I said.

"Yeah," he admitted. "She probably would."

We had made our way over to Polk by now, where I had to explain my status to some of the other boys who had shown up. Before long, I was no longer much of a curiosity. But I was still someone to talk about.

We sat around on the steps of the back entrance to the school. None of us mentioned anything about getting up a game of softball.

"Are you going to work for her again?" Joe asked.

"You mean Mrs. Schweikert?" I asked. I knew whom he meant, but I just didn't want to talk about it anymore.

"You know darned well who I meant," Joe retorted.

"I don't mess around in your business," I said in maybe too nasty a way.

"So, what's the big deal? You think you're something special now, don't you?"

"I don't feel that way at all," I replied a little defensively. "I guess I just got ...you know, lucky."

"Yeah, you sure are," John put in. He said it in such a way as to settle things before they got out of hand. Probably no one really wanted Joe and me to get into a fight. I was glad John had said something. I didn't want to get into a fight, either, although I wouldn't have backed down for anything.

"You're more than lucky," Joe persisted. He wasn't going to let up on me. "You're..." He was trying to think of something to finish it with.

"I'm what?" I asked, getting to my feet, staring hard at him.

When he tried to stand up, I was so close that he brushed up against me, causing me to move back a little.

"Quit your shoving," I said. And I pushed him back a little.

"You quit your shoving, yourself," he rejoined, and he pushed me fairly hard.

Then we were face to face, so close that I could see two little pimples that hugged his face under one of his eyes. And for some inane reason, I relished the thought that he had those blemishes.

We stood apart, but dangerously close.

"You're just jealous," I said.

"Jealous of you?" he retorted. "Who'd ever be jealous of you?"

The rest of the boys had all risen, and the tension was mounting.

"You are," I challenged.

"Yeah?" he said in return. "Who'd ever be jealous of a moron?"

"Are you calling me a moron?" I replied.

"I don't see any other morons around," he said with a sneer, his lower lip moving up to close with his upper lip. And at that point I would have been glad to have closed both of his lips.

"You know, Joe," I said sarcastically, "you always were a jerk."

"At least I'm not a coward," he retorted.

That did it!

I shoved Joe as hard as I could, and he tripped over one of the steps and fell backwards. But he was up in a hurry, and he tried to rush me and to grab me with his arms.

We both fell, then, and rolled around on the ground, and for a minute I thought that he was going to pin me down. He weighed a few pounds more than I, and if he got the upper hand, I figured that I would get a pounding.

But I turned and twisted, and Joe fell off, and then I was on top of him. Because I was so angry, I hit him across the head with my right hand. I was careful not to ball my hand up into a fist; I wanted to teach Joe a lesson, but I didn't want the fight to get too serious.

The other boys were all yelling. I knew that Joe was not well liked, for a lot of old reasons; consequently most of them were yelling for me, trying to encourage me to let Joe have it. I wasn't the most humble boy in Germantown, and there were times when, I'm sure, that many boys and girls would have found themselves pulling against me in a fight. But not when it came to a dispute with Joe.

Joe was yelling up at me, struggling to throw me off, but I had my knees over his shoulders now, and I told him to say "Uncle," but he wouldn't. So I was prepared to give him another slap.

Suddenly I could feel some hands pulling at me, and I heard a different voice.

"Come on, you boys, stop it." And I felt myself being pulled up and off of Joe.

It was Mr. Bond, the janitor of Polk School. He had been at Polk for as long as I could remember, and had even been there when my older sister Marilyn had attended Polk, five years before. So his face was familiar to us all.

A fairly tall, slender man with graying hair, he was a fixture at the school. I used to like to sneak down into the dark basement, where the older boys' and girls' bathrooms were located, just to watch him pull on the rope that rang the bell that started school in the morning and also after lunch time.

"What's going on here?" he asked, holding us each by one hand. I was surprised that he had so much strength.

Joe was glaring at me.

"You're just lucky that Mr. Bond is here," Joe said.

"Yeah, sure," I said sarcastically.

"Who started this?" Mr. Bond asked, still holding each of us by a hand, and looking back and forth from Joe to me.

"He did," John said, pointing to Joe.

"I did not!" Joe yelled. "He pushed me," he added, looking at me.

"You called me a moron," I said.

"That's no reason for fighting," Mr. Bond said. He still held us apart, seemingly with little effort, but by then neither Joe nor I was trying too hard to get at each other. The truth was that neither one of us really wanted to fight.

School was not in session, but there still was the worry that Mr. Bond would dutifully report the incident to Miss Tremayne, and neither Joe nor I wanted that to happen.

"Now I want you two to shake hands." He looked at both Joe and me.

I looked at Joe, but he pulled his hand behind his back. It was his way of saying that he wasn't about to shake hands with me.

"Did you hear me?" Mr. Bond said, and this time there was a more pointed, serious tone in his voice as he looked sternly at Joe. It was a warning.

"You wouldn't want me to report this to Miss Tremayne, would you? Or your parents?" he added."

Joe snapped his head up then, and looked to see just how serious Mr. Bond was. I shook my head. I had had enough encounters with our principal, and there was no way that I wanted to start the next school year by meeting her personally again. And I also knew that Joe did not want his parents to hear anything about what had happened.

"Well?" Mr. Bond said. And he waited, looking hard at both Joe and me.

"Well, I will if he will," I finally said, looking at Joe in as conciliatory fashion as possible, under the circumstances. And I stuck my hand out, somewhat tentatively, not sure if Joe would take it or not. If he didn't reach out and shake my hand, I would lose face. And if that happened, I was ready to pounce upon him.

But he finally and reluctantly stuck his hand out, more tentatively than had I, and his hand briefly touched my hand. Then he pulled his hand back quickly, as if he had touched something unclean.

"Now you boys go on about your business," Mr. Bond said. "I have more things to do than settle arguments. If you're bound to fight, then do it someplace else."

He took one last look at us, and then went back into the school.

I shrugged. It was over, as far as I was concerned. But I knew that this whole thing didn't sit well with Joe, and that he would brood about it, trying to come up with an idea to get even with me.

Such was boyhood!

CHAPTER SEVENTEEN

The Telling of Terror

THE FOLLOWING WEEK passed slowly. Something in me wanted the days to pass, so that I could work for Mrs. Schweikert again. A boy just didn't get that many chances to be rich, and I harbored a lot of thoughts of all the money that I could earn. Greed had raised its ugly head.

Part of me wanted time to go as it had always gone, slowly, deliberately, playfully. Boyhood was too precious to waste, although I seriously doubt that I actually was philosophical about it. I just wanted to get as much out of life as I possibly could. But I have to admit that my mind was mostly on the money to be made at Mrs. Schweikert's.

Friday came. It was hot, typical of our summer weather. The next day I was to be at Mrs. Schweikert's again. Although it was hot, it wasn't so hot as to dull my senses about earning more money.

Money. Money. It seemed as though that was the only thing on my mind. What a powerful hold it had on me.

That Friday night we played kick-the-can until it was pitch dark. There was a really large group of us, both boys and girls, and there were no serious wranglings, for a change. Afterwards a lot of us sat around on the grass at the corner of Minnie and Sixteenth, on a patch of Mrs. Wolfe's yard, where we usually placed the cans for the game. This particular evening some of the older boys and girls were there, including Chetty and Kenny.

"You going to old lady Schweikert's again, LayLay?" Kenny asked.

Everyone turned to me, I noticed. So! My work for Mrs. Schweikert was still a hot topic, apparently hotter than the night air.

"Tomorrow," I said in as offhand a manner as possible, hoping to deflect some of the curiosity. For some strange reason, I did not enjoy it when the other kids became interested in my working for Mrs. Schweikert. I enjoyed the thought of making more money, but I did not want any of them badgering me about it.

"I told you before. You'd better be careful of her," Kenny warned, lowering his eyes. Even in the duskiness of late evening, I could see the look he gave me, and the drama was probably made greater by the shadows across his face, created by the faint light from the street light overhead.

"How come he has to be careful?" one of the girls asked. There was a faintheartedness in the voice, and I couldn't determine who it was who had asked the question, as I was as interested in knowing Kenny's answer as were all of the others, and thus I had my attention drawn to Kenny instead of to the questioner.

"Because she's a witch," Kenny said knowingly and matter-of-factly. He had drawn his words out slowly, to increase the effect of what he said, and also to draw attention to himself. Kenny was haughty, but at that stage in my life, I foolishly considered that to be an admirable quality. Oh, how I longed to be like him!

"Wow!" Don exclaimed. And there were whisperings from others, as well. Don had been there, at our front porch, when Kenny had first brought up the subject of Mrs. Schweikert being a witch, so his *wow* had merely reinforced the thought in his mind. And It also reinforced the idea in the minds of all the others.

"How do you know she's a witch?" Jerry asked. I could tell that there was no disbelief in his voice, just a sense of wonder.

Kenny leaned forward, and the group closed in on him. No one wanted to miss out on anything he would say.

"Have you ever seen her house at night?" he asked, his voice deep and throaty, and there was, in the question, a whole new reason for imagining all kinds of strangeness.

There was a collective shaking of heads. Most of us were too young to have made the rounds in that section of town, especially at night. Her house wasn't exactly foreign to us, nor was it out of bounds at night to the older ones. But we younger ones never ventured so far at night.

"I hear that there are things that float around inside her house," Kenny said, looking around at everyone in order to deliver a greater impact of what he was saying. "They get thrown by the bad spirits inside. Those spirits belong to the devil."

"Wow!" someone said, the dark of night seeming to echo the word around and over us.

And not only that," he added, and here he paused for dramatic effect, "but she can levitate," and he stretched out the last word for emphasis. And having said that, he sat back on his heels, nodding his head knowingly, his face blurred in the shadows.

"Boy!" someone said, then asked: "What's that, Kenny?"

"Levitate?" Kenny said. "Heck, I thought that you'd all know what that is." Knowing something so strange sounding, when no one else knew what it was, made Kenny an authority on most everything.

"It means..." and he leaned forward again, knowing that we would all lean towards him, as though what he was about to share was something so grave and so important that it required absolute secrecy.

"It means," and he paused here, "that she can rise right up in the air, and even fly around, if she wants to." His voice had a kind of whispery huskiness to it. And he sat back, nodding his head, as gasps came out of several mouths.

"How do you know all this?" Joe was impudent enough to ask.

"You calling me a liar, Joe?"

Kenny stared at Joe, and we could see that Joe instantly realized that he had done something dangerous: called Kenny on anything. After all, Kenny was quite a few years older, and he was far bigger and tougher, and thus he was not a person you wanted to mess around with.

"No, no," Joe immediately stammered. And I noticed that he tried to recede back into the night's shadows.

"You'd better not," Kenny said, staring Joe down, and even in the dark of the evening, we could see the sternness in Kenny's eyes. Or maybe it was that we merely imagined it. Whatever! Real or imagined, it had the effect that Kenny wanted, for Joe leaned back as far away as he could from the group, retreating into the outer perimeter. I am sure that, at that point, Joe wanted to be swallowed up by the evening darkness.

I swear that Kenny's look could have penetrated even into the darkness, and Joe must have been aware that all of us were looking at him, or at least were looking into the area into which he had retreated. Not another peep came out of him.

"Besides," Kenny began again, turning to address the rest of us, "I've been down there, at her house, at night, and I've watched it and seen a lot of things."

We all looked at Kenny in a new way. There was no doubt that he had done what he said he had done, and had seen things that we probably would never see and certainly didn't ever want to see.

"You guys should go down to her house some night," Kenny said boldly. "It's spooky, that all I can tell you. I saw lights come on in one of the rooms on the top floor, and then the curtain was pulled away, and you know what?" he asked.

We shook our heads once more, waiting expectantly. We were too scared to use our voices.

"There ...was... no... one. .there." The words were drawn out so much that they accomplished what he had intended: an overwhelming feeling of fear.

Labored voices panted. Looks were exchanged and then quickly dropped. We waited for Kenny to go on, for we knew that he had some more things to say.

"Who pulled the curtains back?" a tremulous voice asked.

"They were pulled back by someone invisible," Kenny replied assuredly.

We waited for more. For we knew there was more coming. He gathered himself into a posture of authority, and then spoke softly.

"*I* watched the lights up there go on and off, on and off, about ten times. About ten times," he repeated for emphasis. "And then..." and when he paused, we pulled even closer to him, our ragged breathing the only sounds in the night air, our dark figures like phantoms in the blackness of the night.

"And then," he finally continued, almost whispering now, "there was this real dark shape, and it was moving across the window, but it didn't have any legs. It was like it was stretched out…kind of like this, like it was lying down on the air." And he put an arm up, horizontally, and moved it slowly back and forth, showing how it might be something floating around. And he made a whistling sound, something like what we might imagine the wind to sound like.

And when we looked around at each other, embarrassed to show the fear that marked our faces, taking deep gulps of air, Kenny sat back again, once more nodding his head up and down in that confident manner of his.

"What'd you do then?" I managed to ask. And no one was looking at me to see how scared I was. Their eyes were all on Kenny.

"I beat it out of there," Kenny replied. "I'll tell you, I didn't wait around any longer."

And we all shook our heads, showing that we understood his reaction. I mean, it might have been one thing for one of us smaller boys or one of the girls to run off, as Kenny said he did, especially the girls. But for Kenny to admit that *he* had run off…well, it made the event all the more frightening. No. That is not the word. Terrifying was what it was.

"Well, like I say, you ought to go there some night, when it's dark," he challenged. "There are some weird things happening there. I mean, besides the stuff flying around and her levitating." And once more he sat back, like a king pontificating to his subjects while seated on his throne

After he said that, there was silence. It was a silence that hung ominously in the air. Most of us kept our eyes to ourselves. We did not want any of the others to know just how frightened we were.

"I'm going home," said Eleanor, one of the girls, her voice breaking into the stillness that had taken hold of us. And we could sense that she was really scared. We watched her as she got up and made her way up Sixteenth Street, walking into the darkness of a night that had been made even darker by Kenny's revelations.

And almost immediately all of the other girls got up, too, making their way home. No excuses were made by them. No excuses were necessary; they were girls.

After they had gone off, Kenny turned to us boys. There were probably five or six of us still there. Not one of us wanted to be thought of as a sissy. It was one thing for the girls to go on home, but for boys it was unthinkable to be the first to admit to being scared out of his wits. Yet scared we were.

"All I can say, Larry," Kenny said, turning to me-and he only called me Larry when he was very serious-"is that you'd better be careful." And the slow nodding of his head gave his words extra meaning.

"She was really nice to me," I said, gulping a deep breath as I replied. I was hoping to put a new face on things. "She even had me sit and talk with her, in her yard."

"Sure," Kenny said, "that's what all the witches do. They get you to think they're just like everyone else, and that they're your friend, and then the next thing you see..."

He left the sentence hanging there, nodding slightly, silently inviting us to fill in the blanks. And I was sure that everyone's imagination was working overtime to fill in the gory details. I know that mine was.

"What about her husband?" I asked, dread obviously having taken hold of me.

"He's dead," Kenny said flatly, and I could swear that there was a spookiness in his tone. It was the kind of spooky sounding voice that might have been expected of Bela Lugosi in his Dracula role.

"How'd he die?" I asked, fear taking my question far beyond mere curiosity.

And Kenny leaned forward again, and once more we all leaned forward, too, not wanting to miss anything he was going to say. Even Joe leaned forward, not wanting to be left out of the group. Besides, there was some comfort in being attached to the group.

"They say that he had a...".-and again there was a dramatic pause- "a strange accident," the last two words spoken slowly, for dramatic effect. He paused to let that sink in. Then: "They found him out in the back yard... with an ax in his chest." And Kenny sat back, nodding his head once more in that all-knowing manner, sitting Indian style, his upper body erect and rigid, fully in control.

Several of us sucked in our breaths, and the night enveloped us even more. It was as though the darkness had not merely crept in, but that it had completely swallowed us up. There were no more shadows of the night, just the blackness, the blackness of atmosphere and the blackness of our thoughts.

Everyone was exchanging looks, and a lot of them whispered to others near them and then looked at me. I shrank back as far as I could. And maybe it was my imagination, but it seemed that the other boys actually shrinking from me.

Contamination? Were they worried that any close association with me might bring the very monsters of evil to them?

"You'd better be careful." That's what Kenny had said to me. That's what he had warned. And that warning had grabbed me and held me in its cold embrace, chilling my very soul. And I noticed that even Jerry had pulled away from me, somewhat, almost as if I were tainted by some kind of mysterious spell.

We sat there a while longer, but there was no more conversation. We were all lost in our own thoughts. Deep, deep thoughts. A cloud moved across the moon, its slow path deepening the suspenseful atmosphere.

That night I lay in bed and looked out our bedroom window at Venus, perched in the western sky. Other stars paled in comparison, struggling to show life, just as I was struggling. And near to Venus, the moon was a sliver of pale light that struggled vainly behind a veil of dark clouds.

I thought Jerry was asleep, he was so absolutely still, but his sudden voice broke the dark stillness.

"Do you believe him?" Jerry asked.

"Believe who?" I said as casually as I could. I knew full well who Jerry meant; I was just trying to make him think that I hadn't been giving Kenny any thought at all, that I hadn't been worrying about anything. I didn't want to appear afraid.

"You know who I mean," Jerry said somewhat angrily, the severity of his voice showing that he didn't believe my pretended ignorance. "Kenny."

"Oh, him," I said, again trying to sound almost careless and casual in my tone of voice.

"Okay," Jerry said even more angrily, "if that's the way you feel, forget it." And he turned over on his side, away from me.

"Okay. Okay," I said, turning over on my side to face him. "Yeah, I know who you meant," I admitted.

Jerry turned back to face me.

"Then, do you think it's all true?" Jerry asked.

"I don't know," I answered. "Kenny's been around. He's probably the only boy in this town who'd go over there and look at Mrs. Schweikert's house at night."

"Yeah," Jerry admitted. "Kenny's got a lot of..."

"Guts?" I filled in.

Jerry nodded.

"But even he ran off that night that he was there," Jerry reminded me.

"Yeah, I know."

"What about Mrs. Schweikert?" he asked. "What's she really like? I mean, is she spooky? And have you seen her husband, or is he really dead, like Kenny said?"

"I don't know about him. I've never seen anyone else at the house. But I've only been there twice. You know?"

"Yeah, I know," he said, softly.

He had been lying there, looking at me, but now he turned over on his back, and I did the same, folding my hands behind my head and trying to get comfortable in the bed. But there was no comfort to be found.

We both were looking out at the night sky, at the slow path that Venus took in her desperate attempt to rival the moon. And the stillness in the room was almost suffocating. And if I hadn't already felt gloomy enough, just then the haunting call of a lone whip-poor-will echoed off the night air and into our room. Was it foreboding something ominous in my immediate future?

I wasn't cold, yet I was shivering. Was I shivering because of what might lie ahead of me? Sleep seemed impossible.

CHAPTER EIGHTEEN

The Garden of Witches

WHEN I WOKE up Saturday morning, I felt as if I had been wrung through the hand wringer of Mother's washing machine. My body actually ached. Jerry was not in bed, so he had gotten up before me, again.

Mother was helping David with his cereal, when I entered the kitchen. Marilyn took one brief look at me, but I couldn't see any telltale signs that told me she was aware of anything disastrous that was about to happen. She hadn't been with us the night before, when Kenny had been *entertaining* us with his tales of witches and all, so she could not possibly have known the particular fate that might await me.

Jerry gave me a brief look, too, but his look was so brief that I knew he was worried about what might happen. In fact, he tucked his head down so that his chin touched his chest, apparently so as to avoid having to face me.

"Do you realize what time it is, young man?" Mother asked. She had come to the table, across from where I was sitting, and was glaring down at me.

"It's after eight-thirty," she said, not waiting for me to answer. "You don't have time for cereal. Take this toast. I'll have a sandwich ready for you when you get home for lunch," and she put a slice of toast smeared with grape jelly in front of me. "You'd better get going."

She stood there defiantly. She knew that I had never been one who liked to work. But I had no other option. I was going to Mrs. Schweikert's house, even if it killed me. And at that moment, that possibility seemed all too real.

I didn't like the idea of dying. Heck, I didn't even like the idea of pain, or discomfort. Marvin's body, lying in his coffin the year before, was ever much in my mind, reminding me all too powerfully that death did actually come, to everyone. But death was something that happened to old people, not to kids. Kids just did not think along those lines. And as far as I was concerned, life was an endless parade of days and nights spent in youth. What had happened to Marvin was an aberration, something which I was able to cast aside.

But Kenny had shattered such youthful philosophy, and had caused me to take a step back and look at things far differently than I ever had before. Death was still not much of a reality, to me. But to be killed...well, that was altogether possible. I just could not relate the two.

Now that I am somewhat wiser, in these my golden years, I realize that my thinking was typical of youth. Foolish, yes. Stupid, yes. But typical.

I wanted to say something to Mother, about what Kenny had told us. But that wasn't something a boy discussed with his mother. That was something that only boys would understand. She probably would have said that Kenny was making it all up. That's the way all mothers were. They just didn't know what really went on sometimes. They lived in their own little kitchens and sewing rooms, completely oblivious to what terrors lay out there.

Besides, Mother most obviously had never stood outside Mrs. Schweikert's house at night. She couldn't possibly understand what I was going through. I wanted to say to her: "All right, you go down there and watch the ghosts fly around."

I picked up the toast, and nibbled at it, but I didn't really feel hungry. It tasted dry. Or maybe it was my mouth that was dry.

"Get going!" Mother ordered, a little loudly. "You know that Mrs. Schweikert told you not to be late. It's just like you to fool away the time, like you always do." And she turned back to the stove, and stirred what must have been oatmeal.

"I'll see you, Jerry," I said spiritlessly.

"Yeah. I'll see you...later," Jerry answered, and he looked up quickly, then bent his head again.

The sky was gray that morning, the sun hiding behind low slung clouds that seemed determined to make the day gloomy. My feet moved me. At least they moved my body. But my brain was somewhere else. I was thinking all kinds of dreary and scary things.

When I got to the corner of Sixteenth and Division, the next block north of our house, Don was sitting on his front porch, reading a comic book, one of the new issues, most likely.

He watched me coming, then pretended not to notice me, turning his attention back to his book. But he had been there, at the corner, the night before, and had heard what Kenny had told us, and I was sure that he had seen me coming.

I kept walking, hoping that he would say something, anything to break the tension, anything to delay my progress, or, to put it more ominously, to delay my demise. But he didn't say anything. I was sure that he was watching me as I walked on further. I understood. He wouldn't know just what to say to me. And I felt his eyes on me as I walked past.

So I trudged on, towards…?

When I got to about a half block from Mrs. Schweikert's, I could see her in her yard, near the front fence. She was pruning rose bushes. I knew that many of the women kept rose bushes near the borders of their yards, for ornamentation, and also for wherever they felt that there was a necessity to discourage young people from entering the yards. Thorns are apt to produce such discouragement. I had had my bouts with those belonging to our neighbor, Mrs. Wolfe.

"Well," she said shortly, as I approached, "I see you're on time again."

"Yes, ma'm," I said, then immediately corrected myself, "I mean, Miss Beatrice."

"It's important to be on time. For everything. You understand?" There was a severity in her voice, but it was slight, not angry.

"Yes, ma'am."

She glanced down at my feet, but didn't say anything this time about my not wearing shoes.

"Well, let's get started," she said. "I left a lawnmower by the front walk."

I looked over to where she indicated.

"You need to cut the front yard, first of all. You have cut grass before, I expect." She looked at me hard, maybe expecting me to say that I hadn't.

I nodded.

"Well, when that's done, I have some more bushes that need trimming. I'll be in the back. When you get done, just bring the mower around to the back and put it in the shed next to the back door."

And she turned, and went out towards the back yard.

The clouds had thickened even more, while I was walking to her house. I suppose that I secretly wished for the rain to come so that I would have an excuse to leave. I had even come close to praying for rain, although a guilty feeling swept over me for wanting God's help with the weather; I didn't need two adversaries in one day. There were so many things that were going through my mind: about her, about the house, about her husband, about witches, and...well, too many things.

I found the mower. It was one of those dependable Sears push mowers. My dad said that they lasted forever, It pushed easily, and it was obvious that the blades must have been sharpened, as it cut a neat swath through the grass, the dew falling away and clearly showing the path where I had just cut.

Her boulevard was the only front yard she had, and while it ran for almost sixty feet across the width of her property, it was only about fifteen feet in depth. So it only took me about thirty minutes to finish the mowing. Each time I pushed the mower along the frontage, I expected to look up and find her watching me. But she had left me on my own. That didn't disturb me one bit, except that it allowed my mind the freedom to think about things that I would have rather pushed completely off to the side.

When I finally finished the mowing, I opened the front gate and pushed the mower onto the brick path, and made my way around to the back. The door to the shed was open, and I put the mower inside, being careful not to disturb any of the other items inside.

She was out in the very back, near the wooden fence, and she had turned when I closed the door to the shed.

"I have a job for you out here," she called.

I walked up the brick path to where she stood. Sheltered underneath the overhanging branches of the trees were some dark green bushes, about five of them. They were all about four or five feet tall. They bordered another brick walk that ran parallel to the fence, and it was plain that the bushes needed trimming, that was for sure. Some of the branches even rubbed against the wooden fence.

"See if you can trim those branches," she said, handing me the shears that she always seemed to carry with her. "And be careful," she warned. "I just had them sharpened. I don't want you to cut yourself."

"I'll be careful," I said.

"Start at the back of the bushes. And try to keep them looking the same, so that they're regular. They're pretty straggly looking, so they'll need a lot of trimming. I used to be able to keep them trimmed back to about my height. But either they've been growing fast, or else I'm shrinking. I"ll be working with my roses." And she turned to leave me to my work.

The bushes had soft, fairly long leaves, each leaf almost opposite another, like in pairs, but not quite. She was right; the shears were sharp, and the cuttings fell away easily. I was moving along the fence, trying to make the bushes uniform-looking on that side, and when I had finished the backs of the bushes, I began to trim the other sides.

I had never trimmed bushes before, so I was a little uneasy about whether she would think I was doing a good job, or not. But she had turned her complete attention to her roses, apparently trusting me to do the job right.

It was hot, but underneath the branches of the trees it felt comfortable.

Like I said earlier, I had never trimmed a bush in my entire life before, so I kept looking around, half expecting her to come and comment about the job, or at least to watch over me. But she remained where she was, cutting away at some other shrubs with a smaller pair of shears.

Time passed, but not so that I noticed. Some song birds were asserting their presence in the branches overhead, flitting in and out of the trees and shrubs, and the summer air was warm and soothing. Finally I trimmed away the last part of the last bush, and then stepped back to look at how I had done.

"They look good." The voice startled me, it was so close by. And I turned around to find her sitting on a bench no more than ten feet away. I hadn't even heard her approach, so I wouldn't have known how long she had been sitting there.

"You sure you've never done this kind of work before?" she asked. It wasn't a challenging question. It was friendlier than that.

"No'm, I mean, Miss Beatrice," I said. "We don't have bushes like these. I think the only bush we ever had was a lilac."

"Ah, lilacs. They're lovely to have," she commented. "They make spring more welcome. I love the smell of the flowers."

"Ours doesn't grow flowers anymore," I said.

"Not enough sun?" she queried.

"No'm," I replied. "My grandmother says that it's because of us boys playing baseball."

She looked up at me, her expression one of questioning.

"It grew right near where third base is, in our back yard," I explained. "Jerry and I used to run over it too much when we played baseball back there. I think we broke it down, a little."

She chuckled at that remark.

"Well, it looks as though you've been handling shears for all your life. I know that I could never have done those bushes as well."

I felt a glow within. No one had ever complimented me on yard work. Come to think about it, no one had ever complimented me on any kind of work.

"I think that they'll hold until next year," she said. "Usually I cut them back twice, spring and fall, but I'm afraid that I didn't get at them this year."

"They were easy to cut," I said, not thinking of anything else to say.

"You ever see bushes like those? " She was pointing to three bushes that ran along the path next to her bench.

"No,m," I answered.

"Then you don't know what they are," she said.

I shook my head. She seemed pleased to have stumped me again.

"They're called boxwoods," she informed me.

I waited for more, which I knew would be coming.

"They're pretty," I said.

"They're easy to care for," she said, "as long as you keep after them. The branches can be kept trimmed back, and the leaves are soft to touch. And they look green the whole year. You like them?"

"Yes'm," I answered, although I was sure that she would have recognized that my appreciation of them would not have been easily come by.

"My, but it's warm," she said.

"It's okay, underneath the trees," I said.

"Well, I'll tell you what. You pick up the cuttings, and put them in this container," pointing to a tall trash can nearby, "and I'll go make us some lemonade." And she rose from her bench.

Immediately I thought of some of the things that Kenny had told us.

"That's okay," I said, maybe too hastily. "I'm not thirsty."

"Nonsense!" she huffed. "Everyone's thirsty on days like these. And I've never known a boy who didn't like lemonade."

"Really!" I said. "I'm not thirsty."

She turned to stare at me, and I lowered my head.

"You just pick up those cuttings, like I asked you to," she said.

"Yes'm," I answered, cowed by her authority.

She left to go into the back of the house, and I watched her, briefly, then grabbed the can and began to pick up the cuttings. I had to get down on my hands and knees, but I found that I could sweep them up with my hands pretty easily, and I moved along from bush to bush. All the while I was on my knees, I was silently praying, too, praying that Kenny could be wrong, for once. Although I had to admit, to myself, that I could find no good reason why a God who was filled with a sense of justice would ever recognize any special plea that I might have. But it was worth a shot, I figured. You know the old adage about "Nothing ventured, nothing gained."

She must have been watching me through a window, because I no sooner had finished my job when I noticed that she was coming back out, through the door, carrying a tray that held a white pitcher and two glasses.

She sat down on the bench, and put the tray next to her. I stood and watched her as she poured lemonade into the two glasses, and then offered one of the glasses to me.

It was obvious that both of us were going to drink the same lemonade. So it must have been okay. She wouldn't drink poison herself.

"Thank you," I said, and I waited for her to take the first sip, and after she did, I gratefully took a sip of mine. She had put ice cubes in the pitcher, and the lemonade was cold, and delicious. And when she took another sip, and I was sure that she had indeed swallowed it, I drank the rest of my glass in one long gulp.

She must have noticed, because she said: "There. I thought so. You *were* thirsty."

"Yes'm. I mean, Miss Beatrice."

"Don't go through life being coy, son," she said then, and there was something warm and good about her use of *son*.

"No'm," I answered. "I mean, yes ma'am. I mean…"

"I know what you mean," she said.

She bent her head slightly and looked at me over the top of her glasses, holding her glass of lemonade in her lap.

"You don't know what *coy* means, do you?"

I was embarrassed to be caught. Again. I shook my head, and waited.

"Well, then, don't be afraid to admit that you don't know something," she said in a kind of scolding way. "You'll never learn anything if you go on pretending to know everything. You understand?"

"Yes, Miss Beatrice." I answered shyly, a little embarrassed.

"Anyway," she said, "to be coy means to be …well, like shy. Except I'd put the word along with the word *sneaky*. *Shy in a sneaky way*. Does that make any sense to you?"

"I'm not sure."

"Well, at least you admit it. Anyway, you don't have to be shy around me."

I had never been accused before of being shy. In fact, there were those in our neighborhood, neighbors and family, who would have given me the label of smart aleck. Of being the first one to open my mouth, and also of being one to open it too often. Rambunctious, yes. Impudent, too, at times. But, shy? That just didn't fit.

"There's only one way to go through life, son, and that is to be honest, in everything. If you have something to say, then say it, but be sure you know what you want to say before you say it."

"Yes'm. I mean, Miss Beatrice."

That's better. Too many people say things before they think. But if you really know what's on your mind, then just say it. It makes it a lot easier for everyone."

I nodded.

"Do you want another glass of lemonade?" she asked.

I was going to say no, but then I thought of what she had just said, about being honest, about being sure to say what you wanted to say.

"Yes, Miss Beatrice."

And she actually smiled, a broad smile that took up all of her face, including her eyes.

"That's better," she said.

She poured lemonade into my glass, and I drank it down fast. When I finished, I told her "Thank you. It's delicious," and handed the glass back to her.

"Well," she said, "I think you've done a good job today." She looked around the yard, taking in the shrubs that I had trimmed.

"If you're available next Saturday, I'll have some more work for you."

I watched her.

"Well?" she asked.

"Oh, sure," I said. "I'm available."

"I don't like to take a boy away from his play too much. I know how important play must mean to a boy. There's only so much time in our lives, and I guess being a boy should be a generous part of it."

She paused then, probably waiting for me to reply to what she had said.

"I get enough play time," I finally said.

"At your age there's never too much time. For anything."

I thought she was talking about play time. But many years later, I thought back to what she had said, and I realized that what she was referring to was life itself, how short it really is. And when I became a teacher of American Literature, it really struck home when I talked with my students about what Ben Franklin said, regarding time, for he proclaimed that the wasting of time was the greatest prodigality.

But at that moment, with Mrs. Schweikert in front of me, I merely shrugged.

She reached into the pocket of her apron, like she had done the previous Saturday, and she handed me the coins that she found there. She didn't even bother to count them.

I looked, and there were four dimes and two nickels. Fifty cents! Fifty cents! I couldn't believe it. Fifty cents! A fortune lay there, in my hand.

"That's too much, Miss Beatrice," I gasped. "There's fifty cents there." I was still looking at the coins in my open hand.

"I know what's there," she said. "I'm not exactly senile."

"Oh, no ma'am. I didn't mean that."

"I know what you mean," she replied, her voice somewhat softened.

"But that's too much," I protested.

"You've been here for almost two hours," she said, "and unless arithmetic has changed since I was in school, two times twenty-five is fifty, isn't it?"

"Yes, Miss Beatrice. It's just that…"

"It's just what?" she interrupted.

"Well…" I managed to stammer.

"It's not too much," she said. "And remember what I said about saying what's on your mind."

She looked at me, and her look was…well, pleasant.

"We'll leave things just as they are," she said then. "You've done a good job, and a good job deserves its own reward. You understand, son?"

"Yes, Miss Beatrice."

And with that, she got up from the bench and began to walk away, carrying the pitcher and glasses, talking over her shoulder again.

"Next Saturday. Nine o"clock. And don't be late."

"No'm," I answered, and I began to run toward the front of the house. "And I'll close the gate," I yelled back, and I swear I could hear her laughing in response.

My feet fairly flew on my way home. Fifty cents! Fifty cents! That's all I could think about. Like the previous Saturday, I kept my hand balled up in my pocket, afraid that running fast might cause me to jiggle so as to lose the coins.

CHAPTER NINETEEN

Uncle Al Brings a Problem

T HE FOLLOWING DAY, Sunday, I was at St. John's Church, which our family attended every Sunday. It didn't take long before I found myself surrounded by friends that were not part of my immediate neighborhood, since many of the parishioners came from all over the area.

Most of the people at St. John's were of German descent, and many lived in outlying areas, like the Campau area. Those either had escaped the confines of Germantown, or had come to Port Huron later. Sundays were the only days that I got to see many of those people.

The Campau area included some of the Carpo family, as well as some Dortmans and Mays, and Zimmers, and Langolfs, and Alberts, and others.

St. John's had been built by German settlers back in the 1870s. Originally it had been called St. John's German Lutheran Church, and the attitude of German exclusiveness is somewhat alive today.

There were two services each Sunday, in those days: an early service in which the German language was spoken, followed by a service in English at 11:00. Any man who assumed the role of pastor had to be master of both languages, and our Rev. Soell was indeed a master. And to make his job even tougher, twice a month he traveled about forty miles north to preach to a small knot of Germans in the lakeside community of Port Sanilac. Rain, hail, snow, sleet, hot sun-it didn't make a difference. He was like the proverbial mailman; he would show up like the faithful servant that he was.

Jerry and I had some good friends at St. John's, some of whom we saw only on Sundays, since they hailed from other parts of town. Roger

Fenner and the Beach boys(Gene and Carl)were there, as were Don May and Karl Schroeder and Ed Krenke. And somehow they had all heard how it was that I had become *rich*, so to speak, and wanted to know everything about my good luck. Of course I could hear the jealousy in their voices. Well, maybe jealousy is too harsh a word; it was more like self-pity for not having the same opportunity. And I couldn't blame them.

I tried to appear modest about my good fortune, but I'm afraid that I probably did not come across that way. When I was finally seated with my family, in our accustomed pew, I was able to escape the relentless question from my friends.

Immediately after church, we headed home. The mile and a half never felt like a long journey when the weather was good. Jerry and I played tag along the way, but Mother put a stop to that.

"You boys stop that," she said. "It's Sunday. And don't you dare get those shoes dirty.

And don't go off playing, when we get home," she added. "We've got company coming today, so we want you around."

I didn't know of any company that required our presence, so Jerry and I looked at each other, exchanging shrugs.

"Who's coming, Mother?" Marilyn asked. Marilyn could ask that question and get away with it, for the question would be innocent enough, coming from her.

"Your Uncle Al and Aunt Mae," Father replied.

"Oh, boy," I exclaimed, for we all loved Uncle Al. And Aunt Mae was a good soul, too. But a second thought instantly cropped up, one that I did not want to consider.

Dad had a wonderful family, all of them good people. But we children had our favorites. Aunt Helen and Aunt Eileen and Aunt Harriett were special to us; their kindness was genuine, and they tolerated children better than did most adults.

But Uncle Al was, by far, our very favorite.

He was a journalist in Flint, a city about seventy miles west of Port Huron. He wrote a regular column for Flint's newspaper. His articles were biting, sometimes filled with earned sarcasm. And he wasn't afraid of taking on some of the political figures, for which he earned their everlasting enmity. Dad told us that Uncle Al actually enjoyed the hostility that cropped up now and then.

Dad was proud of his brother. They had been really close while growing up. In fact, they looked more like twins than did Jerry and I.

Dad and Uncle Al enjoyed their little debates, which usually centered on politics.

I recall many times, sitting in the kitchen, when Dad would pour out little glasses of Peppermint Schnaptz, and Dad and Uncle Al would hold forth on the "New Deals" of President Roosevelt. What I could never figure out-none of us could-was what side either of them was on. They would throw good natured barbs at each other, and then try to deflect the ones that came their way.

I enjoyed those little *talks*, for we all knew that they were never intended to be hurtful or mean. The talks were just good natured banterings that helped to erase the realities of the times, those realities including awareness of the Nazi hordes strutting their stuff in the streets of Paris while their little mustached leader soaked in all the adulation of a misdirected population. And everyone in America was aware of the horrendous bombings that were taking place almost continuously round the clock in England, and of the heroism of the English people. So there was much that could be talked about.

Uncle Al was about two or three inches taller than Dad, Dad only being about five feet, six inches in height. But when Uncle Al was a boy, he had suffered a broken back because of a fall from a railroad car that he had been playing on. Mistreated, the injury led to a hunched back, which caused him to always walk with his head stooped down.

Aunt Mae was almost six feet tall and thus would have been taller than Uncle Al even if he had not suffered from the stoop. She could give and take it, too, in a humorous fashion, and sometimes served as a foil for Uncle Al's jabs.

So we were delighted to hear that they were coming. At least until the next question, which Jerry happened to have the fortitude to ask, unfortunately for him at the time.

"Are they bringing Nancy?" Jerry asked.

Mother stopped, and looked around at Jerry and me, and she was so defiant looking that we did not dare ask anything else. It was her way of saying that, yes, Nancy was coming.

Even Marilyn, who was walking with Sandra, gave us a quick look.

There is no other way to put it. We did not look forward to Nancy coming. We never looked forward to her coming.

Nancy was born with Down's syndrome. She was severely retarded, and her sanitary and social habits were woefully poor.

In those days, many children born with the affliction were often kept inside their homes, virtually imprisoned by parents who did not quite know how to handle such a situation. Others of the children were sent to special state homes to be cared for, often left there to be forgotten by family, as though they had never existed.

Many years later, in 1962, I was to visit one of the state homes, in Mount Pleasant, Michigan, when I was studying to become a teacher; the visit was made mandatory by one of my professors. And it was there that I learned that attitudes had progressed far beyond those that existed when Nancy was born. The *residents* of the dormitory of those with Down's syndrome were able to perform many duties: caring for their own garden, working in the central kitchen, caring for their own sanitary habits, and even playing basketball, some of them very proficiently.

But this was not 1962. It was 1940. And we felt badly for Uncle Al and Aunt Mae because of the burden that they carried. And we felt...yes, a sense of embarrassment for having a cousin who was so-afflicted.

When we got home we were told by Mother not to go anywhere, but to wait for our visitors, who were scheduled to arrive shortly.

Jerry and I were sitting on the front porch steps when Mother gave us the order.

"And don't get your shoes dirty," she said, her speaking coming through the front screen door. "Or your good clothes, either," she added.

We waited for a few minutes, to make sure she had left us alone. We both had things that we wanted to say, but we were afraid to be heard by either of our parents.

"Maybe she'll let us go over to Eighteenth Street and play some baseball," Jerry offered, although there wasn't much hope in his voice.

"Sure, and maybe she'll let us go to Pollywog and dig around in the pond, with our good clothes on," I replied sarcastically.

So we sat there, disconsolate, the warmth of the summer air lying heavily on us. Boy, what a bummer!

"I'm going to ask Dad," I said, getting up from the steps.

"Ask him what?" Jerry said.

"If we can go play some baseball," I answered.

"Why? You know what he's going to say."

Undeterred, I went into the house. There were noises from the kitchen, and when I went in there, I found Dad at the table, cutting up vegetables. Mother was at the sink, working away at something. I didn't know where Marilyn and Sandra and David were. Marilyn might have been visiting Grandma in Grandma's room on the second floor, which she did often.

"Dad?" I began, standing just inside and holding open the swinging door.

He looked up, holding a long paring knife.

"You want something?" he asked.

"Is it all right if Jerry and I go over to Eighteenth Street and play some ball? We'll only go for an hour. And we won't get our clothes dirty."

"No. It isn't all right," Mother intervened in a scolding voice, turning to face me squarely. "You've got your Sunday clothes on, and you're going to keep them on until after company has left."

"That not fair," I said, and the moment I said it, I knew that I had gone too far.

"Don't you tell me what's fair," Mother said harshly. "You hear me? I'll determine what's fair and what's not fair."

"Yes ma'am," I answered, and I turned to go.

"Larry?" Dad said so softly that I almost didn't hear him.

I turned and looked at him, and he laid the knife down on the table.

"Sit down, son," he said, and I took a chair across from him. I knew that I was about to get a lecture. And I knew very well what the lecture was going to be about. Dad wasn't stupid.

"It's Nancy, isn't it?" he asked, getting right to the point.

I lowered my head so that he couldn't see the look on my face.

"You like Uncle Al?" he asked.

"Yeah," I answered, looking up at him. "Who doesn't? Everybody likes Uncle Al," I added.

"Well, he likes you boys, too." He paused, letting that sink in. "And he can't go many places with…"

He didn't finish the sentence, but I knew what he meant. All of us knew that Uncle Al and Aunt Mae didn't feel comfortable visiting with some of their relatives and friends, because of Nancy. But Uncle Al knew that he could be somewhat at ease in our household, since he knew how we children were going to respond, made to respond. And the fact that Uncle Al and Dad were such close brothers, well, that made all the more reason why we were often chosen to be visited.

"Are you embarrassed about Nancy?" Dad asked. I noticed that Mother had turned back to her work at the sink, allowing Dad to work his magic once more with one of his children.

I didn't answer. There was no need to.

"Let me ask you something, son." And when I looked up at him, he didn't take his eyes off mine. "If Nancy understood the way she is, do you think she'd choose to stay that way?"

I thought about what he said, and shook my head.

"I don't either. We don't understand why some children are born that way," he went on. "I don't think it was God's doing, either. It just happened. Just like some children are born blind, or crippled, or deaf."

I squirmed in my chair. I was uncomfortable.

"You're fortunate," he went on. "You were born…well, normal. You look normal, you're built normal, you talk normal. We're fortunate, in our family, that all of us live normal lives. And we should be thankful. And we should feel sympathetic for those who aren't so fortunate."

"Yeah, but whenever we take her anywhere with us, some of the other kids tease her."

"So that makes you feel ashamed?"

Again my silence was my answer.

"You just think about it. Okay?" he asked.

I nodded.

"Think about how Uncle Al and Aunt Mae must feel."

I kept to my silence. Then I got up and went back through the swinging door. It closed itself on the conversation.

When I went back outside, Jerry was still on the steps. Some of the neighborhood kids were busy at play, although the play wasn't as physical or as energetic as it would have been on a weekday. The Sabbath was being given a little bit of reverence, even by those who had been granted a little bit of freedom.

"What'd Dad say?" Jerry asked.

"We have to stay around," I answered. Jerry turned and faced the street, his elbows on his knees and his hands propping up his head.

"But I'll tell you something, Jerry," I said. "If we have to take Nancy anywhere, the other kids had better not say anything to her. If they do, they'd better be able to run fast because they'll get it from me if they don't. And I don't care how big they are, either."

So there we sat, aware of other kids enjoying the day while we had to sit and wait for company to come, and also aware of someone coming to visit us, someone whom we were not looking forward to.

Nancy! Just the thought of her coming and of us having to be her escorts, so to speak, was enough to throw a damper on the day.

Before too long we could see a sharp looking two-door sedan coming south down Sixteenth Street. It made the stop at the corner. I had never seen the car before in our neighborhood-by that time in our lives, we would have been able to recognize almost anyone's car-so we were sure that it must be a stranger's.

It was shiny and black, and looked fairly new. We just knew that it must be Uncle Al's.

"They're here," Jerry yelled, loud enough for everyone in our house to hear, and also loud enough to alert everyone else in the neighborhood. Indeed, those who were outside looked up to see what the yelling was all about, and in a few seconds a few faces came to the front doors, as well. Visitors were always a matter of curiosity, and were welcome if only for the fact that they brought something novel into otherwise humdrum lives.

Sure enough, the car pulled up in front of our house, and Jerry and I got off the steps just as Mother and Dad came out the front door.

Uncle Al had been driving, and he got out of his door, and made his way around the front of the car, his stoop more noticeable than what I remembered, but his grin as wide as expected.

He and Dad met on the small boulevard, and there were the expected greetings and the shaking of hands.

"Well, you ol' son-of-a-gun," Dad said. "It's about time you got here. What'd you do? Walk this old car here?" he joked.

With his head lifting up as much as his stoop allowed, Uncle Al replied: "Well, it looks as though that if I did that it'd still be faster than what you could walk," pointing good naturedly at Dad's little paunch of a stomach.

Aunt Mae then got out, pulling her tall frame erect, and Mother and she hugged.

Jerry and I were waiting in the background, peering around the adults, enjoying their familiarity with each other, but waiting for the inevitable. For there, in the darkness of the back seat, behind the front seat that Aunt Mae had left tilted forward, we could vaguely see a figure, sitting, waiting.

Uncle Al looked up at us kids, for by then Marilyn and Sandra had come out of the house, Marilyn carrying David in her arms. They were standing alongside Jerry and me.

Uncle Al winked at us boys, and then tousled our heads.

"You boys are growing like weeds," he said to us. "I'd say you're growing like daffodils, but that's kind of sissy sounding, isn't it?" And he gave us each a playful punch in the arms.

I smiled back. He was such an enjoyable character, and we loved him as much as it was possible to love an uncle.

But everyone there knew that we had reached the *moment*, the *moment* that must come. For there, in the rear seat, sat Nancy, and her emergence would be somewhat difficult for everyone. And at that instant I thought of Aunt Mae and Uncle Al, of their quandary, and my heart went out to them, especially to Uncle Al. Maybe it was because whenever he was around, he treated Jerry and me almost as if we were equals, as beings who could and would share in his humor and good-natured banter.

Aunt Mae turned then, and she reached into the back seat and offered help to the girl who sat within, and all of us waited, silently, expectantly, but not really knowing what it would be like once Nancy emerged from the car.

It had been more than a year since we had last seen her. She was at least eight or ten years older than Marilyn, and I recalled a tall and fairly heavy girl, a girl whose flat facial features and narrow eyes and somewhat flabby lips immediately made her condition known. And I also remembered her often having spittle coming from her mouth, and I remembered her often wiping her face with her arm, and of Aunt Mae immediately tugging at her arm and wiping Nancy's nose with a handkerchief.

The adults were crowded around the door, and Aunt Mae was saying something to Nancy as the girl came struggling out of the car, and we children were peeking around the adults, trying to get a glimpse of her; and in the interludes of Aunt Mae's urgings to Nancy there was a sort of discomforting silence on the others' part. And I noticed Uncle Al actually looking away from the scene, as though he were deliberately divorcing himself from all that was happening.

Some of the neighbors, I noticed, had happened onto their porches, and were looking discriminately at the proceedings. They tried not to be too obvious about it, but they were looking.

Then Uncle Al and Dad pretended to be engaged in some meaningful chatter, but I sensed that there wasn't anything important in what they were saying. And I also sensed that Uncle Al understood that everyone was somewhat discomforted by it all. It was like a play being played out by the various actors, their roles and dialogue determined long beforehand.

Then I heard a grunting sound, and I turned to where Aunt May and Nancy were. Aunt May was striving to get the girl out from the back seat, and Nancy must have been resisting, for there were mumbled words going back and forth, the sensible words of Aunt Mae, and the grunting sounds of Nancy.

Aunt Mae wasn't exactly pleading; nor did she sound angry. She was just trying to make it easier for Nancy to come out.

Then she was out, and standing, pressing herself up against Aunt Mae's bosom, trying to bury her face so as to not have to look at us. And

Aunt Mae turned her toward us, holding Nancy close to her side, as though she were presenting Nancy to us and was waiting for our reaction. And I realized that the signal moment had arrived.

Nancy was a much bigger girl than I had remembered. A year's absence had not allowed me to expect what I was looking at. Bigger, for sure! She was not only taller than I recalled, but she was also much heavier. In fact, she was probably bigger around the waist than were any of the boys in the neighborhood.

She was trying to hide her face in her mother's shoulder, but she glanced shyly at us from time to time, only to hide her face again. I couldn't tell if Nancy even barely realized what was going on. She did have some kind of a smile, but the expected saliva ran down from her mouth, which Aunt Mae nonchalantly wiped off with a slight swipe of a handkerchief.

Then Mother moved forward, and I could hear her welcome Nancy, and then Mother hugged her, and Dad did the same thing, and Aunt Mae did her best to help Nancy to respond, although by now it was obvious that Nancy could not have understood much about what was going on. Yet she must have had *some* understanding of the situation, as she resisted, somewhat, the attempts by Mother and Dad to be friendly, pulling her body up close to that of Aunt Mae, and constantly turning her face away from everyone.

Nancy's heavy arms surrounded the waist of Aunt Mae. And all the while Mother was telling us kids to greet Nancy. We were hanging back, not sure just what we were expected to do, or to say.

It was an awkward moment, almost like two sides having been chosen, with the space between us seeming huge. For a few seconds, no one moved and no one said anything. Then all of a sudden, Marilyn walked up to Nancy and reached out a hand.

"Come on, Nancy," Marilyn said, and just as though they had always been friends, Marilyn took Nancy's hand, and the two of them went up the steps and disappeared into the house.

Aunt Mae smiled a sense of relief. Uncle Al gave us all that lifted-head grin of his, and Mom and Dad looked on with both appreciation and amazement.

It was easier after that. It wasn't easy, but it was easier.

When lunch was served, Jerry and I sat with Sandra and David, out in the kitchen. The rest of them ate in the dining room, from where we could occasionally hear soft laughter. Jerry and I didn't know what was expected of us after lunch, but we both knew that whatever it was, Nancy would be part of it.

After eating, Jerry and I took our plates to the sink and washed them. There was no sense in hurrying, as we both knew that we would have the chore of washing all of the dishes, so we had to wait for the adults to finish.

Finally, the door between the two rooms swung open, and Dad came into the kitchen.

"I want you boys to go with Marilyn and Sandy and Nancy," he said. "I gave Marilyn a quarter, so you can each get an ice-cream cone at the dairy."

"Nancy's going?" Jerry asked.

I had already had my little conversation with Dad, so I knew that Jerry was going to get his also.

"Is there any reason why she shouldn't go?" Dad asked Jerry in a soft but challenging voice, and the look on Dad's face did not invite argument.

"No," Jerry said, "it's just that…"

"Just what?" Dad asked, his look becoming more serious.

"Nuhhh…nothing," Jerry stammered.

Sandra looked totally innocent. She knew that there was something *different* about Nancy, but her awareness was not something that would have given Sandy any concern about what had been asked of us. For Sandy, it was a bit of excitement, a wonderful opportunity to share in a treat that was rarely enjoyed: an ice-cream cone at the dairy.

"So, it's settled then," Dad said. "As soon as Marilyn is ready, you will go with her. Understood?"

"Yes, sir," we both replied.

When Dad left the kitchen, Jerry and I looked at each other in a way that demonstrated our unhappiness. We had already figured out that Nancy would be in our presence the rest of the day, but we had not figured on having to go out into the neighborhood with her in our company. To be seen publicly?

I have to admit that I personally dreaded it. But there was no getting around it.

About fifteen minutes later, our duties with the dishes being finished, we were all walking down Minnie Street. The dairy was eight blocks away, and Jerry and I lagged behind Marilyn and Sandy and Nancy, Marilyn again holding Nancy's hand. Some of the kids we knew looked at us curiously as we went by their houses, but then they turned quickly away when they realized that we noticed their looking.

And word must have spread, moving at lightning speed ahead of us, because it seemed, as we moved along, that there were more people outside than what would have been expected on a Sunday afternoon. Usually most people, especially the adults, spent much of their Sundays inside, either reading the Port Huron newspaper or one of the Detroit papers. Few were those people who did yard work on the Sabbath. Sundays were noticeable for lazing away.

But this Sunday was different. A fairly large number of people were looking their yards over, or at least they tried to give us that impression. And some of them nodded as we walked by; some of them even said hello. And all of them, in some slight way, gave furtive glances at us as we passed by. So, word had passed, indeed, just as it always had in Germantown. We must have had one of the fastest communications systems in the world.

Well, I figured, at least few of the younger ones that we saw were those of my close friends, so I did my best to shrug it all off. In fact, I could understand the curiosity of the young ones, but I was disturbed by the sideways looks of the adults.

But when we turned up Eleventh Street and began walking by Polk School, I was surprised to find a few of our friends sitting on the front steps. I could never remember them sitting there before, since the back of the school, which was adjacent to the playground, had always served as a meeting place.

But sure enough, there were quite a few boys there, and wouldn't you know it but that one of them just had to be Joe. Of all the boys that I knew, Joe would be the most likely one to find some kind of way to embarrass me.

"Hey, you guys," I called out as casually as I could. I figured that if I acknowledged them first, then maybe they might just let us pass by without any problems.

"Hi, Larry. Hi, Jerry," some of them called back.

Then came the voice I expected, but did not want, to hear.

"What's that you got with you?" Joe shouted in derision.

There were no accompanying chuckles from the others. I immediately sensed that Joe was all alone in his scorn.

I could see Marilyn pause and turn to look, but then she went on, still holding Nancy's hand. Sandra walked on the other side of Nancy.

I stopped. Jerry pulled at my arm, and said: "Come on, Larry. Forget it."

"Nah, you go on ahead," I said.

Jerry began to walk away, slowly, looking back at me. But then he stopped, a few steps further along. I walked up toward the guys, but my eyes were on Joe.

"What'd you say?" I asked Joe. And no one could have mistaken the tone of my voice; it was filled with rage.

He drew himself up as tall as he could, but I could tell that he was beginning to wish that he hadn't said anything at all. Then, with as much bravado as he could muster, he said: "You heard me. I asked what that was you had with you. Is it some kind of freak?"

He had a stupid looking grin on his face, and he looked around at the others, for support, I suppose, but they weren't grinning with him. In fact, they had moved somewhat away from Joe. He was left all alone with his problem, and I realized that he recognized his dilemma.

I looked over my shoulder at my sisters and Nancy, who now were walking more slowly, looking back now and then. Jerry was standing about fifteen feet away. I knew that if it had been needed, he would have been quick to come to my aid.

I moved closer to Joe, so close that there couldn't have been an inch of space that separated us, and I said, in a small voice that was little more than a whisper: "That girl is my cousin." The tone of my voice was stiff. "And if I were you, Joe, I'd keep my mouth shut. Because if you don't, I'm going to lick you so hard that your mother won't even want to look at you."

And I glared at him, never taking my eyes off of him, my face directly in front of his face.

I don't think that I had ever been so mad in my entire life, and Joe must have realized it, because he actually backed away a little.

"Okay. Okay," he said, a little mollified. "I didn't mean anything."

I continued to look at him, and the hardness in my eyes gradually began to soften, and I nodded at him, once, then nodded at the others, and turned and walked away, walking deliberately so as to make sure Joe realized the gravity of the situation. For I wanted to make sure that Joe realized that I would be all too ready to turn back, if necessary.

By the time I reached them, I was breathing a little easier.

Union Farmers Dairy had two sections: the east side of it had a few tables with chairs, and a large curving bar with stools; it was where people bought ice-cream sundaes, sodas and malts; the west side of the building was where people bought ice-cream by pints or quarts or half-gallons, or got cones.

Of course Nancy was stared at, and I was prepared for those stares, but after facing down Joe, I was not going to let people get on my nerves. Nancy was our cousin, by golly, and she deserved better than what she was getting, even though she would not have realized why people were looking. In fact, she would not even have realized that they *were* looking.

I moved up alongside Nancy. Her thick lips quivered a little, as they usually did, but she stared straight ahead, seeming to look at nothing in particular.

Marilyn ordered a single vanilla cone for Nancy and one for herself, and one for Sandy. Marilyn was careful to put a couple of paper napkins around the cones, and she was very careful in getting Nancy to put her hand around her cone like she should. Then the rest of us ordered our cones, Jerry and I both getting double-dip chocolate cones. I tried not to look at the people who were there, for whenever I did look, I saw the same quick, averted glances I had seen from our neighbors along the way.

Once back out on the street, we licked at our cones, and I could see that Nancy was having a difficult time with hers. There is no other way to put it but to tell you like it was. Nancy was actually slobbering away at her cone, but she had a silly smile on her face, and I wondered just then how few times in her life that she actually did smile, or had reason to. And for the first time since I had known her, I smiled with her, not at her.

By the time we got home, Aunt Mae and Uncle Al were ready to leave. In those days it would have been about a two-hour drive, since the highway went through some small country towns along the way, each one with one or two traffic lights.

Aunt Mae took Nancy into the house, to wash away the ice-cream from her face. Uncle Al looked us kids over, winked at us boys, and did something unusual. He walked over to Marilyn, looked her in the eyes, and then hugged her. He didn't say anything. The look on his face was enough. It made a statement, one of thanks. For he knew that Marilyn had done a wonderful and gracious thing when she had taken Nancy hand-in-hand for the afternoon's journey. It had been an act that most likely had not been performed many times before, by anyone.

As they were pulling away in their car, Uncle Al waved his arm out the window. Aunt Mae sat in the front passenger seat, eyes straight ahead. And we expected to see Nancy sitting rigid, just as she had when she had arrived. Instead, the last we saw of her, she was turned in the back seat, and was waving feebly. And all I could do was look at Marilyn, in a new light. In a small way, she had been a miracle worker.

Chapter Twenty

Schooldaze

P OLK SCHOOL OPENED its doors to us kids the last days of August. It was still hot, hotter, in fact, than it had been the previous three weeks. I think that it purposely arrives that way in order to punish children and teachers for taking so much time off during the summer.

I said something about the heat one evening, during dinner. Dad told us that we should be thankful that it wasn't as hot as it had been four years earlier. He said that there was a hot spell during the summer of 1936, when the temperature got past one hundred degrees, and that it got even hotter out on the prairies of Kansas and the Dakotas, where it actually got over one hundred and twenty degrees.

I knew there were times when Dad would kid with us about something, but he didn't sound like he was kidding this time. He told us about how a lot of people in our area went up to the beaches along Lake Huron and slept out on the sand, hoping to catch just the slightest of breezes from off the water, or to take cooling dips in the lake. There was no such relief for the poorer folk, for those who for one reason or another could not get up to the beaches. As for the poor people out Kansas way…they had no wonderful Lake Huron to take refuge in or alongside. How they must have suffered.

Years later I came across an account of that heat wave, and when it was pointed out that literally hundreds of people had died from that summer's devastating heat. From then on, I tried to be a little more positive when summer threw some heat my way. Everything is relative, especially in regards to suffering.

Meanwhile, over on the far side of the Atlantic Ocean, a terrible war was being played out in the skies over England. The newspapers were filled with tales of the awful struggle, and it was a constant source of discussion among Mother and Dad, just as it was for all the adults. For us boys, it did not mean much. Mostly it was business as usual. Life moved on, but only as we urged it to do so.

I continued to work for Mrs. Schweikert each Saturday, cutting her lawn weekly or every other week, and climbing the ladder to get at difficult branches of her trees and shrubs, and she continued to count out those precious coins into my hands. Although I still deposited many of the coins into my metal bank, by order of Mother, I felt much like what a millionaire must feel: on top of the world.

Jerry and I had moved into fifth grade. Miss Penzenhagen was our teacher, a warm-hearted woman whom everyone adored, both the boys and the girls. She was fair and friendly, but she still maintained discipline, without raising her voice.

She was somewhat tall, and pleasant looking. Her hair was blond, and it fell softly down to her shoulders. Mostly I remember her eyes, for they were the clearest blue, a summer-day sky blue.

I was going to miss Miss Sullivan, our fourth-grade teacher, but time moves on, as the saying goes, and we did, too.

Miss Penzenhagen assigned us our seats, and I quickly recognized that there was a method to her organization, as she had me far removed from my brother as well as from most of my best friends, who were scattered around the room so that few of the boys in our special group had direct access to the others.

My desk bore the expected scars from previous years, where no doubt boys before me had surreptitiously carved their names. Rare was the boy who did not carry a pocketknife in those days. Besides carving names into the desks, a pocketknife was handy during recess, for oftentimes many of us boys played a game of flipping the knife into the air and attempting to make it come down blade-first into a target of a small wooden-chip. In those innocent days there was no such talk about zero tolerance and weapons, unlike these days.

Rubbing my fingers under the top of my desk, I discovered the expected dried up pieces of gum, placed there some time before by those who had defied the rule about chewing gum in class and who had deposited it in a hurry when worried about getting caught. I doubt there was a desk without a few of those gummy deposits. It would be difficult-nay, impossible-to determine where there were more of these gummy deposits, either the seats in the theater or the seats at school.

Ironically, eventually I was to discover another place of choice for depositing wads of gum: under the seats of the pews at church. Believe it or not, there are few of those seats without a number of deposits, even to this day. Just recently I told our custodian, Dave Heino, about what I had discovered. At first he was skeptical, but he found me a few minutes later-I was down there with a few other men who share coffee and doughnuts and work details every Tuesday morning-and he confessed that I was right. He had gone into the church and investigated the matter, and found numerous pews with the gummy attachments. One wonders whether anything is sacred.

Anyway, back to the matter of school.

Of course I wanted to get off to a good start with my new teacher, but luck didn't go my way. Before twenty minutes had passed, I was caught passing a note to Jack, who was seated two rows over.

"Larry?" Miss Penzenhagen's voice was moderate, but clear. She had risen from her desk in the front of the room, and was looking right at me.

"Yes, ma'am?" I answered as politely and kindly as I possibly could. I had gotten to my feet, as was expected, my arms at my side, at attention. When called upon by a teacher, in those days, whether it was to respond to a question or to receive a reprimand, a child rose and stood dutifully by the side of his desk. Not to do so might result in a visit to the principal's office.

I am sure that I must have tried my best at looking both innocent and responsive, but I knew that my reputation had preceded me. For anyone to think that teachers do not share information about the pupils is absurd. She would have known all there was to know about most of the students that she had inherited. That was expected of teachers. Consequently my pretended innocence would not have amounted to anything.

"Perhaps you'd like to share your correspondence with all of us," she said, moving slowly down the aisle toward Jack, who had not had the opportunity yet to read my letter and who was in the process of trying to stick the paper under his butt but who was doing too hasty and clumsy a job about it.

She stuck her hand out toward Jack, waited patiently for him to pull the paper out of its resting place, and then unfolded it while she stood there.

I wanted to creep under my desk. For there was a very pretty girl who sat next to me. I adored her. And what's more, everyone knew it.

Her name was Jill. She was a fairly short girl, and a little husky, but that huskiness translated itself into athleticism, which she displayed on the playground whenever we played kickball. She could kick the ball almost as well as most of us boys could, and better than some, and there was no doubt in my mind that she would have beaten more than half of the boys in a race.

She was a smart girl, and was pretty as well as athletic. She had hair the color of summer wheat, and she kept it cropped short, which allowed her facial features to take prominence.

Just about every one of us boys had a crush on Jill, although most of us would not have admitted it openly.

A low wave of laughter swept across the room as Miss Penzenhagen looked at the note that I had written, and I am sure that my face must have reddened, because I felt heat that had nothing to do with the weather. Over the years Miss Penzenhagen had achieved a reputation for reading aloud the notes that she had intercepted. And since all of us were well aware of that custom, we assumed that my letter would also be read. Of course the embarrassment of the public readings was meant to deter us from writing the notes. Still, many were the students who attempted to defy the rule.

In that note I had written some sentences about my admiration for Jill which I would have felt comfortable sharing with Jack but probably with no one else, not even with my brother. Jack had already expressed his similar feelings for the girl.

I had been *in love* once before, the previous year, which I wrote about in my first book, and that love had died as a result of a bizarre mixup in the distribution of Valentine Day cards. No! It had not died. It had been killed! No! It had been smashed. It had been annihilated.

And here, once again, a potential love affair was about to be shattered. Not only that, but I realized that Jill might possibly be somewhat embarrassed by what I had written and might show resentment as a result, and even in those days I knew that a girl's wrath was something far worse than that of a boy's. And I would have been able to understand her resentment, too.

Miss Penzenhagen stood there for quite some time, much longer than was necessary to read the two or three foolishly intimate remarks I had written, and my mind was racing over all the possibilities of what was about to happen. The silence in the room was horrible, for I knew that everyone was being quiet out of a sense of impending trouble for me. There is nothing more satisfyingly to a kid than the feeling that someone else is about to suffer some embarrassment, that someone else *is going to get it.*

And at that moment, I could not have sat lower in my seat. If I could have, I would have disappeared entirely. And I realized that half of the eyes in the room were on me, and half were on Miss Penzenhagen, waiting for the contents of the secret letter to be divulged.

Then Miss Penzenhagen looked at me, smiled, and said simply: "Well, I agree with you, Larry. It certainly is hot today. But I really don't think it was necessary for you to tell Jack about it. He probably already realizes it."

And having said that, she folded the letter, stuck it in a pocket of her skirt, walked back to her desk, and charged us with a reading assignment.

As all of us began reaching into the space of our desks to take out the required textbook, there were two reactions, of course: disappointment on the part of all the others in the classroom that something horrible hadn't happened to me, something embarrassing enough to give them ammunition to launch at me for many days; and a great sense of relief on my part.

I could only smile at Miss Penzenhagen when she announced the lesson for the morning and looked over at me. She smiled softly at me, a knowing smile. And for the rest of my career in that school, and for many years afterwards, as well, I could only think of Miss. Penzenhagen with the fondest of feelings.

"So, what happened?" one of the boys asked first thing during recess.

I had hoped that the incident would be forgotten, and that I wouldn't be called on to provide any answers. Oh, not that I couldn't make up any answers. I had always been pretty good at lying. Lying is such a convenient way to avoid the truth. I've always considered it to be a great form of art.

"What do you mean, what happened?" I acted as innocently as I could.

There were a bunch of guys crowded around. They all wanted to know what had happened. They weren't any different than adults when it came to wanting to know all the juicy gossip.

"You know darn well what he means," Joe put in.

"Yeah," another boy said, "what'd you write in that note, anyway?"

"Nothing," I said.

"Then how come it took so long for her to read it?" Joe asked.

"Yeah," several others said at about the same time, the sound like an annoying echo.

"Ask Jack what it said," I replied, hoping that Jack would rescue me.

"How should I know?" Jack said. "I didn't even get to look at it. She was at my desk before I could even open it."

Everyone was looking at me.

"I bet it was about some girl," Joe said, obviously hoping to embarrass me.

"Probably about Jill," someone said.

"He's probably got a crush on Jill," Joe said.

"So do you," my brother put in.

"Not like Larry," someone said.

I looked at the one who said that, and wanted to argue immediately, but I was worried that whatever I said in return would only open the debate even further. So I decided to keep my mouth shut. I wasn't always good at doing that.

"Nah," Jack put in. "Anyway, if it had been about a girl, then Miss Penzenhagen would have read the letter so that everyone could hear, just to teach Larry a lesson."

They all agreed about that. But they hadn't thought it out very soundly, or they would have realized that Miss Penzenhangen would never embarrass a girl just because some silly boy had written something about the girl. She was much too honorable a person to do that. It was fortunate for me that in their minds it was not expected that a teacher would be so reasonable.

A whistle blew. Miss Penzenhagen stood on the back steps, underneath the archway of the back door, and we all went over to stand in line before returning to the classroom. Miss Penzenhagen led the way, after giving us a brief, serious look that was warning to us not to make any noise as we made our way into the hallway and then up the stairs. And I wasn't sure, but I thought I could detect Jill giving me a quick glance only to immediately look away, just as she was taking her place in line next to me.

Did Jill suspect anything? And had she been talking with the other girls out on the playground, during recess? And if so, who had initiated the talk? Jill? The other girls? And what were they saying? Could the talk have centered on me? On my note? On my character? On my lack of character?

I think, now, that my egotism quite got away from me that day. How else would all those questions about myself have cropped up? Back in my seat, during the rest of the day, I looked up now and then to see if any of the girls were looking at me. I could never catch them, if they were.

It was a long day. Especially for the first day back at school.

CHAPTER TWENTY-ONE

Crisis in the Hole

WE HAD A terrible rain storm one day, and everything was water-logged, including our underground fort. Even the ball field was under water, especially the infield, so that evening, after supper, we wound up playing football in the outfield area. There were about seven or eight guys there, including Carl Petillo and Rich Miller and Charley Miller.

While taking a break, sitting near the tunnels, I ventured into the main tunnel, and was happy to find that the sandy bottoms had dried sufficiently enough for us to use the main room.

Soon everyone had scrambled down, and matches were pulled from where we had stashed them in the niches, and some candles were lit in the tunnels as well as in the great room.

No one brought up the issue of the gang; we were just there, with no real purpose.

"Want a smoke?" Rich abruptly asked.

We all looked at him in wonder.

And then Rich pulled a cigarette out of his shirt pocket, a whole cigarette. Each of us must have been startled, for I noticed that we were all staring at him.

"Where'd you get that?" Carl asked.

"From my old man."

"You mean he gave it to you?" I asked, astonished at what he had said.

"Are you kidding?" he rejoined. "I took it from his package when he wasn't looking."

Now, my dad smoked, as did many of the men in Germantown, although many of them smoked pipes. Dad smoked cigarettes, also, but Jerry and I would never have thought to steal one of his cigarettes.

"What are you going to do with it?" Jerry asked.

"Smoke it!" came Rich's answer, spoken casually so as to make it sound as if that were the only logical answer.

"You mean you smoked before?" I questioned.

"Sure," he said. "It's nothing." He sat back against the wall, with an authoritative air.

"How do you do it?" someone asked.

"You just put it in your mouth and light the end, and then you suck on it. Kind of like you would a balloon, only backwards. You know. Suck your breath in."

And with that said, he put the cigarette in his mouth, bent forward, grabbed one of the candles, and lit the end of the cigarette. I watched him intently, waiting to see how he would suck in on it. I really didn't think he would do it.

But sure enough, he held the cigarette to his open mouth and then closed his lips upon it, and his cheeks kind of folded in on themselves, and then he pulled the cigarette out of his mouth and blew out, and smoke rolled out of his mouth. It filled the air.

Our mouths were open. Although most of our dads smoked, and even a couple of the mothers-they tried to keep that latter fact a secret, without success-the idea of any of the children taking up the habit was forbidden.

Rich sat back, leaning against the sandy walls of the room, and we watched him. He took another puff, and again smoke filled the air.

"You want a puff, anybody?" Rich asked, and he looked around at us.

Then he specifically offered it to me.

Why was it that I was always the one who fell into the traps that were set? Why was I always the one that others chose to do stupid things? I'd like to think it was because I was a leader, of sorts, but looking back on those times, I'm inclined to think the real answer was that I was some kind of a sucker. Or a dope.

I knew that everyone was looking at me. I felt the kind of pressure that only one's peers can present.

So I took the cigarette, and trying to look suave-you know, like Humphrey Bogart-, put it in my mouth and sucked hard on it. Instantly my throat and lungs were filled with a strange, acrid substance, and I coughed, and smoke blew out of my mouth, along with some phlegm. My eyes were watering, also. It was awful. It was terrible. I couldn't imagine why anyone would do it. But pride prevented me from saying how I felt.

Rich laughed, as did everyone else. Of course I resented the laughter, since Rich had handled the puffing so much better and I didn't want to look as though I couldn't handle anything that he could.

So I puffed again on the cigarette, only a little more cautiously this time, and this time I was able to keep the smoke from traveling down my throat, and I blew the smoke out through pursed lips. The others were all staring at me, but I wasn't sure if what I saw on the others' faces was admiration, or surprise, at my foolishness.

"Want a puff?" I asked Jerry in as nonchalant a way as I could. Of course I would offer it to him, for if I was to get involved with something, then it was only natural that I include my twin brother. That's what twin brothers are for, I reasoned.

Jerry took the cigarette, although he didn't appear confident, or eager. I knew right away that he didn't really want to take it. When I look back on those days, I realize that what boys often mistook for bravery was really stupidity or foolishness. And I knew that it was often better if one chose to share the foolishness.

But with the cigarette in his hand, Jerry really didn't have a choice, as everyone was looking at him, and I was sure that he wouldn't back down and look like a coward.

Jerry took a small puff, and instantly spit out the smoke. He didn't blow out the smoke, as Rich and I had done. He spit it out in a manner that should have given us reason to do the same.

He then turned and began to hand the cigarette to Charley, and I would have given anything to see just what Charley would have done.

But just then, before Charley could even grab the thing, we could hear someone outside, yelling.

"Shh," I cautioned, placing a finger over my lips.

"Larry! Jerry!" came the voice, and even though the sound had to travel along through the tunnels, I knew who it was. It was my father.

"Larry!" came the voice again. "I know you're in there. You too, Jerry. Are you boys smoking in there?"

I shook my head at Jerry, in a way of telling him not to answer. I knew that Dad wouldn't clamber down the tunnel, so unless we had been speaking real loud, there wouldn't be any way that he could be absolutely sure that Jerry and I were down inside. He had to be guessing, I figured. And I thought we might be able to wait him out.

But again came the call, and this time it was louder, and to say that the voice was merely insistent is to downplay the matter. He was angry, very angry.

"I'm not going to tell you boys again," he could be heard yelling. "I know you're down there. And I can see the smoke. You come up out of there, and I mean right now."

"How could he see the smoke?" I whispered. And Rich pointed at the iron pipe that we had stuck up through the center of the ceiling many weeks before as a way of making sure we were getting enough air. The top part of the pipe had been left about four or five inches above the ground, high enough to admit air but not so high as to be conspicuous to anyone who might be nosing around.

I grimaced.

"Do you hear me, boys?" Dad said. "I want you out of there. Right now!"

"Answer him," Jerry whispered to me.

"You answer him," I whispered back.

Jerry shook his head. He wasn't about to answer. He was scared. And well he should have been. We were both scared.

"Well, neither am I, then," I replied to his refusal. I figured that I could out-wait him. At the same time, I had little faith in thinking that we could out-wait Dad.

And when Dad's voice boomed once more, this time with more volume than I would have thought possible, I gave in.

"I'm going up," I said to Jerry. He merely nodded.

Slowly I crawled out of the main tunnel, and as I lifted my head at the surface, I could see my father. At that point he was not "Dad." He was a father, the father of a miscreant.

He stood straight, his legs spread wide, balanced on his toes. When I looked into his face, his eyes appeared dark, seriously dark; there was no humor in his eyes, as there usually was.

I slowly pulled myself to my feet, and stood before him, turning my eyes away, looking down at the ground. I knew I was in for it. The famous razor strap would be used this evening, for sure.

"Where's your brother?" he asked.

"I don't know," I lied.

"You mean, he's not down there?" he asked.

"No, sir," I lied, shaking my head. "I don't know where he is," I lied again. I have to admit that I had gotten so used to lying that people could readily take it for granted that I was telling the truth, if that can make any sense. I could think up the most plausible answers to questions, answers that came in a snap.

There was a deathly silence. I could sense that he was waiting me out, waiting for me to commit myself to saying something that would betray the lie.

"I'll ask you once more," he said. "Where is your brother?"

"I don't know," I said emphatically. "I think he might be over at Don's. He wanted to look at some new comic books that Don got."

I might have been a lot of things in those days, but I sure did not want to be thought of as a stool-pigeon. I was relieved when Dad didn't pursue it any further. Instead he took a different direction.

"Who's down there?" he asked.

I didn't want to rat on the others, for I feared that my father would call their fathers, and that would get me into more trouble, not only with my father, but with the guys I would be ratting on. And I would have sacrificed myself a thousand times rather than be a rat.

"Just some of the guys," I said, hanging my head down.

He must have understood the predicament I was in, for he dropped that line of questioning. Even fathers must realize, now and then, that their sons don't want to be called stool-pigeons.

"So you've been smoking," he said. He was not asking me. He said it in such a way that there wasn't any point in arguing with him. He knew that I knew that he knew. How's that for a confusing way of putting it? To put it more concisely, he *knew*. Like I said, there was no use arguing.

"Yes, sir."

When neither of us said anything further for a few seconds, I looked up at him, wanting to know why the conversation wasn't being continued. It was difficult to read his face. No longer was there any anger there. And for those long few seconds, there seemed to be something there that I had never seen before, and that something was made obvious in his next words.

"I'm disappointed in you, Larry." He looked long at me. A long pause ensued then, followed by: "Let's go home, son." And he turned and walked toward home, and I followed, a few steps behind him, all the way.

I was disheartened by his words, by the fact that he expressed disappointment in me. So I lagged somewhat behind him. I figured that the self-punishment I was inflicting upon myself, by conspicuously lagging behind, was as apt a punishment as I could receive.

By the time we got home, my spirits had sagged lower than they ever had before. My father had never before told me that he was disappointed in me. That was what crushed me so. If he had stayed angry and had decided to take the strap to me, as I deserved, then I might have shrugged off the entire incident eventually. But he hadn't.

He was disappointed in me. That hurt me far more than any justified whipping would have. What boy is there who doesn't hate the idea of disappointing his father?

I was sent up to bed, and the long trip up the stairs seemed endless, each step sounding loud, each sound on the steps resonating in my soul as well as in the stairwell, as though the very steps were pounding out the damning words that my father had spoken.

The room was empty, of course. I didn't know where Jerry was, at that moment, whether he had trailed behind Dad and me on that long journey home, or whether he had taken a different route so as to make it appear he had not been with me in the tunnel-fort. Of course he would have heard the conversation between Dad and me, and thus would have been able to *verify* the *fact* that he had been at Don's house.

I lay there on the bed, my conscience working harder and harder on me. I had rarely ever given free reign to my conscience before, but it was making up for all its confinement. I was tormented, and it isn't very often that the conscience of a ten-year boy old takes such control.

I wasn't even thinking of Jerry. I was so caught up in my own misery that when he finally came into the room, I realized that I hadn't even heard him coming up the stairs.

And he didn't say anything, at first. He must have been waiting for me to say something, probably because he figured that I would be angry with him for taking all the blame. But when I hardly paid any notice to him, he finally spoke.

"Did you get whipped?" Jerry was standing by the bed, looking down at me.

I shook my head.

"He didn't use his strap?" Jerry asked, bewildered by my silent answer.

Again I shook my head back and forth on my pillow, my eyes looking up at nothing in particular.

"What'd he do?" Jerry asked, moving so as to stand even closer to me.

I looked up at him then.

"He just said that he was disappointed in me," I answered, and I looked up at nothing again. The words had caught in my throat, so that they must have sounded wounded themselves.

"That's all?" Jerry asked incredulously.

I nodded.

"Are you going to get a licking? I mean, later?"

"I don't think so," I replied.

"How come?" Again his tone professed disbelief.

"Cause he's not mad," I said somewhat testily, as if that were explanation enough.

Hesitantly he asked: "Did you tell on me?"

"He thinks you were at Don's house," I said.

"And you didn't get whipped." Jerry said solemnly, sounding like he failed to understand it all. Only, this time it wasn't a question. He obviously couldn't fathom it all.

He went into the bathroom, and I could hear him washing up, and when he came to bed, he didn't say anything else.

We both lay there, wrapped in our own thoughts, each with our own emotions. Except that I lay in the darker zone; I had disappointed my father.

The stars in the night sky became dim, as a shallow cloud passed between them and earth. And my soul was darkened, as a cloud passed between my soul and that of my father's.

I vowed to myself never to disappoint him again…at least so as he wouldn't know.

CHAPTER TWENTY-TWO

A Dangerous Journey to Town

I CONFESS THAT AT ten years of age I did not really know much about our downtown. Our neighborhood of Germantown was pretty much the only truly familiar place I knew. This was true despite the fact that our church was located very near to the downtown area.

Oh, we had gone downtown every Christmas season to see Santa Claus, who sat in a throne-like chair in the basement of Sperry's Department Store, but our family never had much money and so we were always persuaded to shorten our Christmas visits with him. Any list that Jerry and I might have worked up to present to Santa would have been presented in somewhat of a skeptical manner, as Jerry and I had been prepared ahead of time by our parents to realize that there were a lot more children who were worse off than we were and who thus deserved more of Santa's attention. I rarely met those children. But no matter.

Even without the money for luxurious purchases, we could still appreciate the wonderful main attraction in the basement of Sperry's. It was a running train on a huge oval track. The train had whistles and bells. Miniature villages and railroad crossings gave the whole scene a wonderfully quaint atmosphere. Oh, to own a train like that! And although we knew we could never afford such a thing as that train, still there was nothing to prevent our marveling at it. There was always a crowd of boys and girls standing around the display, their oohs and ahhs demonstrating their admiration.

The whole of downtown Port Huron was a curious mixture of churches, stores, and movie theaters, restaurants, and bars and poolhalls.

There were eight churches within a radius of five blocks of the main intersection, that intersection being where the Black River ran through the main street and under the Military Street Bridge and thence eastward into the wonderfully clear waters of St. Clair River.

Black River was the dividing line between the two ends of Port Huron, and for some strange reason it is still considered a dividing line between what has been erroneously regarded as the haves and the have-nots, supposedly the North End being the halves(the more opulent). Just don't try to convince me of that, since I was born and raised in the South End yet now reside in that "opulent" North End, and I have yet to reach that stage of opulence that so many people have declared to exist.

What was most amazing to us boys, in those days, was the fact that Sperry's had two elevators, one of them immediately off its side entrance. The other elevator was in the center of the store, and was run by an operator. Amazingly, up until the time of this story, Jerry and I had never once ridden in either of those elevators. I can't say why, as undoubtedly we had been in that store a number of times, taken there by our parents during the Christmas seasons. It is also true that most of our friends had never been on either elevator. I knew that for a fact because we boys often talked about someday having the opportunity to ride in one of them.

We were not just curious about the device; we were enchanted by the idea of being conveyed in a metal box up and down the interior of a building. It was more like Buck Rogers stuff to us. And when we learned that Chetty and Kenny had actually ridden in the elevators, why, we were flabbergasted. To have ridden in an elevator was further reason to admire them. . We longed to ride in one. We dreamed about it. We talked and talked about it. But that's about as far as we ever got.

The downtown was a mystical place. Up on a roof of the entrance to the old Orttenburger's store, on Military Street, was a life-sized statue of a white horse. No one visiting Port Huron could possibly miss seeing it.

For most of my youth, downtown had as much commerce on the south side of the Black River as on the north side, which is to say that there was very little commerce. America was just beginning to come out of the severe Depression that had held the country-indeed, the world-in its grip, and the retail business of most American towns was slow in reviving.

Sears had a store along Military Street, on the south side of the Black River. There also was Ritter's Appliances, as well as Dave's Hardware Store, and Montgomery Ward's catalogue store, and Barnett's Drug Store, and also the Howard Furniture Store. There even was a corset shop, but of course I wouldn't have had any idea what was sold in there.

But nothing was more imposing looking on the south side as the Michigan National Bank building. A huge stone building that occupied a large chunk of territory, it had three stories. But the most impressive part of it was the grand main floor. The ceiling was so high that it made the inside of the bank cavernous looking. It also gave the whole structure the look of what a bank was supposed to look like, in my estimation.

My dad took me in there a few times, which usually drew a few stares and chuckles, since Dad shared the same first name as one of the tellers. So when my dad approached the counter, he would be greeted with: "Good morning, Manville." To which Dad would reply: "Good morning, Manville." And others in the bank at the time, both employees as well as customers, would look up from what they were doing, and grin.

Obviously there must have been other *Manvilles* in the area, but I never came across them. And of course Dad couldn't help but to leave his name behind; he named my young brother: David Manville Miller. We all called him Skip, which, I am sure, helped to relieve him of his burden, if he ever felt there was a burden.

But it was the north side of the bridge that was to command my attention one unforgettable day. Of course much of the whole downtown area was still nothing but a great mystery to Jerry and me. It was a great curiosity to us. It was something that we both longed to experience.

The chance to have my dream fulfilled came one Saturday, when I had been given the day off by Mrs. Schweikert. Autumn always slowed down the growing season for grass and plants. Thus I had a day free from work.

I don't recall where Jerry was that particular day. By the time that I had gotten up, he was gone. A cursory look around the neighborhood proved to be useless, and I was resigned to having to look for someone else to share any adventure that might be dreamed up.

I wandered over to Pollywog, but there was no one there. The stagnant pond slept under the autumn sun. The only creatures that enjoyed it were the frogs, whose greenish-yellowish heads could be seen peeking above the surface, probably looking for prospective mates.

I ventured over to Eighteenth Street, but no one was there, either. I scrambled down one of the tunnels, hoping to find one of the guys. But the room was empty. Candles still sat in their niches of the walls. But there was no evidence that anyone had been there in a while.

I was wandering toward home, when Jack appeared. He had also been looking for any of the gang.

"Where's Jerry?" Jack asked.

"I don't know. Maybe at Polk School," I answered. We sat down, near to the fort, sunk into a kind of melancholy. What the heck was going on? Here we had a free Saturday, the sun was out, the air was warm with promise of boyish adventure, and we were just sitting around.

"Are you going to go to the movie?" Jack asked.

"It's the same Hoot Gibson one we saw last year," I said. "You remember the one where he had to take over as sheriff of that one town."

"Yeah," Jack replied. "I didn't like that one, either."

And we continued to sit there. Brooding.

All of a sudden, I had an idea.

"Let's go downtown," I said abruptly.

"Where?" Jack practically shouted, as if he had not heard me right.

"Downtown," I answered. I said it as casually as one grown person might answer another grown person, as if it was something that we were accustomed to doing.

I could see that Jack was mulling over the idea. Downtown was still like foreign territory to us boys; it was so...well, grownup, so exotic.

"It's not that far," I said. "It's only a few blocks past my church."

Jack's face lit up. It was, I was sure, a grand idea, an adventuresome idea.

He looked at me, and I could see the resolve in his eyes. He nodded.

We jumped to our feet, looked once at each other, and started off. We knew that our mothers most likely expected that we would be gone until after the movie let out, so we would not be missed.

We headed up to Griswold, which we knew would lead us to Military Street, the magical street that would take us through the great downtown. The great adventure was just beginning.

We weren't walking. We weren't running a race, either. But our pace was quick. We were about to do something daring, and that made us keep the pace up for the first few blocks.

Once we passed Kuhr's Drug Store, we slowed down a bit. But the excitement had not abated.

Just a couple of blocks further we had to walk by the Gruel and Ott Coca-Cola building, where my dad worked, but we knew there was little chance of anyone, including my dad, being inside. During weekends the bottling operation was always shut down, with the drivers off on their runs.

Shortly we found ourselves at the corner of Griswold and Military, the site of a Rexall Drugstore.

Military was a broad street, built years before to carry transportation to the far north end of the city, up to Fort Gratiot, an outpost built many years after the French had abandoned its crude fort(Fort St. Joseph). The street had many trees lining the sidewalks, and the buildings looked old and worn, even in those days, and there wasn't much traffic, either vehicular or pedestrian, probably because people were just coming out of the lethargy produced by the Depression.

Port Huron was more than eighty years old, and it showed, but that was not so noticeable to Jack and me. We were thrilled to be a part of the commerce that passed by.

Everyone in the town knew that Thomas Edison had once lived in Port Huron, and I remember so well the day when Mickey Rooney and his entourage arrived at our train depot to celebrate the premiere of the movie that was made about young Edison's life. Electricity! Edison! It was all part of our history, and we were made to be proud of it all, by our parents, by our school teachers, by our town historians.

We passed the Desmond Theater, and the excitement was building, as we could see, just ahead, the huge horse above Orttenburger's store. We were, for all practical purposes, Downtown.

On the opposite side of the street from Orttenburger's was William Herpel's barber shop. I had never been inside it or any other barber shop; Mother cut Jerry's and my hair, an ordeal that ranks with the worst childhood torture.

We were there. We were Downtown. It was all so wonderful. And I think our heads swung around this way and that way, trying to take it all in.

We ambled along the sidewalk, making our way north, eventually passing the Sears and Roebuck Store. At the corner was Barnett's Drug Store, which rivaled Cunningham's Drug Store and Van Haaften's, and Tomlin's and Ruff's, most of them sporting an ice-cream parlor.

We crossed over the Military Street bridge, stopping in the middle of the span to lean against the railing on the west side of the bridge. From there we had a perfect view of the Black River as its muddy and sewage-strewn waters wound eastward and under us to the clear blue St. Clair River. We stood there awhile, oblivious to anyone passing by, and watched huge rats playing in the rotting foundations of the brick buildings that lined the river bank. There were hordes of them, scampering around the wooden pilings and in and out of the holes in the basements of the buildings.

"I wish I had a rifle," I said. "Those rats would make good target practice."

"Yeah," Jack answered. "Boy! Some of them are pretty big, aren't they?"

And they were big, some of them as big as cats.

On the other side of where we were standing, just a little ways east, was the ferry boat operation that carried people across the St. Clair River to Canada. The Blue Water Bridge, which had been completed about three years before, had not yet put the ferry boats out of business, probably because there were so many people who did not yet own cars and thus relied on the boats to get them into a foreign country.

The next block took us past the Fanny Farmer candy store, and several men's clothing stores. We walked past Mosher's Jewelry Store (where years later I would buy the rings that would cement my marriage to Carol Washburn). Mosher's was not just a jewelry store; it was in a class all by itself, with real experts in gems and time pieces, a place where quality counted and still counts today. It stood as the hallmark of the jewelry business in Port Huron; its reputation for quality was well deserved. And it still is today.

Finally, we reached our destination, the corner of Military and Grand River Avenue. There it stood: Sperry's Department Store.

J. B. Sperry must have been a wonderful man, as he not only gave the city a great place to shop, but he almost single-handedly sponsored the annual Thanksgiving Day Parade, which heralded in the Christmas season.

In its own way, Port Huron was a wonderful old town. The brick facades, especially those of the upper stories, were aged but comfortable looking. Dilapidated, true. But it was a comfortable kind of aged look.

Not far up the street, past Sperry's, was the J. C. Penney store. Across the street from Penney's was The Coney Island Restaurant, with arguably the best coney dogs ever served to anyone. I remember the man at the grill, his left arm extended and balancing five or six buns and hotdogs, all while loading them with the right ingredients: onions, mustard, and, of course, the famous hot coney sauce, some of the sauce dribbling onto his arm. His arm must have been scarred, over time, by the sauce. And I am sure that nowadays the health department would stop such activity.

But Jack and I were not focused on hot dogs. We knew where we were headed: to that celebrated elevator that sat just inside the side door of Sperry's.

We hurried our pace, without saying anything to each other. It was almost as if there were an accepted, unspoken agreement between the two of us.

There were few people on the side street on which the building sat. I could see a few people either going into or coming out of the building. So when we got to the side entrance that housed the elevator, we loitered outside, trying to look casual and inconspicuous, although at this stage in my life I realize that there is nothing more conspicuous than two boys trying not to look that way.

Finally, when no one was in sight, we hurried through the entrance door and walked up to the closed door of the elevator. There was a button on the face of the wall, but not having had any experience with an elevator, we were hesitant to push it.

"That's got to be the button for the elevator," I said.

"How do you know?" Jack asked.

"What else could it be for?" I returned.

He shrugged his shoulders.

"Maybe it's an alarm," he said finally.

"It's the button," I argued.

"Well, then push it."

I looked at Jack, gave a quick nod, and pushed the button. Shortly we could hear what sounded like a heavy clanking of machinery working, and we looked at each other, and jumped back.

"You broke it," Jack said, a worried look on his face.

"All I did was push the button," I protested.

The sound grew somewhat louder, and we looked at each other in alarm, and then hurried back outside the store, not wanting to be around if someone should happen to investigate the noise.

There we waited, looking back into the store to see what would happen. I really was worried that I had broken the contraption, but then we saw the door of the elevator open. It was empty.

"See," I said, "I didn't break it."

"Okay. Okay," Jack answered. He was probably a little annoyed that he was wrong, but also a little relieved that I hadn't broken the thing.

"Let's go," I said, and I hurried back inside, Jack following. But just as we went through the entrance door, the door of the elevator closed, of itself.

"What happened?" Jack asked, the worried look back on his face.

"How should I know?" I answered, a little angrily. "I didn't touch a thing."

"Then how come the door closed?"

"Quit asking stupid questions," I said to him.

Just then, the same sound of moving machinery could be heard again. We hurried back outside, where we stood alongside the curb of the street, letting our eyes glance back at the elevator from time to time.

We must have waited about a minute or two, when all of a sudden, the door of the elevator opened and this time a tall man walked out of the elevator and out through the door of the store. He was carrying a smart looking briefcase, and he nodded at us as he walked by.

"Boys," the man said somewhat briskly.

"Hi, mister," I answered.

"Who was that, do you think?" Jack asked when the man was a comfortable distance away from us.

"How should I know?" I answered.

And then, the door of the elevator closed again. And once more we looked at each other, as if each of us was waiting for a magical answer to the problem.

"Let's just wait one more minute," I said.

"Then what?" Jack asked. It looked as though Jack wanted to beat it out of there.

"I don't know," I said. "Let's just wait."

So we dawdled awhile, watching a few cars pass by, and some people going about their business. No one paid us much mind. And when about two or three minutes had gone by, and no one else had come out of the elevator, I motioned with my head to give it another try.

With a definite purpose in my stride, I went inside, Jack following, and walked quickly to the elevator, and pushed the button, hard.

The elevator door opened, and the empty car faced us.

"Come on," I said, hurrying into the car before it closed again, and I pulled Jack inside with me.

There was a panel with some numbered buttons, and some other strange looking buttons, as well.

Before Jack could say anything, I pushed the button numbered "three," and the elevator door closed, of itself. And before our astonishment could register on our faces, we could feel the elevator move, with that familiar sound of working machinery. So, that was what the sound was!

I couldn't remember having as much fun in a long time, probably not since we had used the handcar out at the railroad. But Jack had a look of horror on his face.

"What's the matter?" I asked him.

"We shouldn't be doing this," he answered. "It doesn't sound good." He was referring to the sound of the machinery. "I think we're going to break it."

"It's okay," I said, but I don't think there was as much bravado in my voice as I would have liked. "It's just pulling us up."

"Yeah," Jack replied, "but what if the rope breaks? I hear that there's only one rope that pulls it up. What if it breaks?"

"Who told you that?" I queried, a little anger edging my voice.

"Kenny Nelson," he replied.

"Well, Kenny doesn't know everything," I said, but the constant grinding of the mechanism didn't give me much comfort. "It's not going to break." At least I was hoping it wouldn't break, but at that point I was not very sure of myself.

The last part of my remark caused Jack to jerk his head up at me.

Just then, the elevator stopped, and the door opened magically. There was an empty hallway in front of us, and we hurried out of the elevator car.

We could see a glass panel that noted the offices of a few persons, one of them a doctor.

"Where are we?" Jack asked.

"I think we're on the third floor," I said. And just as I said that, the door of the elevator closed again, by itself.

"Let's get out of here," I practically yelled, running over to a stairwell that was nearby, and we flew down the steps, not really knowing just where we were heading. And when the staircase came to an end and we burst through the door, we were surprised to find ourselves in the same entrance where we had started, near the elevator door.

And just then, a woman came into the entranceway, walked over to the elevator, and pushed the button, and as we walked back outside, we could hear the same machinery sounds that we had heard before.

We had had our thrills for the day. We had ridden in an elevator, and while we didn't fully understand its workings, it was enough.

Across from that side entrance to Sperry's was the old Majestic Theater. It looked old and beaten and worn. That's because it *was* old and beaten and worn. But it had enjoyed its heyday, for it had featured a number of celebrities who had been part of what was known as Vaudeville. My dad told us about the great Eddie Cantor playing there; he became famous as a song and dance man, and starred in some movies.

And better than Eddie Cantor, at least in the eyes of the men, was the performance of the beautiful Lillian Russell, an actress who put her best self *forward*. She brought a whole line of talent, along with what the men called a magnificent bust.

Next to the theater, running south, away from Sperry's, was an alleyway. It was spooky looking, and was filled with litter and trash cans and discarded cardboard packing boxes from the businesses that lined the main street. Its twisting route looked like something stolen from some old horror movies, movies that featured assassinations and muggers and shanghaied sailors.

"You're not going to go down there, are you?" Jack asked as I moved across the street toward the alley's entrance.

"Why not?" I answered. I stood on the sidewalk, waiting for Jack to catch up. He wasn't in any hurry.

"I'm not going to go down there," he said.

"You going to walk home alone?" I asked, and I took a few steps into the alley, and turned to see if he would follow.

"There might be somebody down there," Jack said, not identifying just who that *somebody* might be.

I looked down the alley, but I couldn't see anything but a couple of stray cats. I will have to admit that I was harboring some thoughts about what I was doing, and not comfortable thoughts, either.

"Come on," I said, trying to encourage Jack to follow.

And when I turned and started to walk slowly down the alley-it twisted its way downhill, somewhat-I could hear his footsteps behind me.

The alley had its own peculiar smell and junkiness: rotting garbage, broken wine bottles, stale beer from discarded bottles, and discarded pieces of old furniture and clothing. For some strange reason, I thought of Charley Chan, of what an old Chinatown might look like, and suddenly I was not as brave as I had been when I had started. For I recalled stories about Chinese gangs, of knifings and blackjacks and dungeons, and this alley was dark, too, even though the sun was shining. It was as though what was good about life had been denied access to this alley.

"I don't like it," Jack said. He was trailing a few steps behind me. He wasn't any more scared than I was, but he was more practical, perhaps a little less daring, and certainly a lot smarter about not doing stupid things.

We were about half way down the alley, when the sounds of two men could be heard, two men who apparently were angry. A trash can was knocked over. Curse words were shouted. And then I heard what sounded like somebody had struck someone, a sound not much different than one of the countless blows that we had witnessed in the old cowboy movies.

Someone yelled, as if in pain, and more curse words followed. The words were the worst imaginable, and they were filled with anger.

Just then, two men emerged from out of the shadowy depths, snaking their way around one of the various turns in the buildings. I could see the south end of the alley, and the feeble daylight at the exit caused the figures of the two men to blend into the shadows, so that their features were indistinct.

They were making their way toward us, the first man taking stumbling steps, the second man following, and within seconds they were nearly upon us. Jack and I hugged one of the brick walls of a building.

The first man was huge, and heavy. His trousers were torn and stained, and his face was grimy and whiskered, the whiskers rough and ragged, giving him a menacing look. He staggered, falling toward the building almost opposite from us, barely catching himself. He was snorting, his breathing ragged sounding.

The other man was short, and skinny, but it was obvious that he was making his way better. His clothes were not in as bad a condition as the other man's, but they still showed marks of age and use. He was trailing the heavier man, about two or three paces behind.

Jack and I looked at each other. I was scared, and I knew that Jack was scared, too. These were obviously two villains, if ever I knew villains. They lurched and stumbled their way, until they were almost directly across from us. Their heads were lowered, their voices directed at each other with curses that I had never heard before. And as they drew near and Jack and I tried to blend further against the brick exterior of the building, it suddenly became obvious to me why it was that the men had not noticed us as yet; they were staggering drunk, the bigger one apparently more so than the smaller one.

They were arguing with each other, their voices loud and profane, and the smell of old whiskey went before them. I had smelled it enough times on old man Weigant to recognize the smell for what it was.

Just as they were about to pass us, the heavy one stumbled, falling away from the building that he had been leaning upon, and he practically fell against me. His body slammed into the brick wall, and he must have hurt himself terribly, because then he let out a roar of obscenities.

He must have noticed my shoes, because he raised his head, and tried to focus bloodshot eyes on my figure. Jack was about three or four feet away from me, and when I looked at him, he had a look of abject fear on his face.

"Who're you?" the man asked, his voice slow and slurred and gravelly. He was holding himself with one hand against the building, trying to focus his bloodshot eyes, and he was so close to me that I could see his rotting and yellow stained teeth, and smell a breath that made me think of vomit. His figure was bent, but his upper torso was raised, so that he could stare at me. His eyes were opposite mine, and he shifted and staggered, trying to hold his position, the one hand holding himself away from the wall.

I was paralyzed with fright, and for some strange reason I suddenly thought of the ugly blind man from Robert Louis Stevenson's *Treasure Island*. Except that this man was hideously worse than Stevenson's character.

The smaller of the two men came up to me then; he had been drinking, that was apparent, but he was more focused, more alert.

"What're you boys doing here?" the smaller man asked. There was no anger in his voice. It was more like he was surprised to find someone else in the alleyway.

"We're just going home," I said, my voice stammering.

"You got any money?" the bigger man asked, his hand reaching out past me and grabbing at the wall, so that I was practically pinned against the building.

His body reeked terribly. It was a foul smell. I had never smelled anything as bad. He was about as loathsome a person as I had ever seen, or smelled. And he was practically leaning against me.

"Leave them alone," the smaller man said, and the threat in his voice was distinct, and he pulled at the bigger man's arm.

The bigger man turned and stumbled backwards at that, struggling to maintain his balance, and he turned toward the smaller man, swearing at him.

"Who're you, telling me what to do?" the big man slobbered.

Then a look of great anger crossed his face, and he lunged at the smaller man, who merely stepped aside, so that the bigger man fell to the ground.

Jack and I looked at each other. I knew he was thinking just like I was. We were trying to figure out if we could get away, if we should try to take off running. But now the smaller man was on one side of us, and the bigger man, though on the ground, was on the other side.

Then the big man slowly pulled himself up, and the anger in his voice was so great that his face practically turned purple. The veins in his neck and face were pronounced, and his color got redder, and again he yelled at the small man, swearing terribly. He was holding himself up by placing his hands on his bent knees, and he was looking at the smaller man with a look that terrified me.

"You keep your mouth shut," the big man said, his words slurred and harsh.

The small man came up to the big man then, and I could see that he was mad. Considering that he was the much smaller of the two men, he sure didn't look scared, and his right hand was balled into a fist, hanging loose at his side but kind of twitching like.

"You're all mouth," the small man said, standing no more than a couple of feet away from the big man.

Then, from a crouching position, the big man swung at the small man, a clumsy and slow swing, but the blow was useless, as the small man easily turned aside and cracked the big man on the side of his face, sending him to the ground once more, where he lay writhing and cursing.

I swear I heard a bone crack in the big man's face. The big man lay there, on his back, his body rustling around with the garbage and other debris of the alley floor.

"I told you before, don't ever try and hit me," the small man said. He was standing over the big man, glaring down at him. His fist was ready at his side once more.

Then the big man slowly staggered to his knees, and then tried to tackle the small man, and when he got hold of one of the small man's legs, the small man let out a kick with his other foot, striking the big man alongside his face, sending him once more sprawling on his back, where he lay moaning.

"I don't know why I married your sister," the small man yelled down at the big man. "You're both alike. You're just a stupid drunk. You'd be better off dead."

Again the big man struggled to rise, and when he was half-way up, he lunged at the small man once more, but he was clumsy and slow, and this time the small man lifted his right hand from down under and struck the big man viciously in the middle of his face, and the blow was so strongly struck that it lifted the big man up off his feet, so that he fell hard on his back. This time he hardly moved. The moans from his throat were barely audible, as it seemed that all strength had left him.

I looked at Jack, and nodded toward the far end of the alley, and when he nodded back at me, we both took off running. We were almost at the mouth of the alley, when I slowed down, letting Jack catch up with me, emerging into broad daylight, and feeling somewhat safer, especially when I could see people on the sidewalks.

We turned and looked back down the alley, but I couldn't see anyone. Except for a couple of small rats scurrying about, the alley appeared lifeless.

Jack and I turned west and went down Quay Street, to the Seventh Street bridge, and made our way home, talking hurriedly all the while. And we agreed that we wouldn't tell anyone about what we had seen. As far as we knew, the big man might even have been killed, and we would have been witnesses, and there was no way at all that we wanted our parents to find out about where we had been and what we had seen. So we decided not to tell anyone, not even our best friends. I figured that if the guy really was dead, then he had it coming to him. It wasn't a very kind thought, and I felt guilty the moment it came to me. And I carried the thought home with me, back to the comparatively safety of Germantown.

Downtown had turned out to be...well, not as glamorous as we had thought. Even an elevator ride was not worth what we had gone through.

Chapter Twenty-Three

The Warfare of Autumn

A s autumn crept slowly by, it brought changes. The air was less humid, and instead of the evening dances of fireflies, we were treated to nighthawks as they swooshed through the atmosphere, in competition with the zigzagging bats for the mosquitoes and other insects foolish enough to venture out.

It was the time of year when the chestnut trees were bursting with their annual bonanza of nuts. Every boy worth his salt-as the old expression goes-knew where the chestnut trees thrived, and most of us knew the trees that were the most profuse, although each one of us thought that we were guarding secrets from each other.

Of course these were not the kind of chestnuts to be eaten. Apparently the edible chestnuts, I have since learned, are imported from Europe or England or some such place. No, these were not the edible nuts; these were the nuts of war.

Each autumn found us collecting stockpiles of them. We took them to our homes and peeled off the outer covering, where were revealed the shiny, hard brown shells of somewhat-round balls of ammunition. Beautiful brown nuts with tan colored tops, they were almost perfect for throwing.

The chestnut fights came hand in hand with the falling of the leaves of the maples and oaks that dotted our neighborhood. Very few people had large yards in Germantown, but our area-indeed, all of Port Huron-was canopied with the towering growth of tens of thousands of trees, and while those trees were somewhat of a curse to the adults-for the adults only saw in them the necessity of raking up the leaves-for us boys it meant a windfall, for we not only raked up those leaves which fell in our own yards, but we were even known to pilfer the leaves from our neighbors' yards, a kind of stealing for which, I am sure, our neighbors were most grateful.

We carefully raked the leaves into piles near the foundations of our homes. There the piles lay, growing taller and taller, until the day that one of the older boys called for a battle.

The rules of engagement were the same as those for the annual snowball battles that came with winter. Sides were carefully chosen so that the teams were fairly represented by boys of all ages.

Since the Nelsons' house and our house were directly across from each other, the two front boulevards of the houses became the war zone, with the middle of Sixteenth Street being the dividing line. The day of the warfare, the piles of leaves were dragged away from the foundations and out onto the boulevards, and neatly stacked in fair resemblance to what we thought leaf-forts should look like.

When the two sides were established in their respective forts, with supplies of chestnuts at hand, a signal was given, and the war began. Chestnuts were thrown from one side to the other, boys jumping quickly up to make a throw and then ducking down, hoping not to be struck while exposed.

There was a great spirit of adventure in those battles, with each side sending out quick-striking parties in hope of making a *kill.*

It is remarkable, looking back on those days, how accurate many of us were, for there were many *kills* made down through the years of boys who had exposed their bodies for only a fleeting moment. A *kill* was counted when a boy was struck on the face or head or upper body. Of course there were innumerable arguments as to whether a person had actually been struck in what could be regarded as a lethal manner, since it was necessary to hit near the heart, and not just a lesser important part of the body. But rarely were there any arguments when the face or another part of the head was struck; in such a case, the victim was quick to let out a howl that told us that, indeed, a kill had been made.

Most remarkable, to me nowadays, is that there were no serious injuries: no eyes put out, no teeth shattered, no broken cheek bones. And certainly no lawyers were ever consulted by concerned parents about their *precious little* ones having been severely hurt. *In fact, I don't* recall ever seeing any parents witnessing the battles. Most likely they wanted to remain oblivious to what was going on outside the more peaceful confines of their homes. It was just as well, since we did not want our parents supervising our games.

The rules were strictly administered. If a boy was struck on the leg, then he had to fall where he was and try to escape by using only the good leg. If he was struck on the arm, then that arm was considered useless for the remainder of the battle and was not to be used.

Those were exciting times for us, since the battles often took on all the elements of real war, with raiding parties stealthily making their way through various yards in hope of sneaking up on the enemy, and with advance scouts sent out to reconnoiter the other's territory and to report back in to headquarters. Sneakiness, accuracy at throwing, speed in retreating and advancing, these were all necessary skills to develop.

Everyone knew the area well, knew the different fences that could be climbed, knew which garage roofs were easily accessible so as to provide a place for aerial bombardments. And all of us knew the alleys and the small openings into bushes and vines that allowed entrance into neighbors' yards for sneak attacks, hopefully without the neighbors knowing what we were doing.

I don't know of a boy who wasn't *killed* many times, through the course of the years. And not one of us escaped injuries of some kind or another. These *killings* and *injuries* were merely the fortunes of war.

It was during one of those battles, when Jack and I were teamed together as advanced scouts, that one of the scariest moments of my life occurred.

The game had started at dusk, that time of day when shadows turned allies into enemies, when bushes moved by soft evening breezes caused one to be overly cautious. All of us had learned the art of warfare by watching movies; we knew how to creep from shadow to shadow, and we knew when to be perfectly motionless.

We knew that one could find cover way back under Mrs. Wolfe's front porch, where the darkness of night provided excellent refuge, for if one were hiding there, the only way to discover the person was to get down on your hands and knees and look carefully, and to do that would leave you exposed. It was much better to leave any possible enemy there, undiscovered. Besides, the person under the porch had to endure the spiders that resented encroachment on their territory.

That particular night, Jack and I had gone up the alley behind my house, crossed over Minnie Street and then went east across Sixteenth Street, and down the alley that wound past Wingarden's apple tree. All this without being discovered.

Night was creeping on, and the shadows of dusk were being swallowed by night itself. We hoped to sneak down Minnie and cross back over so that we could come up behind the Nelsons' house, with the idea of making a sneak attack from behind. Both of us had our pockets filled with chestnuts and our hearts filled with hope.

At the corner of Fifteenth and Minnie lived "Old Man Schrader." Well, that's what all of us boys called him. Our parents had always commanded us to respect our elders, and there was a time, not long before, when I had made mention of Mr. Schrader with that somewhat disrespectful appellation. Of course, my father had taken me aside and let it be known, in no uncertain terms, that I was never to refer to Mr. Schrader again by anything other than "Mr. Schrader." My butt felt sore with the warning. A razor strap can do that to a fellow.

Anyway, there were two languages spoken by us boys: that which was used in front of our parents and other elders; and that which was used by us boys when we were absent from supervision. Thus we boys continued to refer to Mr. Schrader with our familiar appellation.

Now, there were two notable characteristics of Old Man Schrader's yard. First, he had an apple tree, easily the only one in the immediate vicinity that bore really good fruit. In fact, so good were the apples that everyone knew that the tree was carefully guarded. Word was out that the old man had a shotgun that he kept just inside the front door of his house, and that anyone caught trying to swipe some of his precious fruit would meet a most fateful end. So, while we boys were often bold and foolish in regards to other residents of Germantown, we had long given up on the idea of trying to swipe some of his apples.

The second characteristic about Old Man Schrader's yard was that he had a goat. Yes, a goat. It was kept tied by a rope to the apple tree, that tree standing in the middle of the front yard. That blasted goat was a most cantankerous animal. I had quickly discovered that two or three years earlier, when I had tried to make myself friendly with it.

On that particular day, though I had been warned repeatedly by my parents, as well as by many others, to stay out of that yard and away from that animal-I was about seven or eight years of age at the time-I had walked up very innocently to the goat one day and tried to pet it. Jerry was with me, and he warned me not to get anywhere near the animal, but I was not one who took advice very well. Besides, a goat in the neighborhood was particularly unusual, so much so that I had long harbored the idea of trying to make some kind of contact with it. It seemed like such a docile animal, and I noticed that whenever anyone got somewhat near the animal, he would nod his head up and down. I assumed that he was offering some kind of greeting.

I had always been cursed with a great sense of curiosity, resulting in my venturing into places where I was forbidden and to do things that wiser souls would not have attempted. Of course I often suffered, as a result.

Anyway, at first, as I approached the goat that day, it certainly appeared to be gentle, looking up at me curiously, its head held slantwise. It appeared to be sizing me up.

Emboldened by what I misconstrued as friendliness on the part of the goat, I reached out and petted the back of its head. It shook its head away from my hand, "nahhed" a little bit, backed up a couple of steps, and looked me over once more. And I have to admit that there wasn't much of me to look over.

I wasn't satisfied. In fact, the obstinacy of the animal only made me more determined to get my way. I was bound and determined to make a friend of the animal. All the while, Jerry stood on the sidewalk, about twenty feet away, yelling to me that Old Man Schrader would catch me and thrash me.

I moved nearer to the animal, since it seemed to be at the end of its tether and thus would not be able to come toward me any closer than it already stood, and I reached out and petted the animal again. This time, cocking its head from side to side, it looked me over more intently, its silly looking whiskers hanging down from its face, causing it to look like an old man who was trying to solve a problem. And as I petted it this time, it didn't seem to resist.

Emboldened by what I thought was an act of friendliness on the goat's part, I grabbed hold of the goat 's whiskers. I'm not sure why I did that. I was either naïve about goats, or foolish, or stupid.

Of course, with me holding onto its whiskers, the goat shook its head from side to side, I suppose to free its whiskers from my grasp, which it was successful in doing. That made me a bit too obstinate, for I reached for its whiskers once more, and this time I held on more firmly.

At that, the goat called out "Nahhh," shook its head most vigorously in order to free its whiskers from my grasp, and backed away from me a few steps. That only made me even more stubborn. After all, I was a human, while it was merely a goat. Who was calling the shots here?

So I moved in and grabbed the goat's whiskers once more, this time with determination not to let go.

At that, the goat backed up a couple of steps, pulling me toward it. At that point I lost my grip on its whiskers, and I was just about to reach out and grab those whiskers once more, when the goat "Nahhed" loudly, and jumped forward, butting me in the chest, sending me sprawling on my back. It stood over me, daring me to get up. And when I did, it jumped at me again, butting me once more, "Nahhing" even louder.

This was no act of friendliness. That stupid animal! He needed to be taught a lesson, I figured. He needed one good, quick kick in the rear. That was what he needed. And I was about to get up and do just that, when suddenly the door of the house opened and a woman came out, screaming.

Now, I had heard my share of German words before, although my proficiency with the language was pretty poor. Grandma, who lived upstairs, just down the hallway from Jerry's and my bedroom, had tried to teach us some, but we always resisted her efforts. After all, we were Americans.

But there I was, on my back, looking up at an angry goat, and with a very angry German haus frau charging across the yard with a broom in her hands. She was a small woman, with her hair tied in a severe bun on the top of her head, which made her appear all the more fierce than what I might have imagined. And she was shaking the broom at me as forcefully as the goat had shaken its whiskers.

Meanwhile Jerry was running away, yelling for me to get out of there. I didn't need his encouragement. I was up and out of that yard faster than I could have thought possible. A torrent of German words followed me, as I ran. I didn't know what the words were telling me, but I was sure that they weren't invitations to visit the Schraders again.

So here I was, a few years later, in the darkness of evening, along with Jack, in front of the Schraders' house. We crouched behind some bushes that bordered the property between the Schraders and their immediate neighbor to the west.

It was all quiet. Looking back toward Sixteenth Street, we couldn't see any of the boys from either side, so we figured that it would be easy to sneak around behind the Nelsons' fort and catch some of them unaware.

"Let's run over to the alley," Jack whispered to me. "I don't see anyone."

I was just about to answer, but suddenly there was an old familiar sound, the "Nahhing of the goat in the Schrader's yard.

It spooked the heck out of me, and I must have flinched. And I could hear Jack gasp, so the sound must have startled him, too.

We could barely see the Schraders' house. It was sitting back in the night darkness, and we didn't move an inch, for fear that Old Man Schrader himself might be out in the yard, protecting his precious apples. But there were no other sounds, nor was there any noticeable movement in the yard. Our eyes had become somewhat accustomed to the darkness, and I could discern various shapes and shadows in the faint light that came from the corner street lamp.

"Do you see Old Man Schrader" I asked Jack in a hushed tone.

"I don't see anyone," Jack whispered back. "Why?"

"I'm going to get some apples," I answered.

"You're nuts," was his quick, hushed reply.

I sat in my crouched position, peering intently into the yard, but I couldn't see any person. The tree was barely visible in the darkness, and I couldn't see the goat, although I imagined it standing there, tied to the tree.

"I've got to get a few apples," I said.

"I'm not that hungry," Jack replied.

"Neither am I," I countered, hoping that our whispers weren't being carried to the wrong ears.

"Then why do you want apples?" he asked, bewildered at my stance.

"Because they're Schrader's apples," I answered. I thought that answer would suffice.

"I'm not going into that yard," Jack said resolutely.

Jack lived just a few houses due west from the Schraders, and I remember him once saying that he even was scared of Old Man Schrader during the daytime, the old man was so fierce of temper. Plus, Jack had been warned many times to leave his neighbors alone. And if Jack had one irritating quality about him, it was that he was usually obedient.

"I'm not asking you to," I replied. "Just stay here, and watch."

"If someone comes out," he said, "I'm not going to give myself away by yelling to you."

"You don't have to," I said. "Just make a sound like an owl."

"Yeah," he answered, but he didn't answer with any enthusiasm.

And I began to creep, soldier-style, on my belly, across the grass, edging toward the apple tree. There was a sense of adventure in crawling across the yard like a soldier. It made me think of the many times when I had seen such action in the movies.

My stealthy slithering was done slowly, and the closer I got to the tree, the creepier the night seemed to become, as the shape of the tree, against the backdrop of a small light in the side of the house, became more distinct.

Where the heck was that dumb goat? I wondered. Then, another light came on, in a front room of the house, and I lay flat on the ground, perfectly

still, waiting to see if someone was about to come out of the house. I was
worried that someone inside the house had seen me.

But all was still. Nothing moved. No one came out of the house. So,
emboldened, I crept forward on my stomach, all while surveying both the
yard and the house. Oh, this was glorious adventure!

And then I saw it. In the faint light from that single table lamp, I
could see the goat. It was lying down, about ten feet away, munching at
something. And then I knew what it was munching; it was an apple.

I waited for another minute, and then I stood, cautiously, watching
the goat carefully to see how it would react, but it only glanced up at me,
briefly, and then resumed munching away. I was glad that the stupid goat
didn't recognize my smell from the incident of a few years earlier, else, I
figured, it would have taken it upon itself to give me another butting. I
assumed that goats had the same keen memories as that of dogs.

But the goat nibbled and munched away, seeming not to mind that I
was moving toward the tree. He hardly paid me much attention.

There was only one branch that was within reach of my outstretched
hands, and I couldn't feel or see any apples. Darn! I would have to climb
the tree, if I was to get any.

The tree was easy to climb, its main trunk easy for me to wrap my
arms around, and within seconds I was up in the tree, straddling one of
the branches that spread themselves about ten feet or so off the ground. It
was easy to creep out on the branch. I was quiet and careful as I crawled
out, but as careful as I was, I couldn't help but jar the branch under me, so
that a few apples tumbled to the ground, where the soft thuds sounded, to
my ears, like muffled cannon shots.

I waited a few seconds, in case someone in the house had heard the
falling apples. But there was nothing to be heard. And no door was opened.

There were apples all around me. I found a huge apple, and was in the
act of stuffing it inside my shirt, when the goat began to make that awful
"Nahhing sound," except this time it kept it up, as though it were sounding
out an alarm. The sound scared the heck out of me, and I froze.

I was about to climb down out of the tree, when the front door of
the house opened, and there, in the background light from within the

house, casting a dark silhouette, stood what looked like Old Man Schrader himself, and he was holding what looked like a long, slender object in his right hand. I didn't know for sure what it was, but I felt reasonably sure that the thing he was holding was the feared shotgun.

It was too late to jump, and when a poor semblance of the sound of an owl echoed in the dark air, I was scared out of my wits. That is, if I had had any wits. If I truly had had some, I wouldn't have been up in the tree, in the first place. And Jack wouldn't have been crouching at the edge of the property, making lousy imitations of a night owl.

Then came a fearsome voice.

"Who's out there?" It was spoken from the doorway, and it was a tone far beyond that of curiosity. It was spoken as a challenge.

Then the figure moved, and even though it was almost pitch dark, I could make out that it was, indeed, old man Schrader.

I had only seen him a few times in my life, as he was a very private man. And I remembered him as a rather small man, thin, with graying hair.

He moved slowly, the thing that he was carrying hanging down, along his right side. He came out and stood in the yard, and I tried to disappear into the leaves and branches and apples, feeling miserable and frightened.

He made his way through the yard, walking slowly, and the closer he got to the tree, the bigger his figure loomed. This man, who might not have been more than five-feet, six inches tall, suddenly seemed to be a giant. And I was too frightened to move an inch, so I really couldn't make out for sure if it was a shotgun he carried, or not. But at that particular moment, his reputation led me to *know* that it was a gun, indeed.

There were no more sounds of an owl, so I didn't know if Jack was still in the bushes, or not. I figured he wasn't, for it would have been foolish of him to have stayed. One foolish and stupid boy was enough for one night.

The old man found a spot directly underneath me. His figure was dark, and my fear made him darker yet. He had cocked his head, listening intently, trying to find the one or the something that had caused the goat to make its absurd call. He even got to talking lowly with the goat.

"Is there someone here, Joe?" I could hear him ask.

Joe! Joe! The stupid old goat had a name? What kind of a person would give a name to a stupid goat? What did he think the goat was? A member of the family? But I was in no position to question the old man's sanity.

But another question about stupidity intruded into my mind? Who is it, I thought, who's stupid enough to be up in Old Man Schrader's apple tree, at eight o'clock at night, cringing in abject fear? I didn't need to answer. My knocking knees were answer enough. And I only hoped that the old man couldn't hear them knocking, and I also hoped that the old man wouldn't look up and see who it was that was jostling the branch. I just knew that the branch must be shaking, for certainly my body was shaking enough to make the branch move.

I was almost afraid to continue looking down, for fear of further jostling the branch just enough to cause him to look up, but after a few seconds I cautiously bent my head down, just enough so that I could watch him. He was standing perfectly motionless, except for his head. I could see him carefully turning his head from side to side, looking over the yard, and I knew that he was also listening for any sound, any sound at all.

Please, I begged and prayed, please do not look up.

It seemed as though it was so quiet that I could hear the frogs from a small bog that was about a half-block away. But other than the croaking of the frogs and the insistent mating cries of crickets, there didn't seem to be any other sounds.

Where were the other boys? Was the war game still going on? And why weren't some parents calling for the younger ones to come in for the night?

I stood balanced on the limb, holding to a branch for dear life, afraid to move one inch, for fear of jostling the branch into letting go some more apples.

It seemed like forever that he stood there, but finally he went over to the goat, which was more visible now in the faint light coming from the open doorway of the house, and the old man caressed the goat's neck, still looking out toward the street.

"Good boy, Joe," I could hear the old man say then. And with one last searching look around, he turned and walked slowly back to the house. When he got to the open doorway, he turned, looked out at the yard once more, and spoke once more to the goat: "You keep your eyes open, Joe," he said somewhat loudly, "and you let me know if someone else comes into the yard."

I knew why he had spoken loudly. It was for the benefit of anyone who might be hiding out there in the dark. And there *was* someone out there, in the dark, all right! And that someone was just waiting for the chance to get down out of the tree.

Finally, the door closed, and then the light inside was switched off, and the darkness of the house melted into the darkness of the night once again. But still I did not come down right away. I figured that the old man might be standing behind a window, watching for any sign of movement.

It seemed like it was forever, but after what seemed to be an hour but was more likely a matter of a few minutes, I quickly shinnied down the branch, jumped the last few feet to the ground, and took off.

Again there came a "Nahhing" sound, and I could sense, rather than hear, the front door open again. But I didn't stay around to find out for sure. And until I made it back to the corner of Sixteenth Street, I held my back rigid, feeling that any moment I would feel the pellets of the shotgun.

And when I made my way around the corner, still running, my breath ragged because of the fear I had felt, turning the corner was like a release from unimaginable horror, and I slowed to a walk, fortunate to have survived a night of terror. In fact, I was ecstatic, knowing that I had escaped from a possible load of buckshot.

Just then, while I was still feeling a great sense of relief, a barrage of chestnuts lashed my body. There must have been a dozen chestnuts which had been thrown, and I was pelted on my face and on my chest and legs, and I suddenly realized that I had come into another *enemy's* territory.

Of course *they*-this particular *enemy*-had not known what had been happening to me in old man Schrader's yard. They had been lying in ambush, waiting for me, for anyone of the opposing side, and I had been unlucky enough to stray into their ambush. The game was still going on, apparently, and I was *killed* instantly. Their surprise was achieved, and my body was bruised all over.

And while I fell dead, as was required by the rules of the game, I couldn't have been more grateful for having been *killed* in this game, rather than having been really killed by a shotgun held by Old Man Schrader.

As the years passed, so did my appetite for any of the apples from Old Man Schrader's tree. I figured that apples do not go very well with buckshot. I was quietly acquiring some wisdom. Not much. But some.

Chapter Twenty-Four

Weathering Fifth Grade

THE FOLLOWING SATURDAY I found myself in Mrs. Schweikert's yard. There was little trimming left to do, and the grass barely needed the onceover that I gave it. I could see that my labors were coming slowly to an end. I harbored the feeling that maybe Mrs. Schweikert was merely being gracious, that she was struggling to find any purpose at all for me to be earning the twenty-five cents that she so religiously paid out into my hand.

The warm season of autumn was winding down. Each night the air held a bit of coolness, as though in anticipation of the coming of winter, although daytime still felt much like summer.

In some ways, it was the best time of the year. The leaves had mostly turned, so that the neighborhood was filled with beautiful reds and yellows and golds.

One October day, not long before Halloween, a terrible thunder storm hit the area, while we were in school. Lightning bolts flashed continuously, filling the air with a sense of foreboding.

Even our teacher, Miss Penzenhagen, seemed to be somewhat terrified by all the commotion outside the windows of our classroom. She glanced out the windows often, and her directions to us were often interrupted by the cannon-like sounds of the thunder. I noticed that she stood on the far side of the room, away from the windows.

The air that morning, when we were walking to school, had been unusually warm and humid, and there had seemed to be something like an electric feeling in the atmosphere. Sure enough, that afternoon a storm struck with all the ferocity it could bring, the light from the lightning bolts flashing against the windows and off the hardwood floors of the room. The booming sounds of the thunder seemed to shake the old brick building, rattling the windows.

I enjoyed the storm immensely, for there was fear on the faces of many of the girls, and nothing appealed to a boy more than the pleasure of showing off his bravery in the presence of danger.

The crashes of thunder echoed and echoed throughout the room, the sounds seeming to get progressively worse. I had seen war movies and cowboy movies with gunfire and cannon fire, but nothing from those movies could possibly have compared to what nature was throwing at us now. This was real stuff.

Just about when it seemed as though it couldn't get any worse, a fierce wind blew up, and the howling of the wind came with hard missiles of hail and debris from the playground outside. The hail pelted the windows, and for a few moments it seemed as if the windows might break.

Miss Penzenhagen ordered everyone away from the windows, directing us to the far side of the room, where she was trying valiantly to put up a brave face.

We were all ordered to move quickly to the wall farthest from the windows, where we huddled on the floor. Both girls and boys sought out their friends, many of the boys hoping to share the excitement of it all, while the girls sought mutual comfort.

Jack took his place next to me, sitting Indian style, a position that I had never been able to achieve. I sat with my legs sprawled in front of me, trying to look cool and casual, trying hard to let everyone know that I regarded the storm as something that was wonderful.

"Heck, it's just a bunch of lightning," I remarked carelessly.

Just then a streak of strange light appeared outside, filling the room with a horribly strange illumination, and the accompanying exploding sound was like that of a shotgun fired next to our ears. Many of the kids fairly jumped at it, and I have to admit that I felt lifted off the floor, myself.

"Did you hear that!" Jack said, reflecting what everyone else must have been feeling. He moved closer to me, and I noticed that almost all of the other kids had moved closer to each other, as though it was natural to move into a semblance of a circle.

Eventually the hail let up, but the winds still howled, and the pellets of rain made it almost impossible to see anything beyond the windows. More flashes of lightning struck, a seemingly inexhaustible supply of them. Suddenly I was not feeling quite so brave, and with the next horrible shot of thunder, I retreated within myself, looking around to see if anyone had noticed. But a lot of the girls had covered their faces with their hands, and even some of the boys had tried to find places closer to the wall.

Miss Penzenhagen walked along in front of us, trying by her outward look of composure to instill courage in us, but most of the kids were not even looking at her.

She stopped, about in the middle of our group, and looked down at us. When she noticed how few of us were actually looking at her, she must have felt it necessary to say something. But her words were going to require some effort, as she looked over her shoulder continually, hoping, I am sure, that the storm would subside. She continued to stand there, words having failed her.

Finally, after she had been standing in that position for about a minute or so, the storm began to let up, the strongest of the winds subsided, and the lightning bolts seemed to be retreating, too, moving toward the west, towards my house, and suddenly I was worried for my mother, for she would be home alone with my little brother David.

When school ended for the day, I rushed down the stairs as quickly as I could but not so fast as to warrant being reprimanded by one of the always-vigilant teachers who always seemed to be everywhere.

It had quit raining.. In fact, the sun was trying to break through a thin layer of clouds as Jerry and I rushed through the playground and up the alley that led toward Sixteenth Street.

By the time we got home, we were both panting from the hard run. We burst up the front steps, and rushed through the screen door, only to be met by Mother, who was on her way out. We nearly knocked her over, but she backed up just in time, at the edge of the living room.

"What in heaven's name is wrong with you two boys?" she asked. "You trying to kill me?"

"No, Mom," Jerry said. "We were just worried that…"

"And look what you two just brought in with you," she said, interrupting Jerry. "Mud!" she practically screamed. "Just look at this mud."

And sure enough, we hadn't noticed, but in our trip down the alleyway that ran behind the houses along Minnie, we had picked up clods of mud on our shoes. Of course we had not taken the time to shake the mud loose; consequently the hardwood floor now bore the results.

"I've spent an hour cleaning this floor, and you two have managed to ruin all my work in two seconds." She glared at us.

"Well," she said, "what have you two got to say for yourselves?" Her stern look and hands firmly planted on her hips dared us to argue the point.

We both looked down at the floor once more, and while it was true that the mud had dirtied the entranceway, I wanted to tell her that the floor of the living room still gleamed. I wanted to tell Mother that only a small part of the floor was dirtied, and that I'd clean it all up for her. But she pushed us both out the door, admonishing us all the while, so that a few neighbors who happened to be outside at the time looked up to see what all the commotion was about.

Jerry and I retreated down the front steps.

"You know better than to use the front door," Mother added. "You two get around out in back, and you take an old cloth and clean those shoes. And you clean them good, you hear?" she demanded.

"Yes ma'm," Jerry said.

"Get one of the old cloths in the basement," she added.

I was too angry to say anything in reply. We had worried about her, on account of the story that had passed, and we had rushed home to make sure she was all right, only to be scolded for bringing in a little mud. It never dawned on me that Mother was quite capable of weathering a little storm, and that keeping a house presentable, while raising five children, was a far greater burden.

Mothers, I thought. How exasperating they could be.

CHAPTER TWENTY-FIVE

Ghosts of a Different Kind

T HE FOLLOWING SATURDAY I went to Mrs. Schweikert's for what was to be my last day of working for her, for the season. The grass was barely in need of cutting. Late autumn's cooling had begun the process of introducing us to the prelude of winter.

I still carried in my mind the many things that Kenny had told me and the other kids in the neighborhood. But a part of me felt that there was a lot of exaggeration in Kenny's remarks. Otherwise, I felt, why was I still alive, especially after drinking the lemonade she had made that one day?

There was a slight chill in the air that Saturday, under an overcast sky, and as I approached her house, her garden seemed to be withering, as though it had surrendered to the approach of late autumn.

I could see her out in the back of the yard. She was bending over some plants, the customary shears in her hands.

I opened the gate and entered, remembering to close the gate after me.

She looked up from her work, straightening up. She looked a little tired. Her hair was not as nicely taken care of as usual. And her dress had a few stains on it.

"I'm glad you came," she said. She took a seat on a nearby bench.

"You want me to cut the grass?" I asked.

"In a minute," she answered. "Take a seat," she said, pointing at the bench near where I was standing.

When I was seated, facing her, she wiped away a wisp of hair that had been hanging across one eye, leaving a smudge of dirt on her cheek.

Putting the customary shears on her bench, she folded her hands in her lap, and seemed to lapse into herself. But a little smile flickered across her mouth.

"I see you're wearing shoes," she began.

"Yes'm," I answered. "We usually start wearing them once school starts. My brother and me."

"My brother and I," she corrected.

"Ma'am?"

"Just a little grammar lesson," she answered, but she quickly understood that I still didn't understand, and decided to let it go.

"I suppose school is going all right for you," she offered.

"It's okay," I answered.

"You have a good teacher?"

"Miss Penzenhagen," I said. "She's really nice. Even as nice as Miss Sullivan."

"Ah, yes, dear Miss Sullivan," she acknowledged. "I know her very well."

That surprised me. I hadn't thought that Mrs. Schweikert would know many people beyond her immediate vicinity, let alone our teachers.

"You had her for a teacher?" I asked, not realizing the impossibility because of the respective ages of the two women.

She laughed heartily. "Oh, my goodness, no! Do I look that young?"

"Well, no. I mean…well, I'm not sure. I mean…" I stammered.

"That's all right, son. I know what you mean. I guess it's hard for young boys to keep things like that straight. As you grow older, I'm sure that someone along the way will tell you that you're not supposed to ask a woman what her age is."

She looked down at her hands. It looked as if she were thinking of something. Her shoulders slumped a little. I thought, for a moment, that she was about to fall asleep.

Then she looked up abruptly.

"You get the mower," she said, "and I'll get back at this pruning." And she got up from the bench, and went back to her job.

I got the mower out, and went out in front and cut the grass. It was much thinner, and much shorter, and the job did not take me very long.

From time to time I looked over the fence, to see if she was okay. But she was still pruning, with a small set of clippers that looked like oversized scissors.

When I had finished and had put the mower away, she stopped what she was doing, put the clippers on a bench, and said: "Please come with me."

I saw that she was heading toward the back door of the house. She walked slower than at any time that I could remember, but she did not look back. I couldn't do anything else than follow her. I couldn't imagine not obeying her.

I was a few steps behind her when she opened the back door.

Was she expecting me to follow her into the house? And the moment I thought about that possibility, I recalled what Kenny had said that he had seen while watching her house that one night. I recalled what he had said about spirits, or devils, or whatever he said was floating across the windows of the third floor. About levirating, or levitating, or whatever he called it.

"I think my mother wants me to do something for her," I offered, hoping that I would be believed.

She stopped in the open doorway, her left hand holding the door open. She looked back at me, with a quizzical look. Then her look turned a little more serious. Her eyebrows turned down a little. She looked as if she were dumbfounded a little, as if no one had ever challenged her before, about anything.

"What did you say?" she asked, still holding the door open.

"I think my mother..." I stopped. I didn't want to stammer, and I knew well enough not to lie to her. She was just that kind of person, someone you just did not lie to.

"You have another place you have to get to right away?" she asked. And again there was a challenge in both her voice and her look.

"No'm. I mean, no, Miss Beatrice."

"Then you have a few minutes," she said. And that was enough, for she turned and walked through the door, and I followed, dutifully, closing the door carefully after me.

Four steps up took us into her kitchen. It was spacious, and cheerful, with cupboards lining two of the walls, and I noticed some glass canisters on one of the counters next to the sink. A toaster sat near the canisters. There were shelves with figurines on them, most of them of children at play.

The ceiling was a high one, and a fancy kind of lampshade of various colors of glass filtered the light from inside. It was centered over a large wooden table that looked as if it had been polished recently. Four chairs surrounded the table, and I noticed that they matched the table in color and texture. Certainly they were much nicer than the random pieces of furniture that took up space in our kitchen.

She paused, halfway through the kitchen, and turned to me.

"I have something I want to show you, son," she said, and when I nodded, she went through a wide archway into what must have once been a formal dining room, for there was a huge table in the center of the room, with eight matching chairs.

The room itself was enormous. Polished hardwood floors gave the whole room a look of elegance, and there was a large floral rug underneath the table. A massive piece of a dresser stood against an inner wall. It had three shelves that held painted dishes and cups, most of them painted with flowers. I knew right away that they had been hand-painted, since I had a talented uncle-my Uncle Arthur-who had painted dishes, also, so it was easy for me to recognize the skill. Three drawers were underneath the shelves, and I imagined that they were filled with things that couldn't be found in our house.

Another, smaller hutch occupied a corner of the room, and it, too, was filled with various bric-a-brac, kind of like the things I could find in my grandmother's apartment. Except that these looked expensive.

Along the opposite wall were three large, double-hung windows that stretched almost from the floor to the high ceiling, and drawn back with ties were lacy curtains that offered some little privacy yet made it easy to see the gardens of her side yard. The trees and shrubs could be enjoyed from this room, and it was easy to imagine sitting at the table and looking out over the gardens while eating a meal. And I was sure that she had taken advantage of the view many times.

The lighting fixture over this table was mostly of brass. There were various arms turned out from the center, and each arm had a curious sort of twisted bulb. I had never seen anything like it before.

She had halted at a doorway at the other end of the room.

I had paused to look out the windows, which made her stop at what turned out to be sliding doors.

"You like the view, I see," she said.

"Yes'm," I answered, forgetting to use her name as she had requested. "It must be nice to sit and eat here, and be able to see your garden," I said.

"It used to be," she said simply.

I looked at her, waiting for an explanation, but she gave me a quick glance, and then turned away.

She pulled the two sliding doors apart, and I followed her into what I thought was the most interesting room of them all.

The room was at least as large as the formal dining room, probably even bigger. It obviously stretched along the whole front of the house, and it must have been at least thirty feet in depth. It had a high ceiling that reminded me of being in the city's library on Sixth Street. I had been in that library a few times, a building of large stone and masonry, with huge rooms and high ceilings and a formal-looking atmosphere.

This room had two walls that were lined with shelves, and all of the shelves held volumes of books, many of them in leather bindings. I had always had a great curiosity about books, so I moved closer to the shelves. She stood in the middle of the room, next to a large coffee table.

Two massive couches faced each other across the open expanse of the hardwood floor. She moved to sit on one of the couches.

There were small shelves that dotted the other two walls, shelves that had all kinds of figurines and bric-a-brac like those in the dining room. And again I was reminded of the same kinds of pieces in my grandmother's room. Except that once more I realized, without any expert reason, that these pieces were no dime store articles.

The front of the room had two huge windows, double hung, with beige curtains drawn across them. Heavy maroon drapes were pulled back and tied off to the wall. On both sides of the windows were more shelves with more books.

And off to the left, at the farthest wall, was a staircase with a spindled railing. Obviously it led to the second floor of the house, and almost immediately I again thought of what Kenny said he had seen through the curtains of one of the upstairs windows. I almost shuddered at the thought, and forced my attention back to the rest of the room.

"This was his favorite room," she said simply. "My husband," she explained. She was sitting back into the couch, so that her figure looked even smaller, almost like a doll sitting in adult furniture. It was then that I realized how small she was.

I looked questioningly at her. She was sitting straight, almost formal like. Her hands were lying perfectly centered on her lap. I turned and looked at the book shelves.

"He loved his books," she said, answering my look. "There isn't one of them that he hadn't read. A few of them he read several times."

"Yes'm," I answered, lacking any other words to say.

"I never was much of a reader, myself," she went on. "He wanted me to read, to share my ideas with him. But to tell the truth, I had a hard time understanding what some of them said. I remember once saying to him that it *was all Greek* to me, and he laughed."

I looked at her, and waited for her to continue.

"Some of what he read was *in* Greek."

I had never heard of anyone who could read Greek. In Germantown everyone spoke and read either English or German, or both. But Greek?

"He must have been a smart man," I said.

"A very smart man," she agreed. "I used to think that he was too smart for me."

She got up then, and I was surprised to see that there was still an energy in her actions, as she got up quite easily. She walked over to the wall next to me. I turned to the wall as she got closer.

"Look at the authors, son," she said, pointing her finger at the books on the shelf at our eye level.

Some of the names I recognized: Shakespeare, Plato, Dickens, Hawthorne, Cooper. But I have to admit that they-not all-were only familiar to a degree; I had never read any of them. Oh, I had heard Dickens' "A Christmas Carol," since it was produced on radio each Christmas season, but that was about as far as I had got with Dickens. But the rest of the authors were merely names from long, long ago.

I couldn't know then just how much they would mean to me, later in life. Here they were merely works of writers whose ideas I would not have understood, at that early age. But the fact that they spoke of ideas, of philosophies, of myth and history, made them seem important to me, even though it would be years before I would read them.

"Have you heard of any of them?" she asked, breaking in on my thoughts.

"I'm not sure," I replied. "Maybe I heard of a couple of them."

"That's all right," she said so softly that I barely heard her, and I looked at her, to see if she were okay.

"Once in a while I take one of the books down, and open it up, hoping that a little better understanding of my husband finds its way into my soul."

She sniffed a little, like the day that she had that slight cold, or allergy.

"He did have a couple of favorites that even I could understand," she managed.

I looked at her again, waiting for her to continue.

"Have you read *Treasure Island*?" she asked then.

"Just the comic book," I answered.

She gave out a little laugh.

"Well, at least it's something," she said.

"I hope you will read it someday," she continued. "The real book, I mean. It was one of his favorite books. He said that it never grows old, not even after reading it a dozen times."

I couldn't imagine anyone reading a book a dozen times. I thought maybe she was exaggerating a little. Nowadays I think about that, because I have read some books many, many times. *The Scarlet Letter*, and *To Kill a Mockingbird*, and *Huckleberry Finn*. How times change!

"I've read it two or three times, myself," she continued. And she smiled what was a full smile, as if she were remembering something, and her eyes had a happy look. "I suppose most girls think that it's a boy's book.

"Now, here's one for you." And she reached up to a shelf and took down a leather-bound book, wiping the book across her skirt, I guess to wipe away any dust. And she handed me the book.

I turned the book over in my hands, and noted the title: *The Adventures of Tom Sawyer.* I had never read the book, probably the most famous one by Mark Twain, but everyone had heard of it. In fact, the movie version of the book had played in Port Huron, at one of the downtown theaters, but the cost of the downtown theaters would have been prohibitive for most of us boys, although a few of the older boys had gone to see it. Which is interesting these days of my adult life, because I now own a copy of the movie, and have enjoyed it many times.

She turned to look at me squarely, her eyes level with mine.

"If I give the book to you to read, will you read it?" she asked, turning to face me directly.

I could scarcely believe what she was saying.

"Oh, yes'm, I mean Miss Beatrice," I answered with enthusiasm.

"You know my rule," she said. "Don't say anything that you don't mean."

"I'll read it. I really will." And I was caressing the book as if it were a great treasure, my fingers gently fondling the leather cover.

"I'll trust you to do just that," she said, handing the book to me.

"We'll just pretend that this room is your library. You may borrow any book that's here, but I want you to promise to take very good care of any book that you take."

And she looked at me as though what she had said was really a question, not a statement.

"I'll take real good care of it, Miss Beatrice. I really will," and I clasped the book to my chest, maybe a little afraid that she might change her mind.

But the smile returned to her face, and I swear that the wrinkles seemed to disappear, softening her face dramatically.

"Even as a young girl," she said, "I fell in love with Mark Twain. The writer," she added, pointing to the book I held in my hands.

"Most of my girl friends wouldn't read it. I guess they thought that his books were for boys. But they're not," she continued. "My husband encouraged me to read a lot of Twain's stories. Especially *Huckleberry Finn.* And I have to admit that I never read a greater examination of human affairs than I found in his works."

I looked into her eyes, and I had the feeling that she was thinking of something important, for her eyes had a dreamy look about them.

I could not have known, at that time, just what she was talking about. But later, in my twenties, I discovered Twain for myself. And I came to realize what a remarkable man he was, for he could make a person laugh at human frailties, and yet he got angry with human failings. It was as though he penetrated into the soul of all of mankind. And he hated sham!

But it was 1940, and I was a ten-year old boy standing in a room of wonders, with a woman whom I had come to admire, and respect, and… yes, to love. I held the book more tightly.

My comfort level in the room had increased greatly. Yet there was something about the room that was nagging at me, something that was tugging at me for my attention.

She had turned her attention back to the books, and I looked around the room, across the shelves of books, then at the mantel over the fireplace.

Of course! The mantel, a piece of marble of various colors. I had only seen one mantel like it, I mean, of marble, and that was in Joe's house, so I knew that I was looking at something that was rich.

It was a deep shelf of a mantel, and it held a lot of pictures. Obviously the pictures had been there all the time, but I had not really noted them. I probably had noticed them subconsciously but had overlooked them as merely being a part of a room.

She must have noticed that I was looking at the pictures, for she moved across the room, slowly, deliberately, as though she were being drawn to the pictures by some unseen force. When she got there she stood, silently, with her back to me. I was sure that she had forgotten that I was there, in the room. But she turned partly toward me, without moving her feet, only her upper torso turning.

"These are my family," she said, and she turned back to the pictures.

I knew that she expected me to look at the pictures. She did not say anything more. I walked over to where she was standing.

There were more than a dozen pictures, each standing in its own silver frame. They stood in a regular order, as though they must have been placed with great thought.

In one of the pictures-it was the largest of them-was a grown man. He was standing in front of a large brick building, holding his hat in his hand. He appeared to be very tall. His hair was white, obvious even in a black and white photograph. He was clean shaven. He appeared serious looking, but not somber, typical of the photographs of those days.

"My husband," she said, pointing to the picture. She had said it so softly that I almost did not catch what she had said. "My, but he was a handsome man." She was nodding, as if agreeing with herself.

"Every one of my girlfriends thought I was the luckiest girl in the world when he proposed to me. They all wanted him for themselves."

I looked up at her, expecting her to say more. She did not disappoint me.

"Can't say that I blame them, though. He was tall. Almost six-four. And he had the darkest hair. And when he smiled, he made you feel as though life was just beginning, with all its freshness and good smells."

I looked at her standing there looking at the picture on the mantle. She seemed to be off somewhere else, her eyes no longer looking at the picture but at something straight ahead of her. Or at something unseen.

"He died twenty years ago." The voice came slowly.

"I'm sorry," I said, a little embarrassment in my voice. I couldn't think of anything else to say.

"When you are young, like you are, I'm sure that death is not quite so meaningful. Or understood," she added.

All I could do was nod. And, as I had noticed so many times before, I once again noted how often I nodded at things she said. Perhaps those were times when I kept my mouth shut, displaying a little discretion, not something that I was often capable of.

"You said that you have a grandmother," she said then, and I saw her eyes as though I could see through them. They were gray, in the soft darkness of the room.

She had half-turned toward me.

"Is she a good woman?" she asked.

I was struck by the question. It seemed so...well, unlike anything that anyone had ever asked me before.

"Yes'm," I replied. "She's really nice to me. I mean, she's nice to everyone. Everyone likes her. She lives down the hallway from my bedroom, but she kind of keeps to herself a lot. I mean, she cooks most of her own meals in her own room. She's my mother's mother. I guess she doesn't get out a whole lot. She's really very nice to us kids."

Then I realized that it must have sounded like I was babbling. At least it seemed, to me, like I was babbling. So I stopped, abruptly.

She smiled, a smile that looked as though she thought I had said something funny. Then she turned serious looking. Well, maybe not serious. Maybe thoughtful.

"You treat her nice," she said.

It wasn't a request. It wasn't an order. It was a simple command. And there was no severity in either her face or her voice.

"Life is so short," she continued. "It would be shame not to enjoy it, and to enjoy those who are around you. Especially grandparents," she added. "Grandparents get to the age when all they have is family. And memories of family."

She was looking straight at me, then, in a kind manner. It was almost as if her eyes had softened, if that were possible.

"I'm never going to have grandchildren," she said, so softly that I had to almost bend my head toward her in order to hear her.

This last was said with a touch of sadness.

I really didn't know what to say, so I nodded briefly, once or twice.

She turned to the pictures, and I followed her gaze. Then she took up the picture of the man, her husband, and held it in front of her, and her fingers touched the picture of him, as though she were caressing the figure. Then she put it back on the mantel.

She picked up another picture, this one of a much younger man. I thought it was a picture of her husband when he was a young man.

"Know who this is?" she asked.

"Your husband? From when he was younger?" To me, it was an obvious answer.

"It looks like him. Doesn't it?"

Again I nodded.

"This is our son. His name is Arthur. He was twenty-five when he died. Killed in the war." And she shook her head back and forth, holding the picture up so that it caught more of the faint light of the room. "Such a waste. Such a terrible waste. War." And she shook her head again, slowly.

For some reason, the room suddenly felt gloomy. Her voice was a little angry, with a little leaden quality in it.

"Ever hear of a place named Amiens?" The tone of her question had a bit of harshness to it. And her eyes narrowed, as though she were trying to shut out some memory.

"I don't think so," I answered.

"I suspect you will, eventually. It was an important battle place in the last war."

I looked at her, and waited. I figured she would elaborate. Again I was not disappointed.

"Arthur died there," she said. "He got there just in time to die," and she shook her head back and forth, several times.

"My husband and I argued over that," she remarked then. "It was the only serious argument we ever had. He felt that Arthur should serve his country. I always felt that war, any war, was such a terrible, terrible waste. Arthur really did not want to go. But he went, anyway. I think he did not want to disappoint his father.

"He was full of promise. I expected him to finish college, maybe become a doctor. He liked science. He told me one time that his favorite class was anatomy."

She stood there, motionless, the picture still looking back at her.

She put the picture back down, stood and looked at it for a few seconds, and then moved on down to the far end of the mantle, where she took up another picture. I followed, as though it was expected of me, and stood next to her.

She showed the picture to me, holding it at an angle so that I could see it clearly.

The picture was of a small boy, maybe not much younger than was I. He had on knickers, a curious kind of short pants that the Dutch had introduced into the country. A lot of the boys in our neighborhood longed to own a pair, but only one did: Joe. And he hated them. His mother had bought them, I think, to separate Joe from the rest of the boys in the neighborhood. She did not like any of the boys. She only tolerated them. She thought we were all a bunch of rowdies. Sometimes she was right; many of us were rowdies, at times. Joe thought that the pants gave him a sissy-look.

"I know you wouldn't be able to guess about this one," she said, handing the picture to me.

I took the picture, looked closely at it, and tried to remember what the picture of Arthur looked like.

"Is this Arthur?" I asked. But my question was feeble.

She shook her head, smiling a kind of pensive smile.

"That is Emil, our first-born. He was three years older than Arthur. He died when he was seven. Diphtheria."

I wanted to ask what the word meant, what this *diphtheria* was, but I was too timid. I was not that way with my friends, but this was different. This was something serious, something that young boys, maybe, are not supposed to understand.

"It was an awful way to go," she said, interrupting my thoughts. She was shaking her head again, like she had done when she had held the picture of Arthur. "No mother ever wants to outlive her children," she remarked.

"Some people think that you get over it, eventually," she continued. "But you never do. You really never do." Her hand fell alongside of her, still holding the picture. She was staring straight ahead. It was as though she was trying hard to focus on something.

I watched her closely, waiting for her to go on. For I knew that she wanted to say something else. And she did say something else.

"What you find yourself doing is carrying on. You just carry on. Because you have to. Do you understand that?" She turned and looked at me carefully, as though she was hoping that I did, indeed, understand.

I had opened my mouth to answer, but I couldn't think of what I should say, what I must say. So my mouth hung open, and no words came out.

"Of course you don't understand," she said gently. "It's all right, son. You needn't pay too much attention to an old woman rambling on."

I smiled at that, with what I hoped was a caring smile. I wanted to understand all that she was saying. Any fear that I had had about her had long disappeared. And it was then that I realized that I felt sorry for her.

She put the picture back on the mantel, and we stood there for a few minutes longer, looking at them. They were no longer merely pictures. They were real people, and they seemed to be looking at me. And for some strange reason, I thought of my grandmother just then. And I thought of what Mrs. Schweikert had said about treating my grandmother nice.

She turned slowly away from the mantel, and I turned with her.

"Well," she said over her shoulder, "it's good that all these books aren't going to go to waste, after all." It was an abrupt change in all that we had been talking and thinking about. The tone of her voice became somewhat happier, more alive.

"Now, what do you say that we go back into the dining room and have a glass of lemonade, and maybe even a couple of cookies?"

And she turned on her heels, and I followed her, clasping my book tightly to my chest. *My* book? No! It wasn't my book, but for some inexplicable reason, I wanted it to be so.

Chapter Twenty-Six

A Lesson in Temerity

I T WAS THE middle of October. The air was crisp and fragrant, and the fragrance of ripened purple grapes was a reminder that our neighbor, Mr. Deacon, would be harvesting the grapes for his newest batch of homemade wine.

As the hues of the leaves continued to change, there was no thought of things dying, not for us boys, anyway. For us it was merely the changing of seasons, something which we looked forward to, a part of life's cycles. At that youthful stage of our lives, we were not aware that with each passing day a piece of life also passed us by. We were not philosophers. Instead, each day was a moment in time to be enjoyed, to be fully experienced. After all, we were merely boys.

Some nights, after the activities of the evening had been enjoyed, I took to my room with my book. And it didn't take long for it to take hold of me. I got caught up with a wonderful character: Tom Sawyer. And before long, I was explaining to all of my friends-at least to those willing to listen-of the antics of a boy who would have fit right in with our gang of boys.

I laughed at how Tom had gotten a crush on Becky Thatcher, thus spurning Amy Lawrence in the process. I thought he was a cad. Yipes! Cad! What an old fashioned word! And I met Huck Finn, a social outcast-Twain called him a "juvenile pariah," and I had to look up the words in the dictionary to find out the meaning. Huckleberry reminded me of Marvin, the friend I had lost the year before.

And I practically praised Tom for pulling the whitewash prank on Ben Rogers, for in my mind Ben Rogers was our own Joe, who would have deserved any derision or hardships that came his way.

There followed, in the ensuing pages, the figures of Muff Potter, a likeable drunk, and a vicious, murderous miscreant by the name of Injun Joe. And what boy could have resisted taking a raft down to Jackson's Island? Of course we did not have a great river like the mighty Mississippi. Nor did we have a Jackson's Island. But we had Pollywog, and we had built our share of rafts, and in my mind it did not take much to transfer all of Tom Sawyer's glory to our own lives.

Oh, it was a marvelous book. It had everything for a boy, and even for some girls. It had all the pathos of human life, and mystery and humor, and it spoke to me of a time when life was lived slowly, and humbly.

But there was something else-other than the book-that was important that time of the year, for Halloween was approaching. Although our neighborhood was populated by those who were…well, less fortunate, still there were expectations of receiving treats. Most families were of modest means, and thus not much was expected when Christmas or birthdays rolled around, and with a few exceptions not much was given and received. But Halloween was the one day when we expected things ordinarily not available.

All of the kids in Germantown were looking forward to all of the fun that the holiday promised.

We were hardly aware of what else was going on in the world. In Paris, France, after a Blitzkrieg through Holland and Belgium and Luxembourg, the German army had attacked a demoralized France, and by June the German troops were shopping and dining with unexpected propriety, at their leisure. Apparently they had been warned by Hitler to be courteous and dignified, and that is the way they acted, so that they might just appear to be decent people, after all. I'm not sure that the rest of the world bought into that. As far as we were concerned, those troops represented everything that was evil in the world, and nothing could convince us otherwise. Their arrogant goosestepping left Americans angry.

Meanwhile, back home most of America believed, even at that late stage, that America would never again be involved in a European war.

Supposedly the previous war had taught us to mind our own business and to let the Europeans tend to theirs. People pretended to themselves that what was going on in Europe was solely a European affair.

Thus, here in America, life went on as usual, which meant that Halloween would be celebrated. We kids would celebrate the holiday with all the exuberance that nature had provided us.

For us kids, Halloween was both expected and hallowed.

I was amused, years later, to hear children reciting at my door: "Trick or treat." Such lingo was unknown to Jerry and me. Jerry and I had been taught to say: "Do you have anything for a poor Halloween beggar?" After all, how could anyone turn down a beggar? Even a poor family must have some kind of treat to give. And at most of the homes we visited, we were given candy, or apples, or caramel-covered popcorn balls that were homemade.

Also, it was many years later that I noticed that the name of the holiday was commonly mispronounced. Everyone called it Holloween, and still do so today, even by professional television announcers, as though the first part of the word was supposed to sound like *hollow*. The fact that the holiday had a connection with the sacredness of the church, thus requiring a day when the saints would be *hallowed*, meant nothing to me. Nor to the rest of my friends.

Halloween was a day when we were set free from the restrictions of manners and civility. Well, up to a point, that is. It meant acts of mischief, acts that were never meant to be mean or mean-spirited, acts that rarely ever got out of hand. Over the years we had heard of riotous acts, such as young boys turning over outhouses, but there very few outhouses in Port Huron in 1940, at least not to my recollection. Port Huron had matured and had become somewhat more civilized.

The soaping of windows was expected, with parents warning us not to use wax. Joe was stupid enough to try using wax on Old Man Thiele's house the year before. He got caught, and he was forced to work with a scrub brush and razor blade until the wax had all been removed. Of course he blamed Mr. Thiele for being mean, but all of the kids in the neighborhood had a few good laughs over the whole thing. Many of us purposely went over to Mr. Thiele's house and watched Joe working hard at the task. We figured that it couldn't have happened to a more deserving person.

During the days before Halloween, outdoor lights were mysteriously screwed off, or sometimes they disappeared altogether, only to appear once again the following night. And sometimes small paper bags of manure were left at people's front door steps, especially at the homes of those who had displayed little tolerance for kids. We had heard of some boys setting fire to the paper bags, just after ringing the door bell of the house, so that the owner would come and stomp on the bag, creating an ugly mess on shoe and porch. But I never met any boy who actually took *credit* for such an antic. It's not surprising that that particular story has made its way down to these more modern times. Perhaps it is a myth, although most myths are based on some degree of truth.

The days leading up to Halloween were filled with excitement and the anticipation of even more excitement. Our minds were at work in thinking up what we could do to particular neighbors.

But acts of destruction? Never! It never entered our minds to do anything detestable. The incident of Joe and the wax was probably the most destructive thing ever done by any of us boys. And we had all learned a valuable lesson in that act.

Still, we sat around and talked and planned. That was as important as committing our little tricks. And our conversations often included the horror of goblins, and ghosts, and werewolves, and bats, and Frankenstein and Count Dracula. We enjoyed the scary talk.

"What are you wearing?" Jack asked me.

A bunch of us boys were sitting near the wooden fence that bordered the south side of the playground of Polk School. It was on a Monday, near the end of recess, about ten days before Halloween. Excitement was building just by talking about Halloween.

"I wanted to wear a cowboy costume, with a cap gun and everything," I replied somewhat timidly. "They had one in the window at Kresge's."

"Yeah," Joe put in, "but I bet you your mother wouldn't buy it, would she?" It was meant as a slur, and was so taken.

"So, why don't you have your mother buy it for *you*, then?" one of the boys challenged Joe.

"Who wants to go as an old cowboy?" Joe countered. "Besides, if I really wanted it, she'd get it for me," he replied arrogantly.

The truth of what he said did not sit well with me. Nor did it sit well with the others. None of the rest of us had parents who gave in to the whims of our youth. We all would have gone as cowboys, if we could have afforded the costume. But the entire ensemble cost about three dollars, and that was an enormous amount of money for most of our families. Our envy over Joe's position was enormous.

"So, what are you going as?" Jerry asked Joe.

"My mother bought me a skeleton costume," Joe replied. "It even glows in the dark. She said it makes it easier for me to be seen, in case there are many cars out on the road that night. And besides, it cost almost as much as that dumb cowboy costume, anyway." All of us hated the smugness with which he made his remark.

There was a little grumbling at that information. No one liked to be put down, or belittled. Especially by Joe. It was especially bad at Christmas, when he always showed off all the presents he was given. I remember the previous Christmas, when he showed off the chemistry set he had received. He bragged about all the things he could do with it. Jerry and I hoped he would blow himself up, just to teach him a lesson. Well, not really killed. Maybe hurt a little. Kids do think some bad things.

"What are you going as, Larry?" Joe asked in a snide way. "The same old ghost you went as the last two years?" he added. "I bet you it's the same old dirty white sheet, too."

"You know, Joe, you're a real jerk." That came from Don Weston. Don never was one to say a lot, but when he did, we all listened. He wasn't big, but we knew from the playground games that he was as tough as he was quiet, and no one really knew just how tough he was, and no one really wanted to find out.

Joe looked over at Don, opened his mouth to say something, noted that Don was looking hard at him, and then abruptly closed his mouth. Even Joe showed signs of discretion now and then.

"Maybe Mom will let us wear something else this year," Jerry said quietly. He hurt inside just as much as I did, for he, too, usually dressed up as a ghost in one of Mother's old sheets.

Miss Penzenhagen appeared at the back door of the school just then, ringing a small bell, which meant that we were all to line up to go back to the classroom. All of us got up and started to make our way to the double lines, girls in one line, boys in the other line. I was seething with anger. Joe would pay, somehow, some way. Of that I was sure. I just needed to bide my time.

On that Monday night, just after supper, when the sun still hovered a little above the horizon, Jerry and I, along with Jack, drifted over to Eighteenth Street, hoping to find some of that gang in the vicinity. Sure enough, Charley and Rich and Carl were there, throwing a football around, baseball having given way to the sport of autumn.

Before long, Jack Scahill and Don Cash arrived, plus one of the Gustke boys. Ron Gustke was a pretty good athlete, and was always welcome in our games, although he was not one of the regulars. But often he showed up for baseball and football games.

It wasn't long before sides were chosen. As was the case of choosing up sides, Jerry and I were always designated as captains, I suppose because we were equal in ability and size. Consequently Jerry and I were rarely ever on the same side in athletic contests, which aided in producing a sibling rivalry over the years.

The rules for choosing were the same as for baseball. Whichever of us won the right to choose first always chose Charley, as he was the biggest and best athlete of us all. Thus the one who chose second was given two choices, to help make up for the difference in overall ability, although it had become painfully obvious, from the very first time that anyone tried to tackle Charley, that getting two picks instead of one would never adequately make up for the tradeoff.

Jack B. and Jack Scahill and fleet-footed Carl and I made up one team, that evening, and before kicking off we got together in a huddle.

"Be sure not to kick it to Charley," I cautioned Jack, who was as good a kicker as we had.

"How am I going to do that?" he retorted. "He'll probably get the ball, no matter where I kick it."

"Just kick it off to the side," Carl said. "Just kick it off to the side," he repeated, as if the repeated warning was necessary.

"Yeah," Jack answered with sarcasm, "and if I do, and he still gets the ball, then you make sure you're one of the first tacklers."

Carl looked away at that remark. He wasn't one of the biggest kids, by far. He certainly was one of the fastest, but being fast was not going to count much if Charley got his hands on the ball.

We lined up on somewhat of a straight line. And I noticed that Charley planted himself directly in the middle of the group of receivers. The air was warm, but a feeling of fear cooled my skin.

Once more I cautioned Jack, in a raised whisper, to be sure to kick the ball off to the side, hoping that maybe Jerry or Ron or Rich would receive the ball.

Jack merely glared at me.

Then he walked a few paces in back of the ball, which was being held by Carl on the big toe of his shoe, waited a few seconds, and then charged forward. His foot came through fluidly, and I watched the ball sail off to one side of the field, heading toward my twin brother Jerry. But just as I mentally thanked the gods of football seasons that the ball was going to be handled by a mere mortal, there went Charley, off to that side of the field, where Jerry gave way.

The four members of our kicking team had taken off as soon as the ball had been kicked, and I am sure that each one of us felt more at ease when we first saw the direction of the kick. But I could only guess how my teammates felt when they suddenly noticed how Charley was moving over to catch the ball. I gulped so hard that I thought my throat was going to collapse. Still, I kept running with the others, toward the ball carrier.

Charley could have chosen to run along the sideline, where it would have been a little easier, relatively speaking, for us to shove him out of bounds rather than having to tackle him. Tackling Charley was always painful.

But instead of heading toward one of the sidelines, here came Charley, thundering towards us, heading toward the middle of the field, the sounds of his feet, as they pounded the turf, sounding to our imaginations like the roar of the iron wheels of railroad engines.

I'll say this for our team: each of us still headed toward Charley, not giving way. Now was not a time for timidity. For foolhardiness, perhaps. But not for timidity.

The first time that I had ever tried to tackle Charley in a football game was a half-hearted attempt. It was merely a glancing blow, which Charlie merely shrugged off, as he went on to score a touchdown.

After that feeble attempt on my part, Charley took me aside and gave me a piece of advice that sounded dangerous.

"Don't try tackling from the side," Charley said to me. "You'll miss every time."

I looked up at him, at that massive figure towering at least two or three inches above me, his weight at least ten pounds more than what I carried, and wondered how it was that I could get into such terrible predicaments. My mouth must have remained open, hoping for some appropriate remark that I could come back with, but that is all it did, remain open, because Charley added to his advice.

"Come right at me," Charley said, and it didn't appear like there was anything sinister in his voice, or in his eyes. He wasn't challenging me. He was merely giving me advice about how to tackle a runner.

I wanted to say something like: "Are you crazy?" But I merely looked at him, hoping to see something in his face that would give me greater encouragement. But he wore a look of placidness, and I think it was that casual calmness in him that made me think that all things were possible. Was it possible for me to tackle him head on, and win? Even to survive?

It was a thought that carried itself over to this particular evening. Charley had gone on that previous week to score touchdown after touchdown, sometimes with him on my side, and sometimes with him on my brother's side. I cheered whenever he was on my side, and played scared out of my wits whenever he was on my brother's side. But not once had I attempted to carry out what Charley had advised me to do. Not once had I given myself up to that most dangerous of all events in sports: a head-on collision. I went on with my usual glancing blows that did nothing more than slow Charley up enough for the rest of my teammates to gang-tackle him.

But my fear rankled within me. It tormented me so much that sometimes I had trouble falling asleep. I wanted so much to put my fears to rest. I wanted to meet my fears head on, and meeting Charley head on was the only way I was ever going to be able to rid myself of the demons.

So here it was, a new game, and here came Charley, rumbling toward us, his head held slightly up so that he could survey the field. And there my team members headed, our puny bodies running towards Charley with not much enthusiasm, probably with heads slightly lowered so that we would not have to face the danger with full awareness of what might happen.

There was no diversion in Charley's route, no shifting of the hips that might tell us that he intended to swerve off to one side or the other. No. He came right at us, and at that moment I wouldn't have been able to tell you which one of my teammates was off to either side of me, so intent was I on making that tackle, of meeting both Charley and my worst fears head on. I had it in my head to do the unthinkable: tackle Charley.

On Charley came, and on I went, toward him, like a lamb heading to the slaughter. Foolishly so, I admit. And I think that the strangest thing that occurred to me, briefly anyway, was that there were no blockers in front of him. Not one of his own teammates was helping to clear the way for him. It was almost as if they, too, wanted to get out of the way of that dynamo of power. Or maybe it was that they had gone off to the side so that they could be witnesses to a possible violent act of recklessness.

The gap between Charley and me diminished quickly. In fact, it practically evaporated.

Here came Charley.

There went I.

Time was suspended. It hung in the air, as if it were waiting for that climatic day of Armageddon.

And then it happened. And to tell the truth, to this day I am still not sure just what happened that autumn evening. Over the years there were countless retellings of the event, and not all of the retellings seemed to jell with each other. Such is the nature of eyewitness accounts.

The only thing I know for sure is that darkness came instantly. The dim light of an autumn evening was obliterated as completely as if someone had immediately thrown me into an underground mine.

I felt no pain, at least not right away. There couldn't have been any immediate pain, as unconsciousness had come within a nano-second of time.

I was not aware of anything else. For me, time had taken a holiday. My existence had been given a vacation from reality.

They told me later that I lay there on the ground for at least five minutes. But boys being what they are, I'm not sure that there wasn't a bit of exaggeration in their accounting of time. But it also is altogether possible that they remembered all too well.

And then the light slowly began to come back, and a blurring of thoughts told me that I was still alive, although there were quite a few seconds when I would not have been able to tell you where I was. Or even who I was.

And then there was the pain. I first noticed it in my chest, but it didn't take long for me to realize that the pain went straight down my legs, so that even my toes tingled, a queer sensation.

I must have opened my eyes just then, for I could perceive shadowy figures bending over me, and I could hear voices, although it was almost impossible to distinguish what was being said, or whose voices they were. It was more like rumblings of soft thunder from off in the distance.

Then the words slowly became more distinct, and the cloudiness of the figures cleared up.

"Are you all right?" a voice asked. It was a dim voice, but it was still a voice.

"You okay, Larry?" Another voice.

Then some other voices came through to me, blurred though they were.

And it was then that I began to understand where I was, and what I had been doing. And I began to sit up, for I realized that I had been lying flat on my back. Well, at least I tried to sit up. But my arms, when I placed my hands on the ground as props, gave way, and I fell back.

I looked up, and all around, and faces appeared where before there had been blackness. Then, someone helped me to sit up, and all of them were talking at once, all of them asking me if I was okay.

I looked around, at the others' faces, hoping to discern from their looks just what had taken place. For a little while I was not even sure what all had taken place, what we had been doing.

Then I remembered that we had been playing football, and I recalled what I had been attempting to do.

Then I noticed him: Charley. He was stooping over, looking at me, and there was a big grin on his face. The football was still in his hands, cradled under one arm, as though he was still in the act of running with it.

Charley put one hand under one of my shoulders, and helped me to my feet. I managed to wobble into somewhat of an upright position, a sense of numbness, mingled with pain, taking control of my whole body. And he stood squarely before me, still towering over me, still with the football in his hands, still grinning.

"What happened?" I asked, shaking my head.

And Charley's grin spread across his face.

"You tackled me," Charley said, and the way that he said it, it was almost like he was announcing it to the world, like it was a life-affecting event.

"I tackled you?" I asked, incredulity filling my voice. He must be joking with me, I thought.

"You sure did," Charley answered, and this time it seemed that a sense of wonder and admiration filled his voice. In fact, it almost seemed as though Charlie was proud of what I had done.

And then there were claps on my back from the others, even from Charley's teammates, and words of congratulations from all of them. While the claps were welcome spiritually, I hurt terribly with each well intended blow.

"You're just making that up," I said to all of them, still not believing them.

"No, we're not," my brother Jerry said. "You tackled him. You really did." And the look of astonishment on Jerry's face said it all: I really had tackled Charley. I had tackled Charley Miller. And lived!

I shook my head, and looked up at Charley once more. He was still grinning. He was still holding the football.

I not only had tackled Charley, but I had tackled my fears, as well. And Charley was grinning about it. What other wonders of life still lay ahead of me?

I don't remember much more about that evening. Perhaps I even attempted to tackle Charley again, although I suspect that if I did, then it was probably with a little less bravado, for I'm not sure that the thin, wiry body that I possessed was up to another collision.

All I know is that for quite some time afterwards, there was a little more respect shown to me by the gang. And I probably swaggered a little, also, although it would have been with acute soreness in parts of my body, soreness that reminded me that fame often comes with a price.

CHAPTER TWENTY-SEVEN

All the Demons Arrive

"YOU GOT TO go over there! You got to go over there!" Jack repeated. He was out of breath. And his face was red. And there was such animation in his features that we all knew that something was up.

There was a large group of us, down in the underground fort: Rich and Charley and Carl and Don and Joe and Jerry and I. We had been planning our mischief for the night. It was well after seven o'clock, and all of us had even given up the chance to listen to *Amos and Andy,* one of our favorite radio programs. But this night was important enough for us to make sacrifices, so that we could get things in order. The only thing out of order was the fact that Joe was actually with us, at night, in our underground fort. If his mother were ever to hear of him being in our underground fort, especially at night, she would have made him stay at home for a month or longer.

Jack hadn't been there when we first sat down, but had shortly come down one of the tunnels so fast that I thought someone had been after him. Even in the pale light of the candles that stood in the niches of the walls, we could tell that something had happened to him.

He dropped down into a sitting position, against one of the earthen walls, his breathing labored, gasps of air from his throat sounding loud in the room. He bunched his knees together, and clasped them tightly, as though he was trying to find something solid to hold onto. He was shaking his head back and forth, apparently in an effort to understand something that might have been difficult to grasp. In fact, his whole body was shaking.

"What's the matter with you?" Jerry asked.

"Yeah," Don said, "you look like you've been running from something. What's wrong?"

All of us were staring at Jack. We could see that he was troubled by something, and all kinds of horrible thoughts went through my mind. Maybe someone had been terribly hurt. Or maybe someone in his family had died. Or maybe he had seen...Seen what? Whatever it was, he was upset.

"We went over there," Jack gasped. "You gotta go over there," he said in a shaky voice, his body still shaking. "We went over there. You gotta see it." He was clasping his knees so tightly that it looked as if he was trying to draw his body within itself, as though to make himself disappear.

"What are you talking about?" Joe asked in a challenging way. "Go where?"

Skepticism from Joe was expected.

Jack's eyes were staring straight ahead, not really looking at any one of us particularly. I could tell that he was trying to compose himself. He was still trembling slightly, but his breathing had begun to become a little more relaxed. Still it was obvious that he was struggling to find the words to tell us something, something of importance.

"Yeah, Jack. Go where?" I asked. "What do we have to see?"

Jack turned to me, then, and I had a feeling, from the way that he looked at me, that whatever it was that was bothering him was more directly related to me than to any of the others.

"I really didn't want to go, Larry," Jack managed. "Kenny made me."

"What do you mean, he made you?" Joe countered. "Made you do what?" Again there was skepticism in Joe's voice.

"He said that if I didn't go with him, the demons would come to get me. They're the bad ghosts. He said that if we saw them in the house, then they had to stay inside. But if we didn't go there to see them, then they could leave and come and get us."

"What house?" Don asked. "What demons?" It was obvious that Don was somewhat shaken by Jack's demeanor. I think all of us were.

"That old lady's house," Jack blurted, looking right at me. "Larry's friend. Old Lady Schweikert's house."

Suddenly all eyes were on me.

"The house I work at?" I asked. "My Mrs. Schweikert?"

"Yeah," Jack said almost in a whisper. His eyes were wide open, staring at me, yet not at me, as though his mind was looking at something beyond me, beyond anything tangible. Then, suddenly, his eyes focused on mine.

"And we saw them, Larry!" Jack went on. "The ghosts. The ones that Kenny said were there. We saw them!"

"Aw, go on," Joe said. "You're just making things up." But I could tell that Joe, even with all of his natural disbelieving attitude, was beginning to lighten his tone of voice.

"I don't care what you think," Jack retorted, looking right at Joe. "We saw them. Kenny told me that there were ghosts in her house. And I really didn't believe him. But we saw them. Kenny and I."

"Kenny's always saying things like that," I answered. But I didn't have a lot of confidence in my own words.

And I wasn't trying to put Jack down. I just wanted Jack to know that we didn't always believe everything that Kenny told us. But I really didn't believe myself when I said that. Whatever Jack had seen, there must have been something that had frightened him. Regardless of what Joe said, or thought, it was obvious that Jack hadn't made anything up. He looked really scared.

"Yeah," Jerry agreed. "Larry's been working for her all summer, and nothing has happened to him yet. And he's even been in her house."

"Well, anyway," Jack replied, looking at Jerry, "I don't care about that. We went over there, and I saw them. I really didn't want to go. That place gives me the spooks, even in the daytime. She's mean looking." And abruptly he looked up at me, and I could see that he did not want to get me upset.

"It's okay," I replied. "It's okay," and I reached over and gave his shoulder a gentle tap. I was hoping to calm him down.

With that, things grew quieter. In fact, it was deathly quiet. All of us were staring at Jack, waiting for him to get things together.

"Your friend," Jack said to me. "The lady over on Griswold," he added. And Jack's eyes grew wider, again.

"I know," I said. "You already told us. Mrs. Schweikert," I said as nonchalantly as I could.

Jack nodded his head vigorously up and down, several times.

"Kenny said that he saw ghosts in her house one other time," he said, his voice husky. "He said that they only come out around Halloween. And he made me go over there with him. I didn't want to go."

And Jack began trembling again.

"Go on!" Joe put in sarcastically. "Don't tell us you saw a ghost." Joe's tone was his usual cynical one. But it was a faint remark; it seemed to lack the strength of his usual scorn.

Again Jack nodded his head up and down. I didn't know about Joe, what he actually believed, but I just knew that Jack was not making all of this up. He wasn't putting on an act. He really was scared.

"We saw them," Jack replied.

"Aw, go on," Joe said again, in a mocking tone. "You guys are always making up stories. You're almost as bad as Larry."

But when I glared over at Joe, with my eyes narrowed, he shrunk back against the wall, a little. He was on dangerous ground, with that remark, and he knew it.

"You went over there tonight?" Rich asked.

"With Kenny?" someone else asked.

"Yeah," Jack replied. "But I really didn't want to go, Larry. I didn't," he protested again, looking directly at me.

"It's okay," I said. "So, what did you see?"

He looked at me, and then at the others, as though he was carefully weighing what he wanted to say.

"There weren't any lights on, on the bottom floor," Jack began. "We were hiding out in front, behind the bushes by her fence." And he looked away from me for a moment, and I could tell that he was trying to recall it as best as he could. Or maybe he was trying not to remember.

"So, what did you see?" Joe asked, again sarcastically. "I suppose the next thing you're going to tell us is that you saw ghosts."

"Drop dead, will you, Joe?" Rich put in.

Joe sat back then. He still had a regard for Rich's reputation as a typical redhead, a fighter.

Again Jack looked at all of us. It was easy to see that he already wished he hadn't started to tell us anything, that he wished he was someplace else.

"Just tell us what you saw," Charley said. Charley was not a real talkative person, so when he said something, we usually listened.

Jack looked over at Charley, and then nodded, realizing that no one was going to ridicule him if he said something that might sound stupid. Especially since Charley was the one who had asked.

"There was a light on in one of the rooms upstairs," Jack said. "I couldn't see any lights on the first floor. Just that light in the highest room. And at first there wasn't anything. Nothing was moving at all. There was just that one light on. And I told Kenny that we should go on home."

"Then what?" I asked.

"I'm not sure." He looked around, slowly, at all of us.

"All I know is that suddenly something went by the window upstairs. That top floor. And it went really fast. Then it came back again, only going the other way."

"Well, what'd it look like?" Jerry asked.

"Kenny said that it was a ghost. It was white looking, and it went fast, and sometimes it looked like it was turning around in circles." He paused for a moment. "Then it would go away, and then come back again. And then spin around again. And it was a woman. I mean, it looked like a woman, but it was weird looking, like maybe you could see through her, but you really couldn't. You know what I mean?"

Everyone was watching Jack. Even Joe was unusually quiet.

"Aren't there curtains, or anything up there?" I asked.

"Yeah," Jack answered, "but we could see really good. They aren't dark curtains, just kind of...you know, flimsy-like. Kenny wanted to stay and see if she would float out of the house. He said that if we waited till ten, we could see her come out. But I told him my mother would lick me good, if I stayed out past nine."

"I told you that old lady was weird, Larry," Joe said. "I told you the first time you told me that you were going to work for her. Everybody says that she's weird."

"So," I countered, "now you believe there *are* ghosts."

"I didn't say that," Joe retorted. "I only said that some people say that your old lady-friend is weird."

"Who says that?" I asked, looking directly at Joe. I was daring him to come up with a name. "Huh? Who says that?"

"Lots of people," he replied. But it was easy to see that he wasn't so confident about that charge.

"Name one," Jerry said. My brother was going to stand by me, even though he had never been over to Mrs. Schweiker's house. Even if I had been wrong, he would have stood by me, especially when it came to disputing with Joe about anything. Jerry and I had had our little fights, over the years. But everyone knew that if you picked on one of the Miller twins, you could expect that the other twin would pitch in and defend his brother.

Joe began to sputter something. We all waited. But he retreated into his place against the wall.

Then I turned back to Jack.

"Was it Mrs. Schweikert up there?" I asked.

"No," Jack answered so abruptly that all of us looked questioningly at him. "I mean, it couldn't have been."

"Why's that? How do you know?" Rich asked.

"Because whatever it was…I mean whoever it was, she was moving too fast. All I can say is that no human being, especially a woman, could move around that fast. It was like she was flying. She had her arms out in front of her," Joe said, and he spread his own arms out in front of himself, and waved them, as though he was trying to fly. And his breathing became so labored that I knew for sure that he couldn't be faking it.

"Maybe we should go over there and see," Rich put in.

Suddenly everyone turned to stare at Rich. If he had meant it as a joke, he sure didn't look that way. He was serious.

"I can't," Joe put in. "I told my mother I was going over to Polk, just to horse around. If she ever finds out that I came here instead, she won't let me out of the house for a year."

"It's too late to go," Don said.

That much was true. While we had free rein most nights, within reason, it was generally agreed upon that it was too late to do anything that night.

No one else said anything for a while. The silence was deadening, and the faint flickering light from the candles made the whole atmosphere gloomier than ever. Someone had to say something.

When the silence continued, I was just about to say something when it was broken by someone whom I didn't expect.

"I'd go," Carl said somewhat timidly, "but I want to listen to *The Green Hornet.*" Carl was usually as quiet about things as was Charley.

"Yeah," Don said, "I want to listen to it, too."

I couldn't blame them for hanging onto something that might give them an excuse not to go; timidity requires acceptable reasoning. Besides, there had been so many stories about the Schweikert house that if I hadn't gotten to know her so well, I would have found an excuse, also.

But now everything I had come to believe about her had been turned upside down and inside out. I didn't know what Jack and Kenny had seen, but I felt…well, like kind of sick inside. My stomach hurt, and I felt a little clammy, and the clamminess wasn't because of our sitting down inside an underground fort dug out of sand.

There was only one thing to do. It probably *was* too late to do anything about it that night, but there was always tomorrow.

"How about tomorrow night, then?" I asked suddenly. I looked around at each of the guys. I could see most of them squirming uncomfortably. When no one said anything, I put it to them directly.

"How many of you guys think that Jack here saw a ghost?" And when no one said anything, I nodded.

"I thought so. I'll tell you what, you guys. Tomorrow night, just after supper, we'll meet right here. And we'll go over to Mrs. Schweikert's house. All of us. It gets dark early, so no one will see us there. And we'll see if Kenny is just telling us things and if Jack here is just making all of this up, or if…" and I hesitated a moment…"there really is a ghost in the house."

No one said anything. They were all looking at each other. I knew, for sure, that they were trying to find a way to get out of going, but I also knew that not one of them wanted to be thought of as chicken.

No one said anything. But I had wanted to put it to them, make them know that I thought that Mrs. Schweikert was all right. So I had spoken up.

"I've been in that house two times already," I said, "and I never saw anything scary. She's really a neat old lady. She even had kids one time. And a husband. And I saw pictures of them. And she isn't mean, or anything like that."

I halted. They knew crunch-time was here. No one said anything.

"So!" I said. "Who's going to go with me tomorrow night?" And when still no one said anything, I gave them the big dare. "Whoever isn't chicken will be here. About seven o'clock. And if you don't show up, then everyone will hear who the scared ones are."

Again there was silence. I looked at everyone steadily, then nodded.

And I got to my knees and began to crawl up the main tunnel toward the night air. It was pitch-black dark when I got out. Only a few faint lights from the houses across Minnie Street gave any illumination. The sky must have clouded over, as I couldn't see any stars, and the moon was a pale imitation of one, hanging low over the eastern horizon.

The other guys were a little slow about crawling out of the fort. I knew that I had left something heavy for them, for there wasn't a boy in Germantown who wanted to be called a chicken.

I headed home slowly, and shortly I could hear Jerry running to catch up with me.

"Are you really going to go over there? At night?" Jerry asked, his breathing ragged.

"Sure," I answered. "And you'd better come with me."

"If Mom hears where we're going, we'll really be in for it," he cautioned.

I knew that Jerry wasn't really scared about going to the Schweikert house; he just didn't want to get into trouble with Mother. He'd already gotten into a lot of trouble with our parents simply because he had followed me in one foolish thing after another.

"Who's going to say anything to her?" I asked. And when there was no answer, I asked: "Are you?"

He shook his head. It was answer enough.

Kenny was sitting on his front porch, as Jerry and I turned in on Sixteenth Street. We could barely see his shadowy figure in the faint light that came from the Nelsons' living room window. I kind of expected him to be there.

I tried to ignore him, but just when Jerry and I were at the point where we would turn away from Kenny and head toward the back of our house, he yelled across to us.

"What'd I tell you guys?" he barked. "I told you she was spooky."

I wanted to say something. Anything. But I stood there, looking at the figure in the dark. Then I nudged Jerry, and we went around to the back of the house, disappearing into the night's shadows.

"She'll get you, Larry," Kenny shouted, his words hanging in the night air.

I turned to look back at him, wanting to say something in return. But I could see his figure heading around to the side door of his house.

"She'll get you," he called again, the words following me into our house, echoing in the night air.

And when I lay down that night, sleep eluded me for awhile. I was wondering, myself, just what I was getting into. And what it was that I was getting my twin brother into.

And when a bolt of lightning tore through the night sky, followed by a loud crack of thunder, I turned over on my side, hoping that Jerry was still awake so that I might find someone to bolster my courage. But if Jerry was awake, I couldn't tell. The darkness of the room was enough to spook anyone. And suddenly I felt all alone.

A picture of an upstairs room in the front of Mrs. Schweikert's house was all I could think of. That and the ghostly figure that allegedly flew back and forth in circles behind a thin curtain.

The darkness of night crowded in on me. And then the rain fell, pelting the window, the bullet-like hammering punctuated by more lightning, the flashes throwing strange intermittent light and darkness across the walls.

I pulled the quilt up to my neck, trying to retreat into the comfort of my bed. But there was no comfort to be found.

Chapter Twenty-eight

The Night the Monster Got Loose

T HE NEXT DAY, at school, time passed slowly. And there was an unusual quietness in the classroom. Was it because all of us boys, at least those involved in the business about Mrs. Schweikert, were pledged to silence? But that didn't account for the other boys and girls. Maybe it was simply a matter of expectations about Halloween. Whatever it was, it seemed weird.

As hard as it was to get through the day, it was especially hard to get through supper. Jerry and I must have been unusually quiet, for Mother kept looking at us. We tried to ignore her stares.

"What have you boys got going tonight?" Dad asked.

I must have jerked my head up too quickly, for Mother gave us a curious look, her head aslant. She was waiting for us to answer.

"We don't have anything going," I finally answered.

"Really?" Dad challenged. "Just before Halloween, and you're not planning something?" There was an impishness in his voice, most likely prompted by memories of his own youthful past Halloweens.

"I don't think so, Dad," I responded, maybe too quickly.

Mother glanced back and forth between me and Jerry, hoping, I am sure, to catch something that would allow her to pursue the matter. I avoided looking at Jerry, and was hoping he was wise enough to not look at me. I stared at the food on my plate.

"Boy," Dad spoke to my answer, "that really surprises me. Boys must really be different these days." And when that remark was accompanied by a knowing grin, I realized that he didn't suspect anything. He was just having a little fun with us. He knew that we wouldn't let the holiday go by without doing some kind of mischief, and we knew that he knew, and he knew that we knew that he knew. Are you confused by that kind of thinking? So am I. But, then, a convoluted way of thinking was part of being a boy.

I relaxed then, but only for a moment, for I noticed that Mother was still watching me closely. Oh, she looked once or twice at Jerry, but if she suspected that there was some deviltry planned, then she knew who probably was the instigator of it; thus I got more than my share of her attention. Well, to tell you the truth, I probably got what was rightly my share.

Even when Mother bowed her head to take up a forkful of food, her eyes peered out from under her brows, constantly looking at me, it seemed. It is horrible just how much a guilty conscience can grab hold of a person.

"We're just getting together at the ball field," Jerry said then. "We might play some football."

Jerry hadn't exactly lied. He hadn't said, for sure, that we were going to play some football. It was a clever diversion from the truth. We boys had a natural capacity for avoiding unpleasantness. And as for lying, boys learn early on that the facility for avoiding the truth is a marvelous devotion to expediency. It sure helps in the process of moving through boyhood.

Jerry's remark seemed to mollify Mother somewhat, although she still glanced my way, from time to time. And, of course, she had to make one of her admonitions: "Well, you just make sure that you don't get into any trouble. I don't want to hear from one of the neighbors that you've been doing anything that you're not supposed to do."

I looked up at her, which was expected.

"You hear me?" Mother demanded. Her voice was stern, and her eyes seemed to be boring right through me.

"Yes, ma'm," Jerry and I both said somewhat in unison.

There was no trouble that night with doing the dishes. For the first time in a long time, neither of us argued over who had to wash the dishes and who had to wipe them. We both hated washing them. I can't tell you why. Maybe it was just that neither job was worse than the other but that we both needed something to argue about. What was the good of having to do chores if one couldn't argue about them?

Anyway, we didn't dare rush out too quickly, for fear of making Mother even more suspicious. So we worked diligently, for a change, got the dishes put away, and then made our escape, while Mother and Dad were in the front room, listening to the news on the radio.

The war was intensifying in Europe, and we learned that the Japs, who had invaded China years earlier, had earned the titles of "Butchers." Thousands of Chinese had been murdered in horrible fashion, and the words *Bushido* and *samurai* quickly became part of our vocabulary, as well as names like Nanking and Manchuko and Shanghai. I had no real idea just where these places were; all I knew was that they were half-way around the world and they were places of unspeakable horror.

Of course we boys were not as much tuned in to the war as were our parents. We were still living in that innocent time of life when war was something that we played at, not something that was to be taken too seriously.

Night was falling quickly, and after we heard *The Lone Ranger* show starting, we could see that our parents' interest was diverted, so we hurried out the back door, through the back yard, and down the alley to Minnie Street. Jack and Joe were both heading in the same direction by the time we got to the street, so we waited for them.

"I sure hope no one tells on us," Joe said right off.

"Joe, you worry too much," Jack said, to which Jerry and I agreed.

Charley wasn't there, at the ball field, but Carl and Don and Rich were waiting for us.

"Charley isn't coming," Carl announced. "He says that his mother won't let him out after dark at Halloween time."

We all looked around at each other, our faces dim in the darkness of the night. We would miss Charley, but not too much, since Charley was quiet and had no real deviltry in him. He might have been the acknowledged leader of the sporting contests, but when it came to downright deviltry, everyone looked to me. It's not a reputation that I enjoy looking back upon, but it was deserved.

Dusk had taken hold of the evening. The sun had long before dipped below the horizon, leaving the sky a faint glow of orange merging into grayness. Before many minutes would pass by it would be nightfall.

A very faint light from the corner street light made all the others' faces a little clearer. I could see that they were waiting for me to give the signal to start. But it was apparent that not one of us had his heart in what we were about to do. I felt that probably I had the most face to lose, since I was the one who had dreamed up the whole thing. Part of me wished that I was more prudent about rashly making plans.

"Are you sure about what you saw, Jack?" The question came from Joe, who, I was sure, wanted desperately to find a reason not to go. "We're not chasing one of your made-up stories, are we?"

"Ask Kenny, if you think I made this up," Jack returned.

"You want to go and ask Kenny?" I challenged Joe. But there was no answer.

Everyone knew that Joe wasn't about to do that, since it would be the same as calling Kenny a liar. And no one who had any brains at all would ever do that. We all knew that Joe was looking for any excuse not to go. And we also knew that he didn't want us to talk it about that he was chicken. He was caught. No squirming out of it. Not if he wanted to hold his head up high.

So! It was settled.

I looked around at each of them, our faces grim in the darkness. Then I said: "Let's go." And with just a little hesitation, I started off. Pretty soon I could sense, more than I could hear, the others rushing to catch up with me. There were no voices, no murmurings at all, just the slight sound of soft feet moving through the grass and then out onto Eighteenth Street, heading north. It was not like us to be so quiet.

Mrs. Schweikert's house was only about four blocks from the ball field.

I noticed, as we made our way north, that many of the houses had their outdoor lights on, I suppose in hopes by the owners of deterring any vandalism that any children might have planned. Many nights preceding Halloween, the antics of the children in the neighborhood took on the semblance of amusing contests. Since most of the time the pranks played were of the harmless variety, there was little seriousness to it all. We even entertained a suspicion that many of the adults enjoyed the contests as much as did the children. We might have been wrong.

We moved slowly, often times our feet shuffling though the leaves that littered the road; we avoided the sidewalks, keeping ourselves away from the lights on the porches.

There was no feeling of enthusiasm in what we were doing that night. No whispers, no muted laughter. We were filled, instead, with a feeling of...well, dread. Halloween's season may have always been a matter of nights of fun and merriment in the past, but until this moment, we had always regarded ghosts and demons and witches as the characters in movies and comic books. They were real, to us, but only in an uniquely peripheral way. Still, it was true that we always held a distinct possibility that maybe they were more real than what we might have imagined. And certainly Kenny's tales had lent an absolute certainty to the matter.

When we got to Griswold, we found that it was better lit than was Eighteenth Street, so when we turned west we felt slightly more comfortable, although years later I discovered a verse in the Bible that was most appropriate to our intentions: "For everyone that does evil hates the light." If I had known that verse back then, I am sure that I would not have taken comfort in the increased light from the street lamps.

I looked back, and I noticed that we were no longer moving in a close huddle, but had become a line of stragglers. Either the boys were relaxing in the comfort of the increased lighting, or they were showing a reluctance in moving toward the night's operation.

"Bats!" someone uttered softly, and all of us looked up.

Sure enough, in the shadows of the night, bats flitted back and forth, zigzagging through the night sky in their search for insects. Dad always told us that the bats were beneficial, and I suppose they were, but this particular night they seemed like omens of danger. It seemed, to me, as though they brought an appropriate sense of what Halloween was all about, and I immediately thought of Count Dracula. I shuddered at the thought. And I noticed that all of us seemed to have hunkered down as we walked, hoping that the bats would make insects their targets rather than some small, scared boys. We had heard stories of bats flying into people's hair. Were the stories true? We did not want to find out.

At the next corner we stopped. We could see Mrs. Schweikert's house and its huge yard, just ahead of us. No porch light shone. There were no yard lights. Only the light of two widely separated street lamps gave the scene any illumination, and the illumination was softened considerably by the skeleton-like branches of the trees that lined the street as well as the bushes and trees of Mrs. Schweikert's yard.

I moved a few steps closer to where the wrought iron fence began. The others had moved close to me, so close that I could hear their ragged breathing.

"It looks spooky," Joe whispered, his faint words seeming to hang heavy in the cool night air.

"Quiet!" I whispered angrily. "You want to let her know we're out here?"

But I had to admit that it did, indeed, look spooky. It was the same house and the same yard that I had become very familiar with, yet there was something different about it all. The darkness of night can do that to the environment.

I knelt down on my knees, and the others did the same. Peeking over the fence, I watched the house for any movement, but the dining room was in complete blackness, and I couldn't see any light from where the kitchen would be. In fact, the only light that I could see was maybe from a small table lamp in the living room, in the front of the house, and that light was feeble, at best.

Up above, the windows on the second floor were also dark. No lights there. Not only was it dark, but it seemed-at least to me-forbidding. And foreboding. I shivered, but not from the night air.

Then I turned my attention to the top floor, the floor where Jack had said he and Kenny had seen the ghosts. But again there was nothing. Just darkness. The shadows of night seemed to cover the top floor like a shroud. It all seemed so...well, lifeless.

I could just barely make out the windows of the top story. In my mind I could recall them: three tall windows that stood side by side in their respective gables, the windows and gables occupying most of the front of that story. But they, too, were dark, as though they had shrunk back into the darkness of the house.

After a few minutes, we made our way slowly, creeping alongside the fence, our knees scraping the sidewalk, until we reached the gate that I had always used when entering or leaving her yard. Here I stopped, the others gathering themselves close behind me.

"It doesn't look like anyone's there," Jerry whispered, his breathing close to the back of my neck. He snuggled closer to me, if that was at all possible. I think he was hoping that he was right. And I couldn't blame him, for some part of me also hoped that our trip would be futile.

I looked over my shoulder, and could just barely make out the shadowy forms of the rest of the boys. It seemed as though they were all trying to hug the fence; they were huddled close together.

Bathed in the weak light of the street lights, the house appeared like a spectral three-story ship. Shadows moved across it as the branches of nearby trees waved in the night breeze, the light from the street lamps flickering across the darkened house.

I felt somebody clutch my arm.

"You were in that house?" came a whispered voice.

It was Don. All I could do was nod. I knew that the house must have seemed incredibly strange to them, but, realistically, to me it seemed unbelievable that there would be anything about the house that would be amiss or evil. While I had never been in either of the upper stories, I had been in much of the first story: the kitchen, the dining room, the living room-library. I had shared the pictures of her family. I had been given a book to read. Yet the question was timely.

I didn't answer Don. There was no need to. They all knew that this particular night made things different, even for me.

We waited there, crouched low below the top of the fence. For as long as three or four minutes we crouched, waiting for...what? A thousand thoughts flooded my mind, and all of them scary enough to make me wonder why I was where I was.

Maybe, I thought, Jack had made up the story, after all. I turned to look for him. He was just off to my right. Even in the dim light of the street lights I could pick out his face, and I stared into his eyes, hoping that he could see me staring at him.

"I didn't make it up," Jack whispered to me. He must have read my mind.

"I don't see anything," I whispered.

"I don't, either," came his whispered husky reply.

"Maybe she isn't home," Jerry whispered, and I think that Jerry was hoping he was right. Probably all of us were hoping the same thing. We were there because we wanted to see something scary. But probably not one of us really wanted *it* to happen, whatever that *it* might turn out to be.

"Maybe she's dead," Joe said then.

I couldn't tell if Joe was trying to make a joke, or not. So I looked back at him, but it was impossible to see his face clearly, as he had shrunk into the shadows behind my brother, who was still squatting right behind me. He must have noticed me looking at him, for his shadowy figure suddenly turned away, making it look as though he wanted to see if there was anyone behind him.

"Don't say anything like that," Carl said then, and there was enough anger in his voice to make Joe shut up.

We stayed where we were, our eyes peering over the fence, at the house, waiting for something to happen. Waiting for anything that might keep us there longer, or that might make us wish we hadn't come in the first place. Or that might cause us all to bolt.

"How much longer are we going to stay?" Jerry whispered. I knew that the question was directed to me.

The night shadows had crept over us, over my soul, so to speak. And there was a slight whistling of a breeze that seemed to speak words of caution.

"Hey," came a booming voice suddenly, so suddenly that it was like a bolt of thunder. "What are you kids doing over there?"

At first I couldn't place the voice with anyone, so quickly had it come. I couldn't even begin to place it. I looked all around, but nothing registered. And I noticed that all the others were trying to locate the voice. We were still all huddled together, below the upper bar of the fence.

"Didn't you kids hear me?" came the voice again. It was a bold voice, one with authority.

This time I knew where the voice was coming from. It had come from across the street, and I turned in that direction. And suddenly I wished I hadn't.

There, standing on the far curb, in the weak light from the nearby street lamp, was the biggest man I had ever seen in my life. I mean, he was huge. Not just large, or tall. But huge! And in the darkness of the night, with the street lamp failing to reveal much of his features, it was like looking at a monster from one of our B movies. It seemed almost as if his gigantic figure reached up into the branches of the tree that he stood under.

I was paralyzed. My heart thumped so hard that I thought my chest would explode. Someone grabbed the back of my jacket, and I almost jumped.

The man stepped off the curb then, and stood peering into the blackness of the night, and although the night was dark, it seemed as if the man must have special vision, for he was looking right where we were squatting.

"I'm not going to ask you boys again," came the voice, thundering much like I would have expected it to sound. It was a deep voice, almost like that of the character in the serial *The Shadow*.

I could hardly move, I was so scared. In fact, I was so scared that I no longer looked around at the others, to see how they were reacting. I didn't even give them another thought. My eyes were riveted on the man. On the huge monster.

And then he was moving, slowly, toward us, with deliberate steps, as though each step was meant as a warning of horrendous things to come. So deliberate were the steps that I immediately associated the walk with that of the monster *Frankenstein*. I know. I know. The name *Frankenstein* really was that of the doctor who created the monster, but at that moment I wasn't into making any kind of distinction. To every one of us kids, the monster's name was *Frankenstein*, and at that moment we were staring at one who very clearly resembled that terrifying being.

There were a couple of tall men in our neighborhood, even a couple of men who had large physiques. But this creature stood much taller, and was much larger. Even in the weak light from the street lights he stood huge, and menacing. And the shadows of night made him seem even more menacing.

I finally had sense enough to look around at the others. I didn't know about the others, but I was shaking. We were all still in our crouching position, our bodies leaning against the wrought iron fence, hidden in the shadows. But apparently we were not invisible to this terrifying figure.

"Oh, Lord," I could hear one of the others say, the voice a whispery, hoarse sound. And I was sure that he was speaking for all of us.

The man had stopped in the middle of Griswold Street. It was obvious that he was peering at us, or rather at the darkness that we were crouched in. Then he took another deliberate step, and I could see that he was trying hard to make out just who we were. It was then that I realized we couldn't be fully seen. Crouched as we were along the darkness of Mrs. Schweikert's fence line, we probably made it difficult for him to pick us out individually.

He had stopped again, about midway between the middle line of the street and the near curb. He was no more than twenty feet away. There he stood. I should say, rather, that there he loomed, for there was a threat in his stance, in his hugeness. His long arms hung down along his sides.

"I'm not going to ask you again," he boomed, and he took another deliberate step toward us, as though this time he did not intend to stop.

I think I jumped to my feet faster than I had ever done so in my life, and the others were not much slower, and there was a confusion of colliding bodies and voices, like the famous *Keystone Cops*, as we took off, running east, toward the corner, and toward safety, I hoped. I know our steps sounded loud in the night, and I could hear Joe screaming, but I couldn't tell exactly what it was that he was screaming.

Our pounding footsteps sounded thunderous, and I wondered if people from the houses that we passed would turn out to discover the reason for the noise. But even louder was the horrible noise of the huge steps being made by the creature, who, I was sure, was following us. I was sure that at any moment he was about to pounce upon me, and the noise of his heavy steps spurred me on to even greater speed, if that was possible.

I was gasping for air. But I did not pause.

At one point, just as we turned the corner, at Eighteenth Street, I looked back, but I couldn't see anyone. If he was as fast as he was big, I figured that we didn't have a chance. Our breaths were ragged, and some grunts of fear replaced sensible words. It seemed as if all of us were yelling something, but the words were inaudible, mixed as they were in each other's voices. And while I couldn't distinguish what was being said, I recognized fear in the voices.

I only had one thought, and that was to put as much distance between the man and me. Never in my life had I run with so much fear chasing me. The others-I could tell by the faint sounds of their voices trailing behind me-were laboring. And I might have been glad to glory in the extra speed which I possessed, but this was no race for pride, for personal glory. It was abject fear that was propelling me.

Only Jerry and Carl were keeping up with me.

Much later, when I had the luxury to look back upon it all, I wondered if any of the neighbors whose houses we passed were alarmed by the sounds of our passage, but at the time I didn't give one thought to them; I only wanted to get back to the fort at the ball field, where I felt we could breathe easier.

My lungs felt like they were bursting, and there were cries coming from the others. Jerry was close by, as I expected him to be. But I realized some of the boys were having trouble staying up with the rest of us. So I slowed down a little, letting Rich and Jerry and Jack pass me. Then followed Don and Joe, laboring in their breathing as they finally caught up.

"The fort," I yelled to them. "Go to the fort."

And I took off again, looking at the dark figures ahead of me.

When we reached Minnie Street and turned toward the field, I slowed down, letting the others catch up. By this time, no one was saying anything. I think it would have been impossible for any of us to speak, for I thought my thumping heart was up in my throat, and I was sure that I wasn't alone with that kind of feeling.

When we got to the ball field, we threw ourselves to the ground, next to our underground fort. Our ragged breaths were the only sounds I heard for a couple of minutes, and I noticed each of us looking at each other, as though we were all trying to find comfort in being in a group, albeit a very scared group.

We had our eyes toward Eighteenth Street, the street that we had just come down. Each of us, I am sure, was wondering if the man had followed us. Even in the faint glow of the streetlights it would have been possible to see someone that huge, if he really was there. But there was no one there. The street was empty, eerily empty. It was as though the night's darkness had swallowed up all life.

We lay sprawled on the cold ground, and it seemed as though ten or fifteen minutes passed before we could breathe easier.

No one mentioned going down into the fort. Even with candles lit, the atmosphere would have been too scarily dark, and none of us was ready for anything that might darken the night even more.

The silence was unsettling. A night bird squawked, its lonely cry a plaintive sound in the dark night. I shivered, but not from the cool air.

Finally, Don broke the silence.

"Who was that?" he asked, and it wasn't difficult to sense the terror in his voice.

"I never saw anyone like that before," Jerry said. "That was like looking at a…"

"Frankenstein," I said, filling in the space.

"He was bigger than Frankenstein," rejoined Don.

"Do you think he recognized us?" Rich asked. "That isn't more than a block and a half from where I live."

"Mine, too," Carl said. Carl only lived a block away from Rich, so both of them lived nearby to Mrs. Schweikert's house and, consequently, nearby to the house of the huge man.

I could understand them worrying, for if Rich and Carl lived that close to the man, like they said, then they stood in greater peril than did the rest of us. For even if the man didn't get a hold of them, there always was the possibility that the man would report them to their parents, and...well, the possibilities were endless and not any of them promising.

It was difficult for me to understand how Carl and Rich could live so close to the huge man and not actually realize him, or to know about him. Such a huge man would stand out. Yet Carl and Rich apparently didn't recognize him.

"That guy gave me the creeps," Joe said. And this time there was no one who would argue with Joe. Obviously the man gave every one of us the creeps.

"Weren't you scared, Larry?" Joe asked then. And everyone turned to look at me, but even in the cover of the darkness of night, I wasn't about to try to fool any of them.

"You darned right," I answered. "That man was huge. I never saw anyone like him before, in my whole life. Did you see those arms, and those shoulders? They were like a monster's arms!"

The truth of the matter was that, even in the light from the street lights, it would have been impossible to pick out such details. But our frightened state may have given way to us imagining much more than what we had actually seen. And the more that each of us added to it, the more scared we became. And the bigger the man became. Maybe. But just maybe, the man really was as huge as we were making him out to be. Just maybe.

"Did you ever see anyone like that when you were working for her?" Don asked. "I mean, if there is someone that big near there, you must have noticed him."

"I never saw anyone like that, ever," I replied. And the question caused me to stop and think about the times that I had worked at Mrs. Schweikert's house, and about how I might have been under the huge man's observation. I shivered at the thought.

"Don't ask me to go there again," Jack said. "Last night with Kenny was bad enough. But tonight..." And his hanging thought was left there for each of us to think about.

We had gone there to look for ghosts and witches. But I couldn't put Mrs. Schweikert together with ghosts and witches, and I didn't want to, either. But this huge man, this monster of a man, added a new dimension to it all. We had all seen him, so it wasn't just our imaginations. He was real, all right. But just how real, it was hard to say, especially when one considers a young boy's ability to inmagine.

"I'm heading home," Carl said, and he moved off, Rich tailing along behind Carl.

"Me, too," Don returned.

Each of us took our own paths, toward our homes, toward the most secure places where we could wrestle with our thoughts. No one even said goodbye.

And that night, in our bed, Jerry and I lay quietly. There was no conversation. Each of us was locked into the events of the night.

I looked up, through the window, but some clouds covered the sky; I couldn't see any sign of the stars or the moon. And the expected warmth of the sight of Venus was absent, leaving even the universe in grave solemnity.

It was just as well. The gloomy atmosphere matched my thoughts. I figured that I was being punished, and it was appropriate. I didn't know just exactly what it was that I was being punished for, but considering all the troubles I had been in during my days, there seemed to be sufficient reason. Justice was not always denied.

CHAPTER TWENTY-NINE

Halloween and Its Goblins

T HURSDAY ARRIVED. IT was Halloween. It was, for some kids, perhaps the biggest holiday of the year. The incident of the huge man paled as the excitement of the holiday grabbed hold of us.

Supper was a hurried affair. Mother didn't even complain when Jerry and I rushed through it all. And she even relieved us of our duties with the dishes. Was it possible that she realized just how important the night was to us? Or was it possible that she merely wanted us out of her hair? It might have been a combination of both.

It was just after six o'clock, so it was already dark enough to take part in the great adventure.

Up in our room, we pulled on the old sheets that Mother had set aside. Of course they were sheets that had not only seen their best days, they had seen their worst days, as well. I might have called them white sheets that were fitting for ghosts, but to tell you the truth, not all the bleach in the world would have given them true whiteness. They were actually gray in color. But they would do.

Each of the two sheets had been given small slits for our eyes and nose and mouth, and we had even given the eye-slits somewhat of a spooky look by blackening the edges of the slits with coal dust. Cuts along the sides allowed us freedom with our arms and hands.

Jerry and I each had a large paper bag, which we hoped to fill two or three times before the evening was over. Optimism and greed reigned.

Thus costumed, and armed with our paper bags, we ran down the stairs and out the front door, our noisy footsteps enough to cause Mother to yell out something of a warning, but we were in too much of a hurry to acknowledge it.

Already the streets were filled with cowboys and Cinderellas and monsters and space people. It is curious to me just how clever were so many of the mothers, for most of the costumes were homemade, and cleverly so. And when it was apparent that so many others had gotten a head start, we ran down the steps and raced next door to the Deacons.

Halloween had officially started.

We did not expect much from Mrs. Deacon, as we knew that she did not have much money to spend, but the Miller twins were expected, so we did our duty. Sure enough, we each got an apple, and Jerry and I were polite enough to thank her in as gracious a manner as we could muster.

Then it was off to the races, so to speak. Jack and Joe were waiting for us when we came back down the Deacons' steps, and we all made our way south on Sixteenth Street, hitting each house with enthusiasm, and sharing information with the other goblins about which houses were giving out the best rewards. There were a few houses we simply ignored, not just because they were unlikely to give out acceptable treasures. We did not want to bother Mr. Warner, for example, for he was fighting a serious illness. And quite obviously we did not go to Mr. Schrader's house, for the incident of the goat and the shotgun caused me to give it wide berth.

But for the most part, we were able to reach enough homes so that our treasures mounted up enough that we had to run home, at least twice, to dump our treasures on the kitchen table. And Mother was always there, ready to spirit away most of the treasures so that we wouldn't eat too many at any given time.

Dutifully Marilyn had taken Sandra to several houses, and obviously their treasures did not amount to very much, although Sandra seemed happy. Of course Jerry and I would share our bounty with them, as well as with David, who was much too young yet to participate.

Laughter and unbridled excitement filled the air, and there was an eagerness among all the kids to compare success. And even a cool night air, a promise of the coming of winter, could not dampen the enthusiasm and joy that we knew.

Oh, Halloween! A night of acceptable thievery! How wonderful! But eventually time took its toll on our exuberance, and the streets became less crowded as the beggars returned to their homes. Halloween was rapidly drawing to a close. Like all good things, and bad things as well, there was an ending. And the moment that the truth of it hit me, it seemed as though a cruelty had struck; another wonderful part of life had passed us by.

The next day, in school, there were wild reports of minor vandalism supposedly caused by those who dared to brag about such things, but we all took those reports for what they really were: part fiction, part truth. There was nothing wrong with exaggerating things. It was an acceptable part of boyhood.

"Did you hear what happened to Old Man Burmeister?" Jack whispered to me, leaning away from his desk.

"I had been studying my geography, and was just about to see if I could locate Bolivia on the map in my book. It probably was just as well if I could have a conversation with Jack, since my attempt to locate Bolivia was not going too well. It didn't sound exactly European, but I had tried diligently to put it on that continent. Bulgaria, I found. But Bolivia? They had to be close together, didn't they?

"What happened?" I asked, my curiosity aroused. Some of the other kids were trying to catch what it was that we were whispering about; their heads were leaning slightly toward us. Anytime a kid whispered in class, heads turned; it just had to be something important, or so everyone would think.

"He had a lot of manure dumped on his front porch," came the whispered reply.

"No kidding?" I replied in as hushed a voice as I could manage, snickering at the thought of what might have happened. Old Man Burmeister was a real hard-nosed man. He had a lot of children, including five sons, but none of the boys ever played with us. Four of the boys were much older than we were, but one of them was about our age, yet the boy never had much to do with us.

Their house, not more than a block and a half away from our house, was a huge structure. It was painted dark gray, and I always thought that the color matched the nature of the occupants. The *old man* was a construction worker, and his physique showed it, as he was big, and muscled. And his face was always grave. He had that kind of swarthy complexion that I always expected of a construction worker.

Mrs. Burmeister was short and somewhat stout. She always wore her hair tied in a severe bun on top of her head. And her dresses, gray or black in color, came almost to the ground. And in all my time, I could never remember her ever saying anything to me. Was it taciturnity? Or quiet hostility? I did not know.

I can only remember one time when I was ever in their yard. I had met the youngest boy-he was about a year younger than was I-and for some reason or another, I had found myself in his yard, sitting on the steps of their huge porch, talking about things that most boys talk about, which probably was about nothing of importance. He didn't seem like he was happy, and he was obviously pleased that I had shown him some friendliness.

We couldn't have been on those steps for more than five minutes, when his mother came out to see what was going on, and just who it was that was talking with her son. And after he had introduced me to her, she had scowled at us, and then told the boy that there were some chores he had to do and that he'd better get at them before his father got home.

It was the only time that I ever heard her voice. There was nothing mean about it, but one could expect that there would be no effort to argue with her.

The boy and I never talked again, and since the boy attended a Catholic school, there were no connections in that regard. He was just a part of the neighborhood, like a lamp post, or a curb.

All of us boys gave wide latitude to the house whenever we were in the vicinity, especially whenever the *old man* was around. He only had to look briefly at us to make us want to leave them alone. And so we did, leave them alone.

"Who put the manure there?" I asked Jack.

"I did," Jack said with a big grin. "Old Man Thompson had some that he uses for fertilizer in his garden."

"Did you boys finish your lesson?" came a familiar voice, in a very stern tone.

Miss Penzenhagen was standing in front of the class, her arms crossed, her face questioning and challenging. And she was looking at both Jack and me. How could a teacher look at two boys at the same time? It must have been some special kind of talent that only teachers possessed.

"No, ma'm," Jack replied.

"No, ma'm," I echoed.

There were snickers from most of the kids in class.

"Maybe you'd like to stay after school and finish the lesson," she suggested.

That was enough to make us get back to our books, and me to my futile search for Bolivia. But I smiled at Jack before I did, to let him know that I was pleased at what he had done to the Schultz house.

Manure, huh? It wasn't the first time someone had done the manure bit. But to have the nerve to hit the Burmeister house was a wonderful thing. It was as if Jack had done it on behalf of all of us.

Later, at recess, I had been made to promise Jack that I wouldn't tell anyone else about what he had done. If word had ever gotten out, he feared, there might be all heck to pay. And no one wanted to be party to anything that old man Burmeister might take it upon himself to do. As far as we knew, he wasn't just an old crank, he was mean.

"I promise," I said. And I meant it, although there was an understanding upon both our parts that I would pass the story on to my brother. The news was just too sensational to keep entirely to myself, and the closeness that I had with my twin brother meant that anything I knew just automatically would be shared with Jerry.

"You want to try and see who that huge man was?" I asked Jack. Joe and Jerry had moved in to sit with us against the wooden fence of the playground.

"Who are you talking about?" Jack asked.

"You know who I mean," I said. "That huge guy. The one who looks like Frankenstein."

"You mean the guy over by Mrs. Schweikert?" Jack asked.

I nodded.

"You mean, go over there again?" Joe asked in disbelief.

"Tonight," I said simply.

"You're nuts," Joe said.

No one said anything else, for a few moments. Then Jack spoke up.

"Why not?" Jack said. "I'd like to see him again."

Okay, Jerry?" I asked. "Want to go?"

"I guess so," Jerry replied. Jerry didn't sound very enthusiastic about it, but I knew that he would go. He wouldn't back down from something that involved all of us boys.

"You're all nuts," Joe put in. "You know that? You're all nuts."

"What's the matter, Joe?" Jack asked. "Are you scared?"

Everyone looked at Joe, to see how he would react. It was one thing to be chicken. But it was another thing to admit it to the guys. I knew that Joe wouldn't back down. We all knew that even a guy like Joe had to face up to things in order to remain part of the gang. And I was enjoying Joe's discomfort. Perverseness was not just an adult trait; it is inherent, I now believe.

No one said anything for a few moments. And Joe knew we were all looking at him, waiting for an answer. He was looking at the ground, but the ground wasn't of any help. Finally he looked up, uncomfortable but not to the point of backing down.

"I'll go," Joe said.

There was something like a collective sigh.

"Right after supper," I said. "We meet right after supper," I repeated. "Down at Eighteenth Street. Okay?" I asked.

There were nods all around.

Supper was usually eaten around five-thirty in most of the homes. I can't say why there was such conformity. But there was, which made it convenient for us boys to plan things.

I was worried that Jerry and I might have a tough time getting away, since we had been out somewhat late the night before, on Halloween. But it was Friday, which meant that there was no school the next day. And besides, both Mother and Dad were preoccupied with something going on over in Europe. Some guy by the name of Edward R. Murrow was giving out nightly news broadcasts, and it seemed as if all the adults in our neighborhood were gathered around their radios.

As I learned much later in life, Edward R. Murrow was much more than just a news broadcaster. He actually flew missions over Europe with our pilots, and he lived through much of the German bombardment of England. Thus anything that Murrow had to say, or what Churchill, England's Prime Minister, had to say, was of great importance. And the mood changed whenever the results came over the airwaves, for everyone learned just valiant were the pilots of the RAF(Royal Air Force) of Great Britain. Ol' Adolf was getting what was coming to him, although at a horrendous cost of young men's lives.

I think that almost every radio in Germantown was tuned in to listen to Murrow's reports. I know that the few times that I heard him left me with a feeling of terror and wonder, for Murrow spoke with urgency and seriousness. And I began to understand that war is both urgent and serious. It had no relationship with the little battles that we played at with snowballs and chestnuts.

There were five of us, when we gathered that evening. October was giving way to November and left us with a quickly disappearing sun. Night had come quickly and had pulled a cloud of darkness with it, lending the proper kind of atmosphere appropriate for perilous adventures.

It was a little chilly that night. Don arrived. I had let Don know what we were going to do and he had reluctantly agreed to come along. I had wanted to call Rich and let him know what we were going to do, but that would have meant using the telephone, and since everyone was on a party-line in those days, it was not wise to make our plans available to the general public, as it was well known that people listened in on other people's calls. But Rich was there, word having come to him somehow.

We stood around for a few minutes, shivering in the night air. I wasn't sure if it was the air that caused the shivering or if it was the knowledge that what we were about to do bordered on the downright stupid, if not dangerous.

"Boy," Joe said, "if my mother ever finds out what we're doing, she'll make me stay inside for a month."

"Who's going to tell?" I asked. There was comfort in knowing that none of us would ever talk about such important plans, since revealing the plans would have meant punishment for all of us. We could trust each other, but not anyone outside our gang.

No one said anything else. So, after looking around at everyone, I moved off, and the others followed. Jerry quickly fell in line, alongside of me.

It was a quiet and somber group that trudged toward Griswold Street. Our feet shuffled through the leaves that littered the road, causing a haunting, rustling sound.

By the time that we got to Griswold and turned west, it was real dark. Night had settled in, and the silence that we moved in was strangely uncomfortable.

Shadows of tree branches flickered back and forth in the faint light of the street lamps. Against the feeble light from the lamps, the almost-leafless branches of the trees looked like long, crooked, spiny fingers. And bats were zipping back and forth in the night air, giving the atmosphere its proper scariness, their zigzagging bodies stark against the feeble light from the streetlamps. How proper, I thought, to have their presence on such a night!

At the last corner before we got to where Mrs. Schweikert's house was, we stopped, all of us crouching down behind a large bush. We each had our eyes on the three houses that sat across from that of Mrs. Schweikert's. The trees that bordered the sidewalk on that side of the street looked like blackened sentinels, their upper branches now mostly empty of their leaves, appropriately spooky looking.

"Do you see anything, Larry?" Jerry asked, his voice barely more than a murmur. It seemed as if his mouth was right next to my ear. I could feel his breath on my neck.

"Nothing," I whispered. But I didn't move. And neither did the others. It seemed like an eternity, waiting there. But I'm sure that it was only a matter of a minute or so.

"Maybe he's waiting up on his porch," Joe said.

No one replied. There was too much truth in that possibility. So we waited, hoping that we couldn't be seen by anyone who might be on watch. The minutes passed slowly, finally there was nothing left to do but to get it over with. We wanted to see the man once again. We wanted to prove to ourselves that he was everything that we had thought him to be. And the only way to do that was to hope that he really was there. But there also was a great fear that he was really what we remembered him to be: a horrifying monster. I wondered, at the time, if I were the only one with such conflicting thoughts.

"Let's get closer," I said, and I moved around the bush and began to walk, very slowly-or was it a shuffle?-toward Mrs. Schweikert's house. And then we reached the eastern edge of Mrs. Schweikert's yard, the wrought iron fence marking a boundary to the property.

I stopped abruptly, and dropped down to a crouch alongside the fence, and the others dropped down behind me. But our eyes weren't on Mrs. Schweikert's house; they were on the shadowy area across the street, where it was presumed, the huge man lived. But nothing moved, and the wind had died down, so that the black branches of the trees were silent and still.

Then I peeked over the fence, and up toward Mrs. Schweikert's house, where I noticed a light turned on somewhere on the second floor, its weak glow just barely visible through the front windows. Had it been on before? Or had it just been turned on?

Someone whispered something, and one of the others whispered for him to shut up.

Just then another light came on, in the third floor, and this light was much brighter. It was bright enough so that we could clearly see the filmy curtains of the window in one of the cupolas.

"Someone's up there," Jack said then, his whisper barely audible.

"No kidding," I hissed sarcastically.

We waited a few moments, and when there didn't seem to be any visible movement up there, we crawled further alongside the fence. A lone hoot owl made his presence known, and the sound was enough to make a boy shake. And I shook.

Then a door opened on a house across the street. There was a quick light, and then a hard closing of the door, and the porch of that house was once again swallowed in the night.

Jerry grabbed my shoulder, his fingers tightening hard, and I tried to shake his hand off, but he was persistent. I think he was letting me know that he had seen the light and had heard the door close.

"I know! I know!" I whispered. "You're hurting me." And his hand fell away.

The rest of them also must have noticed the light and the closing of the door, for there was a restiveness that swelled its way forward. A few whispers, a few fears exposed-and we all threw ourselves down onto the ground, hugging the sidewalk. I wanted to bury myself beneath the sidewalk, I was that scared.

Had someone been alerted? Was there someone on that porch, watching us? Was it even possible that someone could see us crouching in the black shadows of the fence line?

I kept my eyes on the house where the door had closed. It was hidden deep in the darkness; I could barely make out the faintest of light from within the house.

There didn't seem to be anything moving over there, but it was impossible to tell for sure, it being so dark. And it wasn't just the darkness of night, but more like a darkness of the soul.

Then there was a flicker of a light, and I could tell immediately what it was. Someone was lighting a pipe. Heaven knows I had watched my dad light his pipe a number of times.

It was eerie to watch the flame of the match as it moved toward the bowl of the pipe, and then the match was snuffed out, and there was a barely noticeable glow of a lit pipe. I knew that a hand was holding the bowl of the pipe, and the wondering of who it was made me shrink into as small a form as I could present.

Was the man watching us?

Then a movement! A shadowy form slowly walking down the steps of the porch, the pipe jiggling with the movement of the form, its glow like a ghostly ember floating in the darkness. But that burning glow was much higher off the ground than what we might have expected it to be. And all of a sudden, I realized who it was.

It was him! Our Frankenstein. Huge! Much larger than what I remembered, as if the shadows gave him greater size. And as he moved slowly down the sidewalk and into the light of a nearby street lamp, it was then possible to see the pipe itself, clenched in his mouth. And who could tell what the teeth were like that were clenching the pipe. Why, they probably were like the fangs of some gargantuan beast.

He stopped. He was just standing there, alone at the edge of the street, a huge form dominating the entire environment, it seemed. And now, in the glow of the pipe, smoke drifted upward into the night air, like vapor from a demon. It curled upward and then lost itself in the darkness.

I lay still, the cold sidewalk creating greater discomfort to an already shivering boy. If I could have prayed, I probably would have asked that benevolent spirit to whisk all of us out of there, like the magician that makes the beautiful girl vanish.

But prayer was not on my mind, just then. Fear had grabbed a fierce hold of me. And besides, looking back on it all and knowing just what kind of a boy I had been in those youthful years, I can't imagine that any God, or any holy spirit or angel, would have deigned to grant me any relief. In fact, it was more likely that He would have seen a reason to let things work themselves out on their own, in, perhaps, a logical way of demonstrating to me just what happens to young boys who deserve the consequences of wayward behavior.

Of course, that is nothing but a fancy way of saying that whatever was to happen, I had it coming to me. I remember my mother telling me that, a number of times.

I looked back over my shoulder, and I could just barely make out the forms of the others, sprawled out behind me. No one was saying anything, not even in whispers. They were practically lying on top of each other, probably trying to gather some kind of collective courage.

There was such total stillness that it seemed as if all life had stopped. I wanted to jump up and run off, but someone was lying on me. Besides it was like my body was imprisoned by the fear that I felt. I was frozen to the ground. Then a voice, barely audible.

"It's him!" Jerry said, his breath even closer to my neck than it had been, his voice barely even a whisper. And I could vaguely hear the whispers of the rest of the boys as the word was passed.

"Don't move," I cautioned in such a low voice that the words had to be passed down from boy to boy, and the sound was like the rustling of dry leaves. And after I had breathed that word of warning, I realized that the warning was not really necessary, for they were just as scared as was I.

Just at that moment, our attention was drawn to the light in the upper floor of Mrs. Schweikert's house. There were flashes of light from within, sudden and violent flashes that sharply illuminated the curtains of the window and escaped into the night air. It seemed as though the light flashed so violently that I expected booming noises to accompany it, as though the light itself was trying desperately to escape from the room.

I looked from there to the monster across the street, and the huge creature must have noticed the lights also, for he had turned so as to face Mrs. Schweikert's house, and he stood there, motionless, the pipe still clenched in his mouth. Had he noticed the flashes, as well? It was impossible to say, but if he had, he didn't react. He merely stood there, looking up at the windows from where the flashes had come. It seemed as if nothing about the lights was unusual, to him, for he continued to stand there, all serene, puffing on his pipe.

"I told you guys what we saw," came a husky whisper, and I recognized the voice. It was Jack's. He must have moved up closer to me. "That's what Kenny and I saw," he added. And there was a tremulous alarm in his voice.

"Quiet" I uttered as low as I could. And I looked to see if the monster had heard our voices. But he continued to stand there, the pipe's bowl glowing eerily.

The flashes of light continued, and one could imagine the demons let loose and flying out through the windows and into the night, where they would seek their victims.

I had never been so scared, not even that night when I had been trapped in Old Man Schrader's apple tree while the old man stood underneath me, his shotgun in his hand.

I wanted to move; desperately I wanted to move, to jump up to my feet and run away as fast as I could, but a horrible dread kept me pinned to the ground. And so did the body that lay atop of me.

And then the man, the monster, moved, turning and walking slowly away from us, his steps deliberate, mechanical, just as I would have expected Frankenstein to move.

And with that, someone jumped up, and I heard a gasp, and then someone yelled, a voice filled with fright. One of the boys had leaped up and begun to run off. And then there was a general scrambling and yelling, as the others jumped up and began to run off. And then I felt Jerry's body lift off from me, and I vaulted to my feet, and sped after the shadowy figures that were running off frantically.

A booming voice followed me, a horribly scary sound of a voice: "Boys! You boys!" And I realized that the voice must have been that of our Frankenstein.

No one had to tell me to keep going. That voice was reason enough. I ran like I had never run before, the darkness of the night causing the voice to grow louder and louder: "Boys! You boys!"

And then there came a heavy, thunderous sound of footsteps behind me, and I almost fainted, as I realized that Frankenstein was behind us, his giant footfalls gaining on us.

It couldn't be! It just couldn't be! No one that huge could run that fast. But the terrible sounds seemed to echo and fill the night air. Death beat a horrible cadence, and I could not run fast enough to escape it, even as I was gaining on those in front of me.

At Eighteenth Street, we all turned south, heading to those old familiar grounds of ours, where the fort and the ball field would provide us some degree of comfort. If only we could make it there before the monster grabbed us.

We were pretty much together by the time we hit the corner at Oak Street. And still the sound of those awful steps behind us continued, bringing with them certain, awful death. I had been running so fast that my wind finally gave way, just about when I caught up with the others, a block later, at the corner of Division Street.

The guys had thrown themselves down, on the grass, at the corner. I yelled to them as I ran past: "Get going. He's coming! He'll kill us."

They all jumped up, gasping for air. One more block to go. One more block to our fort, where I hoped for some kind of refuge. But shortly I realized that the others weren't following me. I was scared out of my mind for my safety, but I stopped. I was not about to leave my brother and my friends all by themselves, at the mercy of the monster.

So I turned, and was determined to stand my ground, even if all of us were killed. But they were sprawled out on the grass, their bodies shapeless in the shadows of the street light, their voices nothing more than ragged breaths. And I looked up the street, to see the monster who had been chasing us. But there was no monster. No horrible, frightening specter pounding his way toward us. And instead of the scary sound of footsteps, all I heard was the collective gasps of the gang, a chorus of collective, laboring breaths.

It was then I realized that the sound of footsteps must have been the pounding of my heart, thumping in alarm. And I collapsed on the ground with the other boys.

In the thin light from the street lamp overhead I looked at the others. It was like looking at shadows. They weren't saying anything. They were all lying on their backs, their breaths ragged. No one stirred.

I sat up and looked back towards Griswold, but there was no one there. All there was to see was an empty street, its gloomy lane looking foreign to me.

We couldn't have been there more than a couple of minutes, no one saying anything. And then the others got up, each of us heading home, each of us looking back from time to time. But there was no one there.

We were heading to the best place possible, each of us, to our homes. Home! That place, I was to learn many years later from Robert Frost's poem, where "when you have to go there,/They have to take you in."

Thank God for home.

CHAPTER THIRTY

November's Dismals

WHEN THE MONTH of November took its rightful place after Halloween, it did so reluctantly. It didn't know if it wanted to keep the calm brought on by the warm days of October or if it wanted to show a sign of coming winter. Most of the early days of the month were filled with dreary drizzles that seemed to take the cheerfulness out of the month that gave us Thanksgiving.

Over in Europe, Hermann Goring, that pompous, arrogant monster who headed up Hitler's Luftwaffe(Germany's Air Force), had found it necessary to change his bombing targets away from London in order to try to destroy England's industries. I admit to not really knowing much about England's geography, but Father must have understood it well, for he became very upset when he heard about the bombing of the city of Coventry, a disaster that included a lot of the city's churches and thousands and thousands of homes.

War was reaching out its ugliness to America. And every little disaster that struck England was immediately communicated up and down America's streets, from house to house, from porch to porch, which was the quickest form of communications in those pre-technology days.

Grandmother came down to dinner more often, sitting quietly at the table, sharing her grief for the people of Europe, and especially for those valiant Britons. Just about the only positive news seemed to be that which involved the heroics of the RAF(England's Air Force). Greatly outnumbered, still those heroes brought down more than two German planes for every one of their own that was lost. Oh, those wonderful brave and daring men!

While all this was going on, we boys were striving to maintain our usual enthusiasm for life, although the weather was trying equally hard to put a damper(forgive the cliché)on our plans.

Pollywog became a darkened bog, its waters slowly swollen by the daily rains. The skies seemed perpetually gray, and the temperatures made it impossible for us to know whether we should put on autumn jackets or winter coats. Most of the trees had shrugged off their leaves, although some of the oaks and chestnuts were still holding on, with their usual tenaciousness.

And then, when November was in its final days, we were hit with a snowstorm, and not just a dusting, either. Four or five inches fell, creating a wonderland of sorts. We boys welcomed the change, and not just because everything became whiter, but because it gave us an incentive to change our daily routine, which had become rather boring.

The first winter war took place, the fortresses of leaves giving way to fortresses of packed snow. The rules were the same, but the ammunition was changed from chestnuts to snowballs. What was most wonderful was that the battles were attended by some of the older boys.. It was as though life had been given a boost by the wintry scene. Maybe the only downside to it all was that when you were struck by a snowball that had been thrown by one of the older boys, you were quickly and painfully reminded about how much stronger they were. But that all goes hand in hand with-forgive another cliché-*the fortunes of war.*

That snowstorm was just the beginning, for winter continued its assault. The temperatures plummeted, and Pollywog quickly froze over. We monitored it every day, waiting for when it would be deemed safe enough for us to lash on the old ice-skates. We waited for one of the older boys, like Knobby Pugh, to tell us that it was okay.

But before we were able to use the skates, Jerry and I, and a few others, learned a new skill: street-skiing, or bumper-skiing as it was also called. I suppose nowadays it would be called street-surfing, but in those days we boys had never heard of the word *surfing.*

Now, I want to offer a word of warning to my readers; bumper-skiing is, and was, a dangerous act; and although it has been done by many boys down through the years, it is not something I recommend. Like I said: it is dangerous. And it needs an explanation.

Kenny was the one who not only told us of it, but he was the first one to demonstrate it to us. That was expected, for he was the greatest daredevil in our neighborhood

The sport, if that is what one might call it, required a frozen, icy surface on the streets, two good gripping-hands, and a bit of foolhardiness.

There was quite a group of us boys out the night we were introduced to the sport. Kenny had told us that the event would be something wonderful to see, and even more wonderful to act out.

That night we waited patiently with Kenny for the city bus to makes its appearance. It came down Sixteenth Street every hour, braking at the stop sign at Minnie. Kenny told us that he had used some cars in the past, but that their drivers sometimes were too clever for Kenny and would spoil his plans. Ah, but the city buses! They were big, they were fairly regular in their schedules, and they always came to a complete stop at the corner. Plus, they had ample bumpers on the back for grabbing.

We pretty much knew the schedule of the bus that traveled down our street, so we were ready for when it finally came.

Hiding behind some bushes that hugged the corner, we watched as the bus slowly rolled to a stop and Kenny made his move. Dashing out to the rear of the bus, Kenny squatted down and grabbed a hold of the bumper, sitting back on his heels. And then the bus took off, turning east on Minnie, and Kenny's trip began. We watched him, skiing along on his feet, the packed icy snow allowing him a thrill of a ride. How far he went was up to Kenny.

We ran out into the middle of Minnie, to watch Kenny's ride of daring. Down the street Kenny's figure slowly went, dragged along behind the bus, until the two of them were finally swallowed by the darkness of the winter night.

About fifteen minutes later, Kenny appeared, a grin on his face.

"Boy, that was really something," I said," speaking for all of us boys.

"Weren't you scared?" someone asked.

"Sure," Kenny replied. "But that just makes it more fun." And the grin spread itself across his face.

"Who's next?" Kenny asked, looking at each of us, challenging us individually.

"Why don't you try it, Larry?" Don asked.

"Yeah," Joe put in, "why don't you try it?"

"Well, why don't you, Joe?" I retorted. I hated the fact that it was always me that my friends turned to whenever some new kind of daring required an old kind of foolishness.

"You're scared to, Larry," Joe dared.

"Yeah?" I responded with a bit of false bravado. "You wait until the next bus comes. I'll show you who's scared." Such rashness on my part was expected, and when a smug look came from Joe, I was more determined to prove myself. Back down to that ignoramus? Never!

The wait for the next bus seemed interminable, and I don't recall just what we did to pass the time, but I'm sure that I was having second thoughts about such a foolish act. I do recall Kenny singling me out by standing by me much of the time, giving me encouragement, and advice.

Finally we could see the bus coming from the south, rolling over the railroad tracks, heading toward my destiny. Jerry was waiting alongside me, which was somewhat comforting. The bus was somewhat slow in its approach, as though it was aware of our plans.

Then it made its stop, and without looking at any of the rest of them, I ran out, and got into the required squatting position, as I had seen Kenny do, and grabbed onto the bumper. And it was then that I noticed that I had company: Jerry. He had dashed out, too, and there he squatted, next to me, his hands also on the bumper of the bus.

We looked at each other with what must have been stupid grins on our faces, and Jerry nodded, as though to say that it was all right. We had been born together, and had grown up together, so we might just as well die together. He was not one to let me down.

Both of us knew, from what Kenny had told us, that the greatest danger in skiing behind the bus was the possibility of hitting a bare spot on the surface of the street. The city did not respond all too quickly, in those days, to lay cinders down in order to provide traction, but bare spots could still crop up.

If we were to hit a bare spot, we would probably be dragged onto our faces in the split second before we would drop our hold of the bumper. According to Kenny, it had happened twice to him, and both times he had suffered gashes on his face, as well as torn jackets and pants.

But with the recent storm, Minnie had plenty of packed snow. At least that was what I had reasoned.

Then the bus took off, and the instant fear of what we doing made me grab hold of that bumper as tightly as I could, and I tried to think of what my feet must do. Having never skied in my life, it was a new experience.

But by the time the bus had turned onto Minnie and headed east, I felt pretty comfortable. The ride was exciting, and if it had not been for the exhaust that was pouring out of the tailpipe and into my nostrils, I would have thoroughly enjoyed it all.

Other than the possibility of bare spots in the pavement, the only other danger that Kenny had warned us about was the possibility of cars coming upon us. It would have been extremely dangerous if that were to happen, for it would mean that if we let go of the bumper, we might get run over by a car.

In the years that we engaged ourselves in that stupid and dangerous winter activity, there was only one time that I hit a dry spot, and luckily for me the bus that I was hanging onto was not traveling fast, so that I hit the pavement on my chest instead of on my face. Even so, it was a sharp and painful reminder of the dangers of boyhood.

I don't remember ever bumper-skiing on Sixteenth Street, since, in those days, the street had not yet been surfaced with concrete. Instead, whenever snow came, Sixteenth Street was covered with the hard clinkers of cinders created from the coal that had been used in heating people's homes. The clinkers, while giving traction to cars, would have made a street impossible to ski on.

Thanksgiving arrived, and once again we were invited to our Uncle Arthur's house for dinner. And that meant, of course, reacquainting with our two cousins, Joyce and Corinne. It was always a treat to be with those girls, for they were charming and gracious.

And, as always, there was the usual turkey, and mashed potatoes smothered under turkey gravy. Cranberry sauce, and celery stalks filled with a special cheese were special accompaniments. Following it all was the inevitable apple pie, which our mother had made as her contribution.

To top it all off, Jerry and I were allowed to use the pool table in the basement. Unfortunately for me it eventually evolved into a passion, during my teenage years, a passion that took me into several of the notorious establishments in the downtown area that had built reputations concerning the various games of eight-ball, and snooker, and nine-ball, all of those games requiring the gambling of money. Of course, that all lay in the future. Enough said about those times.

And suddenly it was over. Thanksgiving had passed. But something else had passed also: a bit of life. As children, we did not realize how momentous was that passage, for we were so caught up in living life for the moment that we failed to realize that those moments could never be grasped again. We were still in that stage in life when life would be the same, day after day, year after year. Or so it seemed to children who still lived in their innocence.,

I had not seen Mrs. Schweikert in quite a while. The end of my summer job with her yard had long passed. But I thought about her, from time to time, especially after the incidents of *Frankenstein* the previous month. But even those notable events faded somewhat.

It was Mother who brought my attention back to her. The book *Tom Sawyer* was sitting on my dresser, and she had seen it during a day when she was cleaning our room. That night she confronted me about it, when I appeared for dinner.

"Are you through reading this book?" Mother asked when I entered the kitchen. She held the book in one hand, while stirring something on the stove with her other hand.

"Yes, ma'am," I dutifully replied.

"Then why haven't you returned it?" she demanded. Her full attention was on me; it no longer was divided between the stirring and the book..

"I will," I countered in maybe too severe a voice.

"When?" she demanded. And I could see that she was not going to back off until she had an answer. Her eyes bore into mine, so that I lowered my head.

"Look at me when I ask you something," she ordered.

"I'll do it tomorrow," I said.

"You'll do it tonight, right after dinner." It was as flat a statement as I could have expected. There was no wiggle-room in it.

"Tonight?" I asked, a slight tremor in my voice.

There was no way that I wanted to go back to that house, to that area, in the dark of night, and at that time of year it was already quite dark by suppertime.

I looked over at Jerry, who was sitting at the table with Sandra and Marilyn. He quickly looked away. And I instantly knew that I would have a devil of a time convincing him to go with me. I also knew that I would never convince any of my friends to accompany me on such a mission.

"Tonight!" Mother answered.

"Your mother's right," Dad added. He had come into the kitchen just as this conversation had begun.

"You don't keep things that don't belong to you," Dad continued. "You told me, some time ago, that you had finished reading it. So, you return it tonight, right after you boys finish doing the dishes."

So, the matter was settled.

Dinner was served, we sat and ate, and conversation took place, although I don't recall taking an active part in the sociality. It was a dark night, even in what should have been the comforts of the kitchen.

Jerry worked with me, on the dishes. But I could sense that he knew I wanted to ask him to go with me. His silence was awful. And I knew that he would not leave the safety of the confines of the kitchen, with everyone there. I couldn't blame him.

So it was that I was soon on my way, the book in my hands, my heart in my stomach, and fear in my whole being.

The night was especially dark. No stars appeared. The moon was not visible. And my thoughts were dismal, to say the least. My thoughts magnified the coldness of the air.

When I *approached* Mrs. Schweikert's house, warily I looked across the street, half-expecting *Frankenstein* to be standing guard. I stopped at the edge of her yard and looked intently. But there was no one there. No one that I could detect. That other side of the street was all in shadows and night darkness. It was cold, but not nearly as cold as I felt. My nerves were on edge.

I unlatched and opened the gate, and rushed up the steps to the front porch. I wanted to get this over with as quickly as I could.

I found the button to the door bell, pushed it hard, and stepped back. Then I pushed it again, too quickly I thought.

The tinted windows that decorated the door were difficult to see through, but then I thought I saw some movement. And then the door was opened.

Mrs. Schweikert stood there, in what appeared to be a dressing gown. She looked wan, almost sickly. Her eyes seemed to be dark, and sunken. Her hair unkempt.

Then she seemed to take notice of who it was, and a faint smile crossed her face. She held the door open, and invited me in.

"Oh, no, ma'm," I remarked, handing over the book. "I can't stay. Mother says that I have to return this, and then hurry home." The last remark was my safety valve. While I had no fear of her house, the specter of a monster living across the street from her was all the reason I needed to find an excuse to escape.

She took the book, and thanked me, and I turned and hurried away, fleeing down the steps and through the gate, almost fearing that she would call after me. But she never did. And I felt bad. I felt terrible. All the way home I felt a terrible guilt about having dismissed her so readily, so... curtly? I was never one to abuse an older person, and my conscience tore at me, all the way home.

December began with a thaw, and the snow disappeared. The days were cloudy and gloomy.

But we were not meteorologists. We were merely young boys in search of things that would entertain us. And success in such a venture was dependent upon our imaginations.

Of course it being December we were all looking forward to Christmas. Although we never expected much, in the way of gifts, there was always the anticipation of something that the lack of gifts could not obliterate: a sense of hominess, a feeling that basically all was right with the world. Nothing could dampen a general feeling of comfort, of family, of good tidings. There would be caroling, more smiles on people's faces, and a general faith in the goodness of mankind. Okay, so the glowing feeling didn't last long. But it still was a kind of reprieve from the usual, mundane affairs of the world.

I think most of the kids-even the girls-hoped that the weather would turn cold again. I know that we boys talked a great deal about it, in school and out. We wanted a frigid December, so that Pollywog would freeze over. A frozen Pollywog Pond meant ice-skates, and a community of kids anxious to skate away from the ordinary. We loved to skate, even though Jerry and I used skates that were still too big for us and thus we seemed always to be skating on the sides of our ankles. I was hoping that each year would see our feet grow enough to give us a feeling of fitting into them.

Daily we went down to Pollywog, to see if the skim-sheet of ice was changing into solid ice. Pollywog was our greatest reprieve from the onslaught of winter, and our hopes grew only as fast as the pace of the ice thickeneing. And daily our hopes seemed dashed by the thin sheet that quickly broke under the weight of the feet of those who dared to risk an icy soaking.

And then it happened. A cold-snap hit us; the temperature plunged. It became cold enough to cause the adults to complain and to cause all of the kids to envision the community of youth that would soon find a haven from adult supervision.

Anxiety built up. And then, Pollywog, hiding its denizen of hibernating frogs, finally gave us what we had been wishing for: a frozen pond.

The first boy to venture onto the ice and safely make his way from one side of the pond to the other side was called a hero. I don't recall who it was that performed the heroic deed, but I do remember that when he made it safely to the far side, there was a feeling of great elation over the triumph.

Word quickly passed, and in many of the homes, skates were dug out from where they had been stored, and scarves and mittens helped to declare that winter had finally been officially opened.

Pollywog became the community center for most of the kids from blocks around. Of course there were still reeds of grass that stubbornly poked their unwanted stems through the ice, but most of them were quickly destroyed by shovels that the most thoughtful of the older and wiser youth brought with them the first few days. Pollywog's surface, although still a little bumpy in places, was a marvel.

There was gayety those evenings, although there were a few nights when the severity of the coldness drove us to the comforts of home.

Pollywog became, for us, the center of the universe. So much so that I did not even recognize all the faces of those who participated. It was obvious that Pollywog's reputation had drawn young people from the remote areas of Germantown. Of course, most of the kids in the immediate neighborhood would be there, thus turning the evenings into social events. Some of the kids came without skates; they were there just for the society. Tag and makeshift hockey games and whirl-the-whip were accompanied by laughter and taunting screams and the cooing of a few of the lovebirds.

Thus December sped by, and along with it went Christmas. That winter was all a blur, time having moved inevitably across God's calendar.

January arrived with snow flurries, which quickly turned into heavy snowfalls. Of course the scene was set for our warfare games. Of course it was only a matter of snowballs. And I do not recall anyone ever being seriously hurt by the snowy missiles. But still it involved the idea of battling one another.

The figure of Frankenstein receded into the back of my memory bank. We boys were more involved in enjoying the season. But it got so cold, that more were the nights when Jerry and I were content to lie on the floor of the living room, and listen to the radio shows that challenged our imaginations.

I was not prepared for the message that was about to be delivered. All of our family were in the living room, where the only radio we owned was playing. Dad was in his easy chair, reading the day's newspaper, smoke rising slowly from the bowl of his pipe. I don't remember which show we were listening to at the time, but I do remember, very vividly, the scene as it was before me, the domestic simplicity of it all. A boy. His family. A radio program. His father smoking his pipe. The sounds of winds blowing on a wintry night.

"I see you've lost a friend," my father said in a simple manner.

For some reason, I knew that he was addressing me. I looked up at him. His face was partially hidden by the newspaper. But his eyes were locked onto mine.

"Huh?" I said. There was something about the way that Dad looked at me that raised more than just my curiosity. Something impending?

"Your friend. Mrs. Schweikert," Dad said, his voice offering something more than mere information.

He hesitated, then went on.

"Olive June Schweikert," he read. "Died Tuesday, January 14."

He kept looking at me, and I felt everyone's eyes on me. And the voices from the radio receded into the background.

"She died?" I asked as if in disbelief. "Mrs. Schweikert?"

Dad put his pipe into the pipe bowl that sat next to him. The smoke curled its way into the shadows of the room. And I pulled something of my soul into my inner self.

"But she can't die," I said.

"I understand she's been sick for quite a spell," a voice said. And I could hear the tenor of my mother's voice. "I just didn't want to tell you."

I looked up at her. She was sitting on the sofa, with my sister Marilyn. Both of them were looking intently at me. And the hush in the room was suddenly too much for me, and I burst into tears.

A sudden flurry of scenes moved across my mind's eyes. Mrs. Schweikert moving among her roses. Mrs. Schweikert carrying a pitcher of lemonade and glasses from the back door of her house. Mrs. Schweikert standing in her living room, holding the pictures of her husband and deceased sons.

And then I realized that Mother was holding me. I had not even realized that she had risen from the sofa. Even Sandra, only six years old, was crying. She did not know Mrs. Schweikert, but she was crying, anyway. And I know now that her tears were for me.

The rest of the evening is mostly lost to my memory. What little of it that remains runs itself together with other losses that I have come to know. But of that night, only bits of grief and a feeling of not being able to understand were left to me.

The sense of loss kept its place in my thinking, all the next day, while I was at school. There was no sense of anticipated gayety during recess. It was evident that the word had been passed about Mrs. Schweikert. My friends were cautious in what they said, when they spoke with me. Even Joe stood off, away from me. And Jerry was wise enough to realize that I was alone in some different kind of world.

"You have to go visit her," Mother said. It was after school. She and I were in the kitchen, where she was preparing supper. It was about four-thirty, shortly after school had let out. Normally I would be at play, or in my bedroom, at that time of the day. But I had gone to the kitchen because I needed to know what I could do, what I should do. What was expected of me. And I did, indeed, feel that there must be something that was expected of me.

"It's what people are expected to do," she added.

I sat in one of the kitchen chairs. It had been a hard day. And by the time that I got home from school, I had thought a lot about Mrs. Schweikert. I did not know what was the responsibility of a ten-year old boy, but I did know that there was something that I must do.

"It won't be easy, Larry," Mother said. She had stopped what she was doing, and was looking at me with a sympathy that I had seldom seen in her. She was leaning back against the kitchen counter.

"But she's..." I did not want to say it. I refused to say it. It was as if I was trying to keep her alive, simply by not saying it.

"They lay them out in the living room," Mother said, by way of explanation. "It's the old-fashioned way of doing it. Usually people nowadays rely on funeral homes. But according to the newspaper, the family is going back to the way it was years ago, and laying her out in her home."

I looked at her, and waited for her to go on.

"Neighbors will pay a call. And about family...I don't even know who her family is," she said then. "All we know is what they put in the paper. And the only one mentioned is a brother."

I waited. There must be something more.

"You probably should go now, while it's still daylight. Most of the adults, especially her neighbors, will probably wait until this evening."

I nodded. I could not say anything. I was still thinking.

Finally, I asked: "Can Jerry go with me?"

She did not answer right away. But it was obvious that she had already thought about that possibility.

Then she shook her head.

"I don't think so," she finally replied. "He never even met her, did he?"

"No, but..."

And I think it was then that I understood. It was all about honoring a person. One should not honor a person just for the sake of appearances. And that is all that Jerry's visit would be. He never knew her. He only knew the things I had shared with him.

So it was that I got my coat and winter cap, and went out into the wintry afternoon. It was bitterly cold, but I confess that I did not fully recognize that.

I passed the houses that contained neighbors that I thought I knew well, and I passed the houses of those who only lived on the periphery of my consciousness. That was the way of Germantown, as I suppose it is for most neighborhoods everywhere. And I shuddered both from the wind and from a sense of grief that I had never known before.

A thousand thoughts rushed through my mind; none of them were helpful. And as hard as I tried, I could find no link between the funeral I had attended, more than a year before, for my friend Marvin, and the death of Mrs. Schweikert. This was not a matter of a young boy, someone I had played with at Pollywog.

No. This was a woman who...Who was what? A friend?

And then it dawned on me. She was more than that. She was someone whom I had come to admire. Someone who spoke to me about life. Someone who was the epitome of integrity, although I would not have recognized that word, at such a young age. It was something that I knew within myself, even if the definition of those words would not come until much later in life.

As I approached Mrs. Schweikert's house, I was hoping that there would be no one there. Maybe I could avoid whatever it was that I felt was my duty. And then I felt a sense of shame for having had that thought. She deserved more than that.

After all, she had been…what? My employer? Just an old lady?

No! Absolutely no! She was a friend! And a dear one, at that.

The steps leading to the front door had been swept clear of snow. And across the street was the house from which had emerged our Frankenstein. I looked over at it. It loomed silent and foreboding, almost as gray as was the sky of the retreating day.

I looked at the bottom of the steps, hesitating. I would not know what to say to whoever would answer the door. A million thoughts swirled inside me, none of them helpful.

The yard looked as desolate as winter could have presented it. I looked at the gate, and thought of her words commanding me to close it whenever I departed on the days I had worked for her. And alongside the wrought iron fence, her rose bushes looked….what? Abandoned?

The huge yard appeared desolate.

And then I went up the steps.

I pushed on the doorbell, and stepped back a little.

Slowly the front door opened, and then the storm door. I looked up, and there, in the vague light that emanated from the room within, stood the biggest man I had ever seen in my life. He was not big; he was enormous. His massive frame filled the doorway

"I kind of thought you might come. Please come in," the man said in an unimaginably soft tone, and he moved aside, and motioned for me to enter.

To this day, I do not know what gave me the courage to enter that house, for I immediately recognized who the man was. He was the…the what? The monster? The Frankenstein of my imagination?

Ironically I cannot say that I was scared, standing before this man of such great stature. He was smiling down at me, and the look that he gave me was comforting.

Once inside, I found myself able to carefully look him over, albeit briefly, and surreptiously.

He actually was a handsome man. His features were soft, especially around the eyes. His smile was sincere. At least, that was what I immediately thought. And I felt a little guilty about trying to find the monster-like features that I might have intended to find.

He had a pipe in one of his hands, which made me think of my dad. And the moment I had that thought, I felt mostly at ease.

Standing there, in that living room of her house, I found myself looking around. I knew it all, so very well. The mantle, with the pictures. The sofa. The shelves of books.

And then I noticed it, over in a corner of the room. A casket! It was blue, and ironically elegant looking, as if death was mocking life.

"You took care of her lawn," he said, interrupting my thinking.

I looked up at him. No hideous face looked back at me. Instead there was a pleasant looking visage. And he was still smiling.

"I'm her brother," he said.

I was startled, beyond imagination.

At first I wondered how that could be. She was so small. Tiny by comparison.

He chuckled at what must have been a look of disbelief on my face.

"Our mother and father used to kid us a lot," he said. "But my grandfather was really big. And his wife, my grandmother, was small, really small," he said in explanation.

I could not think of anything to say. I think I just stood there, perhaps waiting for him to go on. But what else was there to explain?

I looked past him, at the casket in the corner. I didn't know what it was that might have been expected of me. And I realized that I was purposely keeping my eyes away from her figure. I had only seen one other body in a casket, Marvin's. And my memory of that time did not help this situation.

He seemed to understand my plight, for he nodded.

"It's all right. You may go look at her." His voice was gentle, and he motioned for me toward the casket, taking a step toward it. I followed him.

She was dressed in light blue. Her hair had been groomed. There was a necklace that graced her upper bosom. The tiredness that I had last seen around her eyes was gone. And her eyes being closed, it seemed as if she were merely sleeping.

What struck me was how small she seemed, smaller than what I remembered. It was as if she had shrunk within herself. She did not look frail, just small. Maybe even, tiny.

"She would have appreciated your coming," came the voice. "You were special, to her."

I quickly looked up at him, but could not think of anything to say. So I did not say anything, but turned my eyes back on her.

"It wasn't just the lawn. Or the bushes you trimmed," he added. "It was your coming to see her."

I looked up at the huge man standing next to me, and I tried to put it all together. The yard with all its bushes and trees and shrubs. And the lawn mower in the tool shed. And the pitcher of lemonade. And the gate that I had been told to close.

And then I thought of the house across the street, and the gigantic figure that had moved toward us boys as we had knelt in the shadows of the fence that bordered her property. It was all there. Haphazard flashes of a time of boyhood.

I could only stand and stare. I was not sad. I try to recall those moments, and for some strange reason, I remember thinking about how peaceful she looked.

I looked around. Carefully. There was something nagging at me, but I could not pin down what it was. It was as though something was out of place.

My eyes turned toward the mantle. And then I saw it. I saw what it was that was out of place. It was there, on the mantle. The mantle with the pictures. The family pictures. Almost a dozen photos meant to capture the past and the disillusionment of the present.

There was her husband, and their two sons. All as I would have expected them to be. But one small photo caught my full attention, and I moved toward it, wondering how it could be. It was a photo of me, in my